COWARD ON THE BEACH

COWARD ON THE BEACH

James Delingpole

BLOOMSBURY

First published 2007
This paperback edition published 2008

Copyright © 2007 by James Delingpole

The moral right of the author has been asserted

No part of this book may be
used or reproduced in any manner
whatsoever without written permission
from the Publisher except in the case of
brief quotations embodied in critical
articles or reviews.

Bloomsbury Publishing Plc,
36 Soho Square,
London W1D 3QY

www.bloomsbury.com

A CIP catalogue record for this book
is available from the British Library

ISBN 978 0 7475 92747
10 9 8 7 6 5 4 3 2 1

Table from *From Omaha to the Scheldt – The Story of 47 Royal Marine Commando*
by Professor J.O. Forfar
reproduced by permission of Tuckwell Press, Birlinn Ltd.

Typeset by Palimpsest Book Production Ltd, Grangemouth, Stirlingshire

Printed by Clays Ltd, St Ives plc

Bloomsbury Publishing, London, New York and Berlin

All papers used by Bloomsbury Publishing are natural, recyclable products
made from wood grown in well-managed forests. The manufacturing
processes conform to the environmental regulations of the country of origin

This book is dedicated to the boys of 47 (RM) Commando and also to my dear late mother-in-law, Rosemary, who did her bit at Bletchley.

Contents

Twiddling My Thumbs

Well, bugger me, so I'm finally dead. Must be, or you wouldn't be listening to these tapes. And since, unfortunately, I'm no longer available to answer your questions, I thought, in case you were interested, I'd start by telling you how it all came about.

It was on the afternoon you introduced me to your Playstation. A game called Medal of Honor, with the 'honor' spelt in the American way, as inevitably it would be these days. You would have been thirteen, fourteen at the time – 15 September 2006, however old that makes you – and if you remember the moment at all, I'm sorry to say, it's probably because I was so damned irritable.

'Bugger bollocks damnation and arse!' I cried out in frustration, because all those pixelated images on the screen were playing havoc with my eye strain and I couldn't get my arthritic thumbs to coordinate with all those wretched knobs and fire buttons and jump keys and what have you.

'Daddy, darling, *pas devant les enfants*, please,' your mother said.

'Oh, for Christ's sake, Tabs, I'm sure Jack uses language a hell of a sight worse than that,' I said.

'Well if you're going to be difficult,' said your mother.

'Oh, bugger off, Tabs,' I said, because really, it's one of the worst habits she's picked up from your father, this dreary sanctimoniousness – doesn't get enough of the you know what, that would be my suspicion, and with a husband like hers who could blame her? Off she duly buggered.

'Would you rather play L'Attaque, Grandpa?' you asked.

'L'Attaque be damned, I'm going to master this game if it kills me.'

So, very sensibly, you went off to make me a cup of tea.

Took you bloody ages. Must have done because by the time you'd got back, I'd taken out the wire with a Bangalore torpedo and was well on my way to clearing the last of the forward trenches.

'You're a quick learner,' you said.

'Well, I have done it before,' I said.

'Really. Where?'

'Oh, you know. Normandy. June 6th, 1944.'

'Oh. Yes. Of course.' Your disappointment all too obvious but I wasn't going to push it. Not just yet.

You showed me how to pause the game and I took a sip. Dunno what you'd done. Brewed it too long, maybe? Used an old tea-bag? Insufficiently boiled water, with a drop of sea salt, cordite, blood, powdered milk and engine oil in it? Quite revolting, but it took me right back.

'Gunfire,' I murmured, appreciatively. And you gave me a look which said: 'Old bugger's rambling again.'

It could have been the tea, as I say. Then again, it might just as easily have been the game. Either way, in a rush, it was all starting to come back with a clarity and intensity I hadn't known in over sixty years. Names, faces, smells, sounds, sensations – details I'd never expected for a moment I'd ever recall again were suddenly so clear in my head it was if they'd happened yesterday.

Well, when a chap needs to get his head straight, there's no better medicine than another strong hot sip of tea, is there?

On this occasion, though, it only seemed to make things worse.

There it all was, bouncing round the synapses like a rico-cheting bullet. Lt. Frost and his circular swim. The chaplain and his hay box of tea. The Spandau.

I was aware of you looking curiously at me. Worriedly even.

'Gunfire on the beach,' I muttered. 'In a spot just like that. Best mug I ever drank.'

'What was?' you asked.

'My gunfire,' I said, aware that I was about to breach your father's strict orders. Equally aware that there was nothing I could do to stop myself.

'Why would you want to drink gunfire?' you prompted, as, of course, I'd hoped you would.

'It's what we used to call tea, usually with a drop of some-thing added. In the commandos.'

There was a long pause. So long I was beginning to worry you were never going to ask.

'Were you really in the commandos?'

'Once or twice, yes.'

Lovely eyes, you have. Just like your mother. Your grand-mother too. A limpid grey-green. Honest. I remember them turning towards me at that moment, begging me not to lie any more, because it was hurting you, I could see, hearing your old granddad come over all gaga like this.

'It's just –' Sweet boy. You were twisting your arms, writhing as you tried to work out a way of saying it without giving me offence. 'Well, when you took me to that air display – at Farnborough – and we saw the Spitfire, I thought you said . . .'

Then you trailed off, shaking your head, as if in disgust at the unreliability of your memory. Know how you felt.

I beamed a benign smile of encouragement. One of the joys of being a grandfather, deploying the benign smile.

'And that thing on the History Channel about the war in North Africa. I definitely remember you saying about how in tanks, in the desert, how – well, you were talking about it as if . . .'

I nodded a donnish nod, such as one might give to a bright undergraduate making a point so daringly original and baffling he can't quite believe it could possibly make sense, though it does.

'And it was the same when we saw those programmes about Stalingrad; and Burma; and Sicily. But Grandpa, you can't have been in all those battles. No one was. It just isn't possible.'

Unfortunately, with her impeccable timing, your mother chose this moment to bustle in, saying: 'Daddy, I'm really sorry but Robin says he needs to take you back right now. We're out for dinner this evening and we need to pick up the babysitter and – I'm so sorry to have to rush you.'

'No trouble, darling. No trouble.'

'Jack, could you help your grandpa out of his chair?'

I put on a show of fumbling in my pockets.

'Here you are, old chap. One for you and one for your sister.'

You pretended to be impressed by the two two-pound coins in your palm.

'And don't spend it all at once,' I said, with a wink. Because, of course, what your mother didn't know, nor your sister, and certainly not your bloody father, is that on the quiet I'd already slipped you a crisp twenty. To be spent, as per my usual conditions, on something frivolous.

'MILLA!' your mother called upstairs. 'Grandpa's leaving. Will you come and say goodbye?'

From upstairs came some muffled excuse or other.

'Thanks for the gunfire, Jack,' I said with a wink. 'Quite the most memorable cup I've had since you-know-when.'

And I don't know whether I was imagining things, but it seemed to me that at that moment, it finally occurred to you that maybe your father had got it wrong. Maybe your old granddad wasn't, after all, such a deranged fantasist. Still, there was only one way I could make sure.

'Daddy,' your mother asked. 'Is there anything I can get you, before I next see you?'

'Don't think so, darling, no. No wait. Actually there is, though I don't expect you to pay, just let me know how much. What I should very much like is a tape recorder.'

'For music?'

'No. For recording things on. And I should like some tapes. Lots of them. As many as you like.'

2

Going In

Now, tell me, Jack, what's the sickest you've ever felt? I don't mean that glorious, cathartic moment after you've brought it all up and, save the odd chunk of diced vegetable lodged half-way up the nostril and a sweet-sour taste turning your tonsils rancid, you're feeling pretty damned good about yourself, because you're over the worst. I mean the bit just before, when your skin has turned such a grisly green you can feel the chloro-phyll leeching through your pores, your stomach's swirling like a fairground waltzer and you're on the tip of reaching the very climax of your nausea, where you know that something has to give and if it doesn't give soon then by God you'd almost rather die.

And when you've fixed on that moment – maybe it was gastric flu or food poisoning; more likely it was in one of those heaving ferry lounges where the stench of vomit is so strong that merely to inhale is to renew your acquaintance with the stale baguette with limp lettuce and slice of reconstituted ham you ate not ten minutes earlier – what I'd like you to do is to imagine yourself tumbling down a scrambling net with rifle, Bangalore torpedo and pack and into a lurching flat-bottomed wooden boat reeking of puke and diesel fumes on a cold grey day, towards eight a.m., off the coast of Normandy, in seas so choppy you'd think it was November, not early bloody June. Now, throw in an empty stomach; a spray-soaked body chilled to the bone; and the near-certain knowledge that within the next hour you're going to be emasculated, decapitated, eviscerated, pulverised or otherwise obliterated by any one of the numerous devices the opposition has thoughtfully included in your welcome package.

That was my D-Day. That was how it felt in those first numbing minutes. And I wouldn't try to claim that my experience was significantly worse than it was for the other 100,000 poor fellows who had to go ashore that day – except, perhaps, for two small details.

The first was that, unlike most of them, I had an idea of what was coming. There was a theory abroad at the time, not wholly unfounded, that a man fights better if he doesn't yet know where it hurts. And though I was by no means the only one in my unit who'd seen action before, we veterans were in the minority. And there were times, I remember, when one did feel a bit like a character from an H. M. Bateman cartoon: 'The Man Who Didn't Think It Was All Going to Be a Breeze'.

It came up during the final briefing we were given on our mother ship – an ex-Belgian Channel ferry named *Princess Josephine Charlotte* – sometime in the small hours on the morning of the 6th. We'd had a rough crossing; none of us had been able to hold much down, even if there'd been anything available to eat, which there wasn't – half our supplies having been blacked as per usual by the dockers at Southampton; but quite a few of us, invoking naval tradition, had sneaked an illicit drop or two to drink, so the atmosphere was quite light-headed, jovial even, as we crowded round the scale model, perhaps 200 of us, in one of the upper-deck lounges, the light dim, the portholes all blacked so as not to alert the enemy to our crossing.

So we're all giving this model the once-over – the houses, the hedgerows, the flooded area just behind the beach, the strongpoints, the wire, even the tiny signs saying 'Achtung Minen!' – when a voice pipes up from a Geordie next to me. He's a tiny fellow, slight build too: you wonder how he ever got past the medical.

'Sir,' he says. 'I think there's something missing here.'

'Oh, I'd very much doubt it, Dinning,' says our troop commander, Capt. Dangerfield. 'These maps are accurate in every detail.'

'I was thinking of the clockwork model of the *Flying Scotsman*, sir,' says Marine Dinning to much general laughter, because he has hit the nail on the head. It's like looking at one of those elaborate train sets, only with pillboxes and machine-gun nests instead of picturesque stations and jolly bakeries.

'Hoping for an easy ride, were you, Dinning?' And everyone laughs at that too, not so much because it's funny as because – so I've gathered in the week or so I've known him – he's a very popular fellow, this Capt. Dangerfield.

Suddenly the laughter dies and with a clatter of boots we're all standing to attention because our CO's just arrived and he's not a man for jokes.

'At ease,' says Lt. Col. Partridge. But not the subsequent 'Stand easy' we might have hoped for.

'Now, one thing I'd like to remind you men is that however hard it is for you today – and I believe it will be hard – it's not half as hard as you're going to find it tomorrow. This morning you're lucky. You've got the Dorsets and the Devonshires doing most of your dirty work for you. This evening you're very much on your own. But I know that's what you trained for and I know that's why you volunteered to become commandos. I shall look forward to regrouping with you – most of you – tonight at our, ahem, rendezvous. Otherwise, adieu.'

And with a snap of his heels he's off.

'Cheery sod,' murmurs a marine just in front of me.

'What was you expecting: kisses and flowers and a personal message for each and every marine?'

'I thought, just for once, we might have a bit less parade gloss. It being our last day on this mortal coil.'

'Speak for yourself, Harry. I intend to last the duration.'

'Oh, me too, me too. But you know what they say about the best-laid plans. Suppose we're put in the back of the LCA –'

'Now, listen up, chaps. There's little I can add to the CO's heartening words –' Sarcastic sniggers from the audience, though I don't think Capt. Dangerfield means it as a joke. Far too proper to make fun of the CO in front of the men. '– but this may be the last opportunity I have to say how very much I've enjoyed training with you for the last eighteen months –'

'What's wrong with the back of the LCA?'

'– and how thoroughly bucked I feel to be going ashore now with such a splendid bunch of fellows.'

'Most dangerous place to sit.'

'Really, if this proves to be the last day of my life –'

'Bollocks it is.'

'– as, of course, I have every intention of it not being –'

'Oh, it is, yeah. Mate of mine was at Salerno. What happens, he says, is that your 88s and your mortars range in as you comes ashore, giving the first few rows just time enough to get off, while for them poor sods waiting their turn at the back –'

'– honestly say the privilege of being among the first to liberate Europe with the boys of 47 will have made it my happiest.'

'Kaboom!'

'Or perhaps I should say, should my wife have any spies aboard,' continues Capt. Dangerfield, 'my happiest equal.'

'Poor sod. He's only been married a week.'

'Poor sod? Some of us have been stuck with our missus for seven bloody years!'

Capt. Dangerfield waits for the affectionate chuckles to die down. Most of us haven't even a girlfriend, let alone a wife, but that's not going to stop us pretending we know what it's like to be henpecked.

'Still bollocks. What about the Spandaus?'

'What about them?'

'Draw a bead on the landing ramp, don't they. Soon as it goes down: Vrrrrrr,' says Harry, his body juddering in a pretty good impression of the front ranks in an LCA being mown down by an MG34.

'Embarkation in the LCTs is scheduled for 0700 hours,' announces Capt. Dangerfield. 'Till then you all no doubt have plenty to keep you busy. Were there any last questions?'

The marine called Harry makes to raise his hand. I know what he's going to ask and it strikes me it would be a better idea if he didn't.

I prod him gently in the back. 'Makes no difference,' I say softly.

He turns round, looking a bit irritated. 'Eh?'

I notice dear old Price standing next to me isn't much pleased either. Can't open my mouth without putting my foot in it, he's always telling me.

'It makes no difference where you sit,' I say. 'It's a lottery.'

'You there. Marine Coward. Do you have a question?'

'No sir. I was just – no, nothing, sir.'

'Coward, you'll find that in this commando if a man has something to say, he'll say it.'

'I'm sorry, sir, if I was speaking out of turn. I was trying to allay a marine's concerns as to the best place in an LCA to sit during an opposed landing. I was explaining that it doesn't much matter where you sit because, such is the nature of war, the best place to sit in one LCA could be the very worst in another.'

'The nature of war, indeed,' declares Capt. Dangerfield, his voice heavy with scepticism. 'And just how many opposed landings have you experienced to draw you to this philosophical conclusion?'

'To be honest, sir, I try not to count,' I say, which is nonsense, I know exactly. But I don't want to sound immodest. And I certainly don't want to sound like I'm pulling rank on the Captain, who's clearly a decent chap, whatever he now thinks of me.

There's a dull pain in my right ribs from where Price has just elbowed me. Rather too late, unfortunately, because the damage has been done. Some of the men are tutting or shaking their heads or whispering sneerily to their neighbours. Others are staring at me hard, as if trying to fathom whether I'm a lunatic they should steer well clear of or whether perhaps I might prove some kind of lucky talisman.

Capt. Dangerfield, very sensibly, decides to spare us all further embarrassment.

'Does that answer your question, Marine Barwell?'

'Not really, sir. What I was actually going to ask was about the availability of cabin facilities on the LCAs. Only I've been a little disappointed with the sleeping arrangements on this here so-called ferry, and I had a mind to snatching a bit of sleep, just so I'm fresh for when we meet Jerry, like.'

Much laughter, now, of course. Manly laughter. Laugh-in-the-face-of-death laughter. Which, thank heavens, rather lets me off the hook. Capt. Dangerfield takes the opportunity to tell us just one more time what splendid chaps we are and, apart from the last dirty look he shoots me just before he tells us to fall out, that's the end of it.

Well, almost. Our third and final encounter on the *Josephine*

Charlotte – I shan't bore you with the first, for the moment –
is when we find ourselves standing side by side at the stern,
both leaning over the rails as far as we can, looking down into
the dark Channel water being churned to a foaming pallor by
the screws, both of us heaving our guts out. In my nauseous
stupor I scarcely know whether I'm coming or going, and for a
sweet moment I've drifted back to the old mill where my brother
and I used to play for hours on those days when we were getting
on. We'd chuck sticks into the turning blades to see whose, if
any, would survive; then we experimented with paper boats;
then one day, my brother insisted on trying it with my two pet
frogs Mallory and Irvine and I rather lost interest after that.

Something dark and bloated and horrible comes bobbing to
the surface and recedes into the boat's wake, and the childhood idyll fades. I'm back in an unpleasant present, weighed
down with so much kit as you would not believe, enveloped
by a cumbersome life-jacket the size of a car tyre and more
likely to drown you than keep you afloat, dribbling the
remnants of my bile, which rather unfortunately end up being
carried by a sudden cross-wind directly from my mouth into
Capt. Dangerfield's right lughole.

'Frightfully sorry, sir,' I shout. You have to shout because
the din going on all around really is quite something else –
the rasping shriek of the rocket ships' broadsides; the echoing
boom of the battlecruisers' sixteen-inch guns; the deafening
roar of fighters overhead. 'You must think –'

'Do you know, Coward,' he yells back, bringing his face up
right near mine. 'In your case I don't know what to think. If
you're shooting a line, you're clearly not up to the job. If you're
telling the truth then why on earth am I commanding this
troop and not you? And there's no point asking you either way
because –'

'It's like the Minjims and the Monjoms, sir?'

'I beg your pardon?'

'You know, sir. The two identical tribes guarding the way to the secret city. One of them always tells the truth, the other always tells lies. You bump into one of them and you can't tell which he is. So which question do you ask?'

'Coward . . .' he begins, regarding me as one might a penguin which has just marched into one's drawing-room playing 'The British Grenadiers' on a tin whistle. 'Coward, I shan't try to fathom you further because I doubt our human lifespan is long enough. But I want you to know: if at any stage I think that you are about to jeopardise this operation or the lives of my men, I shall not hesitate –' he taps his Colt meaningfully '– to take remedial action. Do I make myself clear?'

'Perfectly, sir.'

'Carry on, then.'

When I look round, he's still there, leaning over the stern rail, head bowed towards the ship's boiling wake, perhaps in nausea, perhaps in contemplation, perhaps in prayer. Perhaps, as it is for most of us, all three simultaneously.

I mentioned earlier, didn't I, Jack, that besides my unusually extensive experience of warfare in all its forms, there was one other thing that set me apart from the majority of the men who landed in Normandy that day: a lamentably over-active imagination.

You'll no doubt be familiar with what Shakespeare said on this score. Ought to be, given your mother's maiden name. He said: 'Cowards die many times before their deaths. The valiant never taste of death but once.'

Act II, *Julius Caesar* and I remember quite vividly when we studied it at school, tripping over those words, pausing, reading them again, then again, and again once more and thinking: 'Crikey! However does he know me so well?'

Because that's me, down to a T, that couplet. Coward by name and, well, I hope not Coward by nature, but certainly Coward by instinct. It's one of the things that has always fascinated me: the grisly business of precisely how and when and where you're going to meet your maker. Thought about it at school, especially that winter we lost Thomas, Lewis and Ottaway to the flu. Thought about it even more during the war, as you might well imagine: the Nebelwerfer that shreds you into 10,000 fleshy rags; the landmine that rips off your testicles; and so on and ever on. The possibilities are as endless as the enemy is ingenious and desperate to kill you; and if you start to dwell on them, why you'd never be able to stop.

What's frustrating is that, most of the time, there's so very little you can do about it.

Whether you live or die is completely dependent on random factors like what the gunners at the Pointe du Hoc battery had for breakfast, the subtle shifting of the tides and the currents and the flotsam of war, the will of God, the luck of the draw and above all your coxswain. Is he a good 'un or a bad 'un? You don't know, you've never seen him before and probably never will again. Yet, all of a sudden the skills of this stranger are all that stand between you and complete annihilation by the 56-pound shell lashed to the jutting stake he's rather unfortunately neglected to circumnavigate.

So there I am, rifle in hand, green beret on head, buttocks – still pretty scrawny after Burma – being bounced and bruised to buggery by the mountainous swell, thinking, as well one might: 'What the devil possessed me to put myself in this ridiculous situation? I didn't need to be here. I'm a bloody fool is what I am. A bloody, blithering, stupid romantic fool.'

And if this is my view, heaven knows what Price's verdict is. I haven't looked at him yet – I wouldn't dare, even if it were possible to crane my neck, which it scarcely is the way we've all been crammed together – but I hardly need to because I can positively feel it oozing out of him, through his skin, through the serge of his battledress and in through mine: the resentment, the quivering rage. If I believed in such things, I'd almost say we had a psychic bond, Price and me. There's a certain physical resemblance too. If he weren't such an ugly old bastard, you might mistake us for brothers.

I offer him a cigarette from my lucky silver case, which he accepts with sullen indifference, staring fixedly ahead. He lets the fag dangle from his lower lip.

'Oh, come on, Price,' I shout, reaching across to light it – 'And gentlemen in England now abed shall think themselves accursed they were not here.'

He takes a number of sharp drags, still staring grimly forrard and I assume he can't have heard above the general din: the burble of the diesel engines; the whipping breeze; the men's vomitous eructations; the scream of artillery overhead – rockets, shells, and God knows what else, mostly ours one hopes.

But then he turns, very slowly, and gives me that sarcastic rheumy look he keeps for occasions just like this.

'I didn't understand a bloody word of that,' he yells back. 'But then, neither did I first time round when some young bloody lieutenant tried it on us at Passchendaele. "What's that yer say, sir?" I says to him. But I never does get a reply. Mostly, I reckon, on account of the fact that a sniper's bullet, attracted in my opinion by the excessive hot air emanating from his overeducated gob, has just taken away half his jaw.'

The marine on his other side – Harry Barwell, it turns out – leans forward, the better to study Price's face in astonishment.

'You was never at Passchendaele?'

'And you'd know, I suppose?'

'So, go on, then. What was it like?'

Price mulls the question for a long while.

'Wet. Very wet,' says Price, with a disgusted look at the sodden butt end which has just been extinguished by the spray. We're sitting right at the back of the landing craft, the wettest place to be.

For reassurance, I pat the damp left breast pocket in which I've stashed my precious letter to Gina. If I hadn't had the foresight to seal it in a condom, there'd be nothing left of it but an inky pulp.

'Should have got yourself a place under here, mate,' says Harry, gesturing above his head to the gunwale, which is half-sheltering the two outside ranks from the spray. 'Dry as a nun's fanny.'

'We're not ashore, yet,' says Price, fumbling in his pocket for another fag.

Now, as a rule, there isn't much talking goes on in an LCA before a landing. It's not exactly that you're struck dumb with terror – that comes later. More that your senses are so overwhelmed by the immensity of what's going on around you that you can't quite bring yourself to accept it's really happening.

'This is it,' you tell yourself, examining the crib sheet kindly provided by General Eisenhower: 'The hour is upon you. The Great Crusade has begun.' But no matter how hard you try, there'll always be a part of your brain that insists there's been some terrible mistake. Perhaps this is just another rehearsal – a bit more realistic than the earlier ones, that's all. Perhaps you're about to wake up and find it has all been a frightful dream.

Of course, there's another part of your brain that does accept what's happening. That's the part that makes you gaze wistfully over the stern of the LCA, watching the wake narrowing to the diminishing speck that was your mother ship, wishing that you could claw back the time. Knowing all the while that the only way to get out of this mess is by moving forward, not away from the danger but closer towards it. Before it's better, the rational part of your brain is telling you, it's going to get a lot, lot worse.

Every few minutes or so, you're jerked from your stunned reverie of vacillating hope and fear, by the sight of the shore-line – each time looking more distinct and ominous than before. At first, it's just a distant grey blur, sporadically illuminated by so many flashes of bursting, rumbling flame that you almost feel sorry for whoever's having to endure such a weight of fire-power. And perhaps, as you begin to be able to make out the greenness of the individual fields and the tall white Norman houses – those few the Germans haven't destroyed to clear their field of fire – you permit yourself yet another sliver of optimism. 'Well, this isn't so bad. It all looks pretty peaceful. Maybe our bombardments have done their job. Maybe our deception plans did the trick. Maybe the opposition was lighter than we'd feared.'

It's at just this point – about 2,000 yards off shore I'd say – that the German guns properly open up and blow your every false hope to high heaven. You can actually feel it – the tension spreading through the ranks like tautening rope – you can smell the fear and loosening bowels as the tracers arc overhead like murderous fireflies, and the shells splashing either side of the craft send up plumes of water, and the first stray shots and shards of shrapnel begin to ping off the armour plating on the side of the craft.

We want to be ashore. God, how we want to get off this bloody boat. But from what I can see of our landing beach, in the bobbing rectangle of view above the heavy, iron-bound bow ramp, we're in for a pretty rough reception when we do. If we do.

The beach, Jig Green, is apparently deserted save for two bottle-green Centaurs crawling forward under the most intolerable fire, the stubby 75-mm. guns on their angular turrets questing with painful slowness for the German positions which could wipe them out at any moment. This was the beach that was supposed to have been cleared two hours ago.

Now one of the tanks has lost a track; another's brewing up, and even from this distance, with the wind whipping in your ears and the shriek of the shellfire, you can still hear the screams of the burning figure lurching from the hatch and flaming across the beach until he's silenced by a jigger of bullets from a hidden casemate. At this rate, we'll be damn lucky if any of us gets further than the water's edge.

Except now, Lord be praised, our LCA is turning to port and ahead we can see the lead craft doing the same. The CO, I later learn, has given the order for us all to turn east, running parallel to the beach, in search of a more suitable landing zone. But in doing so, he has doomed us to spend even longer in our landing craft, now bracketed by the increasingly accurate shellfire from batteries on the high ground above our first rendezvous, Le Hamel.

There's one of our flotilla now, blown clean out of the water in a terrible geyser of spume, twisted metal and limbs. Thirty men gone, just like that.

'We're not going to make it,' says Harry, echoing my thoughts.

'Oh, we are,' I reply, as much for my benefit as for his because if you didn't keep telling yourself these sweet lies at times like this, you'd go completely mad. 'Remember, I told you, the stern is the safest place to sit.'

'You said it made no difference,' says Harry.

'All the difference in the world,' I say, with as much conviction as it's possible to muster when your mouth's half-buried in a Bag, Vomit.

Seeing he's still unconvinced, I tell him something I wouldn't normally mention to men going into battle.

'Harry, one of the many sights at Salerno I'd rather forget,' I say, trying not to picture it as I speak, because I'm quite sick enough as it is, 'were the bodies, so frightfully crushed you could scarcely recognise them as men, of the soldiers trapped beneath the bow doors of the landing craft.'

Harry nods slowly. I see from the twitch of the heads of the three men in front that they're listening intently too. Price bristles.

'Now, I assumed, as naturally one would, that these fellows were already dead when the LCA ran over them. Then I get talking to a beachmaster: "Yes, well, that's certainly what we'd prefer you boys to think," he says. "Because if you knew the truth, we'd never get any of you to sit forrard in the LCAs."'

The magic is beginning to work: there's a thin smile on Harry's lips. Now even the row of marines in front is straining to hear the story.

'– and he explains to me that what happens as the first few ranks start wading ashore is that the LCA gets lighter. And what happens then, if the coxswain is too eager to beach it or it's struck abaft by a wave, is that the whole craft surges suddenly forward, with the result that all those chaps unfortunate enough to be standing in front . . . well, I'm sure you get my drift.'

Harry does, he indicates with a grateful nod. But so, unfortunately, do the men in front and the ones in front of them, as my cautionary tale slowly filters up the line, as in a game of Chinese whispers. Anxious glances are cast over shoulders, especially from the men nearer the front, as they try to establish exactly how far back you need to be to avoid the grisly outcome they have just heard described.

'Well done. A bit of good cheer. Just what the troop all

needed,' says Price, as an anonymous marine three ranks ahead of us is suddenly drawn into focus by the carmine jet spurting from where his missing head once was. The men sitting all around him explode outward in unison, some vomiting, some wiping the gore from their webbing, some trying to distance themselves from the squirting arterial blood. Then, almost as quickly they've resumed their positions and their numbly stoical demeanour because they know there's nothing that can be done. This is war. Seconds ago he was a living friend. Now he's just an item on a casualty list.

Harry is staring, transfixed. I would guess it's the first time he's seen this sort of thing.

I pull three more cigarettes from my case, one for Price, one for myself, one which I pop straight into Harry's open mouth.

'This'll help,' I tell him.

'You reckon?'

'Life saver,' I say, as the side of the boat where Harry was sitting erupts and the world goes blank.

3

Fever Dreams

A pair of blue eyes are gazing into mine with such warmth and love and tenderness that I know I must be dreaming because there's only one person in the world with eyes as beautiful as that and she's miles away back in England. In fact it's very probably a sexual fantasy I'm having. Must be because crowning that severely cropped dirty-blonde hair of hers I've always wanted so desperately to ruffle is a prim, pert and excedingly sexy nurse's cap.

'Hello, Dickie,' she says and this is an unusually vivid one I must say, because I've got her voice to a T. That light, girlishly amused quality it always has. It's as if she finds the very idea of seeing me here killingly funny. Which I suppose, if I knew where we were, it might be. Wherever it is it's much softer and lighter, altogether less jungly than I remember. A down pillow under my head. And, rather than sweat-soaked rags, what feel deceptively like cotton sheets.

It's all very odd. Terribly hot still. Burning hot, pouring sweat, temples still throbbing and pounding as if my head's going to explode, but something's missing. No shellfire. No screaming. No mosquitoes. And replacing the smell of flyblown corpses decaying under tropical sun, the cool medicinal smells of iodine and disinfectant. The addled mind clearly determined to persist with this nurse-in-hospital scenario, it would seem – and perhaps one shouldn't complain.

'Gina?' I say. Croak, rather.

'Shh,' she says, and the fantasy rather threatens to reach a premature climax as she leans closer towards me and presses a soft finger against my lips.

I nod, my eyes lingering on the curve of her throat, me thinking how very, very much I'd like to kiss it, first under that sweet chin, then further down where the skin stretches into a translucent pallor, then ever downwards towards the place where, somewhere beneath her nurse's uniform, those gorgeous breasts even fuller no doubt than that last time I peeked from behind the willow by the mill pond when she was sixteen and I was seventeen and it seemed sure that one day she and I would –

But enough. This kind of dream is something I've always been wary of, ever since that awful occasion when I woke to discover that the bed in which I'd left my puddle of mess happened to be in the guest room of my terrifying Aunt Matilda. And if this isn't one of those it's probably something more dangerous still, perhaps the final hallucinatory moments preceding my death on whichever battlefield I happen to be lying wounded, exposed, vulnerable, perhaps at this very second about to be sliced from ear to ear by some bastard Nip's samurai blade.

I close my eyes and think of England.

Sure enough, England replies with another face, this time one which reveals the true horror and wretchedness of my predicament. It has stained teeth, a broken nose and pock-marked cheeks, one of them disfigured by a livid scar. It glares at me from beneath its dark bushy eyebrows.

'I shouldn't be telling you this, sir, because it's only a rumour and it'll only go to your head. But they've recommended you for a gong,' says Price and I doubt he could sound less enthusiastic if I'd just been given four white feathers.

'For what?' I hear myself saying in utter disbelief.

'Same as usual, I expect. Stupidity beyond the call of duty.'

'Sorry, Price,' I say. 'It won't happen again.'

But it must have done, for I see it now, on my battledress. Not just the white and purple ribbon of a Military Cross, but with a bar, no less.

'They say lightning never strikes in the same place twice,' I hear a voice crowing. 'But I thought you should be the first to know: it does!'

Now the ribbon is being thrust into my face. I reach out to touch it.

'Jealousy will get you nowhere, brother dear,' says a voice, as the ribbon is pulled once more out of my reach, and the next one I hear belongs to my mother.

'Darling, you're so very clever, I knew you'd do it,' she says.

'I got one, then? An MC?'

'Oh, please don't talk about that nonsense. I meant your recovery.'

'From what?'

'Darling, you nearly died.'

'Oh my good God, no, of wounds?' Panic-stricken, I hoick up my bedclothes to check that the essentials are all present.

'Some sort of brain fever. You've been in the most frightful state. Fever. Buckets of sweat. Hallucinations.'

'Pity. Some of them were rather promising.'

'Yes, darling, you rest yourself, that's the important thing. Lots and lots of rest. And when you've finished doing that you can come home and rest some more. You've done your bit now. That's what the doctors are saying. It's over for you, now, my sweet. This whole ghastly war is over.'

*　　*　　*

Hah! Now, Jack my lad, have you been sharp enough to spot my cunning ruse? I gave you a couple of clues: the tropical sun; the samurai sword – neither of them things you encounter all too often in Normandy. That's because what we have going on here, my dear fellow, is a flashback. A flashback to that period a month and a bit prior to D-Day, when I'm lying in bed in an officers' hospital on the South Devon coast, recovering from the bout of brain fever I contracted in Burma.

It's the most idyllic place, this hospital, in a big old house at the head of a wooded valley running down to a private beach. It used to belong to a Victorian collector and the gardens are quite ravishing – formal borders by the big house; ferns and exotic specimen trees bordering the gravel path leading to the sea. Across the croquet lawn there's a monkey-puzzle tree, beneath which I'm sheltering from the late April sun with my two new chums, known to all the patients – though not to the somewhat disapproving nurses and doctors – as Ginger and Fred.

Fred, a dark-haired naval sub-lieutenant, is so called not because of his matinée-idol looks – though he has those, too – but because of the wobbling gait that tends to ensue when you've left your legs behind after your ship has been shot up off Gibraltar. Ginger, meanwhile, is mainly called Ginger because it goes with Fred – though an alternative theory has it that if you were to remove the bandages covering more or less every inch of his skin, this would be the colour of the crispy burnt flesh underneath.

'My flaming ace in Magnolia ward bought it last night,' declares Fred, a plume of smoke drifting from his cigarette towards Ginger.

Ginger begins hacking horribly. His burns are not merely external.

Fred considerately bum-shuffles downwind of him, dragging his stumps behind him.

'So that'll be another five shillings you owe me,' he says to Ginger.

Ginger mumbles something decipherable only by Fred, his official interpreter.

'Yes, well, it's not as though I haven't told you before. There are only two certain things in this world: nurses and the inevitable demise of 90-per-cent-burn victims.'

From beneath Ginger's bandages come sounds of protest.

'Yes, I take your point. Consider yourself the exception that proves the rule,' says Fred airily.

I've been trying to keep my expression neutral, but Fred must have detected my discomfort because suddenly he fixes me with a long, hard look, at once defiant and amused.

'I think Niagara thinks I'm in poor taste,' he confides to Ginger. 'So perhaps we oughtn't to mention the wager we had when he arrived.'

From Ginger's throat comes an awful rattle, which I think might possibly be laughter.

'Niagara?'

'Sweat pouring off you like nobody's business. Certainly fooled me. Half a crown you cost me before the terrible news came through: it seemed that you were on the mend.'

'Charmed, I'm sure.'

'Dear boy, you mustn't take things personally. It's what it does to you, this bloody awful place.'

Out at sea a fisherman is pulling in his net and just beyond his boat, dark shapes – a school of dolphins? porpoises? – are rising and falling in the blue. I hesitate to use the cliché but at a moment like this it's inescapable: today the war seems a very long way away.

'I think I've been in worse,' I say.

'My point precisely,' says Fred. 'Only a fool would deny that this is as lovely a spot as a man could ever dream of being billeted. But you don't honestly think it was just a matter of good luck that we were sent here?'

'Well, no. It'll be the restorative powers of the sea air, won't it?'

'Sea air, my Aunt Millie. The only chaps they send to this place are the ones they think are never coming back. It's our treat, don't you see? Our last taste of paradise before we head off God knows where – the Other Place, in my case, no doubt.'

No one says anything for a while. Ginger, for fairly obvious reasons. Me, because whatever I say will only give him fuel. Such darkness. Such bitterness. Such an intense conviction of doom. I've interrogated kamikaze pilots with less of a death wish than this poor fellow.

'Bloody shame, though, all things considered,' Fred says, after a time, striking up another cigarette. 'I mean, if a man's going to go to the Other Place, at least he ought to do some proper sinning first.'

'Was there anyone you had in mind?' I ask, sensing a way out of the gloom.

'We'll say, eh Ginge?'

A horrible rattle from Ginger.

'The night nurse,' sighs Fred, dragging the back of his hand with a histrionic flick across his forehead. 'Not the new one, God, talk about the Angel of Death. I mean the one just before, pity you missed her. A face that made the Madonna look like a raddled tart; a body, by comparison with which Botticelli's Venus emerging from her seashell is as but a bloated fishwife – tell him, Ginge.'

Ginger mumbles his agreement.

'Such a marvellous liar too. Had me quite convinced it would be wedding bells just as soon as my feet grew back. Got poor Ginger going, too, didn't she? Such a beautiful soul, that was her line, as she gazed adoringly through the crack in his bandages. Though you'd sell it pretty sharpish for a decent set of skin, wouldn't you, old man?'

'Can you remember her name?'

'Oh, no use crying over spilt milk. Should never have brought it up, really. In fact I didn't. It was you who raised the subject, you bloody man.'

'It's just that I think I might know her.'

'And I'm the bastard son of Winston Churchill and Gracie Fields.'

'No, really, I think I might. I thought at first it was some sort of hallucination. That it was too good to be true.'

'Too good to be true? Now, that does sound about right,' says Fred. He glances anxiously across at Ginger, who has become unusually animated, waving his bandaged arms and nodding his mummified head. 'But perhaps we'd better change the subject before Ginger does himself an injury.'

'I have to ask though. Was her name by any chance –'

'Hello, boys,' chimes a melodic voice behind Fred and me. 'I trust you've all been behaving in my absence.'

I look over my shoulder, open-mouthed. Fred wheels round in such frenzied haste, he damn near topples backwards. Ginger gurgles.

Even if Lady Georgina Hermione St Clair Devereux Nevill Herbert had a face like the arse end of a plucked broiler – which, you'll have gathered, she doesn't – she would still be the most eligible girl in the land for at least three excellent reasons. Her American mother – who shares a set of grand-parents with my mother, making Gina and me distant cousins – owns half of Manhattan; her father, most of Monmouthshire; her parents are agreeable; she's an only child.

There, that's four already, and I haven't even mentioned the really important details. Like the curve of the alabaster breasts I glimpsed at the water mill; and the ambrosial breath I last properly imbibed at the age of thirteen during a game of sardines after which her father the earl had me beaten by his gamekeeper for having broken the door handle on his second-best Chippendale wardrobe; and that way she has of fixing her attention on you as if you are the only person in the world who truly matters to her; and the way, when she's dazzling someone else instead, you suddenly know just how it feels to be 'hurled headlong flaming from th'ethereal sky/With hideous ruin and combustion down/To bottomless perdition . . .'

You'll say I'm exaggerating. But I'm doing no more than present the facts as I saw them at the time, which were these: I had adored Gina Herbert since my earliest childhood; I would happily have died for her; no need would have seemed too extravagant to secure her affection, no enterprise too suicidal to gain at least the remote possibility of her hand in marriage. The result of this stupidity you will shortly see.

But let us not get ahead of ourselves. Join me, for a moment, in my brief sojourn in paradise before the Fall. Gina and I, as has become our daily custom, are taking our evening consti-tutional together down the zigzag gravel path that winds past tree ferns, mossy banks and dripping arbours – a little more redolent of the Burmese jungle than I might have preferred, but still – to the shingle cove and the pirates' cave where I like to tease out our moments alone together for as long as I possibly can. Naturally I am still far too weak to walk unaided, which means that our passage is languorously slow and my Gina has to take gentle hold of my arm every step of the way.

And of course, in my Scheherazade-like need to maintain her interest, I have told her everything. Dunkirk. The Battle of Britain. My sudden exit in disgrace from the RAF. Thence to North Africa and Crete.

'So terribly brave,' she says.

'The brave ones are all underground,' I say, as is the accepted custom, while racking my brain for anecdotes in which I come across as braver still.

'If you ask me it's too unfair. Here you, after all that trouble, with not a gong to show for it while your little brother –'

'Ah. You heard?'

'Impossible not to. He telegrammed me. Once for his MC. Then once again for his bar.'

'Good God, he didn't? So what did you do?'

'Fucked him, of course. What else could a girl do? Poor chap was so clearly desperate.'

I was smacked in the shoulder once by a Moisin-Nagant round on the Eastern Front and let me tell you it had not half the impact of that single, unheralded expletive. Fucked! It just wasn't a word you heard used in those days. In the heat of battle possibly, but often not even then. Certainly not from the lips of pretty young girls as nicely brought up as Gina Herbert.

Fucked. Do you know, I think it might have been that single word – more specifically, the thrillingly evocative way she said it – that landed poor Pricey and me in that whole damned mess at Normandy.

For the briefest of moments it raised my hopes, the thought that this remote beauty was capable of thoughts as earthbound as mine.

But joy quickly gave way to abject despair. Not only, it seemed, was my perfect maiden princess not a virgin – and by the sounds of it, quite a few times not a virgin. But at least one of the myriad jammy buggers to have beaten me to the punch, apparently, was my stinking brother.

I'm staring numbly into the depths of the cave, debating how best to volunteer for the surest suicide mission, when I feel my cheek being pinched, really quite hard.

'Oh, you silly chump,' she says, bringing her face up close to mine, the better to be amused by my mournful expression. 'Do you honestly think I'm that kind of a girl?'

'No, of course not.'

'And even if I were, surely you don't have so low opinion of me as to imagine that your brother is my type.'

'I . . . I wouldn't presume to know what your type is.'

'Heavens, Dickie, you look awfully pale.' She feels my damp forehead. 'Perhaps we should be getting you back to bed. Sister would never forgive me if you had a relapse.'

'Not yet. Please, I . . . need to recover my breath.'

'All right. Five minutes and then I must take you back. Now, where were we?'

'You were about to tell me what qualities you looked for in your ideal man,' I'm about to say.

Before I can spit it out though, she says: 'Ah yes. Your brother.'

'Must we?'

'Oh Dickie, I'm sorry. You must feel terribly sore.'

'About the medals? No. Really I'm not. You know what they say: the only person who knows what a medal's worth is the man who has won it.'

'Which, in your brother's case, wasn't that much?'

'I can't speak for the second one because I wasn't there. But the first – no, I've said too much already.'

'Oh but you can't leave me hanging like that, not now you've whetted my appetite . . .' Whetting Gina Herbert's appetite. There's a thought on which to linger.

' . . . anyway, being secretive doesn't suit you. It's one of the things I so like about you. Your American side. Your openness.'

'My American side? Oh dear. Do you think? I was rather hoping I'd kept that under control.'

'Why would you want to do that?'

'Well, it's just not the way we do things here, is it? Speaking your mind, opening your heart, it can get a chap into all kinds of trouble,' I say. 'But you're right. There are times when I do feel like a stranger in my own country. Maybe it's the American thing. Maybe I was just born in the wrong age. Have you read Boswell's diaries? Quite extraordinary, entering the mind of someone who's been dead near two centuries yet speaks to you with more freshness, honesty and intimacy than your dearest chum. And as you're reading it you're thinking to yourself: "Good Lord. Underneath we're all just the same. Same hopes. Same fears. Same desires. So why can't we just jolly well admit it instead of going round keeping it all buttoned up?"'

'You can tell me.'

'What?'

'The secret thing, whatever it is.'

Lucky it's quite dark in our cavern or she'd see me reddening.

'I wasn't thinking of anything specific,' I say. Then, worrying she might find out – that she might guess what I'm really saying is: 'God, Gina, I don't half fancy you' and promptly reject me with a 'But, Dickie, I've always thought of you as an old friend. Never like *that*' – I decide a quick change of subject is called for.

'Oh well, all right, take poor Fred. Seventeen years old, never known what it's like to, ahem, go with a woman – nor even what it's like to drink in a pub. And perhaps now he never will.'

'But of course he'll pull through. He's young, he's strong.'

'Physically, yes. Mentally, I'm not so sure. I get the impression that he's made up his mind that there's really nothing left worth living for.'

'Then I shall make it my mission to show him there is.'

'How do you plan to do that?' I say, a mite nervous, given what she claimed to have done with my brother.

31

'You're his friend. Don't you have any idea?'

'Well, I know it's his eighteenth birthday next week.'

'Perfect. We can make all his dreams come true.'

'All of them?'

'Leave it to me, Dickie,' she says, tapping the side of her nose. Her smile gives way to a concerned frown. 'But now look at you, you're shivering, I was meant to look after you and you've led me astray.'

If only.

As his birthday approaches Fred and I are pretty much on non-speakers. He, of course, is riven with jealousy over the time I've spent hogging Gina. I in turn have begun to feel quite sick with dread as to what exactly Gina might be planning for his birthday treat.

She won't tell me of course. Whenever I try raising the subject, I find the conversation gently being steered back to me, my bravery, my wit, my charm, my extraordinary adventures, my general suitability as future husband to a maddeningly unpredictable, utterly adorable blonde-haired earl's daughter whose name begins with G. At least that's what I want to believe.

Then on the eve of Fred's birthday, she bowls me her most fiendish googly yet.

'Gina, I have to know what you're planning. It's going to be a tough enough operation as it is. I can't let you take all the responsibility.'

'Dickie, darling, I promise you, it's all going to run like clockwork.'

'Oh good, that's a relief, so you'll have arranged us all leave passes from the Colonel? And a driver? And a fighter escort just in case?'

'Now, don't be silly, you know as well as I do that alcohol

is strictly off limits. The Colonel would no more let a man in Fred's state near a pub than he would – well, any of the other treats I have planned for the lucky birthday boy.'

'You're tormenting me, Gina, and I won't have it!'

'I say, is this you when you're cross? How exciting!'

'Don't you see I'm worried, that's all. About you. If anyone finds out, as they surely must – the duty nurse, what about her?'

'Patricia's on board.'

'And the MO?'

'Tell me about your tattoo.'

'What tattoo?'

'You know,' she says, with a simper and a furtive nod towards my buttock region.

'Humph!'

'Dickie, you were delirious for a fortnight. Someone had to bath you.'

'A professional nurse would have averted her gaze.'

'Just like you did that time by the water mill?'

'When?'

'Don't play the innocent. I saw you perfectly clearly. Lurking under the willow.'

'Well – I don't remember you being in any hurry to cover yourself up.'

'Now, that would have been churlish. Poor chap, you seemed so touchingly grateful for what little I could offer.'

'I was.'

'So now you can give me a belated thank-you by telling me about your tattoo.'

'Gina, you know I'm happy to tell you most things. But not that.'

'Leck Mich Am Arsch – I think I can guess what that means. Is it quite rude?'

'It's a quotation from Goethe.'

'But the bit underneath. The skull and crossbones. And those letters that look a bit like German regimental insignia. Very like, in fact.'

'Has anyone else seen them?'

'I think Patricia would have mentioned if she had. You wouldn't think it to look at her — not when she's on duty, anyway — but she's quite a girl.'

'You know what her nickname is?'

'I do and it's so terribly unfair. If she found out it would break her heart. I know she can seem a bit severe when she's doing the rounds. But that's just the way she was taught. She takes her duties very seriously.'

'So how on earth did you manage to persuade her to let us bunk off tomorrow night?'

'You're very clever, I must say. A moment ago we were talking about your tattoo.'

4

Band of Brothers

'Doctor's orders, it's lights out early this evening,' announces Patricia − aka the Angel of Death − drawing the black-out curtains closed with a businesslike tug. She turns around. 'Books away, gentlemen.'

From where I'm lying, propped on my pillow, I try to fathom what on earth Gina can have meant when she described this ashen-faced martinet as 'quite a girl'. The tightly bunned hair, black as a witch's cat; the pallid skin and prim, disapproving mouth, with its sharky array of funny, gappy little teeth. By Chaucer's account, having gapped teeth is a sign of lechery. He'd soon have changed his mind after a bed bath from Miss Sourpuss.

'That's a bit harsh,' I say, playing along as Gina has instructed. 'You're ruining poor Fred's eighteenth birthday.'

'Which until now had been going so-o-o swimmingly,' says Fred with cool sarcasm. 'Oh and I never said: "Thanks for the presents, everyone."'

'The best present I can give you is a good night's rest,' says Patricia, turning off the light.

No sooner has she closed the door than Fred hisses: 'Witch.'

'She speaks very highly of you,' I say.

'I'd rather lose both my legs,' says Fred.

'Then, Sub-Lieutenant Richards, I have some excellent news for you.'

'Oh, just turn on the light, will you?'

'Better not just yet. She's bound to notice.'

'And what's she going to do? Put me on a charge? Send me back to the front?'

The easiest way to shut him up, I suppose, would be to tell him what Gina has arranged on our behalf while she stays behind to cover for us: rendezvous at 1850 hours behind the hedge by the tradesmen's gate; pick-up at 1900 by her father's driver, the earl's generous petrol allowance being one of his perks as colonel of his regiment; 1915 hours, section assault on the Ship Inn; 2200 hours, closing time – tactical withdrawal.

Ideally, though, I'd like to keep it all a surprise. If, that is, Fred and his big mouth will let me.

'No, no, forgive me, you're quite right, I'm being terribly unreasonable,' he's now declaiming in hurt, strident, quavering tones. 'Didn't I always dream I'd spend my eighteenth birthday getting legless . . . ?'

'How about we jolly ourselves along with a game?'

'You and Ginger can. Wake me up when it's all over.'

'Come on. It's your last night before the firing squad, so who will it be: Patricia or Eva Braun?'

'Eh? Oh. Eva Braun, definitely!'

'Patricia or Adolf Hitler?'

'Hitler, no contest.'

'You're not taking this seriously.'

'I would not touch that hag if she were the last woman on earth. Now, can you please stop talking about her, I'm going to sleep and I don't want nightmares.'

'You can't go to sleep just yet,' I say, swinging my legs out of bed. I pad across the linoleum towards Fred's wardrobe.

'Why can't I?'

'If I tell you that, it will spoil everything.'

'Oh God, not a surprise. I hate bloody surprises.'

What with Fred's bloody-mindedness and the awkwardness of trying to fit a uniform over Ginger's bandages (we have to settle for just a greatcoat in the end), not to mention the difficulty of negotiating Fred's passage on crutches down the steps outside our French windows, over a gravel path, across a stretch of lawn, and down a rutted track, it's no wonder we arrive at our rendezvous almost fifteen minutes late.

But still there is no sign of our transport. It starts to drizzle and, though the redwood tree behind which we've concealed ourselves offers reasonable defence against the wet, it doesn't protect us from the damp evening chill. Ginger feels it especially hard. He's soon shivering so badly that I have to take off my own greatcoat and drape it round his shoulders. Now it's my turn to feel cold. I wouldn't normally, I'm sure, but the malaria has weakened my constitution. And all I have on is my shabby, lightweight tropical uniform brought back from Burma.

'I think I've worked out what the birthday treat is, Ginge,' announces Fred. 'Death by pneumonia, the sick man's friend.'

'Look, if you'd rather go back to your room and sulk, feel free,' I say.

Fred passes me a cigarette, which I smoke mainly for the glow of warmth from the stub at the end. Whenever I take it from my mouth, my teeth chatter audibly.

'Come now,' says Fred. 'I would have expected better from the hero of Stalingrad.'

'Who told you that?' I snap, though really it's Gina I should be cross with, because she's the only person I've ever mentioned it to.

'You actually. Babbling away in one of your fever fits.'

'Say anything interesting, did I?'

'Not altogether sure. A lot of it sounded like German.'

'I say, was that a car?'

We listen awhile. Nothing.

'Do you know –?' begins Fred.

'Wait!' I say. 'I'm sure I –'

From the road, there comes a faint squeaking noise and what might be the clip-clopping of horse's hoofs. But whatever it is is drowned by the sound of rapid footsteps on the driveway, and laboured breathing. We edge further behind the tree trunk, just in case. Then Gina appears, looking miserable.

'I'm so sorry, boys,' she gasps. 'Daddy's driver has just been on. There's been some sort of rumpus, the roads are all blocked and they're not letting anyone through.'

Fred, inconsolable, is on the verge of blaming me – I can just see it coming.

'Then we'll jolly well have to walk it, won't we, Fred? Ginge?'

'I'm game,' says Fred.

'Don't be so silly, you're in no state to walk four miles, any of you. And Ginger, my goodness, you look so cold. And you, Dick, you're shivering. We must get you into the warm.'

'Look!'

The others look to where I'm pointing. Above the hedge, just visible in the fading light, is the shaggy head of a giant cart-horse and behind it, on his wagon, a farm labourer with a long whip.

Without local knowledge we would surely never have found it, for the Ship Inn looks not remotely like a pub. It's a long, low whitewashed building – originally farmworkers' cottages, perhaps – with small blacked-out windows, and a rickety doorway with a lintel seemingly purpose built to bang your head on. If there was ever a sign, it must have rotted away years ago or been removed to fox enemy parachutists. The only indications of its current usage are the American military jeeps parked anyhow outside and the raucous laughter from within.

We enter in pairs so as to support one another, first me and

Ginger, then Fred and our new farmer friend Tom. No doubt we make quite a sight, as we negotiate the narrow entrance sideways and at a low crouch, me with my dark eyes and febrile pallor, Ginger in his bandages, but I still don't think it justifies the cry of 'Say. If it ain't Boris Karloff and Bela Lugosi,' as we stumble in, me calling back 'Mind the step'. Nor yet, the beery hilarity that ensues when, too late to catch my warning, Fred collapses on the floor, dragging Tom down on top of him. Tom must somehow have cracked his head on the way down, because he lies there motionless, Fred trapped helplessly between the sawdust-sprinkled flagstones and the labourer's huge frame, flapping like a freshly pinned butterfly.

The laughter is coming from two tables of extremely dishevelled GIs. If I'd been their commanding officer, I would never have allowed them off base. Their faces are blacked as if for an exercise; their uniforms are filthy; and there's something in their expressions I don't at all like – something dark, abandoned, menacing.

'Are you Yanks going to give us a hand?' snarls Fred from the floor. 'Or is leaving your allies stranded till the very last minute written into your constitution?'

Tom, thank heavens, is showing signs of life – rubbing his head, pushing himself upright.

'Lundt. Kowalski,' commands an American from the nearest end of the snug. He's wearing a corporal's stripe. A tall, lean shaven-headed GI in olive fatigues stained with what might be congealed blood springs from the bench to help him. Another, even bigger, seizes Fred under each arm and hoicks him on to a bar stool.

'And now perhaps you'd like to apologise,' says Fred in a voice of icy belligerence.

'Maybe when you thank me for picking you up off your ass,' says the GI.

'Can it, Kowalski,' says the Corporal. 'Sir,' he says to Fred. 'I would like to apologise if my men have given you offence. May I say, sir, in their defence, that they have been training long and unusually hard today, though I realise that this is no excuse. I wonder, by way of apology, if you'd let me buy you gentlemen a drink?'

Fred eyes him up and down for a moment.

'Apology accepted, Corporal,' he says. 'But you can keep your money. An English gentleman is perfectly capable of buying his own drink.'

The Corporal's once-friendly smile disappears. 'Enjoy your evening,' he says, and returns to his men.

From that moment on, the atmosphere in the pub is decidedly strained. In the snug at one end of the room, sit the GIs, ostentatiously chain-smoking their elusive American cigarettes, bragging and joshing and grumbling loudly: 'Uptight Limeys' and 'We come over to Europe to save their asses. But will they say thank you?', drinking the bar dry and generally acting like they own the place. At the other, as far from the Yankees as is possible in such a poky interior, sit the birthday party staring morosely into their half-finished pints of mild and bitter which, perhaps because we're with a local and are being afforded special treatment, have been served to us in pewter mugs.

'Your decision and all that,' I say to Fred. 'But I'm not sure that it would have been such a bad idea, letting our American chums stand you a round or two.'

'I have my reasons,' says Fred, still peering into his mug. 'Just occurs that one ought to take any chance one gets to even out the quite disgraceful pay differential between our two armies. I have one or two cousins in the US military. Do you realise that their lowliest private earns more than a British lieutenant?'

'Overpaid, oversexed and over here. That's what Jim's always saying. Ain't it, Jim?' says Farmer Tom, who clearly shares Fred's knack for tact and international diplomacy. He cocks his head towards the landlord, the better to bellow this hilariously original *aperçu*.

'What's that, Tom?' says Jim the landlord.

'Oi says –'

'Four more pints of mild and bitter please, landlord,' I chip in quickly. 'And please, while you're about it, one for yourself.' Dropping my voice, I say to Tom: 'Sorry to interrupt you but I thought that with there being only four of us and – seven, eight, nine, ten, *eleven* of them, this might not be the moment.'

'What? Even with three and a half of us, I wouldn't fancy their chances,' says Fred. He drains his mug, slams it on the table and glares across at the Americans.

'Now, come on, birthday boy. You've got some drinking to do.'

But even as I say it, I realise that's exactly what birthday boy shouldn't be doing. In our convalescent state we none of us have much of a head for alcohol. After only one pint, I'm feeling decidedly mellow and blurry; Ginger is virtually comatose. But with Fred it appears to have had quite the opposite effect.

'And what exactly do you mean by that?' he says, jabbing a finger in my face. 'You saying I'm not up to defending my country's honour?'

'Fred, I –'

We're interrupted by the creak of old hinges. A welcome draught of clean air penetrates the fug. From the American tables there are whistles and a 'Hey, nice dress, lady'. Turning round I see a young woman standing uncertainly inside the doorway, as if she's debating whether to brave the catcalls or make her exit while the going's good. She looks half familiar, though I'm not quite sure why. And yes, it is a nice dress – rose-patterned and shapely, demure yet leaving the observer in absolutely no doubt as to the splendour of its owner's slender legs and rather magnificent breasts. Mind you, under the circumstances, perhaps a veil and wimple would have made more sense.

'Now, Kowalski, weren't you saying to me only a moment ago that you had as fine a selection of nylons as can be found anywhere in England?' says a loud American voice.

'Why, indeed I was, Barnhardt. And wishing I could only find a pretty lady to share them with, in exchange for the pleasure of a drink in her charming company.'

'And maybe afterwards a damn good scr—'

'That's enough, Johnson,' snaps the Corporal.

'I should bloody well say it is,' says Fred. 'Please, miss. Will you join us?'

The woman looks directly at us for the first time, smiling awkwardly. With a jolt, I suddenly realise why I half-recognised her. She looks quite different with her hair down, her make-up on and a smile on her face – much prettier too. But still there's no mistaking that wide mouth and those gappy teeth.

Fred, though, has apparently yet to notice. 'Landlord,' he calls. 'A drink for this delightful young lady.'

Patricia removes something from her handbag – a glass object? – and passes it across the bar to the landlord, murmuring her order as she does so. Then she moves towards the chair that Fred is patting. 'Would offer you my knee, but as you can see . . .' says Fred, with a sozzled grin. Patricia settles down next to him.

'Now. Introductions. That handsome chap underneath all that wrapping there is –'

'Fred. Patricia knows us already.'

'Eh? You've met before?'

'We all have. Patricia's our uh – night nurse.'

'No, not the night nurse!' says Fred theatrically, rather as one might announce a pantomime villain. He thinks I've made an in-joke, I suppose. Then, seeing nobody smiling, he turns to look at Patricia closely just in case. 'Not . . .' He trails off as the truth begins to dawn. 'But.' He shakes his head. 'I'm awfully sorry, Patricia. I didn't mean to be rude. It's just that you look so, so very different.'

'Should I take that as a compliment?'

'Oh heavens, yes, you should. You very much should. I mean, if you had any idea just how, well, how ravishing you look now and how, um, now how can I put this delicately?'

'By leaving it at ravishing?'

'Good idea. Excellent idea. Ravishing, Patricia, you shall remain. Gentlemen! A toast! To ravishing Patricia.'

Ginger, Fred, Tom and I raise our glasses. 'To ravishing Patricia!' we say.

The mood perks up considerably after that. Further toasts are drunk. Patricia's beauty is praised. More astonishment is expressed at her Cinderella-like transformation between the hospital and the pub. Fred's hand strays on to Patricia's knee and is not rebuffed. But then, quite without warning, Fred explodes in outrage once more.

'Good God, Patsy, what the devil does that man think he's doing?' he says, blinking in disbelief at Patricia's drink. 'Landlord! LANDLORD!'

'Fred, please, it's perfectly normal,' says Patricia nervously, as the landlord lollops over.

'Is it, hell!' says Fred. 'Landlord, can you kindly explain to me why this young lady is having to drink out of a *jam* jar?'

'It's the war, sir,' says the landlord, wearily.

'What? There's a war on? Oh well, that excuses everything. The weather. Our failure to regain the Ashes. Half-baked service in public houses . . .'

'No, really, Fred. It's the same in Dorset, Wiltshire, the whole of the south coast. England has changed since you went away. There's less to go around and there are a lot more people.'

'The wrong sort of people,' says Fred, glaring towards the GIs.

'Overpaid, oversexed –' intones Farmer Tom.

'Look, they didn't choose to be here,' I say, glancing anxiously towards the GIs, whose looks suggest they are in no mood to take much more of Fred's barracking. 'They've come to help us open a second front. To give their lives so that Europe might be –'

'Give their lives? Drink our beer, more like. And steal our drinking glasses. And corrupt our women with their disgusting chocolate and their filthy nylons and their hideous Yankee –'

And all at once there are four of them, looming over us. Kowalski has seized Fred by the scruff of his collar. Lundt has his hand placed firmly on my shoulder. Two more GIs, even bigger, are standing either side of Tom.

'I'll call the police,' says the landlord.

'With your telephone network?' scoffs Lundt.

'How dare you threaten a man with no legs.'

'Lady, I ain't just threatening,' hisses Kowalski, tightening his grip around Fred's throat.

'I know your names. You'll be court-martialled for this,' says the landlord.

'Sir, you are talking to men who are way beyond caring about shit like that,' says one of the GIs menacing Tom.

'Do to me what the hell you like,' rasps Fred, his face turning red. 'You've done your worst already.'

'Jeez, what is your problem, Limey? It wasn't any of us who did this to you.'

'Someone – like – you,' gasps Fred.

'We're your allies, you ungrateful jerk. Your allies,' calls a GI at the back. Kowalski is not so sure. He has loosened his grip enough for Fred to speak.

'One of your aircraft. A P-47. Bloody good shot, I'll give him that. First pass he took off my legs. Second, he destroyed our MTB. Third one – a nice touch, this – he flew over us low and dipped his wings, just so we could be sure to admire those friendly Yankee stars. Then came the fourth, the one that really endeared me to your people for ever. That was the one that took out our life raft, and my commander, and the rest of our crew.'

There is a long silence and, for a moment, no one can meet each other's eyes. But when I look up, I see that Kowalski has once more tightened his grip on Fred, his jaw set firm, his whole body trembling with rage. 'Oh, Lord, here we go,' I think to myself, scanning the room for the best defensive position while my hands instinctively fumble – commando training, don't you know – for the nearest available weapon which, they appear to have decided, is a leg of the oak cricket table I'm about to smash.

Then, all of sudden, something quite extraordinary happens. Instead of throttling Fred, the American pulls him forward and locks him in a tight embrace.

'Those bastards,' he mutters. 'They never know when to stop!'

From somewhere across the room there's a sob. Then another sob. Now Kowalski has buried his face in Fred's chest, Fred is blubbing his eyes out and Patricia, her arms round both of them, is heaving silently. I bite my lip hard and look to Tom for a sense of proportion. But tears are streaming down his cheeks, too. Only Ginger, flopped against the wall, grinning sloppily, seems immune to the general hysteria. I bite my lip harder but it's no damned use. Within a moment, I too have succumbed to this orgy of lachrymosity. And I must say, part of me – the deep buried American part, I suppose – rather enjoys it. When you've had the sort of family upbringing I have – emotions are nasty, dirty things reserved for foreigners and the poorer class of servant – it makes a pleasant change to be among big-hearted, straightforward people who aren't afraid to wear their hearts on their sleeves. But there's one thing that worries me: if this is how your average GI responds to a story which, sad though it is, is not untypical of the ones we in England have been hearing almost every day for the last five years, then how in God's name are they going to cope when they come up against real bullets?

My awkwardness, it seems, is all too apparent, for Lundt has seized my shoulder hard and is looking me straight in the eye.

'You gotta understand, sir, this isn't how GIs are in the habit of acting.'

'No, no. I'm quite sure.'

His grip grows firmer still.

'No, I don't think you do understand, sir. But I'm gonna make you understand. You see, the reason we're all here, now, doing what we're doing –'

'Lundt, that's enough!' says the Corporal.

'I don't care, Corp. Someone's got to know,' says Lundt. 'What you see here, sir, is the total strength of B platoon. Know how many soldiers there are in a US platoon?'

'Same as an English one, I imagine. Thirty, roundabouts?'

'So what happened to the rest of us, you may be wondering. Price. Stein. Ridgeway. Santini. Bryce. Goldman. Murphy . . . Guys you don't know and never will, but guys I loved like they were my brothers. Guys who shoulda been here drinking with us tonight, like we'd planned, like we'd been dreaming of for two goddamned months. But guess what? Same thing happened to you and your buddies happened to me and my buddies. And all because some stupid goddamned jerk –'

'We don't know that, Lundt,' says the Corporal. 'We don't know for sure they were ours.'

'Yeah, so tell me this, Corp. How did Germans suddenly manage to position themselves in the dunes above an English beach? What were Germans doing firing 0.50-cal. Browning HMGs? How come the guy we found at the beachhead, the guy Kowalski wouldda killed if you hadn't pulled him off, was wearing an American uniform and saying: "Sorry. Sorry. We didn't know" in a New York accent?'

'It came on so sudden, so weird, we thought it must be some kinda joke,' says another GI. 'Like, we were feeling real good, real confident, because it was the most beautiful day, the sea was calm, we came off that LCA with our boots dry – real fast too –'

'Like crap from a greased butt. Oh boy, were we hot!' agrees another GI.

'We were the best. I remember saying to Ridgeway, "We're wasted here in England. We should be in France right now." "Hey, why stop there?" he says, and I think he's about to say more but I don't hear what because we're fanning out now into our protective fire positions, like we've been training to do on the moors, coming out of our imaginary boat which for the first time today is a real boat, in three columns, riflemen like me and Ridgeway first, then Bangalore torpedoes, then wire cutters, then machine gunners and mortars, that's how it's meant to work anyway, and the first idea I get it isn't working is when Ridgeway takes a dive. I'm thinking, jerk's joshing around. You think so too, Corporal, because I remember you saying –'

'Yeah, I did. I said, "Get off your butt, Ridgeway." But he stays down. And he's not the only one who's down, there's others falling around us, and that's when I hear the first rounds whizzing past my ear and I scream "Take cover" because I know right then from the sound, those ain't blanks that are coming at us, and even if I didn't know, I'd see the evidence soon enough – guys cut in half, guys with no heads – that somewhere down the line there has been one hell of a goddamn SNAFU.'

'So the shooting goes on for, Jesus, for what seems like for ever, then finally someone gets through on the radio to ask "What the hell is happening?" and the reply comes back "What do you mean what the hell is happening? Why aren't you advancing?" "Because most of us are fucking dead, that's why," our wireless op says, and finally the message gets through.'

'And we're still not done scraping our buddies off the sand when this major appears, guy we've never seen before, from another unit, and says we must return to base and we must not say a word to anyone about this incident.'

'No "Sorry", we notice. No "We have screwed up so bad and we owe you an explanation".'

'"Yes, sir," I say to the Major. And we commandeer these jeeps. And, of course, we don't go to our base. We do the thing we promised our dead buddies we'd do. What they'd want us to do. And, here's where we intend on staying till those fuck-ups – pardon me, ma'am – come and get us, and if they want to court-martial us, well, what do we care? What could the US military do to us worse than it's done to us already.'

'Amen to that!' says Fred, raising his pewter mug. I raise mine, too, though I've seen too much of war to be altogether surprised by what these boys have told me. Friendly fire has always been a hazard of twentieth-century battle, I'm afraid, and never more so when it's my American cousins doing the firing.

Of course, whenever it happened the people upstairs did their damnedest to keep it covered up. Not good for morale, is it, if you've not only the enemy to fear but your own side too? But if you want to know how common it was, here's something I learned after the war: the Allied forces lost more troops while training for D-Day than they did during the actual landings.

'That cup is looking kinda empty. You sure I still can't persuade you?' asks the Corporal.

'Corporal, I would consider it an honour,' says Fred.

'Name's Danny. Danny Jones,' says the Corporal, extending his hand.

'Sub-Lieutenant Bartholemew Richards, RNVR. But please, call me Fred.'

The rest of us introduce ourselves, all but Ginger, who's lying comatose.

'Jeez, sir. Sorry, sir, I had no idea,' he says, on learning my rank. 'You weren't wearing –'

'That's all right, Corporal. Like you, we're not really supposed to be here.'

'I'm glad you are though. Kind of takes the heat off me.'

'How do you mean?'

'Well, if this place gets busted, I ain't going to be the senior ranking soldier, am I?'

'In that case, you'd better make Dick's a double,' says Fred.

My memory of the events that follow may be unreliable. I have an idea of a considerable number of toasts being drunk, massive surprise and delight being expressed that my maternal grandmother hails from New England, vows of eternal friendship being made, addresses being scrawled on scraps of paper, and much hospitality being promised in our respective countries once the bloody war was over. There might well also have been the odd maudlin interlude as we stared into our beer and glumly contemplated the task ahead of our forces, and the large number of young men – several of them, no doubt, sitting here among us – who would die or be wounded before the summer was out. But only two parts of the remainder of that evening do I remember with any distinctness.

The first is when Fred asks if we wouldn't mind excusing

him for a moment, as he's gasping for a bit of air. When I offer him a hand, Fred looks at me as if I'm stupid and says tersely: 'No, you stay here. We can manage perfectly well, thank you.' And so they do – Fred's left arm on his crutch, and his right arm resting on Patricia's shoulder – as it so often has in the sixty-odd years I've known them since.

No sooner has the door closed behind them than Ginger sits bolts upright on his bench – just like the mummy waking suddenly from his tomb, only much more welcome: I'd been starting to get a little worried – and says: 'Fred?'

'Popped outside for some air,' I say. And can't resist adding: 'With his "Angel of Death".'

'Giving him his birthday present,' says Ginger.

'I expect,' I say, with a ribald snort. And you can tell how far gone I am, because it's not until this point that I actually notice. Sure it's halting, mumbling, and indistinct but compared with anything I've heard the fellow say before it's crisper than Olivier doing Crispin Crispianus.

'Gina?'

'Back at HQ, keeping *cave* for us.'

'Shame.'

'Rather.'

'She's sweet on you.'

'Do you think?'

'Thought she was sweet on me, once,' he says, so heart-wrenchingly wistful that for a moment I can't even reply.

'Better get you another drink, old man,' I say at last. 'You've got some catching up to do.'

But when I do get back with my round of drinks, the poor fellow is comatose once more. I'm quite tempted to give him a shake. There aren't going to be many occasions, I tell myself, when I find my ward-mate on such loquacious form. But now Danny's asking me a question about where I caught my malaria, which leads inevitably to Burma and, once there, there's no stopping me.

At least there wouldn't be were it not for the second occurrence in the evening which I remember quite distinctly: the rattle of engines outside the blacked-out windows, and the squeak of brakes – 'MPs' someone cries in alarm, but by then it's far too late to do much about it – followed very soon afterwards by the entrance of five impossibly well-turned-out, chisel-jawed and cold-eyed MPs in their ultra-polished boots, leggings and gleaming white helmets.

'GIs,' shouts one – not that he needs to shout because the room has fallen quite silent – 'you have one minute to leave these premises, form up outside and await transportation back to your base.'

Corporal Jones clasps my hand under the table.

'Good luck,' he says softly and makes to leave.

'Hold it there, Corporal,' says the senior MP, a sergeant. 'Do you know these people?'

'No, Sergeant.'

'I can vouch for this man,' I say, attempting to rise. 'I –'

'Sir, please sit down. If I need your assistance I will ask for it,' says the Sergeant, adding curtly to one of his men: 'Search this corporal.'

'Sergeant, I am a captain in His Majesty's armed forces –'

'Captain, this is a US military matter and I will not ask you again. Please sit down, sir.'

The Sergeant turns to pick through the contents of Corporal Jones's pockets, as they begin to accumulate on the table. Grenades. Spare ammo clips. A wallet. An old envelope.

He picks up the envelope and squints at the writing.

'Captain R. Coward, Great Meresby, Hambledown Lacey, Herefordshire,' he reads, pronouncing the last word as you'd expect – wrongly. 'Who is this. Some English guy?'

'No not "some English guy". Me,' I snap.

The Sergeant ignores me. 'Corporal, maybe you'd like to reconsider the question I asked you earlier. Do you know these people?'

'We met tonight. Had a few drinks, that's all.'

The Sergeant nods smugly, his brilliant hypothesis apparently confirmed, gives me the look of fair but firm, gimlet-eyed officiousness known to military policemen the world over. 'Sir, may I take your name and unit?'

'I'm not sure that it's any of your business.'

'Sir, you may be a material witness to one or more courts martial arising from events this evening. Would you be happier if I radioed the nearest British military-police unit instead?'

Grudgingly, I give the man my details. Farmer Tom offers his.

'And the gentleman with the bandages?'

'Oh, leave him alone. He's been asleep most of the evening.'

'Sir, I need a name.'

'Put down "Ginger".'

'Sir, I'm going to need more than that.'

I realise, with a twinge of guilt, that I've never bothered to find out. Patricia and Fred would know, I dare say. But Patricia and Fred, wherever they are – that rather cosy-looking barn in the courtyard outside, perhaps? – are very sensibly keeping their heads well down.

'Ginger,' I say, prodding his arm gently at first, then a bit more firmly. 'Ginger, old chap. Very sorry to bother you . . .'

But Ginger, propped against the wall, benign half smile on his lips, resolutely refuses to stir.

'Oh, do leave him –' I begin but the officious GI is already leaning past me. He takes a gentle hold on Ginger's wrist and waits pensively.

'Sir,' says the GI. 'I am sorry to say that your friend is not just asleep.'

5

Great Meresby

It's as perfect a May morning as any I can remember and Great
Meresby has never looked so ravishing. At the far side of the
bridge I pause, leaning against the parapet, to admire the grey-
gold of the stonework and the deep flaming red of the ancient
brick mirrored in the still moat, glowing and shimmering
under a cloudless sky.

God, how I've missed this place!

God, what a tragedy it would be if it fell into enemy hands!

By enemy, I don't of course mean the Germans – who've
clearly long since ceased to be an invasion threat. I'm thinking
more, well, to put it bluntly, of anyone who isn't a Coward.
And if that sounds selfish of me, so be it. There've been
Cowards living on this site since the Norman Conquest. Not
in this exact building – the oldest part of which only goes
back as far as 1450; we've added to it here and there, ever
since, giving it a hotchpotch, piecemeal look which some fools
mistake for ugliness – but certainly on this stretch of land,
which was personally given to my ancestor by William the
Conqueror for services at Hastings. Remember that moment
when the Norman cavalry feigned a retreat so as to lure
Harold's army down and away from the advantageous high
ground on Senlac Hill? Well, the chap leading that retreat
was my ancestor.

Now you know how much the place means to me – and I hope it will mean the same to you, one day – you'll better understand my growing alarm as, on my pre-breakfast stroll through the grounds, I start to notice all the changes Father has wrought in my absence.

Every corner I turn a new horror reveals itself: our croquet lawn, widely admired as the most immaculate in all Herefordshire, now furrowed into potato beds; the tennis courts, transformed into a giant chicken coop; the kitchen garden, extended to embrace not just the old rose borders but the seventeenth-century knot garden. Not even the ancient topiaried yew hedge, I suspect, would have escaped Father's ravages – except that it makes such an invaluable windbreak for the soft-fruit plants Father has installed where the summer herbaceous borders used to be.

Just when I'm thinking it can't possibly get any worse there's breakfast.

'Griffiths,' I say to the butler. 'Would you mind telling me what exactly this is.'

I've just been searching the sideboard for signs of anything edible. Traditionally Mother has seen to it that there has always been plenty – eggs, kippers, ham, fruit, buns, Father's stewed prunes – but today all that appears to be left is a tureen of foul-smelling gloop.

'Kedgeree, sir.'

'I think you should have a word with cook. Haddock's definitely off.'

'It isn't haddock, sir. It's snoek.'

'Hmm. Wondered what those speckledy black bits were. Adder, is it? I do hope cook took the trouble of removing the fangs.'

'Not snake, sir. Snoek. It's a variety of fish.'

'Thank you, Griffiths. I'll have a boiled egg.'

'I'm afraid that won't be possible, sir. Cook has reserved our egg allocation for this evening's dinner.'

'For goodness sake, Griffiths. Our estate has five farms.'

'Those are my orders, sir,' says Griffiths, with just a flicker of a glance towards the far end of the long dining-table, where my father sits hidden behind the newspaper. Mother is next to him, dressed for riding, her face carefully made up for some bizarre reason, looking a touch anxious. She's not at all used to hearing me being so forthright in Father's presence – especially not at the breakfast table.

'Morning, Mother.'

'Morning, dear.'

'Morning, Father.'

Father answers with a slight rattle of his *Daily Telegraph*. I'm in disgrace, he told me last night. And so long as I remained in disgrace he didn't see why he should treat me as a full member of the household. When I asked how long he envisaged this state of affairs continuing, he grinned unpleasantly. 'If it ain't over by this weekend, I shall want to know why,' he said.

'Sleep well, dear?'

'Yes, thank you, Mother,' I say. I try a mouthful of the kedgeree. Then push away the bowl. 'Probably because when I arrived last night it was too dark to see what had been done to the grounds.'

Mother purses her dark-red painted lips. Crikey, if it weren't so out of character, you'd almost think she were having an affair.

'See you at dinner, if not before,' she says, rising suddenly from the table. I can hardly blame her for wanting to get out of the line of fire.

I sip a cup of stewed tea. A clock ticks. Father's newspaper rustles. The room feels cold and dark and dead.

'You know, Father,' I say at last. 'We've already given 3,000 acres to the war effort. Was it really necessary, for the sake of reclaiming one miserly acre more, to wipe out 500 years of horticultural history?'

'Just doing my bit,' says my father into his *Telegraph*. But then, vindictive old bugger that he is, he can't resist adding: 'Something you might care to try sometime.'

Steady now, I have to tell myself. Don't rise. If you rise you'll be playing right into his hands.

'Good God!' I explode. Yes, yes, I know. Problem is, as Price would tell you, I'm never altogether in control when I haven't eaten. 'And when exactly during this war would you say I haven't been doing my bit? When my men and I were fighting to the last round in Burma? When my tank brewed up in the desert? When I shot three Messerschmitts out of the —'

'Dickie, old chap, mightn't it be an idea if you saved all this G. A. Henty stuff for someone who didn't lose five brothers and a leg on the Western Front? Because I'm afraid to anyone who saw any action in 14–18, this new one of yours does sound like a pale imitation.'

'Is that really all you think this war is about? An exercise in competitive hardship?'

'The conversation began, you may remember, when you criticised the efforts I had made towards the war effort. I'm merely pointing out that, to someone of my generation, the loss of a croquet lawn and the odd rose-bush scarcely constitutes a familial tragedy,' he says. Then he smiles — the smile he often gives when something truly malevolent has crossed his mind. 'And besides,' he adds, 'your brother found no difficulty with my emergency measures.'

'You consulted him but not me?'

'You weren't here.'

'Because I was away on active service.'

'I'm sure James would have been, too, if he hadn't had to be called to the Palace to collect the bar to his MC.'

'*Touché.*'

'It's not too late, you know. I haven't a friend in the War Office who thinks it will be over sooner than Christmas. Gives you six months at the very least.'

He is referring, of course, to the unconscionable arrangement regarding the succession of the estate. As the eldest of his surviving sons it ought, by rights, to be mine. But Father, in his wisdom, has decided that instead it will be handed on to whichever of us turns out to have the 'best war'.

'To do what, exactly? Plant the Union flag on the Reichstag? Personally remove Herr Hitler's remaining testicle?'

'If you mean to be silly, then I shan't discuss it further. But I should have thought it was perfectly obvious what was needed to eclipse an MC and bar.'

'Yes but most of them are awarded posthumously.'

'And you don't think Great Meresby is worth it?'

'I can tell you who doesn't. Who's going to turn it into a golf course or flog it off to the nearest black-market profiteer the second he gets his hands on it.'

'I am making no conditions. Whoever earns the right to inherit Great Meresby will also earn the right to do with it as he wishes.'

'And the future of this estate means nothing to you? The fact that it has been owned – and cherished – by our family continuously for twelve generations?'

'There is only one thing that matters to me,' he replies, 'and it has been owned and cherished by our family far longer than twelve generations.' He nods towards the family crest carved into the stone fireplace.

COWARD it says on top. And underneath: 'Semper audax'.

*   *   *

If it weren't for Paddy, I don't know what I'd do. Something very rash, probably. Paddy's that shaggy great brute in that photo you have of me out with the Berkeley – half hunter, half shire horse, with maybe a smidgen of brontosaurus – whose even-temperedness, honesty and tolerance for my ineptness in the saddle has done more to keep me alive than anyone in the world save Price.

Before I reach the stableyard, the dreadful thought occurs that he might turn out to be yet another victim of Father's austerity measures. Canned meat for our poor starving boys on the Gustav Line, perhaps. But though the yard itself is looking considerably less kempt than I remember and though most of the boxes are now empty, Paddy, thank the Lord, is still there, nodding his huge head the moment he sees me. And all ready and saddled up, too, it seems.

'Mr Price said you'd be needing him,' says a fresh-faced thing whose shapely buttocks I've been ogling at some length, till I work out who she was when last I saw her. Becky, the Vicar's twelve-year-old.

'That's very prescient of Mr Price,' I say. 'And where is he this morning?'

'Over at the Cottage. He's expecting you. But asks if you wouldn't mind leaving it till after eleven as he has some business to attend to first.'

This gives me an hour to kill, more or less, which suits me perfectly. Just long enough for a gentle, melancholy tour of the estate. Paddy is dying for a gallop, poor fellow, especially down the long oak avenue, which we usually take at quite a lick, and I keep having to rein him in hard with what little arm strength I have. Just staying in the saddle is difficult enough, with my legs like sticks and the muscles wasted. If Paddy weren't such a comfortable seat – he's like a big lolloping armchair, he is – I'm not sure I'd be up to riding at all.

By God it's worth it though, for the fresh air, and that comforting smell of leather and horse, and the equine companionship and all those sights I've so often doubted I would ever see again. It has changed quite a bit of course, now that every square inch of even vaguely cultivable land has been dug up for Father's great scheme to feed the nation single-handed. Once I've noticed who has been doing all the digging, though, I find I'm not bothered nearly so much: my, are those Land Girls alluring, especially the one with the cropped dark hair and glowing red cheeks, who looks me right in the eye as I touch my cap to her and says: 'Nice 'orse.'

I'm sure there's a more debonair response, one that would prolong the conversation, which is what I'd like to do, because from what I've glimpsed of this boyish-looking girl she's mightily fanciable. But all I manage before I ride on is: 'Thank you.'

Then feeling that's not quite enough, I call back over my shoulder – she's still looking at me, hands on hips – 'His name's Paddy.'

And that, I'm ashamed to say, is it.

Not everything on the estate has changed beyond recognition. The crooked Waterloo obelisk on the hill beyond the oak avenue is still the same; so is the lake, with the upturned rowing boat we used to play in as children rotting on the shore; and of course, there's the water mill.

I tether Paddy to the ruined mill house and, for old times' sake, sit on the wall of the bridge – dangling my legs above the clear deep pool wherein used to lurk the terrifying pike reputed among the village children to have swallowed Mrs Wilkins's Jack Russell puppy whole. Just thinking about him now sets the spiders crawling down my back. Funny, how those childhood terrors can still hold a chap in their grip.

Looking up, I see the willow from behind whose branches

I once played peeping Tom and, of course, I immediately start thinking of her again. We scarcely had time to say goodbye after my contretemps with the American MPs and Ginger's demise. Nobody's fault really, as you know, but the way the military works is, when something goes wrong, somebody has to take the rap and as senior officer present that duty fell to me. So first thing the next day, my locker has been cleared and I'm being driven to the station, lest my example spread further insurrection through the wards. And the most I can manage with Gina before I'm carted off is a quick but encouragingly tight embrace, a peck on the cheek and a: 'We never –'

'We never did,' she agrees.

'Then we must –'

'Oh definitely,' she says. 'There was something I meant to ask you. A favour.'

'Granted,' I say.

'But you don't know what it is.'

'Do I need to?' I say, with a smile which is meant to convey uninterest but probably comes out looking more revoltingly cloying than a kitten with a bandaged paw – an image that haunts me through every one of the eight or so hours it takes me to get back to my unit's HQ, because from what little I know of women this just isn't a side of a prospective lover they much care to see. 'Oh God, oh God, I've blown it now,' I keep thinking to myself. It's all I can do to stop thinking about it when the Colonel calls me into his office for what I gather from the adjutant is going to be my official reprimand.

'Consider yourself officially reprimanded, Dick,' he says.

'Yes, sir. Thank you, sir.'

'I'm not sure there's much I need add, except to wish you good luck in civilian life.'

'I'm sorry sir, I don't understand.'

'Ah, did the MO not mention it? We're giving you an

honourable discharge. On medical grounds. Spares us the awkwardness of any embarrassing details which might emerge during the course of a court martial. Spares you the tedium of having to pass the rest of eternity six feet under somewhere sticky and godforsaken on the road to Mandalay.'

'If it's all the same to you, sir, I'd still rather go back and see it through to the end.'

'I appreciate the offer, Dick, but have you looked in the mirror lately? You're like a stick insect with worms. And it's plain to me as a pikestaff that your mind ain't on the job. Take a rest, Dick. Take a long, long break. You've done your bit. More than done your bit. I'm only sorry that it never quite translated into the gong everyone assures me you so richly deserved.'

'Thank you, sir. But if it's all the same to you, I'd still rather have the opportunity to clear my name. Even if it means having to face a court martial.'

'Damn it, Dick, it is not all the same to me. You joined this regiment, let me remind you, under a cloud. The least you owe us for having had the generosity to accept you when few others would is to preserve our good name at no matter what cost to your own.'

'Sir, I'm confident that when the facts emerge –'

'Dick, the facts as I understand them involve your having decided in the heat of battle to put a bullet through the head of a senior officer. Not one of our own chaps, thank God, but still: gloss it how you will, it is hardly an incident from which the regiment is likely to emerge smelling of roses.'

'I suppose not, sir.'

'Then at least we agree on something. As to the thing we don't agree on, well, I'm sorry but, like it or not, honourable discharge is what you're getting. Enjoy civilian life and take up golf, that would be my advice. Golf for the body, bridge for the brain. And chin up, old chap – in another sixty years you'll be dead.'

Whenever I go into the Cottage, I always half-expect to be greeted by a wolf dressed up like an old lady, or seven dwarves or a witch who smells of gingerbread. It was built on the edge of the wood, as a sort of Gothic folly cum stable-girl-rogering zone by one of my more dissolute ancestors. At the moment though, it's the home of our estate manager, Mr Thompsett, currently on active service somewhere overseas.

Price appears to have made himself very comfortable in his temporary residence. There's a fire in the fireplace; and fried bacon on the hob; and what smells like proper coffee as opposed to the muck cook has been fobbing us off with up at the Big House. From the oven he pulls a baking tray brimming with fat brown sausages and rounds of crisp black pudding. He piles it on to a tin plate, sets it in front of me.

'Not hungry, Price?' I say, slightly irritated because I don't like being stared at and smoked over while I eat.

'Eaten already, thank you, sir,' he says, puffing at one of those American cigarettes even I can't afford.

I don't speak again for quite some time because my mouth's always full. I really must have been very very hungry.

'Price, I'm not going to ask how you procured these rare and proscribed delicacies. Just so long as you understand: I'm breakfasting with you from now on.'

'Oh, I can't promise to be able to match this every day, sir. Today's special.'

'Is it, Price? And please, Mr Richard will do just fine now we're out of uniform.'

'It most definitely is, sir, Mr Richard, pardon me, sir, force of habit. Here!'

From behind the black-out curtain he has retrieved a bottle

of Bollinger – vintage 1934, I notice: no prizes for guessing whose cellar that was filched from – and fills up two mugs.

'You bugger. You've had half of it already,' I say, eyeing the liquid-level.

'There's plenty more where this came from,' says Price. 'Your health, sir!'

'Chin-chin,' I say, clinking mugs. 'But I still don't know what we're toasting.'

'Freedom!'

'Freedom?'

'From uniform. From orders. From ever having to risk our blooming necks again. There's three more reasons to drink a toast already.'

'Well, I suppose.'

'What do you mean, you suppose, you stupid sod, sir? There's millions out there who'd give their right arm, their right bollock 'n' all, I shouldn't wonder, and I know whereof I speak, for what you and I have got ourselves right now.'

'But isn't there a tiny part of you that rather wishes you could be there for the final push?'

'Oh, there is, I'm sure,' he says. 'Problem is, that tiny part's out somewhere in Flanders Field, tucked up nice and cosy with the General's leg.'

With a shake of the head I raise my mug, chink it against his and pour the first draught down the hatch.

Of course, he would say that. Rarely does Price let slip an opportunity to draw attention to the orchidectomy he suffered at Passchendaele from the same German shell that crippled my father. It's a matter of perverse pride. Whenever there's a chorus of 'Price-y has only got one ball', it's always Price himself who's leading it. Perhaps it's a way of disarming those barrack-room jokers who might otherwise be tempted to use his disability against him. Mainly, though, I think it's propaganda aimed at the fairer sex. You see, there's a story abroad – where can it have originated, I wonder? – that besides making him sterile, the loss of that testicle somehow had the remarkable side-effect of causing a growth spurt in Pricey's tadger – which, even before the war, was something of a legend in Herefordshire riding circles. 'Twice the fun with none of the risk,' I have sometimes overheard Price boasting in his cups. It has certainly never damaged his chances, as I often had cause to rue in those early days of the war when it seemed that while he was bedding virtually the entire strength of WRAF, I was doomed to spend whatever was left of my no-doubt brief life a miserable virgin.

'And it's not as though you've got much of a handicap in the britches department, sir,' he once observed. This would have been in my flying days about the time when he observed that if things had come to such a pass that not even a Spitfire pilot could get his end away, we might as well have done with it and surrender now.

'What the devil business is that of yours, Price?' I said to him.

'Pardon me, sir. Didn't mean to offend. Just trying to point out, sir, that if you were ever to let it be known among your circle of lady friends, that, ahem –'

'Price, let me assure you that what may work perfectly well with the ladies in your circle would make the ladies in mine run a mile.'

'Is that so, sir? Then I'm sorry I suggested it, sir. I'm sure you know best,' he said in that grovelling, extra-polite way he has whenever he's being especially impertinent.

Cocky bugger. And he's been up to his filthy tricks again this morning, by the looks of it. The smear of dark lipstick on that glass by the wash-basin. The two dirty plates, bearing the traces of breakfast. Oh crikey, I do hope he washed his hands before cooking mine.

Price pours out the remnants of the champagne and offers me a Lucky Strike.

'And there was one other thing I was celebrating today, sir,' he says.

'Are you sure I need to know, Price?'

'My new position.'

'Enough, man.'

'I was referring, if you don't mind, sir, to the unhappy news that Mr Thompsett will not, after all, be returning from his overseas duties. And that consequently –'

'You're inheriting his house. Well done, Price, I'm sure you'll be very happy here.'

'Sir, if you'll let me finish. It's not just his house the General has given me. It's his job too.'

'But – Price. This is splendid news,' I say, wishing I'd managed to come up with the response straightaway rather than after a spluttering of my champagne, a horrified arching of the eyebrows and a long, stunned silence.

'Thank you, Mr Richard,' he says, tersely, as if he knows exactly what I'm thinking. It's not that I don't reckon him up to the job. More that when you've grown up knowing a chap first as manservant and groom, even head groom, later as your batman and your platoon sergeant it's quite a tricky one accepting his promotion to damn near your social equal.

'I suppose I had better get used to calling you Mr Price.'

'Never you mind about that, Mr Richard. You call me what you like. Just so long as you understand that from now on I won't have the time to go chasing round after you and keeping you out of trouble. My fighting days are over. I'm a civilian with responsibilities. So whatever funny ideas you may have at this dinner the General's laid on for you –'

'Jolly nice of him.'

'I shouldn't be so sure about that. He's invited along a few of his high-ranking pals. What you might call a matchmaking exercise. My advice to you is, whatever sweet nothings they whisper in your ear, don't listen. They're only after one thing.'

'You're becoming very mysterious in your new office, Price.'

'Then I'll be blunt. If you finish this evening volunteering for more active service I would ask you never to try knocking on this door again because I blooming well won't answer. And I don't think I'm speaking out of turn when I say Her Ladyship feels exactly the same way. Now do I make myself clear?'

'My dear chap, I'm not even fit for duty.'

'Since when has that ever stopped you?'

'But, with my military record, who'd want me anyway?'

'You'd be surprised what dregs they're accepting these days.'

'Price, don't you worry. From henceforward it is fully my intention to play the Cincinnatus.'

'And that would mean what, in English?'

'You've never heard of Cincinnatus – the great general who, having defeated Rome's enemies, chose to return to his life as a humble farmer, there to eke out the rest of his days in honest toil and rustic simplicity?'

'No. But I'll take your word for it.'

Price cracks open another bottle of my father's champagne and we drink several more toasts to the safe, simple, rural life we now intend to lead. And I quietly thank the good Lord that dear Pricey had such a dismal classical education – for if he hadn't he might be aware of the final twist in the Cincinnatus legend: that having returned to his plough, he was later called to arms yet again.

6

Taking the Plunge

Now, you might have noticed that sex during the war isn't something my generation talks about and the reason, it seems to me, has nothing to do with prudery: rather, it's that the majority of us were getting so little we're too embarrassed to admit it; and a tiny minority were getting so much they wouldn't want to make you jealous.

Price, as you know, was very much one of the minority. I, for the most part, was not, which is something that has always rather puzzled me. It's not that I'm suggesting I'm God's gift to womankind. Merely that times of war do tend to concentrate the mind on one's mortality and, as you might imagine, in the prevailing spirit of 'gather ye rosebuds while ye may', it isn't too difficult to find willing partners.

The tricky part is plucking up the courage to make the initial pass. And this, I'm afraid, is something that I have never been much good at. I can cope with artillery barrages, wading through the surf under fire; charging enemy machine-gun posts, fighting hand to hand and so on. But when I'm confronted with the terrifying challenge of asking a woman even for the time of day, let alone dinner or a quick one, up against the wall, on the perfectly reasonable grounds that we might as well since we could be dead tomorrow, well, almost without fail my courage deserts me.

This morning, though, I am quite determined will be different. Emboldened by Price's – or should I say my father's – excellent champagne, stung by the thought that this ugly brute is continuing to enjoy the flower of English womanhood while I, his superior in class, rank and ephebic beauty, continue to suffer a life of monkish celibacy, I have decided to steer Paddy back to the place I last saw that scrumptious little Land Girl. We shall strike up a conversation. And then, who knows.

'Hello again,' I say to her. (Gosh, what an inspired opener!)

''Ello,' she says. (Cockney, I should guess. But I've never shied from the exotic.)

'I was wondering –'

'Yes?'

'I was wondering whether you might fancy a ride.'

'A ride?' she says, with a crafty smile. Her teeth are a bit discoloured, I can't help noticing. Still she does have a very nice face.

'On Paddy,' I say, flushing.

She stands there a while, surveying Paddy and me, as if weighing up the pros and cons. 'Fanks for offerin'. But I'd better not.'

'You'll be perfectly safe. He's a very gentle horse.'

'It's not 'im I'm worried about. It's the geezer wot I 'ave to work for.'

'Do you mean Price. Mr Price?'

'New bloke. Ugly sod. Very saucy.'

'Well, you needn't worry about him. He works for me.'

'This is never all yours?' she says, gesturing at the field behind her.

'And that, and that,' I say, pointing towards the obelisk hill and the distant lake.

'Blimey. You a lord or somefink?'

'My mother's . . .' I was about to tell her that my mother

is the younger daughter of an earl, but this strikes me as being more information than she needs. 'No, just a humble land-owner's son. Very humble. You know 3,000 acres really isn't that much.'

She laughs. 'Still. Mustn't grumble, eh?'

'No. I suppose I mustn't.'

There's an awkward silence. She shifts from foot to foot.

'So how about it?' I say, patting the saddle just in front of me. 'If I promise to square it with Mr Price?'

Her eyes flicker down for a moment, then back up at me. 'Yeah. All right.'

The girl's name is Patsy and she comes from a family of seven in Bethnal Green; her parents are dead, her big brothers are in all arms of the military and the younger ones and her sisters are now dispersed across the country after their home took a direct hit from a Doodlebug. She doesn't want me to feel sorry for her – 'There's other families 'ave 'ad a lot worse' – but there's a sob in her voice as she adds: 'I don't 'alf miss 'Arry, though.'

'Your father?'

'My 'orse.'

'You had a horse?'

'For the market.'

'But where did you keep him?'

'In the 'ouse. Where do you fink? 'Arry had his room, down-stairs. And when I was sad, when fings got too much, I'd sneak down into 'Arry's room and spend the night with 'im. All curled up next to him, in the hay. 'E never minded. Good as gold 'e was. Just like this one,' she says, giving Paddy a pat.

Ah, I think to myself. So it's not so much me she's inter-ested in as my horse. Still, these things can be worked on, I'm sure. And as we amble forward, squashed together in the saddle, my arms either side of her as I hold the reins, the delicious thought occurs that this might yet prove to be a rather wonderful summer for me, Paddy and our gamine young coquette.

'Have you been to the old mill?' I hear myself asking.

'Wot, the water wheel? Loads of times,' she says.

'Ah but have you been swimming in the millpond?'

'In this weather?'

'Well, if you're not game,' I say, a touch huffily, pulling on Paddy's right rein so that he begins to turn back the way we've just come.

''Ang on. I never said I wasn't game. It's only, well, I ain't got nuffink to wear.'

I bring Paddy to a halt for a moment.

'Who said you had to wear anything?' I say.

'Wot?'

'House rules, I'm afraid. We've been doing it for generations.'

By the time we reach the old mill, Patsy has all but surrendered to the inevitable. Not only has she grown much more relaxed in the saddle – she doesn't even complain when I press myself closer against her and bring my arms tighter round hers – but she has become a lot more flirtatious and giggly.

'This where you bring all your girlfriends, then?' she says.

'I'll have you know I'm an officer and a gentleman.'

'It's the officers, I've 'eard, wot are the worst.'

'Then I shall endeavour not to disappoint you,' I say, with one of those leers I imagine Price uses all the time, but which I'd never dream of essaying myself if I weren't so tiddly.

Jolly well works though. Patsy titters responsively. So I give her a cheeky squeeze of the waist and she giggles at that too.

Things are progressing so swimmingly that when it comes to dismounting I find it exceedingly difficult to slide from the saddle because of a certain awkward lump in my britches. If Patsy were to notice – and I simply don't believe Price's dubious theories on this score – I reckon I would undo all the good work I've done so far. So I quickly flood my brain with the grisliest images I can think of: the cartload of children just after the attack on the refugee convoy; Johnny's head flying towards me, eyes still focusing on me, after being severed clean by a samurai blade.

It does the trick. More or less.

'Don't look,' I say, as I begin stripping off my clothes. Patsy, waiting under the willow, has insisted I test the water first.

'I've got brothers, Dick. Seen it all before.'

Next thing, I'm mounting the parapet of the bridge and – quick as I can, so as not to allow myself any opportunity to change my mind – leaping straight to the spot where I know the millpond's deepest.

The water, when I hit it, feels hard as blue ice and damn near as cold. But as the shock begins to subside, and the chill gives way to a delicious tingly warmth, I realise I'm laughing and shouting for joy:

'Come on in!' I yell, raising my arms in the air. 'It's –'

'Lovely' I was probably going to say, but I don't because, as happens when you try waving your arms in the air in deep water, I've sunk like a stone and I'm talking in bubbles and thinking about pike. Big pike. The sort of pike that could rip your tackle off in no time, I'm thinking as I clench my upper thighs together, wishing she'd hurry up and join me, so we can get out again and move on to the next course. Every time a stray bit of weed brushes against my leg, I shudder.

'Liar,' she says. But she has started to remove her clothes none the less. 'Oi. No looking!' she says, having got down to her underwear.

'I'll shut my eyes. Promise,' I say.

'You'll turn your head till I say, or I ain't coming in.'

So I paddle myself round till I'm facing the opposite

direction, which I continue to do until I have judged sufficient time has elapsed. I've timed it perfectly, too, because I manage to whip myself round and look up at the very moment she's perched on the parapet, ready to jump in.

'Oi,' she squeals, jumping in, but by then I've had my eyeful. Under all those heavy, oversized farmworker's clothes, she turns out to have a very thin, delicate body, the tan on her face and hands contrasting quite jarringly with her natural urban pallor. She needs filling out; looking after. But most of all what she needs is a damn good –

'Urrrbbll'. She's ducking me, and using her whole bodyweight to keep me under, which as near-drowning experiences go is by no means the worst I've had, not with that bony but smooth-skinned naked young body pressed against mine. Reluctantly, I pull myself free to get a breath of fresh air.

'You're a double liar, 'n' all, cos you said it wasn't cold,' she says as I bob up, laughing.

'And it's bloody freezing!'

'We'll have to find some way of making ourselves warm, then, won't we?'

'You, Dick, have got a filfy mind.'

'Really? I was wondering whether we should make a fire. What was on your mind?'

Patsy takes this as the cue to give me another ducking. Then, after we've bobbed about a bit, and flirted some more, another one. But though the sun is shining, there's still a slight chill in the air and the water is hardly Mediterranean. Patsy says she needs to get herself warm – 'By putting my clothes on, thank you very much' – and since she can't trust me to behave myself, I'd better stay where I am till she's done.

While Patsy wades shorewards, I gaze at her retreating buttocks until she disappears from view. Wallowing in the pool, I'm barely touched by the cold or pike fear now, because I'm far too busy thinking filthy thoughts and wondering how best to make my next move. Invite her back to tea with my parents? I snigger aloud at my silly little joke. Offer to marry her? I snigger again. Draw her attention to the convenient seclusion of the mill house –?

'I say, you look freezing,' calls a voice from the parapet of the bridge. A female voice. The very last voice in the world I want to hear right at this moment.

'No, really, it's lovely once you're in,' I say, automatically, as my heart sinks and my body falls limp with the burden of inextricable doom.

'Do you know, I'm so fearfully hot I'm almost tempted to join you,' says Gina, flapping at the lapels of a grey flannel jacket so as to waft some air down her blouse. Her outfit – shapely, exquisitely cut and very expensive: pre-war couture, no doubt – sets off her figure quite gorgeously. 'Go on! How much do you dare me?'

I look up helplessly as Gina looks down at me from the parapet, smiling, inviting, eager and as lovely as I have ever seen her. And in that brief moment, I know what paradise looks like. Paradise, that is, viewed from the perspective of a poor, miserable wretch wallowing in the third circle of hell.

Then Patsy appears on the bank, looking like a drowned rat, and all I can think now is what terrible teeth she has and what a slovenly posture and dreadful shabby clothes. And I know it's bloody awful of me to think that way, the behaviour of a cad, but there's no reason to lie about it now, that's what we're like, we boys, on those rare occasions where we're thinking with our brains rather than our pricks, and that's how it was, I'm afraid.

Gina's expression darkens just long enough to let me know how deep inside the doghouse I am before expertly recovering her poise.

'Oh, I'm so sorry,' she says sweetly, 'I've interrupted your fun.' The way she says 'fun' suggests anything but.

'No, really, it's quite all right,' I say. 'Patsy's one of our Land Girls and she needed to cool off. But I expect you're ready to get back to work now, aren't you, Patsy?'

'Oh yes, Mr Dick,' says Patsy, bowing and tugging her forelock in mock subservience. 'To please the master is my only wish.' Her eyes are dark fury.

Under different circumstances I might find her jealous rage quite flattering. As it is, I just feel a total heel.

'If you wait just a moment, I can give you a ride back.'

'Fanks,' she says, with a sneery glance at Gina. 'But I reckon any girl who'd want a ride with you would need their bloomin' 'ed examined.'

'Um, perhaps I should catch up with you later,' says Gina, making to leave.

'No, wait, I shan't be long,' I say, wading towards where I've left my clothes on the bank.

But too late – they've already been scooped up by Patsy.

''Ere. Allow me to 'elp,' she says. And with a dramatic swing of her arms, she hurls first my britches, then my shirt, and my hacking jacket, and finally my riding boots, into the millpond.

And that isn't the worst of it either. When finally I've got myself out of my dripping wet kit and gone downstairs to find out from Griffiths where Lady Gina has got to, I learn that she has gone out for a walk with Mr James and isn't expected back much before dinner.

'But how dare he! It was me she came to see. Wasn't it?'

'Strictly speaking, Mr Richard, she came at your father's bidding to make up the numbers for dinner.'

'Well, you'll make sure I get to sit next to her, won't you, Griffiths?'

'I'm afraid the placement has already been decided, Mr Richard. Your father has some military gentlemen he should like you to meet.'

Father is forever inviting senior military types round for dinner. Some are old comrades from the trenches, others are lured by the fact that our home makes a convenient stopping-off point after training exercises in the Black Mountains, by the excellent shooting on the estate, and, most especially, by my father's superb wine cellar – which he never touches himself because, since the last war, ever perverse, he has only drunk whisky. No doubt if I had been as proficient in the art of brown-nosing as my twin brother, I might have used these connections to progress much further up the ranks than I have. The problem is, I have this old-fashioned view that the principal purpose of a dinner party is to see how far you can get inside your pretty young neighbour's knickers, not how far you can bury your tongue up a colonel's arse.

Price is right. Whatever I do this evening, I mustn't play Father's game. Which is why, at dinner, I make a point of dressing in black tie rather than the mess kit I'm still entitled to wear pending my discharge. Yes, I suppose it does make me feel a little out of place amid the sea of scarlet-and-black uniforms – besides Father and James, there's a Royal Marines brigadier, a colonel of paratroops, and a major from the Army Film Unit. But just like Price – he's in black tie, too, an old set of mine, fits him perfectly – I intend to signal to the world that from now on I'm to be treated as a civilian. And I'm going to talk like one, too. No mention of all the things I've done and all the places I've been. That's James's domain, and by the sounds of it, he's going to be given more than enough cues by his man-eating neighbour, Lavinia Crumblebeech, the horse-faced vice-admiral's daughter.

'So, come on, James, do tell all, we're dying to know,' she

says in a voice more piercing than a battle cruiser's klaxon. 'How exactly did you win the bar to your MC?'

The table falls silent – though less, on the whole, out of all-ears eagerness than from sheer bloody embarrassment. My little sister Lucy captures the mood rather well when she leans across and says to me in what she thinks is a whisper: 'I wonder how much he paid her to ask that?' Unfortunately it seems to have come out rather louder than she intended.

Lavinia Crumblebeech is looking appalled; mother anxious; my elder sister Isobel – as ever – confused; the tousle-haired director chap from the Army Film Unit evidently tickled in some sort of abstruse intellectual way; Gina mischievous; Caro Ashenden, the rather attractive young war widow stationed next to Price, is simpering prettily; the marine brigadier and his jolly wife both quite purple with mirth; the airborne colonel tremble-jawed with determination to keep a straight face; Price coughing violently into his napkin; and James, who has never taken well to little Lucy's sharp tongue it must be said, on the verge of exploding.

Only shell-deafened Father, presiding from his throne at the head of the table, has failed to register. He's turning his head from side to side in little jerky movements, desperate for someone to fill him in on the joke, which of course no one will because everyone's pretending not to have heard it.

'Mummy,' says James in a voice quavering with barely suppressed hysteria. He knows there's no point pleading with Father: his little girl is the one person in the world he allows to do whatever the hell she likes. 'Why isn't Lucy tucked up in bed at school?'

'Darling, as you know very well –' Mother begins.

'Excuse me, Mummy, I'm sixteen years old and I'm quite capable of speaking for myself. And do you know, I'll bet James doesn't know because the only person he has ever been

76

interested in is Major James Coward I've-got-an-MC-and-bar-don't-you-know-aren't-I-quite-the-thing?'

'Mother,' threatens James half-rising from his chair. I'm sure if there weren't senior officers present he would have got up and strangled her by now.

'James, you must be patient. Lucy's upset because her school house was hit by a Doodlebug and three of her friends are still missing.'

'Dead, Mummy. Patricia and Sarah and Victoria are dead.'

After a flurry of muttered 'good Lord, how awfuls' and 'terribly, terribly sorrys', the dining-room falls even more silent than before, as everyone suddenly decides to find their first course the most tremendously involving thing on earth.

'Jolly good egg,' says the Brigadier, chewing a morsel of his half-an-egg thoughtfully.

'Very good indeed. Hen, is it?' agrees the Colonel, a tall, lean para named Myles Todhunter.

'Hen,' my father confirms.

'How easily one forgets,' says Todhunter.

'Julius hasn't, the jammy sausage,' says Isobel, poking her latest acquisition in the ribs. 'Julius, tell them how many eggs you ate in America.'

Julius flicks his floppy hair from his eyes and removes his glasses, which he begins polishing distractedly.

'One or two,' he says.

'Darling, you're being too modest,' says Isobel. She turns to the rest of the table and announces: 'Julius has been in America, making a film about the build-up for the second front. Very hush-hush so I probably shouldn't be telling you. And every day he had two whole eggs for breakfast, fried, boiled, poached, any way he wanted. If he'd wanted, I dare say, he could probably have had even more than two. Couldn't you, honeybun?'

77

Julius squirms and I'm not sure I feel too sorry for him. I sense that he's far too sophisticated to be wasting his time among bumpkins like us Cowards; whom, of course, he will be lining up first against the wall, come the revolution.

'You can't beat an egg,' declares my father.

'Only when you're making mayonnaise,' quips the Brigadier, prodding with his knife the noisome, yellowish emulsion cook has served with our half of hard-boiled egg.

'I beg your pardon?' says my father.

'You said you can't "beat" an egg. And I said –'

'Oh very good, Jumbo,' says my father suddenly getting the joke. 'Very, very good. Hear that one, Lucy?'

'It's very stale, Daddy.'

'But good in parts, what?' says the Brigadier.

'Ah now there's one you will enjoy, Lucy,' says Father. 'Have you heard the one about the curate's egg? Good in parts?'

'No.'

'You tell it, Jumbo. You're bound to make a better fist of it than I –'

The egg-related mirth continues for quite some considerable length of time and we all have to listen politely while Father and his old pal Jumbo bat their jokes back and forth. All of us, that is, save Price, who is so busy flirting *sotto voce* with Caro Ashenden he doesn't even notice Father's pointed observation that, now he's got a new estate manager, he hopes he'll be able finally to get hold of some hens capable of laying more than one egg a week.

But the laughter soon stops, I can tell you, when people see what the main course is. Woolton bloody pie, would you believe it, which actually knowing my father I would, but I can see the guests are having some trouble coming to terms with the shock.

You know what Woolton pie is, don't you? It's a fearful mess of carrots, turnips, parsnips, spuds all mixed together with an oatmeal stock, invented for the Minister of Food by the head chef at the Savoy, though I can assure you you'd never guess as much from the taste, which is bland beyond measure. Now, clearly, you have to put up with a lot worse when you're out in the field. But when you've been invited for dinner at a place like Great Meresby, with five tenanted farms and the best beef in all Herefordshire, you do rather expect something a little more piquant to go with your Cheval Blanc '32, don't you?

Anyway, no one's quite sure whether to make a joke about it or pretend it's not happening, which enables Lavinia Crumblebeech to seize the moment and ask James once more if he'd care to tell us all about his MC. But this time, she asks it with her eyes fixed in a very beady glare on Lucy, as if to say: 'Any smart remarks, young miss, and you're curtains.'

James tries, not altogether successfully, to arrange his features into an expression of modest reluctance, takes a deep, preparatory breath and begins: 'Well –'

'Miss Crumblebeech, if I may intrude for a moment so as to spare Major Coward his blushes,' says Mrs 'Jumbo' Watson. 'You ought to know that there are few things a fighting man likes less than talking about his exploits in mixed company. Am I not right, Major Coward?'

'I was about to say that very thing, Mrs Watson,' says James, causing Lucy to snigger so much that snot begins pouring out of her nose, forcing her to dive below the table as if she has just dropped her napkin.

'Decent show, all the same, MC and bar. I've not met many who can make that claim,' observes the airborne Colonel.

'And even fewer who can beat it. Only one I know, in fact. Danish fellow by the name of Anders Lassen.'

'Very handy with a knife,' I say, before I can stop myself.

79

The Cheval Blanc is just too damned good not to drink lots of, unfortunately, and I'm afraid it has loosened my tongue.

'You know him?'

'We've worked together occasionally,' I say, with a nervous glance at Price. And a rightly nervous one, too, judging by the innumerable daggers his look throws back at me.

'Have you, by Jove? What, in the Med?'

'I'm not sure I ought to say,' I say, blushing like a schoolgirl.

'Very commendable,' says the Brigadier.

'Rather convenient, too,' says James snidely. Absolutely loathes it, he does, when anyone else even threatens to steal the limelight. Especially if it's me.

I shouldn't rise, I know, but James does have this effect. 'James, not everyone shares your urgent need to go round boasting about how heroic they've been,' I say.

'Boys!' says Mother.

'Please, Emily,' says Jumbo. 'Some of us were rather enjoying the sport.'

'Rather! Pistols at dawn!' says Lucy.

'Same with my paras,' observes Todhunter. 'It's all very well training them up to a peak of aggression, but if there aren't any Germans around, they end up knocking hell out of each other.'

My father leans forward. He was badgering Todhunter at drinks before dinner and now here he goes again: 'Sounds like Dickie might do rather well with you.'

Todhunter comes over all coy and starts muttering about how the recruitment process isn't quite as simple as that. Don't altogether blame him. For all he knows, I could be the tall-tale-telling pansy my little brother is so keen to paint me as. And frankly, that suits me just fine.

'Not to worry, Colonel,' I say, to spare his blushes. 'After what I saw happening to the *Fallschirmjäger* in Crete, you'd never catch me on a parachute again.'

The Colonel nods as if I've confirmed all his worst suspicions: any man who doesn't like jumping out of aeroplanes under fire from 800 feet clearly needs his head examining.

The Brigadier, unfortunately, does not appear to have been so easily put off by my fib. He regards me curiously, as if to say: 'Hmm. So you've done a bit of parachuting too? Dark horse, ain't you?' He's been giving me these looks at intervals ever since the drinks we had in the library before dinner.

What's frustrating is that I've been trying so jolly hard — as per Price's strict instructions — not to give the game away. It's a bugger that the reference to Anders Lassen slipped out, because now the Brigadier has a pretty good idea I've seen commando service. Generally, though, I think I've been doing rather well. Only with hindsight do I now realise that the game was lost within a few minutes of our first chat together when, striving desperately to keep the conversation from anything that had to do with my military service, I happened to mention our summer jaunts before the war to watch Price race Mother's horses at Deauville.

'Lovely there, I've heard,' he says.

'Oh, it is. The whole Normandy coast, absolute bliss.'

'Know it well, do you?'

'Parts of it, yes. We had this wonderful mare — Blaise of Glory — came in first in '37, and to celebrate we spent a week riding from village to village along the French coast, ending up in this dear little fishing village. Port something — I say, Price. Can you remember the name of that place Port whatsit we ended up in on our riding tour?'

'Can't say that I do, Mr Richard.'

'Course he does,' I say *sotto voce* to the Brigadier. 'Etched on his brain, I would imagine, after what he got up to with the village postmaster's wife, which, I might tell you, meant that we couldn't hang around quite as long as we would have liked. Now, what was its name. Port . . . Port-en-Bessin, that's it.'

'Port-en-Bessin? Never heard of it,' says the Brigadier. Which I now know was the most arrant of lies.

Anyway, back to dinner, where Gina has decided to speak up. 'May I ask a silly question?' she says, with the sort of disingenuous simper that could flatten a man at fifty paces. And in an instant all the chaps round the table are prostrate with eagerness to help this radiant young beauty in any way they can.

'Ask away, my dear,' says the Brigadier.

'I was wondering how important it is to be lucky in war?'

'Oh, good Lord,' says the Brigadier. 'It's the most important thing in the world. Makes all the difference between life and death, winning and losing. Wouldn't you say, Ajax?'

'That's what Napoleon always said. Didn't mind what other qualities his generals had so long as they were lucky. But I think it's a lot of superstitious guff, myself. The truth, as Wellington knew, is that you make your own luck.'

'Come, Ajax. You've seen chaps stop bullets with their pocket bibles and their cigarette cases. You've seen ones who just know — they absolutely know — their luck's run out and ten minutes later they're dead.'

'And what of all the men who weren't saved by their bibles and their cigarette cases? And what of all the ones, convinced they were going to die, as all of us have been at one time or another, who've lived to tell the tale. Luck be damned. It's a matter of percentages. Back me up here, Myles.'

'Well, I would, sir, except there's the damnedest fellow in my unit by the name of Lucky Lucas. The men swear by him. Some of them have been with him since Dunkirk and they all say that just so long as you touch his cap badge before an engagement —'

'Pshaw!'

'Yes, well, I thought so, too, but it does seem to work.'

'Good God, man. Don't say you've been participating in this charade yourself?'

'All I know is that I've seen far too many men who haven't touched Lucas's badge come unstuck.'

My father harrumphs. 'This fellow Lucas, must be an NCO now, I would imagine.'

'He's a sergeant.'

'There you are, then, it has nothing to do with luck. It's what an experienced sergeant does. Keeps his men alive.'

'So if experience and luck are the same thing,' says Gina, 'that must mean that a man who has been through an awful, awful lot of battles –'

'Aha,' says the Brigadier, beaming. 'I see what you're driving at. You're worried about your young chap, that it?'

Gina reddens.

'Well, let me reassure you, young lady, that while nothing is certain in war, I'd say a strapping young Guards officer who's been lucky enough to bag himself an MC and bar, stands an odds-on chance of making it past the finishing post.'

While the Brigadier smiles his blessing at what he imagines to be the happy couple, elsewhere round the table there is much embarrassed wriggling.

'Um, actually, sir, it wouldn't quite be accurate to describe me as Gina's chap. Delightful though that might be,' says James.

'Really? I'm so sorry. I could have sworn your father –'

The Brigadier trails off, having suddenly noticed his wife's desperate semaphoring.

'And besides,' says James, expertly gliding past the Brigadier's *faux pas*, 'if it's luck Gina's looking for, she's sitting next to the wrong Coward.'

And would you believe the bugger's actually pointing at me. What's more Gina is smiling at me, as if to say, 'Yes, I know he is. He's the luckiest man on earth and I love him for it.' And I'm thinking to myself, in so far as it's possible to think straight when you're half cut on Cheval Blanc and you've got the world's most beautiful girl looking at you in such an adoring way, 'There's something fishy going on here.' But quite what James's game is, I can't immediately fathom, which makes it very hard for me to decide how to respond.

Do I reply with the modest truth, which is that, really, I'm no more lucky than the next man, and if I were, then how come after all I've been through I'm not a general by now with a VC and three bars?

Or do I play up to this new image as the Dick 'Lucky' Coward Gina is apparently so desperate to believe me to be?

'If I've been lucky, it's all down to one man,' I say. 'And he's sitting over there.'

'You leave me out of it,' Price growls.

And as officers like to do, we all laugh at this bravura display of salt-of-the-earth NCO wit.

'Whatever the reason, you do seem to have made it through a fair few scrapes,' says Gina, blue eyes fixed on me intently as if to say – well, what, I'm not sure. Her behaviour has left me as puzzled as James's. Is she trying to stir things up by taking turns to make each of us jealous? Has she been trying desperately to be cross with me after this morning's incident but now given up because she simply finds me too irresistible?

And frankly right now, who gives a damn what the reason is, I think, as I put on a shy smile and wallow in the sea of warm, admiring looks.

The way James is wriggling you'd think he had a dozen maggots up his bum. Which makes it all the more surprising when he says: 'Absolutely. I sometimes ask myself how on earth it can be that I've landed all this –' he indicates the ribbons on his chest – 'When poor old Dickie has ended up with nothing.' (By 'nothing' he means my DFC. According to my father – from whom my brother takes his lead – a DFC doesn't count as a proper medal. 'They give 'em out with the rations,' he says.)

'You've changed your tune!' observes Mrs Watson.

'Ah well. *In vino veritas*,' says James, which again is pretty rum because he scarcely drinks.

'Still plenty of time, as I keep telling him,' says my father. 'Bit of spunk on the push to Berlin and he'll have overtaken you in no time, James.'

'Then I wish him well. It's about time he had a stroke of luck,' says James, and I can begin to see what his game is, because now everyone's beaming at him instead. Such a nice chap. How fearfully we misjudged him.

'And of course any help that any of our guests might be able to afford Dickie in that direction will be most appreciated,' says my father, looking at Brigadier Watson and Colonel Todhunter. 'The future of this estate may be in your hands.'

'Ah, now, I did hear rumours about this,' says the Brigadier. 'Is it true, then, Ajax? You're really planning to decide the succession on which of your boys has the better war?'

'Sounds like a good film in there somewhere,' says Julius Greene.

'After John died – you remember my eldest boy, don't you? Went down with the *Hood*? – it seemed the only fair decision. Though not everyone would agree,' he says, with a nod towards my mother. 'Think I've been a bit harsh on your Dickie, don't you, dear?'

'It's not about favourites, Ajax, it's about how we do things. When the eldest son dies, the next-eldest son – even if he's only the eldest by a matter of minutes – takes his place. It's the English way and it has worked perfectly well for centuries.'

'Well, I'll tell you what worked for me in the trenches. I'd promote a chap according to how well he fought; how hungry he was for victory. If I'd decided it on where he stood in the family tree, it'd still be stalemate in Flanders today. Isn't that so, Price?'

'Very likely, sir.'

'"Very likely, sir", he says. Bugger wasn't even listening. Always been his own man, haven't you, Price?'

'If you say so, sir.'

'Of course, if either of you were going to take on my Dickie, you realise you'd have to take Price with you,' says my father to the Brigadier and the Colonel. 'Inseparable they are. Have been, right from the beginning.'

'That so? We can never have too many experienced NCOs.'

'What the General appears temporarily to have forgotten, sir, is that since my discharge he has relied on me to run his estate.'

'Quite right, Price. Quite right, terribly good of you to think of me. But we're only talking a matter of months, aren't we, Jumbo? Christmas at the latest? I'm sure we'll manage to rub along until then.'

After dinner I lie in bed trying to read *War and Peace* by candlelight, far too excited to sleep. My eyes are swimming, my head's throbbing, my heart's racing faster than Mahmoud at the '36 Derby. Tonight, against all the odds, has turned out to be one of the best of my life.

Why? Well, if you'd seen all the adulation I got once the ladies had withdrawn, you wouldn't need to ask. A few more drunken anecdotes – Stalingrad (the expurgated version); Churchill; and the time I accidentally pissed on Hitler's leg

– and they were on me like sharks after blood. Todhunter urging me to re-consider my views on parachutes: 'If only I could tell you about the shows our division has in the pipeline. Trust me, old man, you'd rather die than miss out on the fun . . .' The Brigadier pressing the merits of his Royal Marine Commandos: 'Might be tricky squeezing you in as an officer at this late stage, I fear. But I think I can safely say that, where we're going, you'll have earned yourself a field promotion from the ranks within a week, and enough gongs to secure yourself the estate within a fortnight . . .' Julius Greene chipping in with an 'If it's life at the sharp end you want, don't under-estimate the Army Film Unit. You'll find our casualty rate as reassuringly high as anything you could hope for in a red or green beret.' And all the while, James looking miffed and left out, and my father half-beaming at me with something approaching paternal pride, as if, for the first time in my exis-tence, he's finally seen the point of me.

The only person unmoved by this orgy of lionising is, of course, Price. 'Just you dare, just you bleeding dare!' his sharp little looks keep telling me. 'It's all right, old chap,' say the ones I give him back. 'Everything's in hand, just you see.'

It is too. The night draws on, the flattery and the invita-tions to commit myself to one or other combat unit grow more and more desperate, but still I manage to resist them all. Sorry, chaps, I say. Doctor's orders. And while Father can barely contain his crossness, Price looks as pleased with me as I have ever seen him. It might have cost me the estate but even that might not be such a disaster, I'm beginning to think. Not when I know now that just around the corner lies a far, far greater prize.

I'm talking, of course, about Gina. I don't want to sound mercenary here – I promise you I'd love her just as much if all she had to her name was a set of rags and a hovel – but it is quite comforting to think that however splendid Great Meresby may be it pales into insignificance before the vastness and majesty of the lands and properties which will one day be Gina's.

So that's what I'm thinking about now, as I lie in bed. About the extraordinary meaningful look Gina gave me over the Woolton pie. The one that said: 'Yes, you are lucky, my hero Dick! And there's nothing a beautiful girl like me needs more in this troubled world than a stout fellow like you by her side. I love you, Dick. I've always –'

Enough! I swipe the thought away because, really, these Russian names are quite complicated enough, without the distraction of Gina and all that Cheval Blanc swimming about my head.

Very noisy, by night, Great Meresby. Very unconducive to reading a difficult Russian book (in translation, obviously. If my Russian had been that good it would have spared me an awful lot of bother back in '43). All those creaking doors and groaning floorboards and mysterious knocking noises, you'd think the place was haunted – which it quite possibly is. I certainly used to think so as a child. There's one of them now.

Knock. Knock.

Of course, ideally it wouldn't be a ghost at all. It would be Gina. Wearing nothing but a diaphanous nightgown. 'I'm so sorry. I couldn't sleep,' she'd say. 'I can't stop thinking of you.' 'It's perfectly OK,' I'd reply. 'I have just the remedy.'

Knock-knock. Knock.

'Dick?'

My God. I really must be hallucinating.

'Dick?' Louder this time. Loud enough to hear that it is Gina, definitely. Hallelujah. Hallelujah. HALLELUJAH!

'Come in.'

As soon as she does I can see she's terribly distraught –

red-rimmed eyes, glistening cheeks, a grey pallor, the lot — and I would get out of bed to give her a big, comforting hug, but I don't for reasons which, even though she's in a dressing gown not a diaphanous nightdress, ought to be fairly obvious.

'Dick, I'm so sorry,' she begins —

'Gina, darling, don't be. Really don't. Just come and sit here —' I pat the bedclothes. 'And tell me what I can do to help.'

Gina shuffles over, feeling very sorry for herself. Really, I've never seen her looking so distressed. After a moment's hesitation, she perches on the bed and looks at me uncertainly.

'Tell me,' I urge.

'Oh God, I shouldn't have come, you'll think it's too silly,' she sobs into her palms.

I take both her hands and pull her gently towards me.

'It's not James, is it?' I say, hopefully.

'No. It's not James.'

'Then, who? Tell me his name.'

'It's nobody. Nobody who's done anything wrong. It's more . . . this horrible horrible war. I so detest this war.'

'But of course you do, Gina. We all do. But there isn't long to go now. It'll be over by Christmas at the very latest. And then we can rebuild our lives. And get on with living happily ever after.'

I say the last bit with a meaningful caress of her trembling hands, but she's so distraught I'm not sure she notices.

'But what if we don't make it?' she says, pulling her hands from mine and looking at me with the most abject despair.

'We will!'

'Not all of us,' she says.

'Most of us. The lucky ones.'

'Yes,' she says, smiling for the first time. 'The lucky ones.' And she takes my hands once more and gives me another meaningful look, not a million miles removed from the cracker she shot me at dinner.

And if I wasn't feeling too lucky before, I certainly am now. 'Dick Coward,' I'm thinking to myself, 'you have hit the jackpot here.' Indeed, the only remaining imponderable at this point, it strikes me, is how much longer I should decently leave it before lurching forward and giving her a proper kiss, or maybe just pulling her on top of me.

Best not to rush things, I decide. So I content myself with a stroke of her hair and one of those deep, caring looks women like.

'Feeling better?'

'A bit.'

'A bit? I shan't let you leave this room until the answer's "a lot".'

She laughs. Almost back to her old self now.

'James was right,' she says.

'That'll be a first,' I say.

'He looks up to you, you know. He won't admit it but he does. Underneath all that show, those medals, he knows in his heart that it's you who deserves the victor's laurels.'

'Good. Then he should jolly well say as much to the old man.'

'Dick, you know that won't happen. But just because James won't doesn't mean others can't. People whose opinion your father respects.'

'Who?'

'Me, silly.'

'That's very sweet of you, Gina, but –'

'Please don't thank me, it's nothing. I've got a favour to ask of you and it's much, much bigger than that.'

'How big?'

'So big I wouldn't even have dared ask if it hadn't been for what James said and what I heard at dinner and, well, I know you're the only one who can do it and I know it's so much to ask, but if you could I'd love you for ever — well, I do already, but even more than that if that's possible.'

'I'd better say yes, then.'

'Wait. You haven't heard what it is,' she says, in a voice at once coquettishly challenging and trepidatious. 'And especially now that you've acquired a new lady friend —'

'Gina. That girl means nothing to me. Absolutely nothing!'

Gina studies me shrewdly for a moment. Then she goes on: 'You remember how the Brigadier was talking about these feelings soldiers get in their bones about whether they'll live or die? Well, I've been having them about a friend of mine. Family, in fact. He's my cousin. Not one you know, I don't think. From the other side. We've always been close, very close, and if anything were to happen to him —' She stifles a sob.

'Gina, darling, you mustn't. We all get these silly premonitions now and then —'

'Every night?'

'Every night? Since when?'

'Ever since we . . .' She pauses to think. 'You remember when you were sitting under the tree with the boys and you recognised me for the first time? It was just before that.'

'That's a long time.'

'Every night it's the same. It was the same just now. I wake up in a cold sweat — feel.' She pulls my hand behind her head and I can feel the clamminess of her neck. 'And I'm watching him, then I am him, lying on my side and everything is numb and misty, just feeling all my strength slowly ebb away. And I'm dying. He's dying and he doesn't want to die, he's telling me he doesn't want to die, he wants to be with me.'

'Have I met him, this cousin?'

'You might have done, but he's so shy you probably wouldn't have noticed. His name's Guy. Guy Dangerfield.'

'Dangerfield. Is that the . . .' whey-faced drip with dark girlie hair, I'm about to say, because yes I think I do remember him: he was the spod we used to pick on, my brother especially. 'No,' I carry on swiftly. 'I don't think I do. But you must have lots of friends and family in the services. Why Guy in particular?'

'Because . . .' she trails off. 'Aren't commandos especially at risk?'

'He's a commando?'

'You sound surprised.'

'Well, you did say he was "shy".'

'Shy but brave.'

'I see why you're worried.'

'Is bravery a bad thing?'

'So Price is always telling me.'

Her eyes widen and through them you can almost see the terrible thoughts she's thinking. Guy leading a suicidal charge. Guy throwing himself on to the grenade, in order that his comrades might live. Guy volunteering for the mission from which there can be no return.

'I want you to help him,' she says, fixing me with eyes so steady it's like being mesmerised by one of those turbaned stage hypnotists.

'Of course I will. I'll write him a letter, how about that? A letter giving him all the tips I've gleaned in the last five years as to how you survive in battle. Stuff they don't even teach you at Achnacarry.'

'No. Really help him. Be there with him. Keep him from harm.'

'What. You mean — literally?'

'Yes.'

'But Gina darling, you know I'd absolutely love to if I could. Really, there's nothing in the world I wouldn't do for you if it were remotely possible.'

'Really?'

'I swear. But this one, it's quite beyond my powers. You can't simply waltz into any old commando unit you fancy.'

'Oh but Dickie. This is what's so wonderful. You can! *You* can! James told me.'

'How would James know?'

'He overheard the Brigadier talking to you. And I know it was naughty of him to eavesdrop like that but thank God he did because it's worked out so well. Turns out the Brigadier is in charge of Guy's unit. So he'll have no difficulty pulling the right strings to get you in.'

'I say,' I say queasily. 'What an extraordinary stroke of luck!'

7

Back to Basics

'Hands off cocks and on with socks, you 'orrible bunch of layabout pansies. Parade's in five minutes!' yells a voice near my ear so comically familiar I find it hard to take it seriously. And the setting doesn't help. Lumpy bunks in a billowing bell tent redolent of stale fart and cheesy foot; the early wake-up call; the Sergeant's stock phrases: I haven't heard such nonsense since basic training.

'DO YOUR LUGHOLES NEED SWABBING, SONNY MY LAD. I SAID –'

'So sorry, Price. I thought –'

'Price. PRICE? Did I hear you address me as Price, Marine whatever-your-name-is, not that I care because to me you are lower than vermin, you maggot, you rat turd, you dripping green emanation from a whore's syphilitic piss-flaps? It's SERGEANT Price to you and don't you sodding well forget it.'

'Yes, Sergeant. Sorry, Sergeant,' I say, keeping a straight face only with the most superhuman effort of will.

'Who the fook was that?' says the owner of the pair of size-twenty feet dangling from the bunk above mine. He drops to the floor with a thump and peers at me sceptically. 'And while we're abaht it, who the fook are you?'

'Coward. Dick Coward,' I say extending one hand while I pull up my trousers with the other. 'And you are?'

'Never mind about that, Marine Lah Di Dah,' he says, scrambling into his kit as quickly as he can because he can tell, as we all can, that this Sgt. Price isn't a fellow to mess with. 'What I want to know is, what the fook have you done with my mate Legger?'

'I'm not sure we've ever met,' I say.

'Well, he were in your bed till two days ago.'

'Oh, Lamb. Yes. Apparently he had some kind of infection.'

'I know that. When's he coming back?'

'I'm not sure that he is.'

'Well, who's going to replace him?'

'Me, I suppose.'

'That's joost what I were bloody afraid of.'

Now, when you're in a situation like this, of course, you look for a response so witty, so charming, so otherwise impossibly winning that everyone around you comes instantly to understand that you are a splendid chap who they'll be glad to have around. Of course, you never find one. When you're a stranger arriving unheralded in a close-knit group – and they don't come any closer knit than a section in a commando troop – you just have to accept that for the first few days you're going to be made about as welcome as a dose of dysentery in a battened-down Crusader.

So hats off to Price and his devilish clever ruse, I'm thinking, as I hurry after the rest of my section to the parade ground, praying the while that I can remember my drill because heaven knows it's been quite some time. By singling me out for his especial attentions just now, he will have contrived instantly to suggest to my fellow marines that I am one of them.

'PARADE. PARADE 'SHUN!' screams Sgt. Price and my heels click into place, thank God, in perfect unison with everyone else's. We all stand, perfectly rigid in our green berets, eyes fixed straight in front of us, as Price stalks menacingly up and down the lines.

'Now, you are probably wondering, gentlemen, who I am, why I am so angry and why you have been called on parade at a time when you have so many better things to do such as studying maps, improving your marksmanship, and making the most of what little time you have left with the little fellow before he gets shot off in action as mine so nearly was once, which is your second question answered already.'

There are snorts of mirth from the assembled ranks.

'Do not laugh. It was not intended as a joke. I am not Max Miller. I am here at the suggestion of my old friend Sarnt Weaver, who said to me in the sergeants' mess last night: "Gonad," he said. "Gonad, I have a problem and I wonder if you can help me. I have under my command the most splendid bunch of boys – well, most of them anyway – in the peak of fitness and itching for action. But Gonad, I'm a little worried they're getting a bit too cocky. Not many of them have seen Germans up close before and I don't think they realise what an 'orrible bunch of cunts Germans can be. So Gonad, will you do me a favour? Show them what an 'orrible cunt looks like. "Sarnt Weaver," I said. "It will be my pleasure." And since one or two of you still insist on finding my remarks funny, I'd like you all to drop and give thirty press-ups at the double. Now!'

In one, lithe movement the men around me drop to their hands and begin bobbing up and down. God, they're fit. Fitter than any body of trained men I've ever seen – and I've seen a fair few. They've done their basic; they've done their commando training at Achnacarry; spent days on exercise in the Scottish Highlands, the Black Mountains and on Dartmoor; they've been shinning up and down ropes at the climbing school in St Ives; they're taut and lean and well fed and inured to pain and danger; they can kill a man with their bare hands, with a knife, with a Sten, with a Bren, with a three-inch mortar, with a 36 grenade, with a hat-pin, you name it. Thirty press-ups? They can manage that in their sleep.

All of them, that is, bar one.

'You. Marine. What's your name?'

'Coward, Sergeant,' I say through gritted teeth. Everyone else has finished now, and they're all standing in line, waiting for me to finish. I've only done nineteen but that's all I'm going to be able to manage. My arms are like jelly, my whole body is juddering.

'Would you like to give up, Coward?' says Price.

'No, Sergeant.'

'Course, you would. It's what Cowards do, isn't it, Coward?'

'No, Sergeant.'

'Marines. Show him how it's done. I want thirty more at the double. No, wait. Make that fifty. Go!'

After fifty press-ups, even the fitter marines are looking mildly discomfited. For good measure, Price makes them all sprint three times round the camp perimeter, yapping at their heels like an angry terrier, while I struggle to keep up as best I can. Then he calls us all to attention again, before dismissing us for breakfast.

'Coward. You stay where you are.'

I remain at attention while the parade ground empties. Price marches smartly towards me and halts barely an inch from my ear. He leans forward even closer, as if preparing to whisper an endearment. And I just can't restrain my smirk, any longer.

'Price,' I say with a laugh. 'You really are –'

I'm about to tell him what an absolutely first-rate job he's doing, but I'm cut short by the most massive concussion against my eardrums.

'SERGEANT Price.'

'Sorry, Sergeant, but –'

'No buts. You knew exactly what you were doing when you

volunteered for this unit. You've made your bed. Now you can sodding well lie in it.'

Oh dear, I'm thinking to myself as I hurry off to breakfast because there isn't much time – Price has ordered me back by 0800 hours for remedial fitness training, which only leaves me quarter of an hour. Oh dear, oh bloody dear. Because for the first time – and not for the last, let me tell you – it has begun to dawn what a frightful mess I've managed to land us in.

When we arrived at the camp in the small hours of last night – it should have been earlier but as usual the trains were delayed something rotten, and the roads to Southampton were chock-a-block – it all seemed such an awfully big adventure. The weight of traffic and personnel on the road, even late in the night; the ranks of Shermans, armoured scout cars, jeeps, lorries, DUKWs parked under camouflage in readiness for the day of embarkation; the fighters roaring overhead, ready to blast any nosy Jerries out of the sky. It's a thrilling thing being part of a huge invasion force, and it was about to grow more thrilling still. And you'll no doubt think it foolish of me – I certainly did later – but when Price and I finally persuaded the Yankees at the gate that we weren't fifth columnists and we entered the sealed camp there to remain incommunicado from the outside world until the appointed hour, I remember feeling a surge of gratitude at having been allowed to take part in this wondrous new escapade.

Gratitude to the Brigadier for having sufficient faith in Price and me to have first suggested this most unusual arrangement.

Gratitude to Gina for spurring me on.

Gratitude, above all, to the hand of fate for having steered me away from the weed-strewn path of indolence and back to the field of Mars for the final confrontation against the wickedest enemy our nation has ever known.

It speaks volumes for the misguidedness of that optimism

that I hadn't even stopped to consider the consequences of losing all rank and effectively re-enlisting as an ordinary soldier. I know it's what T. E. Lawrence did between the First and Second wars, but then, he was a masochist. Of course, I had a vague idea I was going to miss the officers' mess, and the automatic deference that men give you when you've got a pip or two on your shoulder, but I had a notion that I'd be amply compensated for these losses by being relieved of the strain and responsibility of command. But that's not quite how it worked out. Not at all in fact.

Inevitably, I'm the very last in the queue for the breakfast but to my surprise there's still plenty left when I finally reach the serving station where a cheerful American Negro is doling on to tin plates beans, bacon, sausages, egg. 'You name it, we got it,' he says when I jokingly ask if he has any mushrooms and sure enough he does. The American part of my heart swells with patriotic pride.

'Say what you like about these Yankees, but they certainly know how to feed their troops,' I announce brightly to the table where my section are hunched over their troughs, more to get their attention than anything, because unless one of them budges up a bit I'm not going to have anywhere to sit.

'Fattening us for the slaughter,' says my bunkmate, the big Yorkshireman, whom I think I heard someone address by the nickname Oily. He doesn't look up though. Still less does he try to make a space.

'I say, would you mind?' I ask those two of the marines at the end of the bench who strike me as looking the least obstreperous. With a show of mild reluctance, they squeeze towards the middle so that there's just enough space for me to rest at least one of my buttocks on the end.

Such conversation as there might have been before my arrival has been brought to a halt. Slurping, grunting and belching, the men shovel down their food with no regard for ceremony or the squeamishness of those of their neighbours more used to the decorum of the officers' mess. I try to follow suit. When in Rome.

Only once he's mopped up the last smear of breakfast from his plate does Oily – Wragg, I learn his surname is – address me again.

'You can tell your mate Gonad,' he says, tapping the point of his knife on the edge of my plate to emphasise his meaning, 'that it en't a good idea to treat commandos like they were recruits at Portsmouth. They don't like it.'

'He's probably just trying to cheer you up,' I say. Which isn't my usual emollient style, as you'll know, but with men like Wragg it doesn't pay to back down too soon.

'Are you being funny?'

'Standard practice before a big op,' I say. 'Keep your men busy. Keeps them from worrying.'

'You're sounding like a bloody officer. That what you are? An officer. Come to spy on us?'

'They thought you might need a linguist.'

'Oh they did, did they? And what the fook would one of them be when it's at home?'

'Language, innit? Wot, speak Frog, do you? I speak all the Frog you need. Listen, 'ows this: "Voulez-vous coucher avec moi, Madame?"' says a lanky, gappy-toothed marine with a button nose and tight curly hair. Marine Hordern, I'll later learn.

'You have a penchant for the older woman, then?'

'Wot?'

'If she's over thirty and married-looking, then Madame is perfect. Younger ones might prefer being addressed as Mademoiselle.'

'Blimey. We've got a right know-all, 'ere.'

'Fookin' cocky bastard is what I'd call him,' says Oily and he may be bigger than me and fitter than me and stronger than me, but there is at least one advantage I have over him, and I may have to use it any second now, which is why my right hand isn't holding my table knife any more, it's edging very slowly towards the sheath strapped to my left thigh.

'Where did you get a gob on you like that?' he says.

'The same place as you, I would imagine,' I say, very nonchalant.

'Same place as me?' says Oily, all hurt dignity and puffed-up outrage. He's tensing up now but he's already too late –

I've rounded the end of the table, and come up behind Wragg with my left forearm pulling his head back and my right hand pressing the blade of my dagger against his jugular.

Wonderful thing, the Fairbairn-Sykes standard-issue commando dagger. So beautifully feminine, in its curves; so perfectly balanced; so Wilkinson-razor-edged; and so ideally suited to situations such as these. Whip it out quick enough and, really, there's nothing the opposition can do except gasp, and gag, and turn puce and pray to God you're in the mood for mercy.

'I say, that man, what the devil do you think you're doing?' drawls a voice from the mess entrance. It belongs to a tall, raffish lieutenant whose dark moustache is quivering his disapproval.

I loosen my grip slightly, though not so much that Oily has any chance of gaining the advantage.

'It were my fault, sir,' says Wragg, rubbing his neck. 'I were asking him to remind me of one of them techniques we learned from Captain Fairbairn.'

'Never mind that, Wragg. I wasn't talking to you. Marine – could you kindly let go of Wragg there and tell me your name.'

I transfer the dagger to my left hand, so that I can salute smartly with my right. 'Coward, sir.'

'Ah. Just the chap I was looking for.'

Ten minutes ago, the majority of my troop didn't know me from Adam. Now, I'm more infamous than the snake in the garden himself. What I can't work out as I march out of the mess past tables and tables of men, all of them completely silent, all of them staring at me, is whether this will work to my advantage; or whether it will completely scupper my chances of ever integrating with the unit.

'Know how to make an entrance, don't you, Coward?' observes the Lieutenant as we stride across the parade ground towards a jerry-built hut. 'Name's Frost, by the way. I'm 2i/c your troop. And the chap you're about to meet, as I'm sure you know, is your troop commander, Captain Dangerfield.'

When we enter his tiny office, Dangerfield is typing, worriedly, at a desk almost completely covered with documents, all in neat piles which instantly put me on my guard. 'Stickler,' I'm thinking. 'Pen-pusher. Teacher's pet.'

Physically he has quite a lot in common with the sensitive youth I remember my brother once teasing for looking like a 'Jew boy' – dark curly locks, a long, elegant nose, gentle brown eyes, with a slightly olive complexion. The sort of chap you can imagine a lot of girls wanting to mother – at least when he was younger. Some of that softness has gone now. He's a bit bonier about the face, darker under the eyes, with a determined set to his jaw as if at some stage he's said to himself: 'Damn it, I'm not going to be a mummy's boy any more. I'm going to be a soldier.' Dangerous sort to have around you, that, because they've so much more to prove. And I should know. I could almost be describing myself.

'Morning, Coward. At ease. I understand Sarnt Price needs you for remedial training, so I shan't keep you long,' he says. 'I just wanted to say: Welcome to the troop. And if you have any problems Sarnt Weaver can't sort out don't hesitate in the first instance to speak to Lieutenants Frost or Truelove. And in the unlikely event they should be unable to help, then do please come and see me. Do you have any questions?'

'No sir.'

'Now, I don't mind telling you, Coward, that you have been allowed into this troop against my better judgement. We formed – 47 Commando that is – at the beginning of August last year and we've been training together ever since. We're a tight unit. We work well together. And I'm still not sure of the wisdom, frankly, of parachuting in some Johnny-come-lately with no understanding of our corps, our traditions, nor of the specialist mission we have been asked to undertake. So you're very much on probation and should you at any time fail to maintain this troop's considerable standards, I shall not hesitate to have you RTU'd. Understand?'

'Yes, sir.'

'Whatever unit that might be,' Capt. Dangerfield mutters irritably to himself. He looks across at Lt. Frost and mouths: 'Papers?'

Lt. Frost shakes his head.

'In the absence of any supporting documentation I'm just going to have to take the Brigadier's word of your suitability for this operation. I understand that you have had previous commando experience.'

'Yes, sir.'

'May I ask where?'

'I'm afraid a lot of it's classified, sir,' I say, which isn't altogether untrue, but both he knows and I know that I could be a lot more helpful than I've chosen to be. Problem is, I don't like the man. He's a stickler and a prig and I can't for the life of me think why Gina feels so protective towards him.

Capt. Dangerfield bristles, and is perhaps about to say

something rather unpleasant, when Lt. Frost glides smoothly into the rink.

'I can certainly vouch for his expertise in self-defence techniques, after what I saw this morning,' says the Lieutenant.

'Trouble?' says Capt. Dangerfield, frowning.

'High spirits I'd call it,' says Lt. Frost.

Capt. Dangerfield gives me a hard, sceptical look. 'Coward, I think you've tested my patience quite enough for one morning. Let me ask one more thing. Have we met before?'

'I don't believe I've had the pleasure, sir, no.'

'You're no relation, then, of James Coward. James Coward the war hero?' He enunciates the last two words with a noticeable curl of the lip.

'War hero is he, sir? No, sir. Never heard of him.'

For a moment Capt. Dangerfield half smiles. It's the first time I've seen him almost content.

'Very good. Dismissed,' he says.

Lt. Frost escorts me some of the way towards my appointment with Sgt. Price.

'Thanks for that, sir,' I say.

'Thanks for what?' he says.

'For not mentioning the, er, incident,' I say.

'Oh, don't thank me. I did it for the most selfish of reasons. Couldn't bear to see the troop a man short again. And it would have been, you know.'

'I do know, sir. I've already gathered that Captain Dangerfield expects very high standards of his men.'

The Lieutenant sees instantly what I'm driving at, that I think this captain of ours is an S H one T of the first order, and when he drops his voice confidingly I assume that what he's about to do is agree with me. But he doesn't and at the time I put it all down to brother officers closing ranks. It's only much later that I begin to grasp the sense of what he's said.

'Yes, old boy. But the thing is: they're not nearly as high as the standards he sets for himself.'

The next couple of days are a blur of remedial fitness-training sessions with Sgt. Price, drill, rifle practice and endless last-minute briefings on everything from escape-and-evasion techniques (by a splendid Kiwi brigadier named Hargest with much personal experience of same) and the mores of Frenchwomen (not as lax as we'd been hoping for, apparently) to the topography of our landing beach and mission objective (about which Price and I have made an interesting discovery, of which more later). It's all I can do to snatch a moment long enough to write to Gina.

'Dear Gina, here I am in sunny can't-say-where about to embark for your-guess-is-as-good-as-mine. Wish you were here,' I begin. Then I suck my pen, wondering what on earth I'm going to say next and how to phrase it because it's crucial that I get the balance exactly right here. Not too needy or maudlin because then she'll think I'm wet. Not too gung-ho because she'll think I'm an insensate brute. Not too forward – and certainly no innuendo – because then she's sure to think I'm a cad who's only after one thing. But then, not too platonic either. I've got to show her I mean business. Spare me, Lord, that terrible limbo known as 'just good friends'.

But now my train of thought has been broken by the nasal voice of Arthur Kemp, our section's resident skiver, pilferer and general ne'er-do-well, known to all by his nickname 'Arfinch'.

''Ere, Oily. Bung us over your sewing kit, will you?' he says.

'What do you think I am?' bellows a voice from above me. 'Stupid or summat? You still 'aven't given back that comb you 'ad off me in St Ives.'

''Ere, Rupert,' calls out Kemp, undeterred. This time he's

addressing young Jack Mayhew, whose dark, handsome looks, utter decency and close resemblance to Rupert Brooke are the source of a popular running joke about him being a 'doomed youth'. 'Rupert, give us your sewing kit.'

'Can't you see? I'm using it,' says Mayhew, who, like most of the section, is stitching on to and into his battledress the various pieces of escape kit we were issued after Brigadier Hargest's lecture – the wafer-thin maps of France printed on fine silk; the magnetised buttons which, when cut off and suspended by a thread, act as compasses; the little, pointy-ended magnetised bars, designed to serve the same purpose should the button go missing.

'Bloody waste of time if you ask me,' says Arfinch.

'Why's that?' says Mayhew wearily. 'Because I'm "doomed"?'

'That as well,' says Arfinch. 'But I was thinking more of Hitler's orders regarding captured commandos.'

'Always think positive, that's what the Brigadier said,' says Marine Dent, who may be a bit slow and literal but is just the sort of chap as an officer you like to have in your unit: does what he's asked without question; keeps his head in a firefight – at least one hopes. 'Never ask yourself "if" you can escape but "when", "where" and "how".'

'Yeah but he was never a commando, was he?' chips in 'Lisa' Bridgeman – that's as in Mona – because he's never slow to join in the complaining when there's complaining to be done.

'Could have been though. Did you see his ribbons? MC. DSO and two bars,' says 'Eggy' Calladine, the marine so far with whom I've found most cause to identify. You might assume, as I at first did, that the nickname was derived from the quality of his flatulence but in fact it's short for Egghead.

'Yeah and I wonder 'ow many of his men 'ad to die to win them for him?' asks Bridgeman.

'He's been through a lot worse than we'll ever have to face.

I heard he was at Gallipoli and the Somme and Messines,' says Mayhew.

'Ah but war was easier in them days. Men still fought like gentlemen,' declares Arfinch.

'Did they fook. Not the fookin' Jerries anyway. Remember Edith Cavell?'

'My father said it was quite ghastly. No quarter offered or given,' says Mayhew.

'What were 'e doing writing all them poems glamorising it, then?'

'Oh, ha! Ha!' says Mayhew sarcastically, while everyone else laughs. They laugh more raucously still when Oily declaims a couplet he's just written. 'Stands the clock at ten to three/Slap-up tea for Jerry 'n' me.'

'My dad won't even talk about the war,' says Calladine.

'Probably embarrassed by the killing he made selling black-market baby milk,' says Arfinch.

'More your father's line, I should have thought,' says Mayhew.

'I did ask him again, last time I was on leave,' Calladine says. '"I'll tell you about it once you've seen some action," he says to me. "Only then you won't feel like asking any more."'

'Bet that cheered you up,' says Hordern.

'I still say they 'ad it easy compared with what we're about to do. They never had to do an opposed landing,' says Bridgeman.

'Wot. Not Gallipoli?'

'There's only one person round 'ere who might know the answer and that's Coward's friend, Sarnt Price. 'En't that right, Coward?'

'What's that?'

'Your mate Price. Seen it all, 'an't he? Lost it all too, at Passchendaele, 'en't that right?'

'Why don't you ask him?' I say.

'I'm asking *you*,' says Wragg. When I don't answer, he heaves a long sigh. 'Look, Coward, we're doing our best to get on wi' you but you 'en't makin' it easy for us. If you joined in a bit more instead of moping round and acting all aloof like you were God's gift to humanity –'

'Yes but, to be fair, Oily, last time he did try joining in, you said he was a cocky bastard,' says Mayhew.

'Well 'e were being a cocky bastard,' says Wragg, adding with mock concern, 'Eh. Can anyone see what he's up to? He hasn't got his knife out again, has 'e?'

'Pointing straight up, about where your arse is, Oily,' says Hordern.

'Look, no offence meant, chum,' says Wragg. 'But the way you carry on sometimes, you'd think you were the only one round here who knew what he was doing. But we're not all green, you know. Arfinch 'as been all over – he were a gun layer on *KG V*, weren't you, Arfinch?'

'Yeah, till the Captain discovered 'alf 'is fifteen-inch shells 'ad gone missing and someone 'ad been selling them on the side to the *Bismarck*,' quips Hordern.

'And Sarnt Weaver's been everywhere from Vichy Madagascar to Palestine; even Lisa Bridgeman was MNBDO on Crete,' continues Wragg.

'*Even* Lisa Bridgeman?' complains Bridgeman.

'Steady with them initials, Oily. He's a Pongo, remember,' says Arfinch.

A Pongo, in case you don't know, is how members of the Royal Navy – which of course includes the Royal Marines – refer to the Army.

'Oh, for goodness sake,' I say. 'Of course I know what it stands for. Mobile Naval Base Defence Organisation.'

'Well, it came as news to Bridgeman on Crete. When he volunteered he thought it meant Men Not to Be Drafted

Overseas,' says Hordern. 'Christ,' he says to himself as the German paratroopers come swooping down on his head. 'I'd better FOOOH ASAP.'

'So what we're saying is, just because we don't go round boasting about it, doesn't mean we don't know what it's like to be at the sharp end,' says Wragg. 'We know what we're in for. And we're not bloody scared.'

If he isn't scared, though, all I can say is that he's a bloody idiot. I know I am, after what Price and I learned yesterday about our destination.

We found out at a briefing, which for everyone else was pretty routine by now but which for Price and me was our first chance to discover where we were going or what the operation was about. Up until that point, we could have been heading to the moon, for all we knew.

All right, so we probably had a rough idea it was going to be France, because we had all been issued French money. And we'd guessed it was more likely to be Northern France, rather than somewhere further off, just because it would be quicker to get to. Exactly where in Northern France though, none of us had a clue. Not the men, anyway. Or the NCOs. A few of the more senior officers had been briefed but that was as far as it went. Even at this late stage and despite the fact that we were in sealed camps, guarded by GIs and with a snowball's chance in hell of making any contact with the outside world, it had been decided that the names of the places where in two or three days a good few of us would be laying down our lives were just too damned sensitive for general consumption.

The first bad news we learn is this: 47 Commando has been granted the honour of taking, single-handed, one of the most heavily defended objectives in the whole landing sector. It's a fishing village whose name, as I say, we are not permitted to know. It's guarded on either side by two huge cliffs – marked on the map as the Eastern and Western Features – each of them absolutely brimming with every form of protection you care to imagine: machine-gun nests, weapons pits, ack-ack, bunkers, trenches, mines, even concealed flame-throwers for heaven's sake.

'Now, I don't want you to concern yourselves too much about the flame-throwers,' says our second-in-command, Major Dalby, who's giving today's briefing. 'They sound unpleasant. They damned well are unpleasant. But they're easy to avoid. You're unlikely to be able to see the nozzle, hidden in the ground, but what you might well see is a sudden glow caused by the electric igniter. Soon as you spot that, step smartly to the left or right –'

'Straight into where Jerry's planted his S-mines,' mutters Bridgeman.

'And with luck, you'll miss the jet altogether,' continues Major Dalby. 'The important thing is not to let yourself get bogged down. It's imperative that you capture both heights as quickly as possible because, until you do, your comrades in the port will be sitting ducks for whatever fire Jerry cares to pour on them. Any questions? Well, chaps, I'm not going to pretend it will be a picnic. But I'm quite sure you'll all agree with me that the Colonel's plan has made a tricky job a great deal easier. It's to the Colonel's credit and our great advantage that Jerry will be expecting us – if at all – to be coming at him from the sea, not from his rear. That surprise, I believe, is going to make all the difference.'

'Yeah, all twelve bleeding miles of it,' murmurs Bridgeman – who else?

He's referring to the day's second, possibly even worse, piece of bad news. Sweet though it is of the Colonel to have decided against letting us get ourselves cut to pieces in a seaborne assault, it means that instead we are going to have to make our landfall further up the coast. Twelve miles up the coast. Twelve miles of enemy-held terrain across which we shall be forced to fight every inch of the way.

As Major Dalby finishes, he gestures with a smile, as if in invitation of applause, to the Colonel, who is standing very stiff and awkward and po-faced next to him. There are one or two desultory claps, but that's as far as it goes, perhaps because the Colonel looks so thoroughly appalled, perhaps because the whole thing feels a bit forced and embarrassing – a generous but naïve attempt by the Major to try to engender towards Lt. Col. Partridge a warmth the Commando simply doesn't feel. Respected the Colonel may be; but loved he most definitely ain't.

It's only once most of the men have filed out of the briefing tent that I can get a proper look at the scale model of this anonymous fishing village. Those Eastern and Western Features, it's clear, are going to be a pig to deal with: the defences look all but impregnable . . .

'I know why we're here,' says a voice next to me.

'Well, Sergeant,' I say – the habit's been drilled into me now, see. 'If it's my fault, then I'm frightfully sorry.'

'Course it's your fault. If you hadn't mentioned it the Brigadier would never have been interested.'

'Mentioned what, Price?' (Well – *almost* drilled into me.)

'Look,' he says sweeping his hand over the model.

I look again and this time I see it perfectly.

This anonymous fishing village – we have been there before.

8

The Great Crusade

Picture it: the biggest invasion fleet ever sets sail for Normandy. The waters of the south coast so thick with shipping you could stride from one side of the Solent to the other without once getting your feet wet. Battle cruisers, destroyers, frigates, tugs, cross-Channel ferries, rocket ships – their freshly painted disruptive-pattern stripes of battleship grey and snow and dove and grey green and black stark and handsome in the June sun. And on those ships, 156,000 soldiers, sailors, marines, airmen in slouch hats and kilts and cap comforters and kepis and berets in all the hues of the rainbow, leaning over the railings, waving what may well be their last goodbye to the thousands of tearful wives, excited children, hysterical mistresses, rueful parents and stoical grandparents all gathered on the docks while brass bands play and the bunting and the Union flags ripple in the summer breeze.

Well, that's how it would have been if I had been directing the film. Unfortunately I wasn't – some other bugger was, with a much bleaker outlook. For one thing it wasn't sunny, it was louring and miserable, with seas so ugly you'd take one look and go: 'Thanks, but I think I'll sit this one out by the fire with my stamp collection.' And for another, there weren't nearly the crowds you'd imagine nor was there anything by way of pomp or occasion because the whole thing was supposed to be a secret. Nobody was to know anything about anything.

None of us did in my troop.

One minute we're swinging across the assault course like the monkeys in Regent's Park Zoo – I'm still a bit slower than most, but I'll give Price credit: I'm in better shape than I would have been if he hadn't been such a sadistic bastard these last ten days – the next, the order comes through: we're to be ready for embarkation at 1600 hours.

It all happens so quickly that it's too much to take in at first. Even when we're sat in the back of our truck, watching those humourless white-helmeted US MPs closing behind us the gates of the hated camp we've nicknamed our 'Stalag', not even then can we quite believe that it's really happening; that, after all that waiting, it's on. It's finally on.

'Hey, this is my road. We're about to pass my house,' says one of the younger marines, a sweet fellow named Tobias, peering through the opening at the back of the tarpaulin which is all we're able to see of the outside world. ''Ere, Sarge. Can we just stop really, really quickly, so I can say goodbye to my mum? She doesn't even know I'm here.'

'And that's just how we're going to keep it, Tobias,' says Sgt. Weaver, firmly but not unkindly. We've all been given strict orders that under no circumstances are we to speak to bystanders. Apparently some idiots tried it earlier today – 'This is it!' was all they said, but that was more than enough – and were damned near court-martialled on the spot.

'I can see her. There! There at the window!' says Tobias, straining forward.

'Down, son,' says Sgt. Weaver.

The marines either side of him pull him gently back into his seat.

She's in an apron and she's got her hair up. She's holding a duster but has been distracted by the rumble of this convoy trundling slowly by. She looks nice. She could be anyone's mum.

'Mum!' calls Tobias pathetically.

'Mum!' echoes someone else more loudly.

Then, almost involuntarily, as if in answer to some deep inner call, we all of us find ourselves saying it.

'MUUUM!' we all cry out to Tobias's mother, in a tone which we'd like to pretend is mordant and mocking, but which we know is quite agonisingly heartfelt. You don't tend to talk about these things because if you did you might cry. But those of us who've been on a battlefield know who it is that dying soldiers cry out for and it's always the same.

Sgts Price and Weaver, the only two men in the back of the truck not to join in, look disapproving but make no comment.

It's hard to tell for certain because by the time we call out, the window of Tobias's two-up two-down is very nearly out of view. But it's my impression that the very last thing we see Mrs Tobias doing is begin to turn her head in the direction of the voices she has just heard.

Pity. Next she'll hear of him is a telegram beginning 'We regret to inform you'. Poor Tobias doesn't even make it as far as France. He's killed on the way in when his landing craft is struck by a shell.

Here's another thing none of us was quite expecting: the interminable wait on board ship. On the first day – Friday 2nd – we didn't even leave the dockside. The only excitement, before we were sent to our quarters below, was when a chap on a troopship just the other side of the harbour dived, in full uniform, into the sea.

'Don't blame you, mate,' says Marine Bridgeman, and I'm sure he's not the only one of us who's feeling that way. First the sealed camp; now the sealed ship – there's a horrible

inexorability about this process that makes what little impetu-
ousness that hasn't been drilled out of you on the parade ground
want to resist at every turn. The only thing that stops you
doing so is the certainty that there's no way out.

And now this deserter chap, whoever he is, has gone and
blown that small comfort out of the water.

We watch him swim to the jetty, waiting for the inevitable
moment when the police or the MPs turn up and take him
away. But the moment never comes. To tremendous cheers
from everyone in uniform, he makes it ashore, hobbles, dripping, up a flight of concrete steps, and with a defiant wave
disappears amid a line of onlookers standing on the shore.

The euphoria of witnessing so daring an escape soon evaporates. 'Why him, not me?' is the mostly unspoken thought.

Or as Marine Bridgeman puts it: 'The jammy bastard.'

That night is one of the more unpleasant I can remember.
Cross-Channel pleasure boat our ship may be in peacetime,
but in war, below decks, the *Josephine Charlotte* more closely
resembles a sardine can gone rotten. The officers, no doubt,
get quarters of their own. But we men have to sleep two-to-
a-berth, end to end, and because no one wants to share with
me because I'm nobody's mate, the chap I end up with is Oily
Wragg.

By the time I'm ready even to attempt some shut-eye, Wragg
is already spread over our mattress like a beached whale and
snoring loudly. It's all I can do to squeeze on the mattress –
there's only a tiny sliver, right next to the edge, and because
it's the top bunk there's quite a drop. With every slight roll
of the ship I threaten to crash on to the floor. So all I can do
is lie there, rigid with anxiety, nose thrust as far as is physically possible away from Wragg's pullulating feet, and pray
for morning to come soon.

Sometime in the small hours, I swing myself down and pad

barefoot down a pitch-black slippery corridor to the nearest heads which, needless to say, are awash with urine and yet more vomit. I feel my way back to my bunk, loathing every one of the men I can hear snoring and snuffling away either side of me – How can you, you bastards? How can you? – and I reach to pull myself up when my palm comes into contact with a patch of something slimy and chunky. This patch extends over every last square inch of available sleeping space. Yet the author of this mess is sleeping like a baby.

I give him a good prod: 'Wragg!' I hiss. 'Wragg! You've got to clear up this mess at once. Wragg! Wragg?'

'Oi, pipe down, will you?' comes a voice down the corridor. 'Some of us was having a nice kip.'

Wragg sleeps on, utterly oblivious to all my attempts to wake him.

After that I give up even trying to sleep where I'm supposed to. We've orders to stay below, not to go on deck, but the only person I see when I sneak upstairs is a weatherbeaten matelot who says chummily: 'Bit rich for you down there, is it?'

'Just a touch.'

'Listen, if you need to get your head down, I'd recommend that lifeboat there. It's quiet and no one's going to notice you.'

But still I can't sleep and now the darkness has given way to a miserable pre-dawn grey. I stand at the rails and watch the ships all around us beginning to materialise from the gloom.

'Well, that's bloody it, I've 'ad enough. I'm going home right now,' announces Marine Simpson looking up from his book. 'Crab' we call him – short for 'Crab fat' – because he's so addicted to Brylcreem he should have joined the RAF.

It's the afternoon of 3 June and we're all spread out on deck, sheltering as best we can from the wind singing through the cables above our heads, reading, dozing, staring vacantly into space. For some of us, it has been our first chance of getting any sleep.

'What's that, Crab?' says Bridgeman, sensing a kindred spirit.

'This!' he says stabbing the page of his book disgustedly.

'There's no use pointing. You'll have to read it to him. And very slowly, else Bridgeman won't understand,' chips in Marine Syd Hordern.

Bridgeman shows Hordern his middle finger.

'If you should happen to imagine that the first pretty French girl who smiles at you intends to dance the cancan or take you to bed —' Simpson reads.

'Eh, I like the sound of this. Where did you get that filth?' says Wragg.

'You've got one, too, you chump. It's what Sergeant Weaver give us this morning,' says Corporal Blackwell. '*Instructions for British Servicemen in France.*'

'Should you encounter a British serviceman,' begins Hordern, as if reading out an instruction from the book, 'please handle with care. By all means ply him with alcohol — beer for preference, and none of your pissy Frog stuff, if you will pardon this guidebook's French — but do not under any circumstances expose him to bullets or shrapnel, as he is very delicate and may well break —'

'Oi. Are you going to let me finish?'

'Aye, go on, Simpson. Tell us what these French girls do,' says Wragg.

'They don't. That's the whole point of what it says 'ere. Says if you expect them to go to bed with you "you risk stirring up a lot of trouble for yourself".'

'I should say that was rather the point, isn't it?' says Mayhew. Then quickly regrets it, if his furious blush and downward-cast eyes are anything to go by.

'Hey, did everyone hear that?' says Wragg, as ever displaying his finely tuned knack for homing in on others' discomfort. 'That were our young Rupert making a saucy joke.'

'A saucy joke, Rupert? You naughty boy. Wait till your mummy gets to hear of this,' says Kemp.

'He's got a sight better chance of getting his end away than you, you ugly brute,' says Cpl. Blackwell. He can't be more than two years older than Mayhew, but he treats him like a son.

'Well, if he does, he'll have what's coming to him,' says Simpson. 'Says here that as many as one in eight Frogs may be infected with syphilis.'

'Sounds reasonable odds to me,' says Marine Coffin. 'Better than the ones we're about to face on them beaches.'

'And no problem at all for those of us who are prepared,' says Kemp, reaching into his ammunition pouch and ostentatiously removing what must be at least three dozen boxes of French letters.

'You bugger! Where do you nick them?'

'I didn't. Put in an indent at Southampton, same as you. Just while you were farting about with two or three I put in for two gross.'

'And they didn't query it?'

'Told them I was a specialist, didn't I? Told them I had a lot of extra equipment to waterproof.'

'From what this ruddy book says, they're going to be no use anyway,' says Wragg.

'Well, there is one small glimmer of hope,' says Simpson. 'Says French behaviour varies from region to region, so with luck the place where we're going the morals will be nice and easy.'

'Why don't we ask Chad?' says Wragg.

No one answers. Then I realise everyone's looking at me.

'Chad?' I say.

'Aye, as in "Wot, no fags?" and "Wot, no bananas?". It's your new nickname. Dreamed of it last night.'

'May I ask why?'

''Ent it obvious? You've been fookin' everywhere but you've got fook-all to show for it.'

'I see.'

'So go on, tell us, Chad. This part of France we're going to. Ice maidens or cancan girls?'

'If I knew which part of France we were going to –' I begin.

'Well, if you don't you're the only bugger on this boat who doesn't.'

'Really?'

'Aye. Beach we're landing on is near a place called Arrow-Monch. Objective's called summat like Port on Basin.'

'God, have I missed a briefing?'

'You don't think they were going to tell us any of this, do you? No. What happened is that this afternoon the officers and NCOs were given these maps of where we're going, only with the names all wrong. And a bloke from "I" section, actually living up to the name Intelligence for once, puts two and two together and works out where it is. Tries to keep it quiet, of course, but the walls have ears. So go on, then. Port on Basin: the natives friendly or what?'

'Well, I can't vouch for all of them, but there is one thing I know –'

From the mooring next to us there's a blast of a ship's horn, and everyone turns to look. Moments later we watch as our sister ship, a tramp steamer called SS *Victoria*, carrying the other half of our commando, casts off and begins to pull away from the dock's edge. Now the decks of our own ship are abuzz with activity, the engines are throbbing and soon our ship is slipping from the harbour towards the sea.

'It's on!' says Mayhew.

We all raise a cheer and the thing I was going to tell them all is forgotten, which is just as well really. I doubt any of them would really have been much interested in my story about the marvellous crêpe Suzette served by *Grand-mère* who lives down by the port.

A day later and we still haven't left, only now the weather's much, much rougher and instead of being snug in Southampton we're rolling and pitching at anchor in the middle of the Solent. This morning we saw some of the slower ships setting out for France, and now, here they are coming back again, tails between their legs like athletes who've jumped the starter's gun. The seas are too rough and the invasion's off, definitely today and quite possibly, I heard someone say, for weeks.

Up on deck the conditions are dreadful – sea water sloshing everywhere, thick mists of wind-whipped spray smacking into your face with a wet-haddock slap, and the whole deck heaving like a fat matron's bosom. But I'd rather be up here than in the foetid sleeping quarters down below, where the vomit is flying thick as Scotch broth and each roll of the ship sends you barrelling into the chap next to you which, if he's Oily Wragg, means the constant threat of death by asphyxiation. So, just as I did the night before, I've made my way into my secret hiding place, in one of the lifeboats, underneath a tarpaulin.

Only three of us know about it. Me and two fellows from Q troop – Billy Brown and Ted Walters. They seem very close – so close indeed that if Brown hadn't shown me the photos of his wife and new-born baby, I'd have had them down for queer. Mind you, there's a lot of that goes on in the military. Not homosexuality, which you don't see hardly ever. I mean buddy relationships every bit as strong and deep and caring and, well, loving you'd almost say, as the one between man and wife. He watches your back; you watch his. It works very well, but woe betide you if your buddy gets killed because your world falls apart and the pain's so great you swear you'll never let yourself get this close to someone again.

Anyway, they're a nice enough pair are Billy and Ted, though Billy doesn't half bang on about his kid. It's 'Tommy this' and 'Tommy that', and 'the way he looks at you, it's so wise, so knowing, and he's still only six months – least he was when I last saw him, which was, Jesus, must be three fucking months ago, he'll have changed so much I'll hardly recognise him, he'll be walking almost now', which is quite understandable, I'm sure I'd be exactly the same if I were in his shoes but the point is I'm not and neither is the long-suffering Ted.

'They need their dads at that age,' Billy is saying now and, by the flare of the match with which he's lighting his fag, I catch Ted's eyes rolling heavenwards. 'They do though, don't they? Especially sons. I reckon it's going to make a big difference when this war's over. A whole generation of kids who've been brought up without their dads around. Some of them who ain't going to see their dads ever again.'

'Tommy'll be all right,' says Ted.

'Yeah. He'll be all right,' says Billy. 'I'll see to that.'

'You will, mate. You will.'

'I wonder what he'll be doing when I see him next. Definitely be walking. Might even be talking. "Mama" he'll be saying. "Mama". Not "Dada", though.'

'You don't know. Maybe with you being away, he'll think about you more.'

'Doesn't work like that with babies, I don't think. If you're not there, you might as well not exist. Rips me up, Ted, I don't mind telling you. My son, the person I love more than life itself, and he doesn't know me from Adam. Any bloke could come along, tell him he was his dad, and he wouldn't know any better. A GI, even.'

'You don't want to worry about them, Billy. They're all stuck on boats out here, same as us.'

Somewhere outside, just discernible above the howling wind, we can hear someone shouting.

'Mightn't be so bad though, if it were a Yank. I mean, they're a lot better-paid than us, aren't they? So if anything were to happen to me –'

'Billy, nothing's going to happen to you.'

'Caaaaaarrdddd,' goes the shouting voice again, much nearer now.

'What's he saying?' says Ted.

'Sounds like Coward,' says Billy.

'Oh, very funny,' I say.

'COWARD, YOU TOSSPOT, WHERE IN CHRIST'S NAME ARE YOU?'

'Chaps, I'm going out,' I say grimly, as I pull back the tarpaulin. 'And I may be some time.'

'COWARD, ARE YOU BLOODY DEAF?' bellows my troop's Lt. Ponsonby Truelove – wiry, red-faced, terrifying – about as unlike a Ponsonby Truelove as a chap could possibly be. 'I'VE BEEN CALLING YOUR NAME FOR THE LAST BLOODY HALF-HOUR.'

'Sorry, sir.'

'Save your apologies for the Colonel. He wants your arse for breakfast.'

Truelove leads the way across the lurching deck, with the stealth and sure-footedness of a panther stalking its prey.

Struggling to keep up, spray in my eyes, buffeted and mauled by gale-force winds, I wonder which of my myriad misdemeanours might have attracted the Colonel's wrath. Not sleeping below decks; failure to shave; a top button undone;

insufficiently shiny toe-caps . . . With a stickler like Partridge it could be anything.

'Coward. In.' Lt. Col. Partridge is seated at a small table in a cabin so tiny that there's barely room for two of us. Lt. Truelove has to stand in the corridor outside.

'Sir!' I give him my sharpest, smartest salute while he squints at me in the pale orange light. Thank God it's too dim for him to find fault with my uniform.

'Coward, it has come to my attention that our destination is no longer a secret. Now, apart from designated officers, only two men on this ship were privy to this information on embarkation. Yourself and Sarnt Price. Is that correct?'

'Yes, sir.'

'Having spoken to Sarnt Price I have satisfied myself that this breach of secrecy had nothing to do with him. Which leaves only you, Coward.'

'Yes, sir.'

'I understand from your troop commander that you have not settled in well since joining our unit. That your section hasn't taken too well to your habit of sounding off at every opportunity, even on matters you know nothing about. That you are a blabbermouth. Is that correct?'

'No, sir.'

'It's your word against those of several others. Men I have got to know well since this commando was formed. Men whose judgement I have come to trust. Are you asking me to believe that they are all liars?'

'Not liars, sir, no. Just – mistaken.'

'Coward, let me reiterate. I consider the breach of secrecy regarding our destination quite inexcusable. A slip of the tongue like that, whether designed to curry favour with men who have so far found your character wanting –'

'Sir!' I protest.

'Or whether through sheer witless incompetence, could easily jeopardise the whole operation. Do you understand that, Coward?'

'Yes, sir, but —'

'And were it not for the pressing circumstances in which we find ourselves, let me tell you that I would have no hesitation in having you court-martialled forthwith. As it is, I'm prepared to offer you the alternative of a week's field punishment just as soon as operational demands allow.'

'Sir, if you'll permit me to —'

'I think what Coward is trying to say is "Thank you very much, sir" — isn't it, Coward?' hisses Lt. Truelove.

'Yes, sir. Thank you very much, sir.'

'I shall be watching you, Coward. Any more incidents like this and I shall not be so lenient. Understood?'

'Yes, sir.'

'Very good. Dismissed.'

A sharp salute. An inward curse. Back down the passageway, trying to keep up with Lt. Truelove.

'Word of advice, Coward, born of personal experience,' growls Truelove once we're out of earshot. 'The Colonel's always right and never more so than when he's wrong.'

'Thank you, sir,' I say. 'You know, then, that it wasn't . . .'

'Course I bloody do. I was there when Ross from "I" section blurted out the name for all to hear. And don't worry. I shall be sure to let him know he owes you a favour. Just as you owe me one for interrupting my leisure hours. Now, you sound like the sort of fellow who might know how to play bridge?'

'I do a bit.'

'You'd better do more than a sodding bit because you're now my sodding partner.'

*   *   *

We can't have been playing more than three-quarters of an hour and already, Lt. Truelove and I are seventeen down. Which at 100 francs a point is looking quite expensive – or would do if we knew how much the wad of French money we've all been issued is worth at the moment, which we don't, not really, not after four years of German occupation. What we can be sure of, though, is that the opposition – Capt. Dangerfield and Lt. Frost – is getting smugger and smugger, while my partner is getting angrier and angrier.

'For Christ's sake, Coward,' snaps Lt. Truelove after yet another unopposed rubber. 'Couldn't you see the ten of diamonds I led to your queen was a singleton? If you'd led me another back we'd have had them one off, doubled and vulnerable, you arse.'

'Sorry, sir, I thought you wanted a club.'

'Sod clubs. I wanted a ruff. And for the purposes of this game, it's Ponsonby, remember?'

'Well, you did call me Coward.'

'Jesus, Coward, you've got an answer for everything. Listen, I'll start calling you Dick just as soon as you stop playing like one. Jack, stop smirking and get on with it, it's you to deal.'

While Lt. Frost deals, Capt. Dangerfield watches me curiously. It has taken him a while to grow comfortable in my presence. I don't think he liked it when Lt. Ponsonby suggested at the beginning that we might as well suspend rank and converse on first-name terms. But a succession of outrageously decent hands, finesses and unlikely splits has raised his spirits no end; as too have the tots of exceedingly good brandy Frost is using to doctor the mugs of tea one of the seamen has kindly brought us.

'I know I've asked you this before,' he says, eyes narrowing, 'but are you absolutely sure you're no relation of James Coward?'

'Nice chap, is he?'

'Terrible shit. But if you did know him I was going to ask

you to pass on my thanks, because I owe him an awful lot. Everything, in fact,' Capt. Dangerfield says.

'A shit taught you everything? I don't believe that for a second, Guy,' says Lt. Frost.

'It's a long story.'

'Well, I don't know how else we're going to pass the time,' says Lt. Truelove sarcastically. 'Not playing bridge, clearly.'

'I beg your pardon, Ponsonby, one no trump,' says Lt. Frost.

'Two spades,' I say.

'My partner putting his foot in it again?' Lt. Truelove muses aloud.

'Pass,' says Capt. Dangerfield.

'Ah well, nothing ventured. Four spades,' replies Lt. Truelove.

Capt. Dangerfield leads a five of hearts.

Lt. Truelove lays down his cards, which include a singleton club and five spades to the jack.

'If you mess this one up . . .' he warns, head swaying like a cobra about to strike.

But I don't; it would be almost impossible. Lt. Frost's ace of hearts falls straightaway to my two of spades. Our only losers are the ace of spades and the ace of clubs. Game made with tread to spare.

'Played, Dick,' says Lt. Truelove, as I deal the next hand. 'So, Guy, I must say I'm as puzzled as Jack. What exactly did you learn from this shit James?'

'It had to do with a girl,' says Capt. Dangerfield, slightly hesitant.

'Say no more,' says Lt. Truelove.

'Why do shits always prosper?' says Lt. Frost.

'They don't always have to. That's what this James fellow taught me,' says Capt. Dangerfield. 'You see, when I was growing up, I wasn't very sporty and I wasn't very rich, and one summer, I went to stay with my cousins and ended up among a lot of children who were both those things, and I don't mind telling you it felt awful. There was one boy in particular who gave me a jolly hard time. Good-looking, good at games, big house, the works, and, of course, it was just my luck that he should be sweet on the same girl I had rather a soft spot for. But what chance did I stand of competing against this James Coward? Well, I didn't. The more he teased me, the more I withdrew into my shell and it got so bad that one day – we'd been over at his place, huge pile he had in the Welsh borders, father was a general, difficult chap, won a VC in the last war – I seriously thought about ending it all. I was standing on this bridge, looking down into the churning water below this big water wheel they had, and I thought to myself: "Why not? Why not end it all now?" And I might have done too if I hadn't glanced down to the millpond, where she and James were playing, and for some reason, she wasn't looking at him, she was actually looking up at me. And she smiled. And I smiled back. And I realised: "No. There's a better way. I'm going to win this one. I can win this one." And over the next few years that's what I prepared myself to do. I couldn't make my father any richer – a vicar's stipend is a vicar's stipend. But what I did discover was the sporting skill I never realised I had. I ran a lot. I swam. I kicked balls around and hit 'em with bats. And before I knew it, I was in the school second XI, then captain of the first XI; and the first XV; and head boy; and victor ludorum. And I dare say I might have gone to do similar things at Cambridge, if Herr Hitler hadn't helped steer me down a different avenue. And, well, that's it really. I'm sorry it took so long but you did ask. That's why I'm grateful to this chap James Coward, who you don't even know so it's all pretty irrelevant. But I've been holding you up. Shall we play?'

Well, to be honest, I'm torn. On the one hand, all the while he's been talking I've been looking at the hand I've dealt myself, which is by far the best of the evening – five good hearts and nineteen points – and I'm itching to play it. On the other, I'm quite curious about the identity of this girl he fancied. My immediate thought is Caro Ashenden. She really was a cracker in her day –

'You bidding, partner?' says Lt. Truelove.

'Er. One heart,' I say.

Capt. Dangerfield passes.

'Three hearts,' says Lt. Truelove.

'Double,' says Lt. Frost.

After a nervous pause I say: 'Four no trumps.'

The look Lt. Truelove shoots me says: You'd better know what you're doing . . .

The contract we eventually settle on is seven hearts doubled and the game play is so tense I find myself half-wishing I could somehow skip forward twenty-four hours so that I might find myself doing something less nerve-racking. Storming the Atlantic Wall, say.

Lt. Truelove's commentary is not much help. 'And we're fucking vulnerable,' he says, when Capt. Dangerfield shows out on the very first round of trumps, meaning Lt. Frost has all five missing ones, including the jack, and if you're unfamiliar with the rules of bridge it really doesn't matter, the point of all this is that the contract I'm trying to make is awfully difficult and more important than life itself.

'Well done,' says Capt. Dangerfield sullenly, once I've made it.

'You bugger!' says Lt. Frost.

'You, Dick my lad, are a ruddy genius and if ever I have the chance to lay down my life for you I surely will,' says Lt. Truelove, leaping from his chair and twisting round my head with his muscly arms so he can plant a huge kiss on my forehead.

Bridge. What a marvellously useful game it is. Wards off boredom when you're young; keeps the brain active when you're old; holds couples together (and the opposite, I'll concede); cements friendships; quickens the senses. But what I like best about it is the way it transports the mind to a place where your quotidian anxieties seem suddenly irrelevant, for all that now matters is the next deal and the next bid and the next card and the next game and the next rubber. Time slips by. The real world is miles away. For all you care, you could be anywhere – in the grandest mansion or the meanest hovel, in a luxury hotel or a prison cell; for, so long as you are playing, your universe extends no further than that square of green baize.

All of which doesn't half come in handy when you're in a cramped, musty cabin on a rusty, swaying old ship as dawn breaks on what may quite possibly be the last full day of your life. Of course the four of us should be trying to get some sleep, we all know that. But when you can count the remainder of your life in hours, you don't want to waste any of it in oblivion, do you? You want to wring it out, like an orange, and extract every last drop of sweet juice. And with hindsight, how right we were to do so! I don't want to spoil the story but I can tell you right now that two of us aren't going to come out of this mission in one piece. One dead; one wounded; which, out of four people, is a pretty fair representation of the casualty rate 47 Commando is going to suffer in the next few months.

If you want chapter and verse on this you should have a look at the book our medical officer 'Doc' Forfar wrote, called *From Omaha to the Scheldt*. Our casualty rates, he shows, were damn near the equal of those in the First War.

From 6 June until VE day on 8 May the following year an

Other Rank (i.e. non-officer) in one of the five fighting troops stood an 86 per cent chance of being wounded and a 32 per cent chance of being killed. For an officer, meanwhile, it was odds-on you weren't going to make it. You had a 75 per cent chance of being wounded, and a whopping 63 per cent – that's two out of every three officers – of being killed. Or, put another way, that's a casualty rate of 116 per cent for fighting-troop Other Ranks and 132 per cent for fighting-troop officers, meaning that anyone in 47 Commando who didn't get killed or wounded wasn't merely lucky, they were an out-and-out freak of nature.

So don't be surprised if, in the course of the next few hours, several of these chaps you've come to know and like end up being mutilated, drowned or blown to buggery. It's what happens in war, I'm afraid. It's why, whenever a soldier is offered the chance to take his mind off things, he'll grab at it as a drowning man grabs at a floating branch. And it's why when, round about seven a.m. on 5 June 1944, a flushed marine from HQ troop comes knocking at our door, we're all still gathered round the bridge table.

We look up, bleary-eyed.

'It's on!' says the marine.

'Fook me. Will you look at that. Poor Jerry doesn't stand a blooming chance,' says Wragg, leaning over the rails on a morning so grey and grim it seems scarcely credible that the people in charge have decided to go ahead. The LCAs dangling from the side of our ship are swinging like a donkey's knackers; the seas are a maelstrom of peaks and troughs and breaking crests and flying spume. If it carries on like this we'll be swamped and drowned long before we reach the shore.

'What?' says Dent.

'That, you blind git. What – is it so big you can't see it?'

Wragg is nodding towards the gargantuan object chugging past our port bow. Even amid the extraordinary variety of strange and wonderful seaborne shapes we have seen passing in line astern across the Solent, this one really does take the biscuit. It's a long, low, very slow-moving craft with no arma- ments or vehicles and very few men aboard: just this vast, great drum amidships, like some — well, there's nothing to compare it to really. It's simply a huge dark mysterious cylinder.

'What do you reckon it is?' says Calladine.

''Ent it fooking obvious?' says Wragg.

'A secret weapon?' says Dent.

'Oh. Aye. See how well they've camouflaged it,' says Wragg sarcastically.

'Well, I've never seen one before and I'll bet nor have you,' says Dent.

'Aye but I'm not so stupid as I don't know what it is. It's for bustin' bunkers, 'ent it?'

'Is it?' says Calladine.

'Course it fookin is. You rolls it ashore. Shoves it in front of a pillbox. Then boom! Because that whole middle bit is stuffed with high explosives. Needs to be to get through all that concrete.'

'So which poor sod's pushing it ashore?'

'I dunno. Somebody from t'engineers, I'd think.'

'What? Suicide unit? If that drum's full of high ex, he's never going to make it to the bunker, is he? Not even close.'

'Oh, for fook's sake. It's armour-plated, 'ent it?'

'Then it's not going to float, it'll sink.'

'Hey, don't expect me to know all the details. I didn't invent it,' says Wragg.

'But don't you think —' I begin.

'Oh, 'ere we go. Chad's off,' says Wragg.

'I'm merely pointing out that, if it were for busting bunkers, it's setting sail a little late. The rate it's travelling, the beaches will have been cleared by the time that thing arrives.'

'You know, Chad, you're not just a fookin' know-all, you're a killjoy too,' says Wragg.

'Yeah, sorry, mate, but he's right,' says Simpson. 'Of course it's not a bleeding bunker buster. But we all of us felt a fuck of a sight happier when we thought for a moment it was.'

What the drum actually is, though we don't discover this till long after the event, is a segment of pipeline. That pipeline – known as Pipeline Under the Ocean, PLUTO for short – is to be extended from Ventnor in the Isle of Wight all the way to a carefully selected destination on the French coast. A destination whose capture will be absolutely vital to the success or otherwise of the Allied breakout, because it will be the main source of the million gallons of fuel each Allied army will require each day.

I wonder, perhaps, if you can guess which 420 poor sods out of the 156,000-strong invasion force landed the short straw of having to capture it?

9

On the Beach

As I burst to the surface and heave a deep gasp of air, I'm
overwhelmed by a surge of shivering elation. I'm alive, by
God. I'm alive. The worst that could happen has happened –
our LCA has been sunk by a shell or a mine – yet by some
miracle I'm still in one piece.

It's my battle jerkin, I reckon, which must have saved me.
You might not have heard of them before because they weren't
standard issue – only meant for D-Day, in fact. But whichever
bright spark thought of them, I owe him my life and so do
many more men besides me. You slipped it on, a bit like a
waistcoat – on top of your Mae West, if you were sensible,
not underneath – and did it up at the front with toggles which
you could release in a flash.

Now this battle jerkin, it's designed to carry all the things
that would normally go into your webbing and your small
pack. It has pockets for your water-bottle and pockets for your
grenades, your .303 rounds, your side-arm, your fighting knife
and your entrenching tool. Someone must have helped me
jettison it when I hit the water. If they hadn't done – together
all that ammo weighs a ton – I'd have gone down straight to
the bottom.

Of course, this does mean I'm now going to have to wade
ashore and face the enemy armed with nothing more deadly

than a vicious sense of humour. But for the moment, I have more pressing things to worry about – such as the numbing iciness of the water, far, far colder than you'd expect of the Channel in summer.

Then there's the fact that I'm floundering two or three hundred yards offshore, utterly unprotected and vulnerable, in seas fizzing, hissing, splashing and erupting with tracer rounds and shellfire. The grey landing craft streaming past me are oblivious of the human flotsam in their path. And the mangled torso bobbing next to me can only be Price's: I recognise it by the sergeant's stripes on its one remaining arm.

Funny, the tricks the mind plays. Through the screaming of the artillery and the crump of explosions, and the dull roar of the sea water stuck in my ear, it's almost as if I can hear his voice.

'Next time you can blow your sodding Mae West up yourself.'

'Price?' I paddle myself round 180 degrees to find a figure floating just a few feet behind me, his face and uniform so blackened with oil that it's only by his misshapen teeth that I can recognise him.

'Beach is that way,' he says, nodding forwards.

We try to swim shorewards, which isn't easy. Battledress soaked with water drags like a sheet anchor and it's hard to work up a decent kick when your feet are being pulled down by a pair of clodhopping boots. I would try to remove them except I know from experience that the kit you throw away before an action will always come back to haunt you. Boots especially. No one who was on the Eastern Front is ever going to throw away a pair of good, fitting boots.

For all the noise and chaos going on above our heads, it feels strangely peaceful at sea level, as if we're not actually part of the mayhem around us, just idle spectators. Time appears to have frozen. Rising and falling in the swell, I keep getting glimpses of the shoreline: the shattered remnants of once-elegant beachfront houses, the plumes of smoke and flying debris, slow-moving vehicles, little khaki dots scurrying to and fro, but none of these things looks any closer than it did five, ten, twenty minutes ago or however long it is we've been here; my watch has stopped and so has Price's.

We must be making some kind of progress, though, because, as we paddle forward, we encounter more and more floating refugees from our landing craft, most apparently unharmed, all swimming doggedly on. Except, there's a chap just in front of us, in some kind of trouble. His head is lolling and he's paddling round and round in a very slow, gentle circle.

'You all right there?' I call out to him.

'Oh splendid, thanks. Water's lovely once you're in,' he shouts back, in that cheery manner English officers are expected to put on when *in extremis*. It's Lt. Frost.

'Well, you ain't going to get dry very soon if you go on like that, sir,' says Price. 'You're swimming in circles.'

'Am I, by Jove. What can I be thinking of?'

Price swims next to him. 'Your left arm's at a bit of a funny angle. How are your legs?'

'Do you know, I can't actually feel them. Sergeant, you wouldn't mind checking?'

As Price is rummaging below the water's surface, Lt. Frost lets out an agonised cry.

'Both legs are still there but one of them's broke. You stick with me and Coward and we'll get you to some help.'

'I say, Dick, is that you? Didn't recognise you with your face all black. Seven no trumps!'

'Double!' I say.

'Do you play bridge, Sergeant?'

'No, sir.'

'Jolly well ought to, you know. Marvellous game, isn't it, Dick?'

'Oh, very.'

'But listen, you fellows, haven't you something more important to be getting on with? I'm sure I can manage perfectly well.'

Price shoots me a look I've seen all too often. It translates as: 'Bleeding officers. I ask you. No wonder so many of them never make it.'

'I'm sure you can, sir,' he says. 'Only I was hoping you might give me a bridge lesson.'

'Ah well, in that case, Sergeant – are you familiar with suits? You play rummy, do you . . . ?'

With me tugging on one side, Price tugging on the other and Lt. Frost burbling cheerfully about contracts and high-card point counts and opening bids, we float, paddle and kick slowly shorewards. Whenever a landing craft passes – and some of them come unnervingly close – we wave desperately for help but get nothing but pitying grimaces. All boat crews have had the same strict orders: no one is to stop to pick up stragglers until they've landed their occupants. One might have hoped by now that we'd bump into one of the craft on its way back. But the troublesome fact is, I've yet to see a landing craft actually making the return journey.

Once we've reached the first obstacles it becomes clear why. The whole landing area is a scrapyard of broken, twisted landing craft, burnt-out tanks and floating corpses. Nothing can escape it because all the channels between the mined posts and clusters of Czech hedgehogs are now blocked with wrecked, swamped shipping. When the first assault waves went in, the sea was much lower, which meant that the obstacles were still visible. Now, concealed by the rapidly rising tide, the Germans' Teller mines are ripping the bottoms of almost every vessel that comes in. And somehow, Price, Lt. Frost and I have to negotiate our way through this mess.

We need to strike a delicate balance: swim too near the poles and we risk triggering one of the mines; swim too far away from them and we'll end up crushed by one of the landing craft trying to avoid them. Not, it must be said, that we have an awful lot of choice in the matter. The waves and the undertow are making most of our decisions for us. As we're picking our way through them, we hear cries for help. Looking across to the next channel, about fifty yards away we see a submerged DD tank, only the tip of its turret still visible above the surf, with a crewman standing on top as the waves buffet his legs.

'Help! Someone! Please! I can't swim.'

'Sorry, mate, we've got our hands full,' mutters Price more for our benefit than the hapless tankie's.

'But we can't just leave him there. He'll drown.'

'Please don't abandon him on my account,' says Lt. Frost.

'What good is he to us anyway, now his tank's broke?' says Price.

'Help! Please!' The waves have now reached the tankie's knees.

'Excuse me for a moment, sir, will you?' I say, about to set off towards the tank.

'By all means,' says Lt. Frost. 'You're a good –'

Fellow presumably but he never finishes because his mouth, eyes and ears have filled with water as our whole world turns a murky green and we're being whirled round like socks in a laundromat, hurled we know not where by the vast wave which has hit us broadside, dragged us under, shaken us about and just as suddenly spat us out amid the oily, bloody flotsam of seaweed, and body parts strewn along the shore.

The wave has taken the wind out of me, sucked out my every last drop of strength. I'm lying face down, arms outstretched, too tired even to spit the sand from my mouth or flick off the thousands of tiny hopping things which have begun to congregate on my face and hands. Sand flies, everywhere. The beach is black with them. It's what happens when for four years a seaside resort has been *verboten* to holiday-makers and it's probably what will happen come the apocalypse: the creepy-crawlies will inherit the earth.

Just above I can hear what sounds like more insect life. A swarm of furious bees buzzing inches from my head, then disappearing into the sand with a tremendous sucking noise.

Twisting to my left, I see Lt. Frost, lying face up, perfectly still, the incoming water lapping at his legs.

'Don't fucking move!' comes a scream.

It's Price, keeping himself as low down in the water as he possibly can, clinging on to a post for support.

'I'm perfectly aware what the problem is, Price,' I call back. 'And I'll thank you to remember, as your officer and your employer –'

'I'll thank YOU to remember that you're neither, right this minute. And that, what's more, the correct term of address is Sergeant Price.'

'Sorry, Price, but as you know in my family old habits die hard. When no one else is listening, Price you shall remain.'

'Who said no one's listening?' says Lt. Frost.

'I'm terribly sorry, sir. I thought you were dead.'

'Feel like it, too, Dick. Must say, though, your chat just now has given me the most tremendous fillip. Best gossip I've heard in ages. Are you going to fill me in?'

'Oughtn't we get ourselves out of this mess, first, sir?'

'Oh Lord. Are we in another mess?'

'"Fraid so, sir. You might have noticed that dreadful din just above our heads. I'm afraid we've been pinned down by a Spandau.'

'I say, that is a blow. I'd been rather hoping the Hampshires and Dorsets would have dealt with that sort of thing by now.'

'So had we all, sir.'

'Do you have any bright ideas?'

'Well, sir –'

'Oi, Coward, if you don't mind, I've got the situation in hand,' says Price. 'Sir, there's not much we can do until Jerry gets bored and finds something else to shoot at. We seem to be below his angle of maximum depression. Do you think you can hold on, sir?'

'I seem to be getting terribly wet.'

'Yes, sir, but if you can just hang on that might be to our advantage. There's a burnt-out Crab not twenty yards up the beach. If we can just play dead till then, we can let ourselves be carried there by the tide.'

Which is exactly what we do. Lying doggo, not even shouting to one another, lest it draw the attention of the machine gunner – who, sure enough, has been distracted by a more active target – we wait for the rising water to lift us up, and the waves to push us to safety.

And a very sensible plan it is too but for one small problem, which becomes apparent when, about half-way towards the cover of the tank, a wave rolls Lt. Frost over on to his front. Having watched him bob face down for some time, struggling with increasing feebleness to right himself, I realise I'm going to have to intervene – and quickly – to stop him from drowning. No sooner have I splashed towards him, though, than the MG is on to us once more. Worse still, the sea has very nearly risen to such a height as to bring us within the scope of the MG's fire.

It's a terrifying weapon, the MG42. That distinctive sound it makes, like ripping cloth, is the sound you get of bullets being fired so close together that the human ear cannot distinguish the individual shots. Which, of course, is why we all so fear it. Our Bren guns might be more accurate, but they're slower to load, and they can only fire a maximum of 600 rounds a minute. The MG42 – or Spandau, as we call it – can fire 1,000 rounds a minute. And being belt-fed, it never seems to run out of ammo.

'Price,' I shout. 'You got us into this mess. For heaven's sake – Hey! Where are you going?'

Price, it seems, has had enough and I'm not sure I can altogether blame him. He didn't choose to be here. He didn't need to be here. He did tell me he wasn't going to save my bacon any more, and now he's been true to his word.

'Just you and me now, is it, eh, Dick?' says Lt. Frost.

'I'm afraid so, sir,' I say, as Price, paddling like a terrapin, pulls surreptitiously out to sea. The Spandau tracks his movements. Doesn't hit him, more's the pity. But at least it buys me just enough time to drag Lt. Frost across the two or three yards of beach to the nearest tetrahedron. Though it doesn't offer us much protection, it will give Lt. Frost something to cling on to and keep his head above water, as the sea rises.

'Well, do call me Jack, won't you?' says Lt. Frost, as I help him hook his good arm round a steel post. Which movement, of course, attracts the machine gunner's attention once more, a stream of 9-mm. bullets whining, ricocheting and sending sparks off the girders just above our heads in the most unpleasant fashion.

'You're a stupid bugger, Dick,' says Lt. Frost, when it's apparent I'm not going to go. 'If by some stroke of luck we manage to get out of this in one piece, I shall put in a jolly good word for you with the CO.'

'Thank you, sir.'

The sea is almost up to our chests now. Before it's too late, and with the greatest difficulty, I reach into my breast pocket and extract the condom in which I have wrapped my letter to Gina.

Lt. Frost furrows his brow bemusedly.

'It's a letter to my girlfriend,' I yell, arms round the tetrahedron for support, my numb fingers wrestling with the slippery knot at one end.

'French, is she?'

'No, English.'

'You sure? Looks like a French letter to me.'

'Oh yes, sir, very good. Sorry, I must have lost my sense of humour.'

I've often wondered since how I managed it: frozen fingers; slimy condom; wet pen; nothing to rest the paper on. But when you're convinced these are the last words you're ever going to write to the woman you wished you could have married, you do somehow find a way, don't you?

'MY DARLING,' I scrawl (anything other than block capitals would be too difficult). 'I THINK MY NUMBER'S UP. SORRY IT HAD TO BE THIS WAY. BE HAPPY. LOVE YOU ALWAYS. DICK.' Then I knot it back inside the condom and replace it in my breast pocket where, with luck, it will be found by whoever finds my body.

'Hullo! Who's this?' says Lt. Frost.

Stealthy as a log-shaped crocodile, Price is cruising purposefully towards us, towing something bulky – a wounded man? – by his side. Not quite stealthily enough though, because now the Spandau has directed its fire at him. At first the bullets splash into the water some way beyond him, but now they're drawing closer and closer and –

Oh God.

An awful juddering and the terrible, dull thwack of lead in flesh. Yet still, miraculously, he keeps on coming.

'Brought an old friend,' he announces, keeping his head to

the safe side of what I now recognise as the drowned corpse of the DD tank crewman, which he is using as a shield. 'Quick. He's not going to stand up to much more of this.'

I pull Lt. Frost towards our unfortunate human shield who, sure enough, is disintegrating rapidly in noisome shards of flesh and bone and bloodied sinew, much of which ends up all over our faces. Only his leather jerkin is holding him together.

'Do you know what your problem is, Price?' I gasp through a mouthful of gore, when finally we've reached the safety of the brewed-up Crab. 'You're all substance and no damn style.'

But, of course, our problems are far from over. There's a Spandau still gunning for us the moment we break from our cover; there are mortar bombs erupting all over the beach; we've none of us a clue where the rest of our unit is; and we've a wounded man with us who, for all his stiff upper lip and courage, is starting to look extremely shivery and pale.

'We'd better get you a medic, sir. And a nice cup of tea,' says Price.

'Lord, you really WERE Coward's batman,' says Lt. Frost.

'A very, very, VERY long time ago,' says Price.

'Oh very well. I'll go,' I say, taking the hint.

'Poor chap needs one now, not in three days' time,' says Price.

'Bugger off, Sergeant,' I say and, before he can stop me, I'm scuttling along the beach – taking extra care, obviously, to keep the dead tank between myself and the Spandau – for the cover of a promisingly deep-looking shell crater into which I've seen several men disappear, about thirty yards further east.

Diving over the lip and sliding to the bottom, I look up to find myself in the midst of the most extraordinary scene, somewhere between a vicar's tea party and a Bacchanalian orgy. Sprawled around me in various stages of undress, some with no shirts, some minus their trousers, and a couple of unfortunates stark bollock-naked, are a half-dozen members of my commando, being served tea and biscuits by the padre.

'Another 47. How nice of you to join us!' says the padre, the only one of us who is dry and with his uniform completely intact. I learn later that, of our fourteen landing craft, five have been sunk on the run in and seven others badly damaged, leaving only two fit to make it back to their parent ship. The padre was on one of the lucky ones which not only negotiated the mines and obstacles on the way in, but managed to drop its ramp on dry land, allowing him to step nimbly ashore with something far more useful to soldiers *in extremis* than prayers, blessings or extreme unction: a hay box full of steaming tea.

'Laugh and you're fooking dead,' says Wragg, who's one of the naked ones.

'Perish the thought,' I say. 'No more would I laugh at such naked magnificence than I would at Michelangelo's *David*.'

'En't that the famous statue with the very small willy?' says Hordern.

'Hey, it's that fooking water — pardon me, Padre, but if you'd fooking fell in it you'd know what I fooking meant — it's fooking freezing.'

'Methinks our Oily doth protest too much,' says Hordern.

Wragg is bunching his fists to defend his honour when he's interrupted by a terrible cry from the crater lip.

'What in sweet Jesus' name do you think you pederasts are up to? My apologies, Padre — excepting you, sir. Your orders were to clear off the beach immediately!' bellows Lt. Truelove, hands on hips, crotch thrust forward for all the world as if he's about to piss on us.

'We tried, sir, but that Spandau pinned us down and we had no weapons to engage.'

'You're not meant to engage till we reach our objective,' says Lt. Truelove, as the sand a few yards to his right suddenly kicks upwards and that familiar tearing noise rends the air once more. Lt. Truelove sidesteps slightly to the left but remains upright – having worked out in a flash that the burnt-out tank is protecting him from the Spandau's field of fire.

'Now, get your arses off the floor, all of you, and get yourselves to that sea wall over yonder, where you'll find Captain Dangerfield. He's been watching you through his binoculars and he's not impressed with what he's seen so far. Coward, what are you waiting for?'

'Sir, I'm afraid Lieutenant Frost is down –'

'I would be too, if I played bridge the way he does,' he says. 'Not serious, I hope.'

'He's by that Crab over there. I was going to take him some of the Padre's tea.'

'Very well, Coward,' he says, handing me his hip-flask. 'You can add some of that with my compliments. Better have some yourself, too. You're looking a little shaky.'

'Bit chilly, that's all.'

Lt. Truelove looks me briskly up and down with his mad, intense blue eyes – an experience akin to being flayed by birches. Then drops his voice and says with unexpected gentleness: 'You won't let us down, Dick?'

'Do you think I would?'

'I never think, you know that. But there are others.' He raises his eyes heavenwards, presumably to indicate Capt. Dangerfield. Or Lt. Col. Partridge. Probably both.

'Lord, but it's so damned unfair.'

'Try being called Ponsonby Truelove sometime. Now, enough chat, I want to see you, and more importantly my hip-flask, by the sea wall in ten minutes. I'll send the medics for Lieutenant Frost.'

By the time I reach the tank, the waves are already lapping the lower part of its tracks and with it the rising tide has carried all manner of flotsam up the beach – jerry cans, empty Mae Wests, crates, a life ring saying SS *Victoria*, corpses and blackened bits of corpses, advancing inexorably inland like an army of the dead in a rolling mass of oily seaweed and filthy spume. Occasionally, with a revolting crunch, it will be over-taken by the army of the living as another landing ramp crashes down, swiftly followed by an urgent splashing of boots; or the clank of tracks as a Bren carrier or tank manoeuvres through the accumulating debris across the narrowing strip of sand leading towards the nearest beach exit.

'With the compliments of Lieutenant Truelove,' I say, helping Lt. Frost to a sip of tea. He's conscious but only just. Cold and greenish, he has been propped up against the tank's track, and wrapped in a gas cape.

'Landed dry, did he? Jammy devil.'

'And he's promised to send you a medic just as soon as he can,' I say.

'We can wait. We've been having a wonderful time here, haven't we, Sarnt? Go on. Tell him what you need for a one-no-trump opening bid?'

'Twelve to fourteen points, sir.'

'Very good, Sarnt, but that's not all, is it? Go on. You know. What's the other requirement? Begins with "B".'

'Balanced?'

'Bravo, Sarnt. See what a fast learner your man is, Coward? At this rate, by the time you reach Port-en-Bessin, Captain Dangerfield will have his new partner ready-made.'

'You hear that Spandau?' asks Sgt. Price, suddenly.

'No,' I say, half-listening, half-distracted by the LCA which is preparing to drop its ramp not fifteen yards from where we're sitting. Full of green berets.

'That's what I thought. Reckon it's been taken out. You feel up to moving, sir?'

'MEDIC!' I yell towards the body of men pouring from the LCA's bows and one of them peels off to attend to Lt. Frost.

As we shake Lt. Frost's hand and wish him luck, we can't help but hear an agitated exchange just beside us between a corporal and his troop commander.

'Sir, two of the men are refusing to get off the LCA,' says the Corporal.

'Then use that,' says the Captain – meaning the Corporal's Colt .45.

'You mean, sir, to threaten them with, like?'

'I mean, Corporal,' says the Captain, with slow, deliberate menace. 'If they persist in disobeying orders, shoot them.'

'Very good, sir,' says the Corporal, swallowing hard. He watches the Captain sprint off to rejoin his troop, then looks wonderingly at his side-arm.

In the LCA, two crewmen in grey tin helmets are remonstrating with the two commandos cowering in the back of the craft. Frankly, I'm surprised they haven't done the sensible thing and simply buggered off to the support vessel with the refuseniks still aboard. But I suppose, being Royal Marines themselves, these men feel a greater than usual sense of solidarity with their passengers. The honour of the Corps is at stake.

One of the commandos looks familiar. He has his arm draped round the shoulders of the other one, who's sobbing into his fists. A crewman has lost his temper now: 'You should have thought of that when you volunteered,' I can hear him scream. The consoler gestures, arms open, to the crewman, that he's doing his best.

'It's not me, I'm not scared about me, it's my kid, my kid. If you had kids, you'd understand,' says the weeping one and, now his face isn't covered by his hands, I recognise, Christ –

146

it's Billy! The chap I've spent the last three nights with in that lifeboat. And the other one is his friend Ted.

A rifle cracks. The Corporal with the Colt .45 has collapsed on the ramp of the LCA. The crewman in the portside cockpit gun swivels his Lewis gun uncertainly towards the direction of the fire. As the LCA's coxswain bends down to inspect the Corporal's body, another round pings off the armour plating barely an inch from his head.

'Sniper!' he cries. 'Stoker, hard astern!'

'Shan't be long,' I say to Price.

'Leave 'em, you bloody fool,' he calls after me, but I'm gone.

When the bow ramp of the LCA begins to rise, I'm already half-way across the beach.

'Wait! Just give me a moment,' I say to the crew. 'Ted! Billy! It's me. Dick! You're not going to leave me here all on my own, are you, chaps?'

Ted, his arm still draped round Billy's shoulder, greets me with a look of despair. I take Billy's other arm consolingly.

'Forget it, mate, we're off,' shouts the coxswain, above the growl of the twin V8 engines straining to drag the craft from the beach.

'I'm not scared. Tell 'em it's not because I'm scared,' says Billy, his face so twisted he looks more gargoyle than human.

'Of course you're not scared. It's Ted and me who are scared. We're bricking it, aren't we, Ted?'

'Too flipping right.'

'That's why we need you to look after us. Because you're a dad. The world's greatest dad and you know how it's done.'

Billy looks at me. His hideously contorted features begin to unknot and, for just a moment, it seems as if I might have penetrated that fug of wild terror.

'Your last chance!' says the coxswain, as the LCA begins to pull away.

I glance at Ted. Ted glances at me. We're going to have to drag Billy off.

But, before we're able, Billy stiffens and bristles, and, as if suddenly possessed of a superhuman strength, he explodes from our grip, yelling: 'I'm not the world's greatest dad. I'm the world's fucking worst.'

And he scrambles past the stoker on to the wobbly stern of the LCA, where he stands struggling to keep his balance, staring wild-eyed into the lurching green. Then plunges in.

'He can't swim,' says Ted, climbing after him. He stands where Billy stood, scanning the oily, turbulent grey-green waters for his missing friend, then dives after him.

It takes me a few seconds more to reach the same vantage point. By the time I do, I can see no sign of life anywhere in the water. Only weed, waves, protruding spars, Teller mines, shattered metal and the grisly floating detritus of war and sudden, violent death.

10

The *Hauptmann*'s Britches

Gold Beach, Jig Green Sector, towards 1100 hours on 6 June 1944: crikey, what a dog's breakfast!

Pretty much everything that could have gone wrong has gone wrong. Neither the RAF's bombing nor the Navy's shelling has managed to neutralise the enemy's heavy-gun positions. This means that most of our tanks – those few that even made it ashore – have been knocked out before they can clear the German bunkers. Our two assault waves – first the 1st Hampshires and the 1st Dorsets, then the 2nd Devons – which were supposed to take the beach before our arrival, have either been dragged to the wrong sector by the strong easterly current, or held up by the 75-mm. gun concealed in a fortified sanatorium building in the middle of Le Hamel.

Meanwhile, at 47 (RM) Commando, we've lost about a fifth of our strength and we haven't even got off the beach. Our rendezvous was supposed to have been the church in Le Hamel, but with the church still very much in enemy hands, all we can do is take what shelter we can, brew up with whatever equipment we can muster, try to smoke our sodden fags, and await further orders.

'Oi! Watch where you're bleeding stepping,' snaps a green beret, as I collapse breathless beneath the sea wall which is sheltering the remnants of our commando. It's Hordern, understandably peeved at having had sand kicked into his enamel mug of rare and lovingly prepared tea. On seeing that it's me, though, he appears to cheer up no end.

'Well, look who it ain't,' he announces. And the rest of the section all look up from their business. Bridgeman, Kemp, Calladine, Dent, Wragg, Mayhew, Coffin, Simpson –

No sign of Sgt. Weaver, yet, and my mind flashes back to the body I saw with three stripes on its arm, floating near where our LCA went down. Pray God it was someone else's. It can play havoc with a section's morale when you lose a popular NCO.

Under the circumstances, the chaps seem to be bearing up remarkably well. Some of them are without boots; some, without trousers, almost all of them, without weapons. They're pale, they're shivery, they're damp and in the eyes is the stunned, far-off look of men who never expected to see quite so much so soon. But for all that, spirits are high, elated even. It's like that when you've narrowly cheated death. For a time, you feel almost immortal.

My return, it would seem, has made them happier still.

'Bad luck, mate,' says Kemp. 'Nice try.'

'Yeah, bloody heroic effort,' agrees Bridgeman.

There are titters and I'm not sure how to respond. Most soldiers, quite sensibly, have an aversion to putting themselves unnecessarily in the way of danger, and are consequently suspicious of those idiots who do. On the other hand, maybe they are, in their gruff pretend-sarcastic way, trying to express their backhanded admiration for what I've just attempted. It was, after all, their comrades I was trying to save from ignominy; and, by extension, the honour of our unit.

'Did you know them?' I ask.

'Who?' says Wragg.

'The chaps I was trying to help off the LCA. Billy Brown and Ted Walters.'

'Names too,' comments Kemp, knowingly, to the general company. 'I like his style.'

'Very crafty,' Bridgeman agrees. 'I've seen courts martial fooled by alibis a lot lamer than that.'

'And what do you mean by that?'

'Outraged dignity too. That always plays well with your officer class,' comments Kemp.

And whether it's the delayed shock or the combination of Kemp's ratlike features and whiny voice, or yet the sheer effrontery and terrible unfairness of his allegation, before I can stop myself I've leapt on top of him with both hands round his throat.

'Would you care to elaborate, Kemp?' I hiss.

'Go on, Arfinch. Tell him his new name,' goads Wragg.

'Coward. Let go of him,' says Sgt. Price.

'When he apologises,' I say.

'I ain't apologising. I saw what I saw,' gasps Kemp.

Before I can mash flat Kemp's pointy, rodent snout, I've been seized tightly by both wrists, my arms are being twisted behind my back, I'm dragged backwards and left lying in a heap on the sand.

'Save it for the enemy,' says Price, pressing down on me.

'Sarge, I think that's the problem. Yeller doesn't much like fighting the enemy,' says Hordern.

That'll be my new nickname then. 'Yellow' Coward. Ah the richness and originality of the squaddie's imagination . . .

'Belt up, Hordern,' says Sgt. Price.

'Are you going to put him on a charge, Sarge? Sarnt Weaver would have done,' says Bridgeman.

'I'm not Sarnt Weaver, am I?' says Sgt. Price.

'No, you're not, Sarge. Sergeant Weaver never had favourites,' says Kemp.

'That's enough, Kemp,' says Sgt. Price in a low, menacing

voice which brooks no further insolence. And it's just as well he has one because, without it, I think we'd have a mutiny on our hands.

Maybe there'll be one still, for now here's a runner, come to ask Sgt. Price to report to Lt. Truelove at once.

'See to it there's no more trouble, Corporal,' says Price.

'Sarge,' says Cpl. Blackwell with a confident nod. He's the Commando's heavyweight boxing champ – fists like legs of ham – and, though a gentle soul in the main, you wouldn't want to cross him.

Even if we did want to carry on arguing we couldn't now anyway, because of the noise like a dozen express trains roaring simultaneously overhead: our battle fleet's twelve-inch and sixteen-inch guns have decided to open up on targets which can't be more than thirty or forty yards ahead of us. You don't want to be at the end of a bombardment like that, you really don't. Just lying under it – belly down, eyes closed, palms pressed in prayer – is quite bad enough.

Berets, mugs, stoves, gas capes, cigarettes, letters, magazines, hot tea and sand, it all starts flying all over the place as the vacuum from the shells' passage lifts each one of us, bodily, off the ground. Then, a moment later, it drops you down again with a thump that takes the wind out of your lungs, while your eardrums are all but shattered with the noise of explosions like you'd never imagine. The earth's shaking; your ears are ringing; your bowels are on the verge of emptying. Then silence. Or at least what seems like silence in your freshly deafened state.

Soon as it's over, Kemp, as chief scrounger, is volunteered to scavenge more tea and cigarettes. Those with weapons clean them lovingly and jealously, while the rest of us sit back and watch the unfolding action, quietly relieved that we're under the strictest orders not to take any part of it.

'Christ, what the bleeding hell's that?' yelps Hordern, leaping back, as a huge, thrashing, rust-coloured snake comes hissing from the skies and lands with a thump by his boots. Another couple of inches and he would have lost both his feet.

'I think it's his,' says Calladine, nodding towards the Sherman Crab tank advancing slowly up the beach, its rotating flail carving an explosive passage through an area marked 'Achtung Minen!'.

'Oi, do you mind?' Hordern yells at it, shaking his fist.

'Wouldn't do his job for all the tea in China,' says Coffin.

'Piece of cake, compared with what we've got to do,' says Bridgeman.

'Oh, you reckon, do you?' says Coffin.

The Crab has just taken a hit on one of its tracks. Moments later, smoke starts emerging from its hatches, closely followed by choking crew members. At once machine-gun bullets start pinging off the armour, almost tearing in half the crewman who was trying to escape from the forward hatch.

'Bastards!' cries McMahon. He's our section's sniper, or would be if he had a rifle.

The rest of the crew makes it, just, to the rear of the tank. Beyond them, a team of Royal Engineers is trying, under fire, to fill a crater on one of the beach's main exit routes with a bundle of fascines. Behind them, an AVRE Churchill noses forward towards the emplacement which took out the crewman from the Crab. Something large bounces off its armour – a dud, thank God – as the tank swivels its hefty armament towards the target.

'Big one,' observes Mayhew.

'Almost as big as mine,' quips Simpson.

'It's a Petard,' I say.

'Trust Yeller to know. Driven tanks too, 'ave you, Yeller?' says Wragg.

'Italian ones he likes best, with the extra reverse gears,' says Bridgeman.

I flick them both a V sign.

'Go on, Yeller, what's the calibre?' teases Hordern.

With a tremendous boom, the Petard's 26-lb. high-explosive charge crashes into the reinforced concrete. The hole when the dust clears isn't as deep as one might wish, but it's the concussion caused to the men inside that really does the damage. Groggy, dizzy and bloody of ear they come stumbling out from the steel doors at the back, there to be machine-gunned on the steps by infantrymen who've neither the time nor the inclination to notice the hands raised in surrender.

'Right then, lads, who's in need of a fag?' asks Kemp, laying a bulging pack on the ground.

A dozen grateful hands shoot up.

'One for you, one for you and one for you. Courtesy of your brigade commander.'

'Brigadier Stanier?' says Calladine.

'No word of lie.'

'But, Arfinch,' says Wragg, examining his moist fag in disgust, 'they're bleeding wet.'

'So's the Brigadier. His LCM went down on the way in. "Sorry, these cigarettes aren't as dry as you'd like, dear boy," says the Brig. – or Sir Alex as I prefer to call him. "But I'm sure it won't be beyond the ingenuity of a commando to get them working in the end."'

'You don't half talk some shite, Arfinch,' says Wragg.

'You ain't heard the half of it yet. I've got news,' says Kemp, pulling out from his bag of tricks a tin of tea, a tin of powdered milk, a tin of sugar and a solid-fuel stove – all of which he tosses in my direction. 'There you go, Yeller. Get brewing.'

'If you ask me nicely.'

'Jesus. Do you want a bloody brew or not?' says Kemp.

'Still thinks he's an officer, I expect. Wants his blooming batman to do it,' says Bridgeman.

'Eh, is it true what I heard? Was Sergeant Price really your batman?' asks McMahon.

'Go on, I dare you, Yeller,' says Hordern, waving a damp banknote at me. 'Bet you this hundred francs you daren't ask Gonad to make us all a nice cup of tea.'

'I think he's having a sulk,' says Coffin.

A bedraggled field-grey line of old men, young boys and frostbite-hobbled Eastern Front veterans files past, herded at bayonet point by a jumpy-looking Hampshire. Christ, I'm thinking. If second-raters like this can hold up our advance so effectively, how the hell are we going to manage when we come against crack troops like the ones from 352 Infantry Division garrisoning Port-en-Bessin?

'If he's not going to join in, he's certainly not getting any of my tea,' says Kemp.

'Lay off him, Arfinch. Can't you see he's had enough?' says young Jack Mayhew. He reaches for the tea equipment and sets to work making the brew himself.

'He'd had enough before we even landed,' says Bridgeman.

'That's enough, Bridgeman,' warns Cpl. Blackwell.

'Well, he needn't have worried. Mission's off anyway,' says Kemp, casually.

'Get away,' says Cpl. Blackwell.

'What? Colonel Partridge give you a private briefing, did he?' says Wragg.

'Now, don't be stupid. The Colonel's dead.'

'What? Since when?' says Mayhew appalled. Whatever, Kemp's announcement has certainly had the desired effect. Everyone's sitting up, listening in.

'Well, if he's not dead, he's definitely missing. Major Dalby's in charge of the mission now.'

'So. Dalby will do exactly what the Colonel would have done and press on regardless,' declares Calladine.

On which cue, Marines Hordern and Bridgeman break into the popular musical refrain 'We're pressing on regardless for the Colonel's DSO'.

'What, without artillery support? Because what I haven't told you yet is that we've got no Forward Observation Officer either,' says Kemp.

'You're 'aving a laugh,' says Hordern.

'Yeah, well, you know what they say: "If you can't take a joke you shouldn't have joined."'

'Crikey, you had me there for a moment, Arfinch. I thought you were serious,' says Dent.

'Wait till you hear the rest. Not only have we got no colonel, no FOO, but we've got no three-inch mortars neither. Nor any HMGs. Bloke from Heavy Weapons troop says they lost everything on the way in.'

'Careless sods,' says Hordern.

'You can talk. Where's your Bangalore?' says Dent.

'On the sea-bed next to your two-inch mortar, I would imagine.'

'So when we get to Port-en-Bessin, what are we supposed to use against all them bunkers? Well-aimed pebbles? Sharpened sticks?' Kemp sucks through his teeth, and assumes an expression of world-weary solemnity.

'Major Dalby's no fool. He's going to look at the evidence before him and say "Sod this for a game of soldiers". And wait till we can get reinforcements.'

'What reinforcements?' says Calladine.

'Well, how should I bloody know. I'm not the brigade commander.'

'Too blooming right you're not,' says Cpl. Blackwell. 'I've been watching you, Kemp, and you know what? All this time you've been talking I haven't seen your lips move once.'

'Just his arse cheeks, eh, Corp?' says Hordern.

'Blooming right,' says Cpl. Blackwell.

'You think we'll press on regardless, then, Corp?' says Mayhew.

'I do,' says Cpl. Blackwell.

'It ain't going to be pretty,' says Bridgeman.

'It ain't,' Cpl. Blackwell agrees.

'For Jerry, I was thinking,' says Bridgeman. 'One sight of Oily's white legs with all them horrible pimples all over them and he'll be half-way back to Berlin.'

'If you think it's so funny, Lisa, you give me your trousers, then you'll see how fooking cold it is,' says Wragg.

'Well, you know where to get 'em, Oily,' says Simpson, nodding over the parapet of the sea wall. 'Yours for the taking.'

'Fook off.'

'I'm serious, Oily. If you don't get them there, where are you going to get 'em?'

'Maybe I'll wait till you cop one,' says Oily.

'Sorry, mate, that won't be for another sixty years. Why don't you try Yeller? You haven't asked him yet,' says Bridgeman.

There is sardonic laughter.

'Ask Yeller what?' I say.

'Fifteen, twenty yards the other side of this wall there's a dead – what do you say he was, Corp?'

'A *Hauptmann*. A captain.'

'A dead *Hauptmann*. Oily-sized. With them special baggy britches that German officers have and shiny black boots and everything. Problem is, Oily's worried that if he goes there on his own, he might get himself shot.'

'I just need someone to cover me, that's all,' Wragg explains. 'These bastards are all too windy.'

'There are things worth dying for, Oily, but the warmth of your tackle isn't one of them,' says Hordern.

'I already told you what's in it for you,' says Wragg, exasperated.

'Oh ah. The imaginary Luger which even if it exists is bound to be booby-trapped,' sneers Coffin.

'Go on, Yeller,' says Wragg, almost pleadingly. 'You'd like yerself a Luger, wouldn't you?'

Without committing myself, I shuffle sideways across the sand towards the sea wall and I take a quick peek over the lip. On the other side is a stretch of road and beyond that what must once have been an elegant parade of *fin de siècle* seafront houses, now about as inviting as the teeth of a Glasgow tramp. Slumped, face down, in front of one of them is the body of a huge German officer. The holster of his pistol, if he has one, is concealed beneath his bulk. Not, it must be said, that the Luger is the main reason I'm considering this assignment. A decent souvenir's always nice but, right now, I have a far more pressing need: to restore my good name to the section.

'I'll need a weapon,' I say.

'You can borrow this,' says Kemp, passing me a Sten gun whose mechanism is still encrusted with the blood of its previous owner. 'I said borrow, mind.'

'If you're that worried, you can always go yourself,' I say.

I take another peek over the sea wall. There don't appear to be any dead Tommies in the *Hauptmann*'s vicinity and there has been no sign of any sniper activity, which suggests that this area is more or less clear of enemy.

'After you,' I say to Wragg.

He pulls himself up over the wall. I follow. With quick glances left and right and up and down in every window and open door frame, we scuttle across the road. I take position with my back against the wall of a burnt-out house, while

Wragg goes frenziedly to work on the *Hauptmann*'s jackboots.

Whether because of rigor mortis or because his legs have swollen, the *Hauptmann*'s jackboots are refusing to slip off without a fight.

'Are you just going to stand there watching, you booger?' hisses Wragg, sitting down with his legs astride one of the *Hauptmann*'s boots, a foot thrust unceremoniously into the *Hauptmann*'s crotch for the purposes of leverage.

I signal him with a jerk of my downturned palm to be quiet. I've seen movement in the high window of a mansard roof four houses away, towards the centre of town. A sniper? No. Wragg would be dead by now. An artillery observer, maybe?

'Unnggh!' grunts Wragg and, for a second, I think he's been shot. But it's just the exertion of getting the first boot off.

'We've been spotted,' I whisper.

'I ain't stopping half-way,' says Wragg, working at the other boot.

Now, from down the road, just out of vision, can be heard the sound of urgent, purposeful footsteps, hurrying for advantageous cover.

'We've got to go!' I say.

'Give us a hand, then,' he says.

Looking, all the time, towards the direction of the footsteps, I sidestep at a ginger crouch towards Wragg.

''Ere. You sit on his leg and I'll pull.'

I sit reluctantly on the hard, dead leg.

'There!' says Wragg, holding the second boot in triumph.

'Let's go,' I say.

'Trousers first,' says Wragg, reaching down towards the *Hauptmann*'s midriff.

'Jesus Christ, you'll get us –'

''Ere,' says Wragg, handing me the blood-congealed object

he has just retrieved from beneath the *Hauptmann*'s belt. 'Told you he'd have one.'

I weigh the dark, sticky Luger sceptically, still not altogether convinced that it has really been worth the risk, and shove it into my belt. The scurrying of boots has stopped. Keeping down low, now, using the *Hauptmann*'s body for cover, I scan the empty road with my Sten for any approaching targets. Nothing. But then there's a dull metallic clink, not unlike the sound an LMG makes when it's being cocked.

'Now!' I hiss to Wragg.

'I'm done,' he says.

Before he's even finished speaking, we're back on our feet and racing across the road. It's only a twenty-yard stretch we have to cover, but the few seconds it takes us seem to last an eternity. Especially when, midway, we hear that familiar 'tonk' 'tonk' 'tonk' that all infantrymen learn to dread. We thought we were going as fast as we could already. But you'd be amazed how much fleeter of foot you become when you've just heard three mortar bombs being fired directly at you. We take the last leg of our journey headfirst at a flying leap, not caring about whatever obstacle we might hit on the other side of the wall because, whatever it is, it's bound to be preferable to the red-hot shards of screaming, burning metal now bursting in the spot where we were lying not ten seconds earlier.

Wragg and I both land heavily in the sand, winded, but otherwise unhurt.

Once it's safe, Hordern takes another peek over the sea wall.

'Come and have a look at this, Rupert. You'll love this,' he says.

Mayhew peeks over.

'What am I looking at?'

'The *Hauptmann*.'

'What *Hauptmann*?'

'Exactly. Now you understand what a fucker it is that we've lost all our three-inch mortars.'

As I sit down with my back against the sea wall, wiping the worst of the blood from my battle souvenir, Kemp passes me a mug of tea. So I made the right decision, then.

Wragg, meanwhile, just can't stop crowing about the glories of his boots.

'Eh? En't they beauties?' he announces, giving each one of them a kiss. 'None of your riff-raff grenadier numbers, these. They're your proper officer's boots. Handmade, I expect. 'Ere, Arfinch, fancy a sniff?'

'I can smell 'em from here,' says Kemp.

'You're just jealous.'

'I'd rather have Yeller's Luger. 'Ere, Yeller, I'll swap you my Sten for that Luger.'

'No, thank you.'

'A Sten and a tin of fags?'

'You just wait till you see them on,' says Wragg, pulling a leg inside his new britches. 'Then you'll know what jealousy is.'

'Field grey's never suited me,' says Simpson.

'The bastard!' says Wragg, yanking his trousers off even faster than he put them on.

'Don't tell me, the bugger's crawling with crabs?' says Simpson.

'Worse. Far worse,' says Wragg, grasping a handful of sand and rubbing at the sticky brown mess adhering to his leg. 'The bastard's gone and shat himself!'

Not long afterwards Sgt. Price returns, scowling.

'Right, gentlemen, do you want the bad news or the even worse news?' he says.

There are groans from the men.

'Sarnt Weaver is still missing which means that, pending his return, I am taking over his section.'

'And the bad news, Sarge?' says Hordern.

'We've seventy-six men posted missing, including the CO. Heavy Weapons only have one three-inch mortar and it's missing its sight; Sparks have lost three out of their four long-range wireless sets; we've no HMGs; we've virtually no LMGs; we're short on rifles, Stens, grenades, mortars and ammo; we've still seen neither hide nor hair of our Bren Carrier section. Orders from Major Dalby are to prepare to advance at 1200 hours.'

'You mean the plan is to press on regardless, Sarge?' says Hordern, glancing at the others with a knowing, cheeky, smile.

'That's exactly what –' Before Sgt. Price can finish, the whole section is wetting itself with laughter.

'If you can't take a joke, Sarge, you shouldn't have joined us,' says Kemp.

Sgt. Price snorts crossly. Then turns to me. 'I need a word.'

'Sarge, before you give him his bollocking, can I put in a plea of mitigation?' says Wragg, who – such are the exigencies of war – has scraped what he can from the *Hauptmann*'s soiled gusset and is wearing the trousers again. 'He risked his life to get me these 'ere trousers –'

'Did he, fuck. He did it for his Luger,' says Kemp, who would seem to have gone off me again, now that I've proved unwilling to do a trade. Sgt. Price glances at my belt.

'Does it matter why he did it? He did it, didn't he?' says Mayhew.

'Ah now, that's a good question, young Rupert. There's some who might say that a commando whose only motivation was the booty he could get his grubby hands on –'

'Belt up, Kemp,' says Sgt. Price.

'Just theorising, Sarge.'

'Well, don't.'

'Yes, Sarge.'

'Coward?'

Keeping low, Price and I pick our way carefully through the straggly groups of commandos huddling in the lee of the sea wall. We pass our new acting CO, Eric Dalby – a tall, quiet, affable fellow with a gentle, smiling face – poring over a map with his troop commanders. Capt. Dangerfield looks up and nods at Price, but not at me, his expression sour.

At last, green berets give way to the tin hats of a company of the Devons, which means Price and I are free to talk without being overheard by anyone from our unit. We sit at the foot of a Bren Carrier – our units have still to arrive, unfortunately – whose crew are listening on the wireless to the BBC announcing the successful opening of the Second Front.

'Do you believe it? I don't,' jokes one crewman to his mates. 'Nor will I until I've seen the evidence with my own eyes.'

'Then I, your fairy godmother, will make your wish come true!' says another, pretending to swish a magic wand in front of his comrade's face.

The joker rubs his eyes and blinks. 'Bloody 'ell. Who'd have thought it? The BBC speaks the truth!'

Sgt. Price scrounges a fag for each of us. He takes a couple of deep drags and stares thoughtfully ahead of him.

Then he turns to me and says: 'Did I ever tell you before what a stupid sod you are?'

I laugh. 'Once or twice, I believe. Why? What have I done now?'

'It's not what you've done, it's what Capt. Dangerfield thinks you've done. Which amounts to the same thing.'

'But surely you explained to him?'

'Yes. He thinks I'm just covering your arse.'

'So what's he going to do?'

'He wants to lose you as soon as he conveniently can.'

'But that's outrageous,' I say, making to get up. 'And I shall jolly well tell him so.'

'You will not,' says Price, with a firm grip on my arm. 'Do you think a troop commander hasn't got enough on his plate, right now?'

'But it's so unfair!'

'You always say that. You were saying it even when you were a young lad and I had you cantering on the lunge blindfold without stirrups to get your balance right. And a fat lot of good it did you.'

Something about Price's tone of voice bothers me. He never normally gets this wistfully nostalgic.

'And if you take my advice,' he adds, 'you'll let him lose you and be grateful for it when he does.'

'What and let him think I'm — a coward.'

'Well, you are a Coward, ain't you? And I'm sure that's how your mother would like to keep it.'

'Price, that's terribly unfair bringing Mother into it.'

'There you go again. Can't you just, for once in your life, take a piece of advice? You're about to be given a chance to escape this bleeding mess.'

'Like a rat deserting a sinking ship?'

'At least you've worked out that we're sinking.'

'Sure, I recognise things aren't ideal. But when has that ever stopped us?'

'And I'll have less of that, too.'

'What?'

'There's no "us" any more. You're an ordinary marine and I'm your sergeant — no more responsible for you than I am for anyone else in the troop.'

'But I never expected otherwise.'

'Stubborn bugger, aren't you?'

'Soon as you fall, get back on – that's what my old riding teacher always used to say.'

Price tries to suppress his smile. Succeeds too: 'So you're not going to take my advice?'

'I'm sorry, Price, but another thing you taught me was always to keep my word. I promised her I would look after Captain Dangerfield and that's what I must do.'

'You couldn't look after a bleeding teddy bear.'

'None the less I gave her my word.'

'Are we talking about who I think you're talking about?'

'You know very well who I mean.'

'If that young lady told me the sky was dark at night-time, I'd go outside to check. She has no loyalty to you.'

'How dare you malign her when she's not here to defend herself!'

'Do you know, before the last war, that's how a lot of fine gentlemen used to talk. Buried quite a few of them myself and do you know what? Before they died, not one of them could remember the great and noble causes they'd come to fight for.'

'Price, I do know what war's like.'

'Do you? I wonder sometimes.'

'Excuse me. 'Ere, Sergeant, excuse me,' calls one of the Bren Carrier's crew. 'Nice of you to join us, and all that, but I think you'd better get a shift on. Your lot's starting moving out!'

11

Sniper

Advancing in open file towards hostile territory is never the most relaxing of activities. But if you want to know what real tension is, try doing it without weapons.

All right, so I've got my Luger; Kemp has got his Sten; Sgt. Price has purloined a Colt .45 from somewhere or other; and two others have managed to retrieve a rifle from one of the casualties on the beach. But in a section of fourteen men, that doesn't constitute what you might call overwhelming firepower.

'If we make contact,' announces Kemp cheerily, as we make ready to climb over the sea wall. 'We are going to be fucking fucked.'

'If you make contact,' corrects Sgt. Price, 'you deserve to be fucking fucked. But since you're going point, you'll be able to make sure we don't.'

'I'm not going point. Why should I go point? Why not Coward?'

'Because you're the only one with an SMG.'

'Take it, then, I ain't that attached to it,' says Kemp, offering his Sten with outstretched palms, eyes begging someone, anyone, to be stupid enough to take it. 'Quis? Quis?' he cries, like a schoolboy trying hastily to rid himself of a catapult which has just been used to break the headmaster's window.

'Oh, for God's sake,' I mutter under my breath, because really, this is too pathetic. 'Ego!'

I grab his Sten.

'Cheers, Yeller. I always knew you was a decent bloke,' he worms.

But before I can take my position at the head of the section, the Sten has in turn been taken off my hands by Wragg.

'I owe you for me shitty trousers, mate,' he says.

'Really. Are you sure?'

'Course I'm not sure, so piss off quick, in case I change me mind.'

Of course, the person who should really be making these decisions is Price, and though he's careful not to show it, I recognise by the faint facial twitch and the set of his jaw that he is very angry indeed. And understandably so. Kemp has just refused to obey his sergeant's direct order – an offence which Price has been forced to overlook only because of the most desperate exigency: viz. that at this delicate stage of his relationship with the section he doesn't want to make himself any less popular than he is already. But Kemp won't get away with this insubordination for much longer. Not if I know Price.

With Kemp smirking, Price glowering, and Wragg leading, we advance in silence through the shattered village.

Rather optimistically in my opinion, our acting CO, Major Dalby, has decided that the Commando – what's left of it – will attempt to proceed to our agreed rendezvous. I say optimistically, because it's perfectly obvious from the amount of shooting we can hear going on ahead that our rendezvous – the church in Le Hamel – is still deep inside enemy territory. As we march, we're overtaken by a platoon of Hampshires hurrying forward to reinforce their unit in the slow, messy, house-by-house battle for the town. The dead and freshly wounded have yet to be cleared. This was not part of the plan.

Every now and then, Price will call a halt and signal for one or other of us to go and investigate a likely corpse he has spotted, down an alley, dangling from an upper-floor window or half concealed at the mouth of a bunker. This is how Mayhew acquires the Schmeisser which he's now caressing like a new pet kitten and how McMahon gets hold of a Mosin-Nagant sniper rifle so elegant – the grain on the stock resembles polished rosewood – that I can quite understand why its late owner felt compelled to drag it all the way here from the Eastern Front. Unfortunately, so can Simpson, who spotted the gun first, and sniper or no sniper, he's buggered if he's going to give such a splendid battle souvenir without a struggle.

When we first hear the scuffling and cries of pain from the building into which McMahon and Simpson have disappeared, we naturally assume they have met some sort of resistance. Price signals that Mayhew and I should go first with our Schmeisser and our Luger, while he follows, Colt .45 at the ready. We nose stealthily through the blackened door frame to find McMahon and Simpson wrestling and straining like puppies in a sack.

'Sarge,' gasps McMahon, 'will you tell that wanker a sniper rifle is for snipers, not thieving Cockneys who couldn't hit a barn door at ten paces?'

'Tell that Fenian tit it's finders keepers,' says Simpson, his nose dripping blood, a livid mark beginning to appear above his left eye,

'Quiet the pair of you,' hisses Sgt. Price. 'McMahon, the rifle's yours and you owe Simpson a tin of fags.'

'Sarge, I don't smoke.'

'Well, you should, Simpson, it will do you good. A lot more good than that rifle. Know what the Germans do when they catch you with one of them?'

'Bollocks, Sarge, see if I care. Soon as we look like being overrun, I'll chuck my rifle over to that Scouse git. "Oi, son, grab 'old of this," I'll say. And being an inbreed Fenian tinker —'

'Up yours. Cockney wanker.'

'It will be far too late by then, Simpson, old chap,' I say. 'You see, the dead giveaway is the bruising caused by the recoil of the telescopic sight round your eye.'

'You mean like that shiner Simpson's got now?' says Mayhew.

'He's never given me a shiner?' says Simpson, touching the damaged area gingerly. Then without warning, he launches himself with renewed vigour at McMahon. 'You bastard —'

'Bastard yourself,' says McMahon, laying into him once more.

'I've had enough of this,' mutters Price, grabbing each of them by the scruffs of their collar and bringing their heads together with an almighty thud which sends them both crashing to the floor, dazed, if not concussed.

I must say it's proving quite an eye-opener, seeing Price's *modus operandi* from the under-side. As an officer, I don't recall having ever been particularly bothered by his brutish efficiency. It kept the men in check; it got things done. From an ordinary soldier's perspective, though, I can recognise that his approach might have its disadvantages. NCOs who make themselves too unpopular do run a nasty risk that come the next firefight they'll stop a 'stray' bullet in the back of their head.

After what he does not long afterwards, I'd happily put one there myself. Price has spotted — poking through the slit of a roadside pillbox so brilliantly concealed that we would all have been dead by now had it still been occupied — what looks like and indeed turns out to be the barrel of an MG42. Needless to say, I'm the one he sends to investigate.

There's a gaping hole where the entrance should have been, as if a shell has gone straight through the embrasure and out the other side, leaving the interior eerily intact. The scene, as I push cautiously through the rubble, is like a waxwork tableau.

The crew are still standing in position, one hunched over the gun and staring sightlessly at his target, his number two with the belt of ammo draped across a pale hand – dusty and still. There's a third German, resting in the corner, eyes open, half-smiling. None of them looks remotely damaged. It can have that effect, sometimes, a large-calibre shell. You might escape the shrapnel, but not the pressure wave which simply crushes all your internal organs.

Having inspected it for booby-trap wires, I retrieve the machine gun and call for help removing the cases of ammo, which, as we've seen on the beach, it consumes at quite a rate.

Sgt. Price is delighted, though you'd never guess it from the reward he gives me: 'Right. I'm making you number-one gunner. Coffin, you can be his number two.'

'Coward and Coffin. There's undertakers who'd murder for that monicker,' chortles Simpson.

'Kemp,' adds Sgt. Price. 'You can borrow Coward's Luger.'

Now, the thought of humping that blasted MG42 cross-country for the next twelve miles is bad enough – twenty-five pounds the bastard things weigh: you carry them across both shoulders, like Jesus *en route* to Golgotha – but what really takes the biscuit is Kemp's expression on seeing he's going to 'borrow' my Luger. Like the Cheshire cat that got the whole Jersey herd.

'Borrow,' I stress, reluctantly unbelting the pistol and its bloodstained holster. I can't think what has got into Price, I really can't. Sure, he knows that after what I went through in Russia, I'm quite a dab hand with a Spandau. Even so, if anyone ought to be manning any captured LMGs, it's Kemp. He's our section's number-one Bren gunner and Bridgeman is his number two. So what on earth does Price think he's doing picking on me and Coffin? Is he nervous about being disobeyed by Kemp yet again? Is he going out of his way not to show any favouritism?

'Oh, you can trust me, Yeller. I'm good at borrowing,' says Kemp, as he tries the Luger for size. He's grinning so hard that you'd think his face was about to split in two.

'Price,' I mutter under my breath as I heave the wretched Spandau on to my shoulders, 'you are a prick of the first order.' And I find myself drifting into the most delicious reverie in which I inherit the estate and create for Price the new position of Head of Privy-Cleaning, Sty-Swilling and Septic-Tank Maintenance.

We're turning away from the centre of Le Hamel now. Word has come down the line that we're going to bypass our rendezvous and head instead for somewhere rumoured to be in our possession, a place called Les Roquettes. *En route* we pass through two minefields, sticking carefully to the paths cleared by the two flail tanks trundling just ahead of us. So long as we stay between the two trails of chalk that pour down from the side of the tanks as they move forward, we should be reasonably safe. It's a very comforting thing for an infantryman, armour. But it's slow-moving; it's noisy; and it's deeply ill-suited to negotiating the tall-hedged Norman fields we've begun to encounter, now that we're moving beyond the coastal strip.

Les Roquettes, once presumably a tranquil Norman hamlet, is now a pile of rubble.

We pass through a gap in the hedge, where a section of the 1st Dorsets are setting up their defensive positions. 'They went thataway,' says their corporal, leaning on the gatepost, smoking a fag, thumbing behind him. Ahead of us, keeping close to the hedgerows, an undulating line of green berets vanishes towards the horizon.

From now on, we are behind enemy lines, which in some

respects is a safer place to be than in front of them. For one thing, your enemy is not expecting you so you have the advantage of surprise. And for another, when you do see a stranger in uniform, you don't need to worry overmuch whether he's one of yours or one of theirs: you just shoot.

The great disadvantage, though, is that the whole time you're there you have to stay on full alert. You may be cold, damp, and exhausted; you may not have eaten for hours, or slept properly for days; yet not for a moment can you let your aching body sink into the dull stupor it craves: if you do you'll end up a goner.

It's twelve miles as the crow flies from Le Hamel to Port-en-Bessin. About half as much again, if you take the meandering cross-country route we took, and do you know, even after six decades, I can recall every inch of that nerve-racking trudge as if it were yesterday: the menacing swish of the tall grass; the quavering shadows; the camouflaged 88 that turns out to be a rotting farm wagon; the cloying pollen which burns your lungs and eyes like mustard gas; the murmuring and whining of the superabundant insects, so loud to our hypersensitive ears they might almost be a squadron of heavy bombers with full fighter escort; the confounding sense of unutterable peace.

Now here's a herd of creamy Charolais – perhaps the best indicator there is of the presence, or otherwise, of mines – come to greet us over the hedge, lowing plaintively, their unmilked udders fit to burst.

And there's an old farmer with a gnarled, medieval face, ploughing his field with two horses, with an innocence and unconcern that makes you wonder whether the destruction you witnessed not half an hour ago wasn't a figment of your imagination.

If it weren't so fraught it would all be so beautiful. You hear everything, smell everything, see everything. It's like being born anew. The greens are richer; the wildflowers brighter; the scent of the uncut meadows more grassy and verdant.

Can this really be war, you wonder? The smell of cordite and death has vanished. The naval bombardments are being directed elsewhere. There is birdsong in the air, such as you never find on a battlefield. We are advancing with purpose, at last. Indeed, I've just begun to ask myself whether perhaps I've misjudged the threat we're facing. The Germans will be directing all their attentions to the front line. As long as we remain unseen –

A shot rings out. A green beret drops.

Almost simultaneously, the rest of us drop, too – 'instantly, as if dead', says the bible – *Infantry Training* (1944) – then roll and crawl for what cover we can find, before pausing to take stock. I rest my MG on its bipod, pointing uncertainly in the vague direction of the single shot, while Coffin crawls to join me with a box of ammo.

It's no use, of course. The sniper's not going to give away his position.

'How is he?' calls forward Sgt. Price.

As next in line, Bridgeman has crawled forward to inspect.

'Dead,' he calls back.

'Sure?' says Sgt. Price.

'Dead,' he repeats, disbelievingly. He's in a very shocked state – we all are, but none more so than Bridgeman. Kemp was his mate. His brother in moaning, bad jokes and petty crime. Arfinch Kemp, who was never in a million years going to cop one. With his gift for ducking and diving and shirking, not even the Grim Reaper himself was ever going to get one over on him.

There's nothing to be done. We can't even stop to bury him. While Bridgeman kneels, pathetically cradling the broken, bloodied head of his dead comrade, Sgt. Price stoops to rip off the red cardboard ID tag from the string round Kemp's neck. Then he gives the signal that we should move on.

We pick ourselves from the ground, and file quickly past, unwilling to intrude too deeply on Bridgeman's grief, but quite unable to resist a prurient glance to see what a mess the sniper has made of Kemp. Sometimes, these shots are quite clean. But the results of this one remind me rather of a childhood picture I remember, of a cloven-shelled Humpty Dumpty: the skull split right down the middle, the brain spilling out like Humpty's yolk.

As I pass, Bridgeman says bitterly, 'I suppose you want this back?' And begins unbuckling the Luger from Kemp's waist.

'If you'd rather keep it to remember him by,' I say because I feel so damned awkward. The way he's looking at me, you'd think I was personally responsible.

'Oh no,' he says. 'I know what your game is. You and your mate Sergeant Price.'

He holds out the gun and holster.

'Thanks,' I say.

'"Thanks" he says. "Thanks",' repeats Bridgeman. 'Bloody idiot.'

You say some funny things when, without warning, your mate has vanished from your life for ever. You want someone to blame and, since there's no German to take it out on, who better than the newcomer, the alien, the Jonah? But as I trudge on, turning his remark over in my head, it occurs there might be something more sinister, even life-threatening, in what he has just said.

Before I can mull this one over properly, though, I find myself being distracted by a matter of more immediate concern. About a minute ago, our section passed through a gap in one of those tall, impassable Norman hedges and into one of those sunken Norman lanes from which there appears to be no exit.

If you were prone to claustrophobia, this would be your cue. It's dark, it's enclosed, you've no idea what's round the next corner – like being stuck half-way through the maze at Hampton Court, but with no dad or mum or nanny waiting to get you out again.

We've been wandering down this lane for what seems like an age, all of us quietly wondering when it's going to end because in combat you never like to put yourself in a position you can't get out of sharpish. The hedges are too high to climb over and the only cover is provided by the meagre drainage ditches running either side. It's at just this point that we hear in the not too far distance the sound that every infantryman dreads: the ominous clanking of chain on cobbled stone and then the roar of rapidly approaching engines.

Armour. Tanks if we're really unlucky. Half-tracks, if we're to stand a prayer. German, almost without a doubt.

Perhaps it's just as well that I'm not in charge at this moment, because my instinct is to chuck my MG into the nearest ditch and leg it as quickly as I can.

'Section, hold fast,' Price commands.

'You are joking, Sarge?' mutters Hordern.

'And no one go near that ditch. It's booby-trapped!' Price says.

Calladine and Simpson step back from the edge, only just in time.

We flatten ourselves against the road. You'd be surprised by how intimate you can get with cobbled stone when it's the only protection you have against umpteen tons of Panzerkampfwagen.

'On my command, fire at will,' hisses Price.

The clanking draws nearer. Whatever it is, it's moving fast. If we'd tried running, it would have outpaced us, for sure. But, as we wait for it to come into view, it seems to take an eternity.

'Gawd, I wish they'd hurry up,' says Coffin, beside me.

'I wish they'd drive into that ditch,' I say.

'You reckon it really is booby-trapped?' says Coffin.

'I've never known Sarnt Price wrong yet,' I say.

'What is he, psychic? If this is what I think it is, I fucking –'

And suddenly, they've rounded the corner and they're upon us. One, two, three of them. Bren Carriers. Ours.

'Fuck me, I think I've been hit,' says Coffin, straightening up. 'I don't want to look. Is it bad? Is it bad?'

'Where?'

Pale-faced, he nods towards his crotch.

I quickly assess the damage.

'That isn't blood. You've er –'

'Oh my God. I've pissed myself!' he says, genuinely delighted.

We have now reached a hamlet called Buhot and, though we're badly behind schedule, the Commando has had to pause for yet another halt, apparently so as to allow the Hampshires to carry out some kind of flanking manoeuvre.

Like most of the hamlets round about, Buhot is dominated by a handsome château encircled by a high wall. By the time we arrive, the four lead troops – X, B, HQ and Q – are already well ensconced, partially concealed behind laurel bushes and in the undergrowth around the walls, but fairly evident none the less owing to the profusion of cigarette smoke and the sound of low, contented chatter around the billycans and stoves.

Sgt. Price sends me off to find our section some tea. 'What, no char?' says a surprised marine from X troop, one of the luckier ones which managed to reach shore with its full complement of officers and men. 'I'd have thought that that thieving bastard Arfinch could have nicked you some by now.'

'I'm afraid he's dead.'

'What? When? Poor bugger.'

'Just now. Sniper.'

'Bastard snipers!' says someone.

'Aye. Fuckers.'

Another marine starts telling his mates what, according to his brother, they do to captured snipers in Italy. I leave them to it and return to my section with my booty of tea, powdered milk and sugar.

As I push my way through the bushes, I hear Bridgeman say something which gives me pause.

'– fucking murdered him. That's my view and you won't change it.'

'You know, mate, I can see a great future for you after the war. Lisa Bridgeman – the new Agatha Christie.'

'You wouldn't be laughing, Hordern, if it were your mate those bastards killed. And I swear to you now – hey, who's that?'

'Char wallah,' I say, pushing on through, hoping to God I'm not blushing too obviously.

Bridgeman scowls and looks away.

'Any news?' asks Mayhew.

'The CO's back. Hitched a lift on the ammunition sledge of an SP gun.'

'Any *good* news?' asks Hordern.

'You haven't heard the best of it yet. First thing he asks Major Dalby is what the hell we're doing brewing up when we could be digging slit trenches.'

'And what does Eric say?'

'Oh, you know. Jolly bad form to dig up a Frenchman's lawn, unless strictly necessary. Tea good for the morale. Departure imminent, so is it really worth it? At which the CO explodes that there's never a time when it's not worth digging a slit trench and the only reason he's going to make an exception just this once is that Eric has given an order and if he goes and countermands it now, it'll only make Eric look a fool in front of the men.'

Bridgeman is the only one who doesn't laugh.

Just as the brew is ready, the order comes through to move out, but we'd rather scald our throats than give up such a hard-earned pleasure, so scald our throats is what we do. While I'm relieving myself up against the tall garden wall, Oily comes and stands close next to me. So close indeed, that as he unzips his fly I'm about to make some sort of ribald joke, when he says *sotto voce*: 'You'd better watch your back.'

'Bridgeman?'

He nods.

'I did have an inkling. What's his beef?'

'He thinks you killed his mate.'

'That's ridiculous.'

'He thinks it was all a plot. He says everyone knows that snipers are always looking out for pistols because it's the sign of an officer. He thinks that's why Price gave him your Luger: to save you because you're Price's mate and kill Arfinch, to punish him for being difficult.'

'The man's barmy,' I say, though the thought does occur that, yes, this was exactly Price's plan.

'All the more reason to watch yourself.'

'Thanks, Oily. Does Sarnt Price know?'

He nods. 'Bastard knows everything, doesn't he?'

We form up by troop outside the château and set off once more in single file, with the standard five yards between us so as to minimise casualties in the event of an ambush.

Now that the Bren Carriers have arrived, I've been able to offload the MG42, for we no longer need it. We finally have more than enough weaponry and ammunition of our own with which to engage the enemy. And not long afterwards, as we're proceeding down another sunken road we make our first visual contact with them: three Germans, two with rifles and one with a Schmeisser, scrambling towards us down a hill. We freeze and line the road, as the Germans carry on, oblivious, their weapons still slung over their shoulders.

Then the one with the machine gun senses something is wrong and starts unbuckling his weapon.

Too late. From our section, a volley of shots. The one with the Schmeisser collapses, wounded, while the others quickly throw up their hands.

Being the first live Germans we've seen since landing, they are naturally the subject of considerable curiosity.

'Scrawny buggers, aren't they?' says Calladine, eyeing the younger of the two riflemen in his ill-fitting fatigues. He can't be much older than sixteen.

'Aye,' says Wragg, taking a pinch of the boy's triceps. 'We're not going to get much meat off that.'

The rifleman looks anxiously to his older colleague, who is dressed, not in field grey but in a camouflage uniform. His face is stubbly. He has about him a lean, haunted look. But his most striking feature, the one I notice straightaway, is the circular bruising around his right eye.

'Was sagt er?' the boy nervously asks his older comrade.

'Nichts.'

'What's he saying, Yeller?' says Wragg.

'I think the lad's a bit worried you're going to eat him,' I explain. 'All that black propaganda they've been fed, there's nothing they'd put past a commando.'

'Tell him he's not to worry. I've never fancied foreign food.'

I translate and the boy laughs weakly. But not his comrade, who is looking queasier by the second. And then I notice Bridgeman, just staring at him. Unblinking. His focus all the time on the bruising round the rifleman's eye. Very likely he

179

suspects what I suspect. A suspicion, indeed, which the man's nervous behaviour is doing little to allay.

Bridgeman needs watching. I'd like to warn Sgt. Price, but Price has gone to recce up the hill with Hordern, Dent and Calladine in case there are more Germans where these came from.

'Coward. Translation, please,' calls Lt. Truelove, kneeling next to the pallid form of the wounded German.

I have to bring my ear almost to his blue, bubbling lips to hear what the fellow's saying.

'He's asking for a cigarette,' I say.

'Tell 'im they're bad for his 'elf,' someone jokes.

'Is the doc coming?' I ask Lt. Truelove.

'On his way.'

'Only, I think it's a lung injury. A cigarette mightn't do him much good,' I say to Lt. Truelove.

'Give him one,' says Lt. Truelove.

'Can anyone spare a cigarette?' I call.

Wragg steps over to join us. 'Here,' he says, handing me one.

I place the cigarette between the German's bloody lips.

'Ey, if I'd known it was for him –' protests Wragg.

'Just give us a light, Oily, there's a good fellow,' I say.

He's an old man. Mid-forties, I'd say. In one bloodied hand, he's clutching a photograph of a beaming Fräulein and two children, a boy and a girl.

'Ihre Familie?'

The German nods.

'Who gave him that cigarette?'

It's the doc, a small, wiry Scotsman, never a fan of smoking at the best of times.

No one confesses. We just keep out of his way as he flits about his examination like a restless bee, unbuttoning the

German's tunic to inspect the wounds, feeling his pulse, peering at the carmine froth in the corner of his lips.

'Is he going to make it, Doc?' says Wragg, with unlikely solicitousness.

The doctor shakes his head.

'Well, he won't be needing that, then.' Swift as a darting crane Wragg plucks from the dying German's mouth the half-smoked cigarette. He takes a couple of deep drags – smoking it using the cupped-hands method: to avoid the German's blood touching his lips I suppose – then, seeing the appalled looks several us are giving him, says: 'Oh, for fook's sake. There'll be plenty smoke enough where he's headed.'

Shortly afterwards the German expires, in my arms.

'Did he say anything, Coward?' asks Lt. Truelove.

'Not really.'

'What was all that stuff at the end?'

'My children. My children. My darling children. I don't want to die. Why must I die?' I translate.

It's as if the whole section has suddenly been draped in a blanket of introspection and melancholy. All conversation has ceased. No one can look anyone else in the eye.

'Coward, old chap,' murmurs Lt. Truelove. 'When I say translate everything, can you please not take it quite so literally.'

My concern now is for the safety of the two remaining Germans. You might think this rather wet of me but I've been captured too many times not to feel a good deal of empathy when the boot's on the other foot. Of course, prisoners are an encumbrance; of course, they're a drain on manpower and resources; of course, it makes far more tactical sense to shoot them out of hand. But if every soldier had thought that way, I wouldn't have survived the war, nor yet would a good many of my mates, Price included, though it has never been an argument he has found particularly compelling.

Some idiot has decided to put Bridgeman, of all people, in charge of them. He has been given a rifle with one of the narrow, round-steel 'pigsticker' bayonets we normally only use for opening cans and which he's clearly itching to try on something more squealy and yielding. And those two Germans, God, don't they just know it. One of them, the older one, has become more withdrawn and still and silent, as if so resigned to his fate he's practising for what comes next. The younger one has got it into his head that it's still not too late to befriend his captor.

'Ich heisse Hans,' he says, in his high-pitched, shaky voice, through a rictus grin. 'Wie heisst du?'

But Bridgeman isn't having any of it. Every time Hans gestures, Bridgeman jabs at his stomach with a cruel little feint of his bayonet.

And still Hans goes on trying. 'Nein. Nein. Ich bin dein Freund. Ich heisse Hans . . .'

'Give him a break, Lisa. He's only a kid,' says Mayhew.

'So was Arfinch,' says Bridgeman.

'But look at him. He's never fired a shot in anger in his life.'

'And now he never will,' says Bridgeman, with soft menace.

There's a tap on my shoulder.

'Enough chat. We're going,' says Price, brushing swiftly past. I move to catch up with him.

'Sergeant, could I have a word,' I say, quietly. 'I'm a little worried about our prisoners.'

'Well, you needn't be. Bridgeman is escorting them to the rear.'

'Bridgeman?'

'You'd rather have him hanging around your back, would you?'

'No, but –'

'Good. Then, if you'll excuse me, I've got a section to command,' he says, marching off.

I look back at the two prisoners. They're a pitiful sight, shoulders hunched like starved vultures, bodies limp, eyes blank. The boy too has now given up the ghost. But when he sees me looking at him, his hands twitch open in what I take for faint, last-ditch supplication.

Lt. Truelove is standing over the German's body, clutching some slightly bloodied papers.

'Ah, Coward, how do you fancy getting yourself back in the CO's good books? I found these maps on our late friend. Wondered if you might care to run on ahead and see if HQ troop can find a use for them.'

'Yes, sir.'

He hands me the papers. 'Very good, then. Bugger off. What are you waiting for?'

'I'm a bit worried about the prisoners.'

'Don't be, it's not your job.'

'No, sir, I appreciate that but can I be frank? I think Bridgeman holds one of them responsible for the death of –'

'Yes, I know. Sarnt Price has already explained to me. I've spoken to Bridgeman and he's perfectly aware of the conventions on the treatment of prisoners. Now, will you kindly mind your own business and do as you're sodding well told.'

'Yes, sir. It's just –'

'Christ. You really think you can do my job!'

'Sorry, sir. It just occurred that since we lost half our medical orderlies on the way in, an extra stretcher bearer or two might come in handy. And that German boy . . . he's quite skinny but –'

'Oh, have your sodding way, Coward. If the doc can make use of him, he can have your wretched boy. But not the sniper. The sniper's going back with Bridgeman.'

'He might not be a sniper.'

'Don't push your luck, Coward.'

'Sir.'

The doc, as I'd suspected, is grateful for the extra help.

'Danke. Danke. Danke,' the boy murmurs pathetically, pawing at my arm in gratitude, when he realises what I've done for him. I wish he wouldn't. The more he goes on, the more nauseous I feel for what I've failed to do for his friend.

Desperate to escape the dismal scene – and, most especially, the sniper's terrible blank stare – I accelerate up the line at a jogging pace, in search of HQ troop.

Needless to say, every marine I pass has something witty to say: 'It'll still be on by the time you get there', 'You're keen', 'Don't work too hard now', 'The beach is the other way', 'Knees up', and so on, so that it ends up feeling more like another training exercise than real warfare. Then, from not at all far ahead, I hear the tearing-cloth sound of a Spandau burst and the scream of men in pain, followed by sporadic rifle and machine-gun fire. And then silence.

The men I pass are still advancing but with increasing slowness and caution. By the time I reach the head of our troop, the Commando has come to a complete halt. I find Capt. Dangerfield in earnest conversation with a medical orderly and one of the lieutenants from Q troop.

'Still with us, Coward?' says Capt. Dangerfield nastily.

'Sir, I have some captured documents I'm taking to HQ troop.'

'Not any more you're not, there's been another hold up. Q troop's been ambushed. They've taken casualties and we need to find some locals, pronto, willing to house them. You speak French?'

'Yes, sir.'

'Then, here's the passage out you wanted.'

'Sir, I resent –'

'No need for that, Coward. We all have our breaking point

and I don't think any the worse of you for what happened on the beach. But when we move on our objective, I simply can't afford to have people I can't rely on a hundred per cent, you must understand that.'

'I do, sir, but —'

'Just do as you're told, Coward, there's a good chap, and I'll be sure to put in a favourable report. You've some wounded men to look after now. That's just as important as anything we're about to do in Port-en-Bessin, wouldn't you say?'

12

The Deserted Farm

'What's yer name?' he says.

'Coward,' I say.

'Any relation of Noël?'

'Distant.'

'So go on, what's he like?'

'Very droll. But we mustn't talk.'

'I'm sorry. I always talk when I'm nervous,' he says.

'Me too but you mustn't be nervous,' I say.

'I can't help it, I'm worried about me sight,' he says.

'It'll come back,' I say.

'How do you know?' he says.

'It happened to me once,' I say.

'And it came back?' he says.

'It came back,' I say.

'Thanks — what did you say your name was?' he says.

'Coward,' I say.

'Any relation of Noël?'

We're moving in file on yet another sunken lane, overgrown and rutted, more like a drover's path than a proper road, which means with luck we shouldn't run into any opposition. If we do, we're in trouble, because one of us is unconscious, two of us are carrying his stretcher, one of us (the chap holding on to my back and asking me the irritating questions) is blind and only one of us – me – has his hands free to do any shooting.

Behind us, in the village of La Rosière, the firefight is getting hotter – MGs, mortars, small arms, grenades – which is good from our personal point of view, because it'll draw any Germans in the area away from us. But for the purposes of the mission it's a small disaster. That village was supposed to have been cleared two or three hours ago, and not by us, but by the army advancing from the coast. Unfortunately, it appears we've had no option but to waste time, ammo and manpower taking it ourselves. And damnably frustrating it is that I'm not there to help them do it.

'With 47 on D-Day, were you, by Jove?' I can already imagine them asking me in the Travellers' Club bar, after the war. 'Bet you didn't half feel bucked once you wrested Port-en-Bessin from the grasp of the Hun.'

'Well, the funny thing is, I never actually got that far,' I'll have to reply. 'My troop commander decided I'd be far more useful looking for shelter for a couple of wounded men, instead.'

'Quite right too, old boy. They also serve who only carry the wounded. Now, have you met "Tiger" Compton? Let me introduce you. "Tiger" won the VC and three bars in Norway, Alamein, Normandy and Burma . . .'

If I thought I could get away with it, I might even cut and run back to the action. I'm sure Lumley and Jones, the two stretcher bearers, could do perfectly well without me; as for Charlie Cox, this young fellow who's clinging on to my coat tails like one of the characters from John Singer Sargent's *Gassed*, he could just as easily clutch Jones's back, couldn't he?

But then I remember the disconcerting exchange between Jones and Lumley, just after we set off.

'Pity. We're missing all the fun,' I say, meaning the firefight that's going on in La Rosière.

'You'll get over it,' says Lumley with a sarcastic inflection which makes Jones chuckle and me wonder, given that we've only just met, what the hell I could possibly have done to offend them. Nasty-looking pair, they are. Lumley has a face like a bloodhound and long, dangly simian arms; Jones is small, dark and angry, like a malign pixie. Half an hour in their company, and you almost look forward to the prospect of being ambushed.

'We're bunching,' I say. 'How about you give me a twenty-yard lead? Then, if anything happens, you'll have time to get the wounded into cover.'

'Better stay where we can see you,' says Lumley.

'If you feel safer that way.'

'It's your safety we were thinking of more,' laughs Jones, as if it's the world's funniest quip.

'Yeah. And in case you were wondering,' says Lumley, 'Jonesy's a very good shot.'

'Christ, what on earth is wrong with these inbreeds?' I'm wondering to myself.

Cox, the blind chap, twigs sooner than I do. But in his innocence, he thinks they're joking.

'What, you mean in case he tries doing a runner,' he says, with a laugh. 'Like the feller on the beach. You see him, did you? "A" troop, I think he was. LCA's just about to pull off the beach and on this feller hops, bold as brass, trying to hitch his lift back to Blighty. You should have heard Captain Dangerfield. "Give me that bloody rifle," he says, "I'll teach that man a lesson he'll never forget." If it hadn't been for Lieutenant Truelove, I think he might have shot him, too. You not see it, then?'

'I think . . .' I'm on the verge of telling Cox what really happened when two things strike me. First, it will take far too long. Second, no one will believe me anyway. '. . . no. I didn't.'

188

'I did, clear as day,' says Jones and I don't look round but I can feel his eyes boring into my back. 'I'm sure I'd know him if I saw him.'

'Me too,' says Lumley, with a nasty laugh.

There's a farm just up the road, according to the map, and it's here that with luck we'll be able to leave our wounded. Rather than approach it from the front, however, I suggest to the others that we recce it first from the rear. It's the sort of place which might easily be being used by German troops as a billet.

Lumley stays behind with the wounded, in an overgrown hollow at the foot of an old oak, while Jones and I advance cautiously down a narrow track. We find ourselves in a large, fenced enclosure almost waist high with thistles and nettles. Poking up through the middle are some rotting posts and crossbars, and rusting steel drums, the sorry remains of what was probably once a not half-bad cross-country course. No sign of any horse, though, which isn't perhaps so surprising given how desperately the fuel-starved *Wehrmacht* has come to rely on horse-drawn transport. At one end of the enclosure, there's a stone wall with an ancient door set into it. Jones and I pick our way carefully to the door, sticking close to the stone wall so that we can't be seen from the farmhouse's upper windows. Something about this place seems not quite right.

The latch on the door doesn't want to give at first. And when it does it makes a sound which breaks the stillness like a gunshot. Standing either side of the door, weapons ready, Jones and I listen for a response. Nothing. Not even the barking of a dog. Complete silence. Which, for a farmyard – even a farmyard after four years of Occupation – strikes me as just a little odd.

The door creaks open with a deafening grating noise. We enter a courtyard, bounded on one side by an open barn, on the other by a handsome, L-shaped stone residence, part of which gives on to the main road. Still there is no sign of life. No dog. No hens pecking in the cobbles, though there must have been once because you can still see their feathers gathered in downy brown drifts.

I glance nervously towards the house – first at the half-open door, then at the dark windows. There's no movement but I have the definite feeling that someone is watching us. So does Jones, clearly, because – rifle pointed at the house – he's side-stepping as swiftly as he can across the courtyard, and, after a quick look over his shoulder, backing into the barn for cover.

As I move to join him, I stumble and nearly trip over something heavy and soft. Regaining my feet, I look down to see the corpse of a dog, its teeth bared in an ugly grin, with gunshot wounds in what is left of its head. This is worrying. But what worries me more is, when I kneel down to touch it, the body isn't quite cold.

Jones has made another discovery. Concealed beneath a pile of straw, but not nearly well concealed enough, are the strings and silk of a parachute. American, at a guess. Did its owner perhaps kill the dog to try to stop himself being discovered? But if so, why did he use a gun and not a knife? And why was he worried anyway, when surely the balance of probability must be that a French farmer would wish to help him, not give him up to the Germans?

I indicate to Jones that he should cover me. Then, eyes flitting from window to window, gun cocked, nerves like piano wire, I step smartly across the courtyard, prod the door further open with my boot and push inside.

'Monsieur? Madame?'

In front of me, running perpendicular to the entrance is an empty corridor. No one answers. But there's a creak of a floorboard upstairs and I know there's someone around, for why else would there be the smell of baked bread wafting from one end of the corridor. Whatever went wrong, assuming anything has gone wrong, it must have happened very suddenly.

Then, like a startled gamebird breaking cover, a figure bursts from a side door and comes hurtling towards me. My instinct is to shoot. God knows what stops me but I'm glad it does, for the figure belongs to a plump, middle-aged woman, her face drawn and pale with fear.

'Je m'excuse, Monsieur. Je dormais,' she says, red-eyed and quite clearly terrified. It's obvious that this lie she's telling me – 'Sorry. I was sleeping' – is intended not for my benefit but for someone else who is listening in.

'Oh pardonnez-moi, Madame, de vous avoir dérangé,' I say, playing along with her lie. 'Tout va bien?'

'Oh oui, Monsieur,' she insists, her smile about as merry as that of her late dog. 'Tout va bien. Mais partez. Je suis très très pressée et j'ai beaucoup à faire. Vous comprenez?'

But of course I understand. I've interrupted her sleep, yet now she's telling me she's very busy and she has lots to do. And there's definitely someone upstairs, I heard another creak of the floorboard.

'Merci, Madame. Au revoir,' I announce loudly for the eavesdropper's benefit, while beckoning Jones to come quickly. But the woman isn't happy with this at all. She's shaking her head vigorously, her face a mask of agony, her eyes pleading with me to go. 'Mon mari!' she whispers. My husband.

I raise my eyes ceilingwards. 'Combien de Boches?' I mouth.

She raises an index finger.

Jones has now joined me.

'We'll have to go,' I tell him.

He pulls a face. 'What about the – ?'

'We're leaving. Now!' I say.

And we would have done, too, except at just this moment there's the snap of a gunshot upstairs, and suddenly all hell has broken loose.

The woman's screaming. 'Non! Non! Non! Jacques!'

The floorboards above us are thudding.

Jones and I are heading in different directions down the corridor, trying to find a route upstairs.

'There's just the one,' I call to him, before I disappear round the corner and find myself in the main entrance hall at the bottom of a stone staircase. Pelting up the stairs, fully expecting that at any moment the fugitive is going to appear and take a shot at me, I make it, gasping, to the top and carefully approach the mouth of another corridor. At the other end is a man with a gun.

'Hände hoch!' I shout.

'It's me,' says Jones.

'Jesus. Where's he gone?'

We run towards each other and meet in the middle, where there's a half-open door. Jones boots it hard, but it barely budges. Something's blocking it. Under normal circumstances, one might prefer, at this point, to lob in a grenade or two – I've no doubt Price would – but it isn't the sort of thing that goes down well in private houses, so, with a resigned sigh, I squeeze through the crack, adrenalin and rage overriding caution and fear. Once I'm through, it becomes clear what the problem is. Slumped in front of the door is the body of a middle-aged man with a hole in his temple. Propped up with pillows on a large *bateau lit* on the far side of the room there's another man, equally dead, his head bandaged, the sheets that are covering him now soaked in dark, sticky blood, eyes still open and staring as if in surprise towards the open window in front of him. Outside a horse whinnies.

'There!' I say, rushing towards the window, to be greeted

with one of those picture-postcard Norman views that in peacetime quite make your summer hols: the rolling fields undulating towards the grey and gold towers of a twelfth-century abbey; the lush hedgerows; the orchard, enclosed with an old stone wall.

Tethered to one of the trees is a horse – a gorgeous-looking beast, far superior to anything you'd expect to be owned by a French farmer. He's a dappled grey with muscular jumper's hindquarters, at least seventeen and a half hands – perfect for hunting, I should imagine, if only they did such things round these parts.

But I see that he's already spoken for. There's a chap in a peaked cap and a dark military coat hurriedly untying him and preparing to mount him.

I raise my machine pistol. Somehow I've managed to keep hold of a German weapon, rather than any of our inferior British ones. But the Schmeisser is a close-quarters weapon and at this range I stand every chance of hitting that splendid horse, and missing that murderous Hun altogether.

At this rate, if I'm not careful, the bugger's going to get clean away.

'Halt!' I shout.

But, of course, our friend doesn't. Why should he? His left foot is already in the stirrup and he's swinging his right leg over the saddle.

'Allow me,' says Jones, elbowing me to one side, no manners, the Welsh. He raises his rifle and takes aim. The German jerks, falls backwards, and collapses at the foot of his mount with a dull thud.

'Couldn't have happened to a nicer person, eh?' crows Jones, all but slapping himself on the back. But under the circs, I find his vaunting more than forgivable. In fact, damn it, I've almost grown to like the fellow.

Still, war's not all fun and games and manly bonding, you know. Just listen to the wails of that poor farmer's wife as she grinds her forehead into the chest of her dead husband.

'Madame. Je suis desolé,' I say and she looks up blankly, then clutches at her husband and begins sobbing once more. God knows who the other fellow is. The owner of the parachute, I would guess. But whatever the story behind it all is, I never do find out because now Jones and I are pushing past the distraught woman and haring to inspect the German officer.

He's lying where he fell, his loyal horse standing over him, nuzzling the body.

'Shot, Jones,' I say.

'You any good with horses?' says Jones, warily, as the horse tosses his head and scuffs the ground with his front hoofs.

'Depends on the horse,' I say.

'We could always leave him,' says Jones hopefully.

'He's an officer. SS. He might have some useful information on him,' I say.

'I was worried you might say that.'

Twice the horse drives me back with his terrifying hoofs. On the third attempt, though, I manage to hook a hand through his reins and then, deftly avoiding his kicks, to position myself close to his shoulder, with a good hold of his bridle, my hands close to the bit. Once I've stroked him on the neck a few times, he appears to settle and I'm feeling rather pleased with myself. If only Price were here to see me now.

'Nothing,' says Jones, once he's rummaged through every pocket.

'I can't believe — wait! I wonder if he's got a saddle bag.'

So, indeed, he has. It's not immediately obvious. It's a slim, fine leather bag which he has concealed beneath the saddle, where presumably he thought it would be safer than on his person. Or maybe he was just worried its bulge might ruin the lines of his uniform. Bespoke, by the looks of it. Swanky buggers, these SS.

'There's some useful-looking stuff in here,' I say to Jones. 'Maps. Orders of battle. The whole damn shooting match.'

'We should get it back to HQ,' he says.

'We should. And quickly,' I say.

The cogs are grinding slow. But to judge from his dazed expression, he's working on it.

'You don't ride by any chance?' I prompt.

'No but you do.'

'God, so I do. Do you think, perhaps, I should –'

'We were given orders,' he says.

'To shoot me if I looked like running away?'

'Yeah. How did you know?'

'Captain Dangerfield is an old friend of mine. You didn't take him seriously, did you?'

'He was joking?'

'In a manner of speaking.'

Jones is persuaded. I get him to relieve the dead officer of his greatcoat and peaked cap – both slightly too big for me, but they'll serve well enough to get me through enemy territory and back to our lines – and, having paused just long enough to scrawl a few more words to Gina, I'm up into the saddle, wheeling round and heading towards the road at what I dare say Price would call a collected canter.

Now, I've done some pretty odd things in my time – perhaps, if I live long enough, you'll hear a few more of them – but I don't recall many sensations quite so strange as the one I experienced mid afternoon on 6 June 1944, riding behind enemy lines on a handsome grey charger in the coat and cap of an SS *Sturmbannführer*.

You might think I'm asking to get myself shot by mistake

by my own side. But the way I see it, when you're riding on your own through enemy territory, you're far safer dressing like one of the opposition than you are with a green beret. And besides, the moment I get anywhere near our lines, I'm going to whip off this Nazi uniform to reveal the British one underneath.

As I trot back down the drover's path whence I came, heading towards the distant gun battle, I can scarcely believe how dramatically my luck has changed. Not half an hour ago, my military career was in ruins, with the stigma of cowardice hanging round my neck. Now though – like some impetuous young scout in the Peninsula with urgent news for Lord Wellington – I'm about to gallop back into my unit's favour in the most dramatic style.

If there weren't so much physical evidence to the contrary – the coarseness of the salt-sodden battledress against my skin; the damp chill which even on a midsummer afternoon has refused to dissipate; the rattle and pop and thump of the continuing skirmish round La Rosière; the leather of the reins between my fingers; the equine muscles straining against my calves – I might almost think I were dreaming. And it's only when my reverie drifts Price-wards and I suddenly hear his voice in my head going 'Look sharp, sir, you dozy sod, sir. Or you'll get us all killed' that it occurs to me that this isn't just another hack in pleasant Norman countryside, that in fact I'm in a war zone and getting closer to the action by the second.

Round the next bend, as if I were in any doubt, is one of those bizarre sights you see so often on battlefields that after a while you take them almost for granted. It's a German staff car, the top completely crushed, the driver and passenger still in their seats and apparently unharmed, save for the fact that neither of them has a head. On either side, the hedge bordering the sunken lane has been pulverised by the passage of an armoured vehicle the exact width, I'd guess, of a Bren Carrier. It can't have been deliberate: a Bren Carrier's so noisy you can't hear the person next to you, let alone the purr of an approaching Mercedes engine. I doubt either fast-moving party even saw the other until it was far too late to do anything about it. I'm sure they never felt a thing.

The lane is completely blocked, unfortunately, and the hedge is too high to jump over, so I'm forced to retrace my steps and find another route. After many false leads and dead ends, I eventually find one. Soon, I'm sufficiently close to the outskirts of La Rosière to start wondering whether perhaps it's time to slough off my Nazi kit and turn back into a commando.

Just a bit further, I persuade myself because, damn it, it does go to your head, after a while, when you dress in SS fig. One minute, it's an innocent game of fancy dress, the next you're all ready to roll across the Ukraine, massacring every Slavic *Untermensch* that comes your way.

Besides, there's no point dismounting just yet because my elevated position gives me a better view of what's ahead. I've slowed my horse to a cautious walk – not easy, I might tell you: the gunshots have made him jittery – and, by listening out for the distinctive tone of the gunfire (English .303 sounds quite different from German 9 mm., though of course, in this case, matters have been confused by the fact that a lot of our weapons are captured enemy ones) I've given myself a pretty good idea of where our respective forces lie.

Now, all I need to do is reassume my guise as a British commando. Which I'm on the verge of doing when, not fifteen yards away, there's the most almighty bang from a stray mortar bomb, and whether my horse is wounded or just startled I don't immediately know but the result is exactly the same. First he rears up so violently that only an instinctive clutch of his mane stops me being tipped off backwards ('If only!' I later wish). Next he pulls sharply forward, damned near dragging me headfirst over his shoulders, takes off like a starter at Aintree and accelerates rapidly into one of those insane gallops even the most experienced rider knows he'll never arrest.

No one likes being on a bolting horse. When it's as big and powerful as this one, you've only two real options: make a tactical exit and pray for a friendly fall, or cling on as if your life depended on it and hope the bugger's strength wears off before he can kill you. This is the problem with a horse. He's not really your friend, you're reminded at times like this. When the chips are down, he's as wild and intractable as any lion or rhino or croc. About as bloody dangerous too.

So dangerous in fact that my immediate response as the bullets start to sing and whine about my ears is 'Thank God!'. At least if I'm hit, I'll have an excuse to abandon my desperate struggle to stay on. This may sound odd, but if ever you've been on a runaway horse you'll know it's true: almost the hardest part is to resist the siren voices urging you to end your misery now.

As the bullets draw closer, however, I begin to reconsider my position. The bullets — all from my own side, that's the galling thing — are coming really too close for comfort now. One shot has hit my cap and whipped it clean off, another has nicked my reins. Really, you want to be clinging on with both hands at times like this, but I'll just have to risk it. So I pass the bridged reins into my left hand and, quick as I can, I dip my right one into the front of my officer's coat, where I've stuffed my green beret, and try to get it on to my head. Well, of course, it's a two-hand job, putting on a beret. Doing it with just one, while simultaneously trying to keep control of a horse galloping over uneven ground under intense small-arms fire, is, I have to say, one of the most maddeningly difficult tasks I have ever undertaken.

I manage just in time.

'Cease fire! He's one of ours!' a voice cries.

'Fuck me, it's Coward,' says another.

'Heels down! Get his head up! Lose the beret,' bellows Price.

Then I'm leaping over the hedgerow where our chaps are hiding, and bombing straight towards whatever they're firing at. The firing behind me has ceased. But the firing ahead of me has flared up with renewed intensity and most of it seems to be directed at me.

'LOSE THE BERET!' repeats Price.

And this time I do.

'Nicht schiessen! Nicht schiessen! Ich bin deutscher Offizier!' I yell in front of me, for good measure. There's a blur of coal-scuttle helmets, field-grey uniforms and startled faces looking up, as my horse bounds over the German positions. Then I'm safely past, heading I know not where, and not really caring that much either, just so long as I stay on because, having got this far, I'm damned if I'm not going to stay the course.

And somehow, miraculously, I do. Some of the hedges we jump would challenge a Galway Blazer. And the galloping is more than equal to the swiftest, straightest run after an Exmoor stag. We travel down cobbled roads, and high-banked lanes; we wade through bogs; we fly across meadows and fields of young wheat; we leap streams and stone walls and – ugh – far too many wire fences; we terrify several herds of Charolais; we see dead cows everywhere. I don't even attempt to make up the horse's mind for him. Cling on, that's all I can do, for his strength cannot last for ever.

Our journey ends, suddenly and unexpectedly, when my shattered, gasping, sweat-drenched grey finally decides to turn off the road and stagger through an open gate. It belongs to the most elegant château. Its walls are white; its lawns beautifully tended; and in the middle, a round linen-draped table has been set for tea. Beside it a woman in white sits all alone.

13

French Oral

Sometimes, when I'm in one of my clubs, and in my cups and in the company of kindred spirits, I'll have occasion to be asked by one sozzled ex-roué or another: 'Tell me, Dick. What's the best blow job you ever had?'

'The best blow job?' I'll reply, stroking my furrowed brow at length.

'Oh, get away with you,' someone will eventually chip in. 'You've probably never had one.'

'Well, I'm not sure I can immediately call to mind the best,' I'll say. 'But I can certainly tell you the most interesting.'

'What. Not the old pinkie-up-the-shitter method?' one of my dissolute companions will invariably observe and the barman, Parkes, will set about restacking the shelves or polishing ashtrays and generally making himself scarce because they're very discreet in the Special Forces Club. Besides he's heard the story so often he could probably tell it better than I can.

But it is such a bloody good story.

Now, you'll probably assume that the woman responsible for this memorable experience is the one in white who is sitting at the linen-draped table set for two on the clipped verdant lawns of the magnificent white château through whose gates my horse and I stumble after our terrifying bolt through the Norman hedgerows. At this stage I'm keeping mum. All I will say is that, if it is the same woman, I'm going to be a very lucky boy, for this girl – I say girl, though she's probably a bit older than me. Twenty-six, maybe? Twenty-seven? – is an absolute knock-out, the stuff of fairy-tales, almost.

You've read *Le Grand Meaulnes*? Well, if you haven't, you should, and do it while you're young, when it makes the strongest impression, as it did on me. The key scene is the one where our scruffy, low-born hero bunks off school and goes for a wander, and finds himself quite by chance at the most extraordinary party held for a beautiful young girl in a magical domain which he spends the rest of his brief life trying desperately, unsuccessfully to regain.

Yvonne de Galais is the girl's name in the Alain-Fournier book.

Virginie is her name in my story and though it's quite likely she does have a surname beginning 'de' it's not something I ever managed to ascertain, for reasons which will shortly become clear. She's just as lovely to look at, though, that I know. Creamy skin you can't look at without wanting to lick and nibble. Hair dark as Snow White's. And best of all, these big, green, almond-shaped eyes, such as you might imagine belonging to the choicest courtesan in a sultan's harem.

First thing I notice, though, as I ride through the gate, is not her fantastical beauty but her expression of absolute horror. And no wonder, really, given we're not five or six miles from an Allied battle fleet which has been thrashing the Norman coastline to within an inch of its life. Even if you're not a direct target, the cacophony and relentlessness of a bombardment like that could drive you half mad. And if it's had that effect on you, just imagine what it will have done to your hated Boche occupiers. Like wasps from a nest that has just been splattered by an urchin's catapult, they'll be swarming round with vengeance on their minds, not caring who they hurt, so long as it's someone. The beautiful vulnerable chatelaine they've spent four years lusting after but never till now dared touch for fear of facing Nazi Germany's especially stringent brand of military discipline? Why not?

'Ne vous inquiétez pas, Mademoiselle,' I call as my horse, suddenly pliable, draws to a halt on the edge of her lawn. 'Je ne suis pas allemand. Je suis soldat anglais.'

The woman, who has risen from her seat and was probably on the verge of fleeing, now manages an awkward smile.

'But, Monsieur, you frightened me. Your coat –'

'Ah, pardonnez-moi,' I say unbuttoning the coat and flinging it contemptuously to the ground. 'Un officier allemand me l'a prêté.'

A German officer lent it to me. Just the sort of manly understatement a girl likes to hear, I'm thinking. But not this one. She's after the full gory details.

'The German is dead?' she asks, her voice quavering with bitterness and hatred.

'But of course,' I reply, dismounting now. I tether the horse to a nearby tree.

'You are sure?' she calls after me.

I turn round to flash her a piratical grin. 'I killed him myself.'

Well, a little poetic licence never did a chap any harm, did it? And, you know, contrary to popular myth, we gallant Allied liberators needed all the help we could get. This idea that the Liberation largely consisted of boundlessly grateful, sex-starved French minxes sticking flowers in our rifles as a prelude to letting us stick our whatnots any damn place we pleased simply isn't true. Not in my case, anyway. Not in the case of many frontline troops, I don't imagine – we simply didn't have the time, we were too busy pressing on with the advance, not to mention far too exhausted.

But naturally there were exceptions. Such as this one. And if there's one thing you learn as an infantryman, it's to press an advantage, using every means at your disposal.

My little porkie pie smooths the path, clearly, because after a shudder of vindictive satisfaction which I can't pretend doesn't put the willies up me ever so slightly, her mood changes completely. Suddenly, she's all floaty grace and manners – breeding will out, don't you know – and won't you join me, Monsieur, and please, enough of this formal 'vous-ing', my name is Virginie.

'Enchanté, Virginie,' I say, rolling the name round my tongue and thinking 'Well, not for much longer, I hope' as you do when you meet a beautiful girl with a name like that. Well, you do, don't you? 'Et je m'appelle Dick.'

'Deek,' she says, nodding towards the seat next to her. 'Assieds-toi.'

And here you're about to learn the true meaning of self-discipline because, instead of taking up her kind offer, I say politely but firmly: 'You're very kind, Virginie, but I'm afraid I must rejoin my comrades. We have an urgent mission to fulfil.'

'Quand même,' she interjects, 'I cannot imagine there is any mission so important for an Englishman that it cannot wait for a small cup of tea.'

And, do you know, she has a point there. I do deserve some kind of breather after my narrow escape from death on Pegasus just now; and I'm bound to have the very devil of a job relocating my troop. The very least I owe myself, surely, while I collect myself and plan my next move, is a nice cup of tea.

Not, of course, that it will be nice. Tea in France, tea abroad generally, never is – except when it has been brewed by an Englishman. Or possibly an Indian servant. Foreigners, on the whole, just don't understand the importance of using freshly drawn, freshly boiled water; the milk's never up to the standards of English milk; and nor, most of the time, is the tea. But I think under these particular circumstances, we can afford to let our standards lapse, don't you?

Virginie insists that I should rest while she goes to make the tea. Normally her staff would take care of such matters, she explains apologetically, but they have all been lost to the war: some have been deported to labour camps, some have joined the Resistance, others the Milice. Such bitterness and division there will be in France, once the war is over. Life will never be the same.

She's right, of course. About France, certainly. But about England, too. It happened after the First War. And it will happen after this one. Men will come home and ask themselves why, when they've given so much for their country, their country shouldn't now give back at least as much to them. The old order will slowly wither. Good manners and deference will fall into abeyance. It will be impossible to get proper service in shops and restaurants, let alone staff prepared to work for an affordable wage. Perhaps, all things considered, it will be better for me if I don't end up burdened with the family estate; at least then I won't spend the rest of my life running myself into the ground trying to sustain a cause that was already half moribund by the end of 1914.

And yet, and yet, I think, as I sprawl in my chair and cast a lazy eye over the high walls and clipped hedges, there really is an awful lot to be said for the country house, French or English. I'm sure if push came to shove, I could eke out a bearable existence at a place like this, maybe tinkering away at the odd novel – wartime potboilers? God knows, I've done the research – until such time as my green-eyed wife appears in the doorway, yawning in a nightdress which leaves nothing to the imagination, saying huskily: 'Tu viens, cheri? Tu travailles trop dur. Viens coucher avec moi un tout petit peu . . .'

God, will you just listen to me? All this bromide they supposedly shove in our rations to stop us being distracted from the main event, it doesn't seem to be having much of an effect. And me an engaged man, too. Well, semi-engaged. Not, of course, that if I do get up to anything, Gina is going to be any the wiser. *Carpe diem* and all that. I could be dead by tomorrow. By this evening, even.

'Le voilà, Monsieur!' she announces, setting down the teapot as elegantly as any maid in a grand hotel.

'Merci, Mademoiselle,' I reply, and smile as she makes a dainty little curtsy.

Her face is flushed, I later remember having half-noticed, and there's a redness about her eyes, as if she might have been crying. But at the time her sadness, if it is sadness – maybe it's nerves, or excitement, or merely the frustration of having had to perform a task she was once used to having done by servants – doesn't much register, for I'm far too busy enjoying our little game.

'Shall I be mother?'

'Pardon?'

'An English joke.'

She laughs prettily and we could be in quite another time and another age, the war a distant nightmare.

The tea, which I pour into the china cups before the milk, looks and smells like real tea. Tastes remarkably fresh, too, and I'm about to ask how on earth she managed to get hold of it when I'm transfixed by a pair of bewitching green eyes peering at me over the lip of some expensive-looking eighteenth-century porcelain. Then a voice saying: 'Eh bien, Deek. Now that you are here, you must tell me everything.'

'Everything?' I repeat, with a slight gulp, because, with the best will in the world, I'm not sure there's quite the time.

'Your vital mission, perhaps?'

'Bof. Ça,' I say with my best dismissive Gallic shrug. 'Ce n'est rien.'

'Nothing, Deek? Mais non. You are a commando. You are being too modest. Or perhaps is it that you think that I am a spy?'

Well, of course it's not that. Spies don't sit around in beautiful country houses, waiting for informants to drop into their laps. Rather it's just that, well, frankly I can think of far far better things to do with a beautiful woman than sit around talking military planning.

When I tell her as much – and I promise you, it isn't normally my style to be so blunt in matters sexual, I fully expect to be rewarded with a sharp slap. Instead, what I get rather to my surprise is a delicious blush and a decidedly naughty smirk, before she recovers her composure and says in a tone of great formality: 'Mais, Monsieur. Forgive me, you must be very tired. Would you perhaps like to lie down for a while?'

Certainly I should like to lie down, if only you would care to join me, is what I'm tempted to reply. But you don't want to push your luck, do you? The wheels are in motion. From now on, I'm quite happy to let fate – or rather the libido of a French girl who has likely been starved of eligible male company for a good four years now – take its delicious course. In fact I'm enjoying it all so much, I think I might just tease out the moment that little bit longer.

'Une bonne idée, Virginie,' I say. 'Mais d'abord, ton thé est excellent.'

And by God it really is excellent tea. I doubt, even in the Georges V or the Ritz, you'd get a better cup this side of the Channel.

'Tu l'aimes?' she asks.

'Mais oui. C'est formidable.'

'I was keeping it for a friend,' she says.

Of course. The friend she was expecting. I'd quite forgotten.

'Oh dear, what will your friend think?'

'Nothing, I imagine,' she says, with a trace of wistfulness. 'Don't worry. He has probably been held up by the war.' She gazes in the direction of the distant gunfire.

'La guerre. La sale guerre,' I say.

'But there are ways of forgetting all about it,' she says, rising from the table. 'Tu viens, Deek?'

A standing prick knows no conscience, they say. Well, quite. And no brain either.

Time and again since that day, I've cursed my idiocy in having failed to pick up so many of the tell-tale signs.

The tea – there was a pretty obvious one. You'd need pretty astounding connections, in Occupied France, to get hold of something as rare as that.

Her studied indifference to the absence of her tea-time guest, there was another.

The fact that she was sitting in the middle of her lawn in a war zone – there's a sign of madness or a death wish if ever there was one.

And what of the behaviour of my horse – the way, having gone completely barmy, it suddenly became all docile on passing through her gates? Or the fact that her lawns and shrubs – despite the apparent absence of her domestic staff – were yet so well tended? Or her unsettling eagerness to learn every detail about the fate of my SS greatcoat's previous owner?

Were I Miss Marple, I would no doubt have twigged instantly. But then, were I Miss Marple, I probably wouldn't have had my analytical powers muddled by the thrilling thought that in two or three minutes I stood an odds-on chance of enjoying rampant, unbridled, possibly-my-last-fuck-before-dying sex with a ravishing, green-eyed Frenchwoman.

I follow Virginie (Virginie? How cruelly disappointed your parents would be, if only they knew!) into a lofty hallway, still resplendent with unlooted portraiture, up a curving flight of stone stairs and along a broad corridor.

We enter a large room containing a writing-desk, an elaborate dresser and a huge four-poster bed.

'You had better take off your clothes,' she suggests in a matter-of-fact voice which even at this stage has me guessing as to her intent.

'Tu crois?'

'Mais bien sûr. Your clothes are damp,' she says.

'Comme tu veux,' I say, unbuttoning my blouson. It does feel awkward, I must say, the way she's staring at me like that. Voluptuous hunger? Or merely the interest a conscientious nurse might show in a needy patient?

I'm about to slip the jacket of my battledress on to the back of a chair when a better idea occurs. Beyond the tall, half-open French windows there's a balcony. I step outside – overcast and dampish, but you never know, a hint of watery sun might yet break through – and drape my blouson over the cast-iron balustrade so as to give it a bit of air. It occurs that I'm probably committing some terrible *faux pas* – like carefully folding your clothes before sex, rather than tossing them around the room with wild abandon – but as it turns out this fastidiousness will serve me well.

Virginie joins me briefly on the balcony and surveys her domain. Then she returns to the bedroom. 'Too much light,' she decides, making to shut the shutters. I follow her back inside.

Promising.

Before she shuts the final shutter, Virginie crosses the room to light a bedside gas lamp. As she passes me, she brushes my arm gently with the back of her hand, gives me a quick, cheeky look and says: 'Tu as quelque chose de dur, dans tes pantalons, Monsieur Deek?'

Tally-ho, chaps! Here we go!

'Peut-être,' I agree, grateful suddenly for the dark, because it hides my blushes. I'm not complaining, obviously. But I've always found it a mite daunting, this manner so many of the French girls I've encountered seem to have: at once icily distant and ball-breakingly direct.

'Puis-je voir?' she asks, once she has shut the last shutter. The room is dark save for the gas lamp's orange glow.

'Comme tu veux,' I say, dry-throated.

She kneels in front of me.

But she doesn't head straight where I was rather hoping she might head.

'Your boots,' she says. 'You haven't taken them off.'

'I'm a soldier,' I say.

'Commando, même,' she says, approvingly.

'Commando,' I agree.

She begins unlacing my boots. Fine – if lingeringly and teasingly is how she wants to play it – I shall not object too violently.

'It is the battery, n'est-ce pas?'

'Comment?'

'You have come to destroy the battery at Longues-sur-Mer?'

'Is it near here?'

'Mais, Deek. You know very well. It is not more than a kilometre away.'

'No, really, I didn't. When my horse bolted . . .'

'Ah yes, I understand.'

'But it's damn good news to hear I'm so close. The battery's right on our route.'

'I am glad to be able to help you, Deek. Un vrai commando.'

She pauses for a moment to examine the dagger she has pulled from my unlaced boot. She feels the edge. Then looks up at me. 'Do you like killing les allemands, Deek?'

'Not especially,' I say, with a shrug.

'But you are a commando.'

'Even so. The Germans are soldiers just like us.'

'But is it not true that commandos never take prisoners?'

'Non. It's not.'

'That's a shame.'

'Do you think so?'

She has been working her way slowly up my trouser legs, like a sexier version of those ghastly body searches you have to endure at airports nowadays. I'm wondering what the Germans could have done to give her such macabre interest in the thought of their deaths.

'Maintenant, ton pantalon,' she says, making for the buckle of my belt.

'Mon pantalon,' I agree.

'Well, then, if you have not come for the Longues battery, then you must have come for – what?'

'Can you not guess?'

'I don't know. Bayeux?'

'Yes, that's it. We've come to destroy the Tapestry of Shame. Hastings revenged at last!'

'Le sens de l'humour anglais,' she says, unamused.

'Sorry. Can't help it.'

'Non, it's not that,' she says crossly. 'It's because you don't trust me.'

Hell's teeth, what kind of a mess have I made of things now? Chocks away. Engines roaring. And suddenly, the very real and exceedingly ghastly prospect of a last-second mission abort. French girls, really. Talk about walking on eggshells!

'Mais non!' I say – or rather squawk desperately because if ever there was a sexual encounter that stood on a knife-edge balance this is it.

'Si,' she says, a slight sob in her voice. 'Yes!' And I fully expect her at this point to pick herself up off her knees, perhaps to flee tearfully, perhaps to find some suitable vase to chuck at me – you never quite know with these crazy Frenchwomen.

Instead, to my considerable relief, she stays where she is, forehead resting pitifully on the front of my bare calves as I stand there with my trousers round my ankles, my poor confused pecker at half-mast, racking my brain for something to say that might yet rescue the situation.

Well, what the girl wants is proof that I trust her, my brain decides.

'Do you know Port-en-Bessin?' I say.

'That is your objective? Port-en-Bessin.'

'Yes.'

And yes, yes, I know what you're thinking. 'What a damn, damn fool, blurting out military secrets for the sake of a woman's snivelling! Just what kind of imbecile are you?'

Well, I'll tell you what kind. A male imbecile. You show me a man out there who says he wouldn't have acted differently, in that particular situation with that particular woman, and I'll show you a poofter liar. And let me tell you, I know how to keep secrets. I've been tortured a lot more than you have, for one thing. By the Gestapo. By the Kempeitai. But it's one thing keeping secrets when you're under extreme duress: a sort of cold, they-shall-not-pass, self-sacrificial ruthlessness sets in, which allows you to allow them to inflict any number of exquisite vilenesses on your tender flesh. Quite another when the only thing that stands between you and nirvana is a tiny hyphenated three-word name, which most certainly won't be of any use to anyone, even if this girl does prove to be a spy because if she is, what's she going to do? Get on the blower and say: 'Watch out, boys. I've just fellated a commando and now he's coming your way'?

So that's what I do and there's an end to it. I've no regrets, even now I've had sixty or more years to think about it. One reason I've no regrets is because, if it was the wrong thing to do, I was soon enough punished for it afterwards. The other reason I've no regrets is because, damn it, it worked.

Yes. No sooner have I uttered those magic words than, with a little gasp of gratitude, she's on me like a leech. The very nicest sort of leech that you certainly wouldn't want to burn off with a cigarette like those bastards in Burma; the sort, rather, that you really wouldn't complain about if you had dangling from the end of your tadger for all eternity.

God, she's enthusiastic. The pumping of her mouth. The rolling of her tongue. Yes, I know, poor dear chap, this is far more detail than you need to hear. But you'll understand, one day. And I do think it's important that I convey to you just how marvellous was the bliss of that moment, in order that you appreciate the full dreadfulness of the plunge from paradise I was about to experience next.

So I'm standing there with this enormous satisfied grin on my face, thinking about battle drill, section assaults, speed marches because if I don't it will all be over very quickly whereas ideally I should prefer this to go on until at least June next year, when suddenly Virginie does the worst thing imaginable, and with a gentle release of pressure pulls herself clear.

'Ça va?' I ask, as concerned as you might imagine.

'Oh oui, tout va bien. I have had an idea. Stay there and close your eyes.'

I wonder what the minx has got up her sleeve. Something thoroughly depraved and disgusting, one hopes.

I close my eyes, not daring to open them again till I'm told, hugely tempting though it is, because I can tell she's watching me like a hawk. From the direction of her escritoire I hear a drawer being pulled open and the sound of rummaging.

Crikey, what was that? For a nasty second, there, I thought I heard what might be a male voice. And the sound of foot-falls on the driveway. I strain to hear more, but just at that moment the *Belfast* or *Erebus* or *Warspite* decides to fire another salvo at the Longues battery and everything is drowned in a succession of ground-juddering crumps.

Jesus, what if she's married? Hadn't thought of that.

What if, in the throes of passion, we're burst in on by some irate count wielding his ancestral halberd?

And if he did, would this qualify as Killed in Action?

Suddenly, I'm not sure I do want this business to last for ever. I'd like it to get it over with, reasonably quickly, so I can head off and do something less dangerous – say, assaulting a heavily defended French fishing village, with an under-armed, understrength commando unit.

'Suis-moi, Deek,' says Virginie, leading me forward gently by the hand.

'Can I open my eyes, yet?' I ask.

'Patience, mon cheri.'

Mon cheri. Well, that's something.

I've never felt too comfortable being led around when I can't see: too often it's the precursor to prison or the firing squad. But in this case I'm prepared to make an exception. Especially when her warm wet mouth closes once more round my you-know-where.

Well, surely it must be safe to look now, the position of her head at this point rendering her in no way capable of seeing whether or not my eyes are open.

It turns out she's got me facing the bedside cupboard. At first all I see is the blur of flickering orange light from the gas light on top of it. But, as my eyes become accustomed to the glare, I see a framed portrait of a soldier.

An officer.

A German officer.

An SS officer.

The SS officer who, not two hours ago, was so expertly drilled by my sharpshooting comrade, Marine Jones.

Her lover.

In moments of extreme danger everything starts to happen in slow motion. It's the brain's cunning method of giving you that extra burst of mental agility with which to think your way out of trouble. There are some times – when, say, your Spit's in flames or your tank's brewing up and you need to bail out sharpish – when it can serve you very well. But there are others when it serves you no bloody use whatsoever. Makes things almost worse, in fact. Because instead of getting the business over nice and quick, it merely drags out the agony.

All at once I have come to understand everything: I realise the SS officer was Virginie's lover; that he was the man she was expecting for tea, for what they both knew would be their last tryst; that the horse found its way to Virginie's château because that is where he lived; that the reason Virginie looked so shocked on my arrival was because she recognised her dead lover's coat; that the reason she positioned me by his portrait was so that I could work this all out for myself, in my brief last moments before she killed me.

How do I know she plans to kill me?

Because poking up between my legs, its tip pressed eye-wateringly hard against my perineum, the woman with my little chap in her mouth is holding something very sharp and very horrible. Her SS boyfriend's dagger? My trusty Fairbairn-Sykes? It scarcely matters. The point – God, what a point – is that she's got me on two counts. The slightest false move, now, and either she'll bite my tackle off or thrust eight inches of steel right up into my privates. And there is nothing I can do about it.

Nothing.

That's what I mean when I say I wish my brain hadn't gone into slow-motion mode. Because how in hell am I going to get out of this one? How would you get out of it?

You couldn't.

All that's left for your brain to do is go: 'Why me?' You can't live through a war without witnessing a pretty rich selection of horrible ways to die. But try though I might, I find it hard to conjure up one that outgrizzles the end that is facing me now.

My only slight chance might be if Virginie pulls away to give me a final lecture on how vile it was of me to have killed her boyfriend and how much she's going to enjoy killing me. Unfortunately, in real life, would-be killers tend not to behave like James Bond villains. Real killers, successful killers, just get on with it.

Besides, she knows she has made her point well enough. She can easily tell by the fact that the once proud and magnificent specimen clasped between her lips has now shrivelled smaller than a starving shrimp.

The knife's going to go in now. Any second. And as my eyes search the room wildly for something (though God knows what) to use (though God knows how) to spare myself, I notice the strangest thing.

The bedroom door is now ajar.

In the gloom behind it is a man. In front of him, in his outstretched hands, is a .45 Colt pistol down whose barrel he is taking very careful aim.

I wince and close my eyes just as the shot rings out.

I feel something splat against my chin; there are spongy,

salty, strands between my lips. The pressure between my legs has gone.

But oh my God. What else has gone?

I scarcely dare look down. I daren't not look down.

I look down.

Then feel for confirmation.

Glory be!

It's all there.

Price is beside me now, standing over Virginie's headless body. Next to him, Hordern is clutching at his mouth and making gurgling noises, apparently uncertain whether to vomit or piss himself laughing.

With my sleeve I wipe the gobbets of brain and hair and skull from my lips, quite speechless with shock and relief. Price fills me in on the background to my remarkable reprieve. A French schoolboy approached our unit, demanding cigarettes and chocolate in return for information regarding the where-abouts of a horse-riding SS officer and his filthy whore. He was about to be sent packing when Price stepped in and questioned him further about the horse. Realising I might be in danger, he volunteered Hordern to help him come and rescue me.

'It was me who spotted you. Taking succour from the enemy, as you might say,' he jokes, and I'm still far too grateful to hold it against him.

At last, I manage to blurt out, 'Thanks. Thanks both of you.' Then I add to Price, 'You kept a damned steady hand there.'

'So I did,' he says. 'But, then, it wasn't my tackle.'

14

Mont Cavalier

Now, in a minute, it's going to get confusing, so while there's time let me plant in your mind's eye a rough layout of the town we're about to attack. Imagine, if you will, a crab with his claws out in front of him and the claw tips almost touching to form a near-complete circle. These left and right claws are the two sea walls, and the sheltered area of sea between them and the town is what's known as the outer port.

On the outer port's landward side, about where the crab's mouth is, is the opening of the inner port. It looks less like a harbour than a fat canal – a deep-water channel which runs at an angle down the crab's back, half-way to its arse, and cuts the town in two. This is where the fishing boats go to unload their catch – those few small boats, that is, that haven't been requisitioned by the Boche.

There are only two ways across this deep-water channel. Either you skirt round the back, via the crab's arse. Or you use the retractable footbridge, near the crab's mouth. The body of the crab is, of course, the town itself, a modest, picturesque fishing port comprising a sturdy church, a handsome seafront hotel, a fire station, a cinema, and a motley collection of smaller buildings, grey stone fishermen's homes mostly, housing a population of around 1,600.

On top of that indigenous population, you can reckon on

a garrison of maybe a thousand German troops from the crack 352 Infantry Division, manning an intricate network of pill-boxes, trenches and deep bomb shelters which have been built into the 200-foot-high cliffs extending outwards either side of the crab's eyes. On his left, as he faces out to sea, is the Western Feature; on his right is the Eastern Feature. Both offer a commanding view of the port and the town, enabling anyone on top to pick off, almost at will, any troops trying to advance through the town. Both must therefore be taken, at whatever cost.

I can see them now, brooding darkly on the horizon, as the last of the sun dies in the sea beyond. There's a very good view from the hill where I'm standing, which is the top of what's known to our planners as Point 72 (in military parlance, hill features are designated by their height in yards above sea level) and which the more poetically inclined Frogs call Mont Cavalier. When I last came here, a few years back, it was a popular picnic spot. Now it's so pitted with holes, it's more like the Klondike in the second month of the Gold Rush.

Dig, dig, dig. Everyone's digging, with picks, with entrenching tools, with whatever they can lay their hands on. Digging as if their lives depended on it – which in current circumstances they very likely do. Save for the Eastern and Western Features themselves, Point 72 is the loftiest strategic point for many miles around. Scarcely the sort of place you can imagine any sensible German commander allowing to fall into enemy hands uncontested.

'Anything happened?' Sgt. Price asks one of the pickets as we broach the summit.

'Not a lot,' replies the marine. 'Jerry's been here all right. Defence works everywhere. But when we got here the place was empty. We took it without a shot fired.'

'Someone's going to pay dear for that,' says Sgt. Price.

'Yes,' says Hordern. 'Us.'

Word comes that Capt. Dangerfield wants to see me. It's almost dark when I find him, studying a map by torchlight. Lt. Truelove, who is with him, looks up and sees me first.

'Good ride?' he says with a smile.

'Christ, news travels fast,' I think. Then I realise it's the horse he's talking about, rather than Virginie.

I put on a very serious face. 'Not my best, sir,' I say, with what I hope is the right note of contrition. This isn't the moment for light banter and witty rejoinders. As, indeed, the expression on Capt. Dangerfield's face would seem to confirm.

'Ah, Coward,' he says. 'Can't seem to get rid of you, can we?'

'No, sir.'

'You were under orders to stay with the wounded.'

'I was, sir, yes but –'

'Right, then. Fire away. Tell me why it is you think you shouldn't be court-martialled for your tomfoolery back there, and make it good.'

I tell Capt. Dangerfield the story of the events in the farm-house, the killing of the SS officer, and my mad cross-country dash leading to my strange encounter in the château. In my new expurgated version, however, I discover Virginie hunched over a radio set, relaying our movements to the Germans, and shoot her.

'But you warned her, first?'

'She was relaying dangerous information, sir.'

'You shot an unarmed woman without first giving her the chance to surrender?'

Oh God. Why didn't I just keep it simple and stick to the blow job?

'I think she had a knife, sir.'

'You think she had a knife?'

'She did have a knife.'

'But her back was turned, you say. You had the advantage of surprise. Yet still you took it upon yourself to play the role of judge, jury and executioner on a lightly armed Frenchwoman —'

'Sir, she was a spy.'

'Coward, I don't care whether she was Mata Hari herself. The right thing to do — the only thing to do — would have been to have detained her and pass her on to Intelligence.'

'Yes, sir.'

'Coward, you disgust me. I need hardly tell you that it is my intention to have you RTU'd the moment our task is completed. In the mean time, perhaps you'd like to hand me those documents.'

'Documents?' I say, patting my pockets, as my face burns an ever deeper red.

'Yes, Coward. The ones you liberated from the SS officer. The ones you felt it so urgent to bring to my immediate attention.'

By the time Capt. Dangerfield has finished his rocket, Hordern has spread his joke about my exploits far and wide.

Twice, while seeking directions in the darkness, I have been asked whether taking succour from the enemy is an experience I'd recommend. And on reaching my section, I'm asked it a third time by Dent — which is the last thing I'd have expected from such a sweet, quiet, unassuming fellow. But I suppose he's probably still elated after his first taste of real action at La Rosière.

'Lively afternoon?' I ask him, as I begin clearing away the turf from a spot just ahead of him and Simpson. It's more exposed than I'd like, but the best defensive positions have already been bagged.

'I've had duller,' says Dent, like the bluff old veteran he

thinks he's suddenly become. Normally, I'd expect one of the others to laugh at this, take him down a peg or two. But whatever they all got up to at La Rosière seems to have induced in the section a new sense of cohesion.

It turns out to have been quite a ruck. Q troop lost two corporals and six marines wounded, two seriously, after being caught in the flank by an MG. X troop charged and overcame another German position, probably the one I jumped over on the horse. Our own troop acquitted itself pretty decently too, with Dent and Mayhew (cricketers both) hurling the grenades that took out yet another MG post while Simpson and Lt. Truelove personally captured three German prisoners.

Dent recounts it to me with a slight air of *de haut en bas*. As if those who weren't there could never fully understand.

Then Simpson says to me with a snigger: 'I hear you had it pretty rough at your end, too.'

Much ribald laughter from the darkness.

'Aye, didn't you hear? He nearly got his DSO,' says Wragg. 'Dick Shot Off.'

More laughter.

'Save your energies, lads,' says Cpl. Blackwell. 'Those of you that ain't standing guard tonight are going to be out on patrol.'

'What about our beauty sleep?' says Simpson.

'There'll be time enough when you're dead,' says Cpl. Blackwell.

We're still digging well beyond midnight, hands calloused, bones aching and nerve endings frayed from the impact of endless juddering stabs into the unyielding, chalky soil. We're not allowed to smoke or brew up but we do at least get to scoff our rations from a self-heating tin. Then Lt. Truelove arrives looking for volunteers. He only needs two of us because recce patrols tend not to go out mob-handed.

'You and you,' he says, pointing to Mayhew and Coffin.

'Yes, sir!' says Mayhew eagerly.

Coffin suddenly develops a terrible cough, which no one has noticed until this second.

'Coughin', Coffin?' asks Lt. Truelove sardonically.

'It's nothing, sir,' says Coffin, coughing still more.

'Keep it that way,' says Lt. Truelove.

'Sir.' The coughing stops.

'The rest of you, grab some kip,' says Lt. Truelove.

None of us needs much prompting. I lay myself down sideways in the narrow, shallow slit which is all I've managed in the time available to excavate from the stony ground, pull my gas cape over my head, and listen to the sounds of murmured conversation, the clink of entrenching tools, and the crack of sporadic rifle shots.

Next thing, I'm being shaken awake.

'Our turn, kiddo,' says Cpl. Blackwell.

'What time is it, Corp?'

'0200,' he says.

Not even two hours' sleep.

The third member of our patrol is Calladine. We travel light – me with my Schmeisser, a Sten for Calladine; a Tommy gun for Cpl. Blackwell – and as much ammo as we can cram into our pockets. Not, of course, that we expect to use it. The job of a recce patrol is to plot the enemy's positions, not to engage.

We file grimly past the pickets guarding the edge of the woods – password, they remind us, is St Ives – and, treading with great care, move slowly down one of the network of paths leading to the base of the hill. I should know this spot. When we were last here, Price, Brigitte – a local woman with whom he was having a fling – and I came here for a picnic. Feeling a bit of a lemon, I went in search of the pyramid and bee orchids with which the hill is abundant while Price got on with his business. But for all the difference my local knowledge makes now, this might as well be Mars. The moon is obscured by cloud. The darkness is so thick you could spread it like Marmite.

We've been stealing our way onwards for what's probably no more than twenty minutes but which feels like an age, as things do when you're creeping at the pace of an elderly snail and with every step, at every crunch of a breaking twig, you're half-expecting to be greeted with a sudden flash and hail of bullets. Then my foot catches under something or other, a protruding tree root perhaps, and down I go, arse over tip, tumbling to the ground with a booming crash louder than the Day of Judgement.

'Now I'm done for,' I think, rolling defensively, steeling myself for the inevitable.

But the inevitable never happens. Nothing happens. No shots. No shouts. No whispers from the dark of 'You all right, mate?' No Calladine. No Cpl. Blackwell. Nothing.

So I lie there a while, catching my breath, knowing that sooner or later they're going to come back. Bound to. We've been sticking pretty close. You have to in these conditions. Lose contact with the man in front for even a moment and, well, what happens is exactly what has happened to me now.

Now what to do? If I call out, I stand a good chance of alerting the enemy. If I don't call out, I may end up stuck on my own all night.

I decide to give it another minute – long enough for them to notice, if they're going to notice, that they're now minus their tail-end Charlie.

After yet another minute has gone by, possibly two, I realise that if I was going to call out to Calladine and Cpl. Blackwell, the time to have done so should have been much, much earlier.

As a last resort I make an owl sound, such as our game-keeper, Chatterley, once taught me to do. He taught me well.

My owl call sounds far too much like an owl, and not enough like a lost soldier attempting to impersonate one.

I wait another ten minutes, listening, nerve ends on fire, hearing everything: the crump of distant artillery; the bark of a dog somewhere near the hamlet of Escures; the whispering of leaves; the crunch of approaching footsteps –

From somewhere in front of me a shot. Then another. Then a volley and, from behind, a quick burst of Bren fire. Jesus!

The German assault on Point 72 has begun and I'm about to be caught in the middle.

I pick myself off the floor, alert once more, synapses primed for fight or flight.

Nothing.

Schmeisser at the ready, I regain the path and push on cautiously down the wooded track. At the bottom, it opens into a field. Beyond it, by my reckoning, there should be a road. Rather than cut straight across – there's moonlight now and I'd be fearfully exposed – I stick to the hedges which border it. Eventually, I reach the lower edge and, sure enough, a gate which opens on to what's probably the Escures road.

I ought to turn back. But an impetuous voice, the one which insists on rearing its head at the most inopportune moments, is urging me to keep going just a little further.

The broad grass verge on the far side of the road ought to make it easy to move silently and quickly. And below it, there's a bank down which I can dive at the first sign of trouble.

'Pssst!'

I freeze.

'Pssssttt! Monsieur! Venez. Vite!' It's coming from the bottom of the bank and it must be friendly or I'd be dead by now.

I slide down the bank. At the bottom, a figure in black emerges from the shadows. He's a young man of about sixteen, apparently unarmed.

"Suis Jean. Bienvenu à Port-en-Bessin,' he whispers, extending a hand. Or rather, a stump, which is all he has at the end of his right arm. I try to stifle my surprise at feeling the warm, smooth little lumps on his scarred stubby flesh, but, of course, he notices. As indeed he does when I glance down to see whether his other arm is similarly impaired. It is.

'Oui, Monsieur. Grenade allemande. Il y a trois ans. Mais vous venez?'

'Où?'

'Port-en-Bessin!'

Not bloody likely, I want to say to him. Not without artillery support, a smoke screen and another 300 men. But, before I get the chance, he has darted into the shadows and I'm forced to make an instant decision.

I decide to follow. You might think this is bloody stupid of me and perhaps you're right. It could be a trap. He could be a fool who's about to get us both shot. But you don't survive as long as I have without developing a certain instinct. So, I trail this mysterious, eager, nimble boy through fields of tall, swishing meadow grass, along hedgerows, over stone walls, and into ditches, sometimes running, sometimes creeping, often crawling on all fours, never pausing to take a breather or consider what a thoroughly crazed and suicidal mission this is shaping up to be.

At the time it's all just a sweating, palpitating blur but what I discover subsequently is that we're more or less following the line of the Escures–Port-en-Bessin road, past the enemy's first major line of defensive weapons pits, and into the inner port.

To negotiate the weapons pits, we must leopard-crawl through a ditch no more than fifteen yards from a German sentry post. I overhear part of the conversation.

'It could be worse. They say the Englanders make very good

225

breakfasts. Our comrades behind the wire in Russia should be so lucky.'

'Defeatist talk like that will get you shot.'

'Defeatist? Realistic, more like.'

'Then you're a bigger fool than I thought. You heard the noise from the west yesterday? That was the sound of our comrades driving the Americans back into the sea. Today we will do the same to the Englanders. If they dare come . . .'

He's talking, presumably, about the landings up the way towards the Cotentin Peninsula. All lies and propaganda, obviously. I'd like to hang around, eavesdrop a little more, see if there isn't anything useful I can relay back to HQ. If the Americans really are in trouble in the west it means we'll have to rethink the security of our left flank; and the likelihood of getting any extra fire support or medical or logistical back-up. But, already, Jean is pressing on.

We're over the worst. Things only get more difficult again once we've entered the town proper. The streets are empty. There's a curfew. From at least two directions we can hear the rhythmic crunch of patrolling feet on cobbled stone – so any open movement would be fatal.

Instead, we negotiate our way through a maze of back gardens, climbing over fences, tripping over garden tools, clattering buckets, startling chickens and generally making what seems to me the sort of din that would alert the whole neighbour-hood. But the people of Port-en-Bessin know better than to expose themselves in the window on a night as fraught as this.

We stop outside a small, shabby cottage with shuttered windows. Jean stands by the back door and blows a short sharp whistle through his teeth. From within come the sounds of stirring. A bolt screeches, then another. The door is pushed half open and I follow Jean quickly into the pitch-black inte-rior. The door is closed behind me and it gets darker still.

'Bonsoir, Monsieur,' croaks a voice from the darkness.

'Uh, bonsoir,' I say, trying to get my bearings.

'Ne vous inquiétez pas, Monsieur. Mon grand-père, il est aveugle.'

A blind old man living with a handless teenager. A recipe for domestic bliss, I'm sure.

'Vous êtes américain?' asks the elderly voice.

'Non. Anglais.'

'Soyez le bienvenu, Monsieur le libérateur,' says the voice, much closer now, and next thing I know I'm being embraced, and three watery kisses redolent of onions and alcohol have been placed either side of my mouth. Just my ruddy luck. Do you know, since the war, I've met no fewer than five chaps who've sworn blind that on the very night of D-Day they managed to insinuate themselves into the arms of sex-starved young Frenchwomen. One of them, for God's sake, ended up sharing a bed with three of them, all sisters, one sixteen, one seventeen, one eighteen.

And what do I get? Three fat smackers on the lips from a blind, pongy-breathed old Frenchman.

'Asseyez-vous, Monsieur,' he says, guiding me into a wooden chair. I settle into it, feeling what must be a large table in front of me.

There's a blinding flash which makes me shut my eyes. When I open them again, the room has been illuminated by a gas lamp. We're in a small, whitewashed, stone-floored room whose furnishings comprise a basin, a table, a cupboard and two chairs. On the table is set a dusty old bottle, a knife, three glasses and a sausage which looks as if it has been hanging around since the Franco-Prussian War.

The old man feels his way to the bottle and carefully pours out three large measures.

'Vive l'Angleterre!' says old Pongy Breath, raising his glass.

'Vive l'Angleterre,' Jean and I repeat, Jean holding the glass between his stumps with admirable dexterity. He downs his drink in one, as does Grand-père, leaving only me with most of my drink intact. It's Calvados. Exceptionally fiery Calvados.

'Il a fini son verre, l'anglais?' asks Grand-père.

'Pas encore,' says Jean, urging me with a sharp nod to finish. To do otherwise would be the height of bad manners, clearly.

I raise the glass once more – the fumes alone are almost enough to get me rat-arsed – and tip the flaming liquid down my throat.

'Ça lui a plu?' asks Grand-père, on hearing my rasps.

'Ah oui, ça lui a bien plu,' says Jean, who has considerately chosen not to report back to Grand-père the agonised face I pull and the fact that I'm shaking my head vigorously to indicate never, never again. My tonsils feel like the interior of a German bunker, moments after it has been cleared by a flame-thrower.

'C'est du Calvados special reserve,' adds Jean for my benefit. 'Grand-père l'a gardé pendant cinq ans, juste pour la libération! Et le saucisson, aussi.'

I glance nervously at the sausage, which up till now I'd rather fancied. Five years old, eh?

'Et maintenant, la France!' announces the old man, charging the glasses once more – almost to the brim, this time.

I lean as close as I can to Jean's ear. 'Jean. Je suis soldat. J'ai mes devoirs!' I murmur in protest.

'Qu'est-ce qu'il dit, Jean?' Grand-père asks.

'Il dit que c'est un grand honneur, boire votre magnifique Calvados à la gloire de la France,' he says, nodding at me encouragingly.

'Vive la France!' toasts Grand-père.

'Vive la France,' Jean and I echo, Jean watching me over the lip of his glass, to ensure that I don't cheat.

And I don't. But the second glass almost floors me.

'Mangez, Monsieur!' commands Grand-père.

Perhaps it's as well I have something to do, trying with my shaky hands and a blunt knife to slice the hard, dry sausage into digestible chunks, because otherwise I'm pretty sure I would collapse. In the military you develop a head for alcohol. But remember, this is on an empty stomach and barely two hours' sleep.

While I share out the sausage – salty, piggy, almost edible after the fiftieth chew – Jean and Grand-père tell me a little more about themselves. After his elder brother and father were taken away to work in labour camps in Germany, Jean and his grandfather would like to have joined the Resistance; both were rejected, but both vowed none the less that when the Liberation came they would do everything in their power to help the gallant Allies. Before his accident, young Jean would explore the German defences under the pretence of taking his blind grandfather for some sea air and even got to befriend some of the German garrison, by responding kindly to their overtures when so many of his schoolmates did not. It earned him the reprehension of his peers, but Jean was playing a longer game than they knew: he was building relationships which might one day prove valuable to the Resistance. Or so he thought. The problem was that when he made his first, tentative approach, it was curtly suggested to him that since he apparently loved Germans so much, he ought to join the Milice instead. A few months later, he was planning to try again, this time carrying as a token of his goodwill a stolen grenade detonator. But before he could do so, it blew up in his hands.

Others might have seen this as a fatal set-back. For Jean it was an opportunity. After the accident, he began to act slow and half-witted, as if his brain had been damaged, exploiting the Germans' sympathy for an accident he persuaded them to imagine was their fault. Sometimes they would let the lolling half-wit sit and watch their training manoeuvres – it was here that Jean learned the arts of movement and concealment – and sometimes they would even allow him into their cliff-top observation posts to watch their E-boats patrolling off the coast.

Most of that stopped when the construction of the Atlantic Wall began in earnest and security tightened. Some of Jean's German friends were sent east, while the ones that replaced them tended to be much harder and less sympathetic, many of them brutalised, convalescing veterans of the war against the Soviets.

Then, in the very early morning of 6 June, attracted by the sound of naval gunfire and ack-ack and the rumble of plane engines overhead, Jean sneaked out for a peek, only to find himself being arrested by a German patrol. The *Oberleutnant* was all for shooting Jean on the spot; but his sergeant, who knew Jean, persuaded him to relent. Instead, the *Oberleutnant* had Jean frogmarched up near the top of the Eastern Feature, mock-solicitously offering him a better look of the invasion fleet gathered out to sea.

'Hast du genug gesehen?' asked the *Oberleutnant*.

Jean didn't know what to reply.

'Ja, hast du!' decides the *Oberleutnant*, giving orders to his men. And next thing poor Jean knows, he's being hustled against the outer wall of one of the bunkers, clearly on the verge of being executed.

It's at this trouser-soiling moment that a salvo of shells from the fleet begins crashing down on the cliff-top defences, and the Germans, *Oberleutnant* and all, start hurrying for cover, their prospective victim now forgotten in their rush to save their skins.

'Fuck off. Quickly,' says the German sergeant to the stunned Jean.

Which, of course, he does. But not without first having the

presence of mind to grab an eyeful of the new, improved German defence system, and to note that the broad zigzag path by which he has been escorted up the hill and down which he is now fleeing for his life is apparently clear of mines.

After that incident, his grandfather's understandably reluctant to let Jean risk breaking the curfew a second night in a row. But Jean insists. On hearing small-arms fire from the direction of Escures and the sniper school at Fosse Soucy – a sniper school? There's another small detail Intelligence neglected to mention – he knows there must be Allies near by and determines to bring one back, so that he could give him the map.

'Le plan?'

'Oui. J'ai fait un plan des defenses allemandes. Ce n'est pas très bien dessiné, mais vous comprenez, Monsieur . . .'

Yes, yes, of course I understand it's difficult to draw a map when you've got no hands, but just get on and show it me, you bugger. The worst of the alcohol has started to wear off and the horrid thought dawns that unless I get back to my lines soon I may well never make it at all.

Jean disappears briefly into a neighbouring room and returns with a sheet of frayed, yellowing paper scratched with faint pencil markings. Beaming with pride, he sets it in front of me. I try not to look too disappointed. It's not drawn remotely to scale and the markings are in places scarcely legible.

'Il faut que je te l'explique,' says Jean, as if reading my thoughts.

Pointing with his stub, he tries to impress on me the most important details. The weapons pits we had to pass on the way into town; the zigzag path which leads to the top of the Eastern Feature; the German boat which he thinks may be in the harbour.

Boat? What sort of boat?

'Je ne sais pas. Je ne l'ai pas vu.'

He hasn't seen it? Then what makes him think –

'Des marins. J'ai vu des marins.'

'Kriegsmarine? Tu es sûr?'

'Absolument.'

It may not be an immediate contender for the Louvre, this map he's drawn me, but he's done us a damn useful service, this French lad.

'Il faut partir,' I say.

'Pour l'Escures?' asks Jean.

'C'est possible?' I ask.

'Tout est possible, Monsieur, quand vous êtes avec Jean Lionnet.'

After another trio of garlicky, alcoholic kisses from Grandpère and an enormous hug, we creep out into the night.

It's much lighter now. Dawn is about to break and we have almost two miles of enemy territory to weave through before we reach our lines.

You'll ask me how we manage it and I really couldn't say. I suppose it helps that we're moving in the opposite direction to the one the Germans are expecting their enemies to be heading in; that Jean knows every ditch, every bump, every scrap of cover like the back of his hand (rather better, in fact, when you think about it); that at just the moment we're passing the weapons pits, the sentries are distracted by a flight of bombers overhead, no doubt about to dump their loads on Bayeux. It might even be an advantage that I'm still half cut from all that Calvados, and consequently more fluid in my movements and less prone to panic.

By the time Jean and I get back to the foot of Point 72, dawn has begun to break. Far too light, I would suggest, for Jean to risk the return journey.

'Reste avec nous,' I urge him.

He shakes his head. 'Mon grand-père m'attend.'

After making me promise to come and join them both for another drink once the battle's over, he heads off back in the direction of the village.

'Bonne chance, mon brave!' I whisper.

But he has already vanished.

It takes me another half-hour's crawling, skulking and creeping to cross the few hundred exposed yards from the Escures–Port-en-Bessin road up the base of Point 72 to the tree line. Once in the cover of the wood, though, I can move much more freely.

Before long, a bush calls out to me: 'Halt! Who goes there?'

'It's me, Coward.'

'Advance and be recognised.'

I take two careful steps towards the bush.

'Password?'

'Um . . . oh God, um . . .' All that Calvados has muddied my brain. 'St Michael's Mount.'

'Stay where you are or I'll shoot,' commands the voice. Then, a little later, I hear him calling back to someone else. 'Sir. Sir. Excuse me, sir. There's someone here, dressed like one of us, says he doesn't know the password. Do I let him in?'

'If his name's Coward, shoot the bastard!' says a voice.

There are stirrings in the herbage. A marine appears, his face heavily blacked, his body draped in netting, twigs and leaves, and beckons me with his tommy-gun.

I pass inside our defensive perimeter to find Lt. Truelove waiting for me.

Before I can apologise, he pats me on the shoulder.

'Bad luck, old boy. I did my best for you but I'm afraid . . .' Lt. Truelove purses his lips.

'Oh God, what now?'

'You've been detailed to escort back the prisoners that

Corporal Blackwell and Marine Calladine brought in a couple of hours ago.'

'Prisoners?' I groan.

'First-rate ones too, apparently. "I" section are milking them now. Such a pity you weren't around to share the credit. And I do mean that, old chap. Others may disagree, but you're not at all a bad soldier. Just a damned unlucky one.'

'I've a feeling that luck might be about to change, sir,' I say passing him Jean's map.

He stares at it with an expression of puzzlement, then brings it closer to his face to see if that helps. Then examines it from different angles.

'The German defences, sir. Drawn by a member of the Resistance.'

'By God they're recruiting them young these days. How old was he? Three? Four?'

'Chap who drew it doesn't have any hands.'

'Were the Resistance wise to pick him as their cartographer?' says Lt. Truelove.

The CO is busy holding an O-group briefing for the troop commanders, most of the NCOs and a man in civilian clothes I don't recognise.

'And Monsieur Dupont,' he says with a nod towards the civilian, 'has most kindly agreed to guide A and B troops towards the centre of the harbour, bypassing the weapons pits, which are of course the task of X troop. On reaching the harbour mouth they will divide in two, with Captain Dangerfield leading A troop to capture the Western Feature, while Captain Albright —'

'Sir, excuse me for interrupting, but mightn't this leave their flank fearfully exposed to fire from any German shipping still in the harbour?'

Far, far too brazen of me, I know. But when not so long

ago you were an officer yourself conducting briefings just like this, it's quite easy to forget you're now just an ordinary marine whose opinions amount to less than sod all. And besides, dire straits call for desperate measures.

All eyes turn to me, with a mixture of surprise, devilish amusement and – from Capt. Dangerfield – pure disgust.

The only person who completely ignores me is Col. Partridge, who looks instead straight at Lt. Truelove and snaps: 'Why is this marine interrupting my O group?'

'I'm sorry, sir, but he's just back from recce with potentially useful documents. I thought it wise that you should see them straightaway.'

'Where are they?' barks the CO.

Lt. Truelove passes Jean's map to the nearest officer – Capt. Albright – who in turn hands it to the CO. The CO studies it with a growing puzzlement similar to that shown a moment ago by Lt. Truelove. I notice the officers edging forward expectantly, like schoolboys vying to get a better view of the imminent pummelling to death of the class swot by the twelve-stone playground bully.

'It may need some explaining, sir,' I say, my voice rising in panic. 'The chap who drew it had no hands.'

'Lieutenant Truelove, has this marine lost his mind?'

'I don't believe so, sir. He received the information in good faith from a young Frenchman he met in Port-en-Bessin.'

'He's been to Port-en-Bessin?' says the CO, richly sceptical.

'Yes, sir,' I say with vehemence.

'And this Frenchman. Does he have a name?'

'Lionnet. Jean Lionnet.'

As I mention the name, the civilian, Monsieur Dupont, snorts derisively.

'Vous connaissez cet homme?' asks the CO.

'Oui. C'est un collaborateur,' says Dupont.

'Hear that, Lieutenant Truelove? He says your marine's informant is a collaborator.'

'That doesn't mean he's right,' I say, unable to hide my exasperation.

'Lieutenant Truelove, could you inform this impertinent marine that Monsieur Dupont is the local gendarme and therefore in a stronger position to judge the reliability of individuals he has known for years than is someone who bumped into them not ten minutes ago.'

'I know how to bypass the weapons pits,' I say.

'As does Monsieur Dupont.'

'What about the shipping in the harbour?'

'Lieutenant Truelove, I'm growing rather weary of this marine's presumptuousness. Could you explain to him that as this unit's commanding officer I am privy to all the latest intelligence, including the most recent aerial photographs, and am therefore far better acquainted with the facts than an ordinary marine.'

'Sir, please, I'm not trying to question your authority. I'm merely asking you at least to consider the possible veracity of new information which, if ignored, might result in wholly needless loss of life.'

'Lieutenant Truelove, is this marine telling me how to do my job?'

'I'm sure not, sir.'

'Only, if I thought he were, I'd be having him charged under Section 42.'

'Sir, I am sure he thinks he's acting purely for the good of the Commando and if his judgement has been clouded by the strain of recent events, then I'm sure he would like to apologise unreservedly. Wouldn't you, Coward?'

When I don't immediately say anything, Lt. Truelove gives me a quick, painful little jab of his elbow into the soft of my upper arm. And I know what I should be saying at this point, of course I do. I think I'm on the verge of saying it, too. It's what all the officers' pleading expressions are urging me to do, certainly. 'For God's sake, man,' they're saying. 'This isn't the time or the place.' Nor is it.

But then, my eyes happen to catch the CO's – it's the first time he's been prepared to hold my gaze, in fact – and I see something there that I don't at all like. That same something, as it happens, which in more extreme form I saw in that idiot in Burma, seconds before I made up my mind that his regiment would be better off without him.

'No, sir,' I say, still looking the CO directly in the eye. 'I'm afraid I'm not in the habit of apologising for any action which I believe is going to spare the lives of my men.'

'Your men, Coward? I wasn't aware you had been given command,' sneers the CO.

'Sir, I'll deal with him,' says Capt. Dangerfield stepping forward, face flushed with embarrassment on seeing one of his own troop show him up so badly. 'And perhaps, Doc, if you could spare a moment to look at him –' he adds to the medical officer.

'This is ridiculous, I don't need medical help!' I say, as Capt. Dangerfield seizes the arm that isn't already being held by Lt. Truelove. As they try to drag me away, I turn my face pleadingly to the assembled officers. 'What the hell are you all playing at? You're supposed to be commandos, capable of independent thought! Will none of you speak out against this folly?'

'By God, is that alcohol on your breath?' asks Capt. Dangerfield loudly.

'Drunk too, eh?' says the CO.

'You bloody idiots! He's going to get you all killed!'

'That's quite enough of that,' says Lt. Truelove, squeezing my arm so hard I can scarcely breathe.

Before I'm dragged out of earshot, I just manage to catch the CO murmuring to Major Dalby. '"Good in a tight spot but be careful. He has a habit of shooting COs he doesn't like." That's what Jumbo Watson told me. Damn fool that I am, I thought he was joking . . .'

15

Taking Flak

All too often, when I revisit the grey modern towns of northern Europe – places I knew before the war when they still had their oak-timbered medieval districts and a charm you'd never guess at now – I find myself thinking: 'What a terrible bloody waste. Did our bombers really need to be so brutal; our artillery so thorough?'

But it's not how any of us felt at the time.

I remember watching from my vantage point near the top of Point 72 on the afternoon of 7 June as our pre-assault bombardment opened up on this quiet, pretty fishing port and thinking to myself: 'Bravo! Bravissimo! Encore!'

First to go in (so I learn later from our medic Doc Forfar's official history) is a pair of LCG(L)s – that's Landing Craft Guns, Large, to you, Jack – hammering away at the buildings on the seafront, house by house. You can't see them, from where we're standing, just hear them.

'Ach,' announces one of my prisoners, optimistically, to his comrades. 'Our flakships are making mincemeat of them.'

'What?' I want to say to him. 'You'll be lucky if the Kriegsmarine has a single rowing boat afloat anywhere off the coast of Normandy, let alone a bloody flakship!'

But I don't, obviously, first because I don't want to give away the fact that I speak German, and second because he strikes me as a dangerous type, this flakship fellow. A committed Nazi, a troublemaker and not the sort that one wants to goad any further than is necessary.

Shortly afterwards, with a sigh like a winded giant, comes the first salvo from the six-inch guns of HMS *Emerald*, a First War-era cruiser, nicknamed 'the Irish Flagship'.

'Put that in your pipe, Fritz,' I mutter, treating Herr Flakship to a disdainful toss of the head. He stares insolently back with one of those 'Tomorrow belongs to me' looks the Nazis do so well. Jolly uncomfortable it makes me feel, too, though quite why, I cannot think. Is it that he reminds me of someone I know? Is he planning to engineer a mass breakout?

If he is, he's with the wrong lot, because most of the other prisoners – twenty-one of them in all, squatting just below me, in a depression encircled with rolls of wire – look more than happy to be *hors de combat*. As the shelling continues, they chunter to one another morosely, speculating as to the fate of those comrades still trapped in the network of bunkers on the two Features. Even from two miles' distance, you can feel the ground shake. And as her shells rain down remorselessly on the Eastern Feature's defences, you almost start to feel sorry for the Germans who are having to sit, cowering, shaken and deafened underneath.

'Sweet Jesus. It will be a miracle if anyone survives,' gasps one prisoner.

'Let *die Engländer* think that. They'll be sorry,' says Herr Flakship with a sly Teutonic smile. He catches my eye and I give him a big dumb smile back. 'Stupid English arsehole thinks I'm being friendly,' he confides to his young friend. I smile more broadly still.

Suddenly the prisoners become very quiet, assuming the studiedly blank, not-me-gov'nor expressions that POWs tend to adopt before a capricious-looking enemy. Glancing back, I see the rest of my section, armed to the teeth and itching for combat, come to bid me a last goodbye.

'Anyone fancy a swap?' I call out miserably.

All morning, while they have been making ready for war – cleaning and recleaning their weapons; sharpening their daggers; being briefed by their troop leaders and section commanders; studying maps; writing final letters; synchronising watches; wishing one other luck – I've had to sit here, frustration mounting, like a spare prick at an orgy.

'What the fook 'ave you got to moan about, you jammy booger?' says Oily, prodding me in the back with the sole of his boot.

'Important job, guarding prisoners,' says Sgt. Price.

'Thanks, Price, for that heartwarming platitude,' I reply.

To my surprise, he doesn't respond with: 'For the last bloody time, it's SARNT PRICE.'

Nor, when I add sullenly, 'I dare say I'll see you later,' does he come up with that rejoinder he picked up from the Aussies that time in prison in Crete: 'Not if I see you first.'

Instead, he edges closer and hands me a letter.

'In case anything happens, this is for the General,' he mutters sheepishly. Then, not meeting my eye, as if as an afterthought, he hands me another letter: 'And this is for Her Ladyship.'

'What's this? What's this?' I'm thinking to myself, really quite stunned. He's always had a special fondness for my mother, what with the riding and hunting and what have you, so that one I can understand. (Though it does rather put me to shame, given that I haven't yet written anything to dear Ma myself.) As for the one to my father, well, clearly there are all sorts of estate-managerial matters that need tying up. No, the thing that has taken me aback is this 'in case anything happens . . .' caper.

I mean, of course, in war there's always a fair to even chance that something will happen. But most chaps most of the time have the decency not to mention it except in jest.

'Something up?' I say.

Price just forces a scowl and grunts: 'And mind you don't mix them up or there'll be hell to pay!' He turns away and pretends to be busying himself with a final check of his equipment.

What on earth can have rattled him? Another of his premonitions? I rather hope not because in the past his forebodings have too often proved spookily prescient. Not that he'd ever acknowledge it: Price doesn't hold with psychic powers, or indeed mumbo-jumbo of any kind. I remember once telling him why it is I never carry photos of my loved ones with me – the people who do, always seem to end up dead – and you should have seen the look he gave me. Since then I've always been careful to keep all my superstitious tics, talismans and rituals to myself.

'Then I suppose you'd better look after this, Price,' I call out to him.

He spins round, irritably. 'Eh?'

I hold out my letter to Gina.

'Well, if we're going to play the "in case anything happens" game, here's my letter to you-know-who,' I say, to rile him mainly, take his mind off what's coming. Does the trick too.

'If it says half the rubbish I think it does you're better off burning it,' he snarls.

'Do you mean the passage where I ask her to instruct my solicitor to pass on all my worldly goods to my dear, friendly, smiling companion-in-arms Sarnt Tom Pr–'

'Sarky sod,' he says, snatching the letter and slipping it into his battledress. By the time I've thought up a suitable rejoinder, he has already gone, leaving behind only the incipient bruise on my shoulder where he has thumped me with an affectionate knuckle. Now it's the rest of the section's turn to bid their farewell.

'Hey, Yeller,' says Hordern, leering at my prisoners. 'What's German for "We're off to mess up your mates, good and proper"?'

'I wish I knew, Hordern, you ass,' I reply with a significant glare. 'But as you've clearly forgotten, I only speak French.'

Hordern, of course, misses my point completely and is about to put his foot still deeper in it when Simpson chips in: 'Hey, Yeller, I've just thought. You never did finish telling us how loose the girls were round this neck of the woods.'

'Insatiable,' I reply. 'Quite insatiable.' Got to sound jaunty, even if I don't feel it.

'Give 'em one from you, then, shall I?'

'Just isn't fair, is it?' says Mayhew, as ever looking rather awkward as he attempts to sound like one of the boys. 'You stuck up here while the fair ladies of Port-en-Bessin wait to welcome their gallant liberators.'

'Oh, Yeller's already had his welcome treat. From Mademoiselle in the château just now,' says Hordern.

Ribald laughter.

'Anyway, he's got plenty to keep him happy up here. What with two dozen strapping Bavarian lads to choose from,' jokes Oily, prompting an evil glare from the bolshie grizzled German, who clearly has understood every word.

'You want to watch that one, Yeller. He looks like trouble,' observes Oily.

'Yes, well, if you will insist on goading him,' I say.

'Quite attractive now I look at him, in his brutal pig-ugly way,' says Oily, making as if to unbutton his flies. 'Do you think I might have time for a quick –'

'Enough of that, Wragg,' says Cpl. Blackwell. 'Lads, if we don't get to that start line soon, B section will have done all our fighting for us.'

'Best idea I've heard all day,' says Coffin.

'Good luck, chaps. Give 'em hell,' I say as they file off.

Last to go is Calladine, ashen, withdrawn, eyes directed list-lessly at the boots of the man in front of him.

'Mein Sohn, was birgst du so bang dein Gesicht?' says Herr Flakship in a mock-sympathetic voice. ('My son. Why do you hide your face so anxiously?') It is, as I'm sure you know, a quote from Goethe's 'Erlkönig', in which on a ride across the foggy moors a child is stolen away from his father's arms by the dreaded Alder King.

'"Siehst, Vater, du den Erlkönig nicht? Den Erlkönig mit Kron und Schweif?"' chips in another of the prisoners. Literate lot, clearly.

Then together, four or five of them chorus – and I have to stop myself joining in too, because it's such a haunting line: 'Mein Sohn, es ist ein Nebelstreif.'

My son, it's a streak of mist.

And with that, we all find ourselves impelled to gaze in the direction of the shelled port, which – not unlike Goethe's father and doomed son – has begun to disappear beneath a fog of smoke, dust and burnt cordite.

It's a spine-tingling moment. Quite the second most memorable occasion on which I've ever heard those lines quoted. Which will no doubt make you wonder when the first time was, but that story will have to wait for another day. Suffice to say that it was on the Eastern Front, and that the two men singing it – Metelmann, one of them was called; God knows the name of the other because he was twenty yards away on the Russian side – had the most beautiful tenor and the richest bass it has ever been my privilege to hear.

Well, as you'll imagine, the moment I hear those lines being quoted by my prisoners I'm no longer on that hillside overlooking Port-en-Bessin. I'm back on the Eastern Front, reliving that *Götterdämmerung*. The mixture of emotions that comes rushing back is quite overwhelming. Fear, certainly, because all of my *Truppe* – Metelmann, Heine, Strauss, Ostermeyer, Oberleutnant Kimmelman – were doomed to die horrible deaths, and we knew it; nostalgia, too, for the boys who didn't make it; but, most of all, an intense determination to do whatever necessary to survive; and not just to survive, either, but to crush the enemy and win.

As the softening-up barrage builds to a fortissimo and the smell of cordite drifting up from the town grows ever stronger and more intoxicating, so my urge to be part of the action rather than an idle spectator rises to a frenzied pitch.

There's only a few of us left on the hill now: medics, forward observation officers, sparks, men from HQ troop. Everyone else has moved down to the base, dumped their packs at the Regimental Aid Post (RAP) and passed on, thus unencumbered, to the start line.

You can tell it's not going to be long now. Nine rapidly enlarging dots on the horizon reveal themselves as a squadron of Typhoons come to strafe enemy ground targets with their rockets and cannon.

'Arseholes,' comments Herr Flakship, pointedly not looking up as the squadron overflies our position after its second pass, dipping its wings in acknowledgement as one or two of my comrades rise up and wave their green berets (a self-preservation gesture as much as anything: ground-attack aircraft do have a nasty habit of firing on their own side).

Next it's the turn of 231 Field Battery to open up, and now the attack really is imminent. It's laying down a smoke screen to cover our advance, though at this point it's scarcely necessary. With the dust and smoke from the naval bombardment, and the grey-brown fug from a grass fire which has broken out on the Eastern Feature, the town has already all but disappeared from view.

And now, piercing the low rumble of shellfire, I can hear the crack and staccato rattle of small-arms fire from the southwest, as the fighting troops start to engage God knows what. The weapons pits? Wrong direction. More likely that verminous sniper-training school at Fosse Soucy. Oh Christ, this is frustrating. Why can't I be there?

'Coward?' It's one of the sergeants from HQ troop. 'We've had three RASC lorries just turn up at the RAP. Get your PWs down there sharpish and you've your ticket home.'

I need no further prompting. 'OK, you lot. Raus! Schnell! Und Hände hoch!'

I herd the prisoners from their pen with the barrel of my Schmeisser. None of them tries to escape. Perhaps they have sensed my edginess.

'Come on! Come on! Schnell! Schnell!' I order as we wind our way down the hill, the Sergeant leading the way, the troublemaker Herr Flakship right up close to me where I can see him. The engagement at Fosse Soucy is growing fiercer; and now, by the sounds of it, another skirmish has broken out, this time in the direction of the weapon pits which X troop have been ordered to attack.

'Imperious bastard, isn't he?' calls Herr Flakship to the prisoner behind him.

'Yes. And they're always calling *us* the arrogant ones,' says his mate.

'Well, the worse he treats us, the worse we will treat him when our positions are reversed,' says Herr Flakship with a relish which cries out for a Schmeisser butt in the mouth. Not that I would, obviously: not my style; and besides, he might well give something away.

'You believe they will be?'

'Of course. *Die Englischen Arschlöcher* are completely surrounded and quite oblivious, it would seem, to the warm reception our dear naval comrades have been preparing for them in the harbour.'

With a ghastly stab in the pit of my stomach, it hits me: they already have. Of course! That remark the Nazi made when our LCG(L)s opened up on the harbour front. He thought they were Kriegsmarine ships, not British ones. Why? Because Jean Lionnet was right and the gendarme was wrong: there really are Kriegsmarine in the harbour. They're the crew of a flakship; a flakship which for some reason has eluded our intelligence reports and which could jeopardise the whole mission.

I'd like to stop my unwitting informant for further questioning, but there isn't time, he wouldn't speak anyway and besides, he's just this second dropped straight to the ground with a large chunk missing from his skull. The bullet was presumably intended for me. Student snipers, eh? God bless their wobbly paws.

Such is the noise, the prisoners in front haven't even noticed. So I bend down just long enough to be sure that the hole I saw in his head wasn't merely wishful thinking, then step quickly over the body, and catch up with his twenty oblivious comrades.

The RAP is a large concrete bunker at the foot of Point 72, which until yesterday belonged to the Germans. One of our sergeants stumbled on it by accident last night, capturing two German medical officers and several wounded. This morning, it helped us capture some more: led by a corporal, a party of German soldiers reporting for sick parade wandered in, quite unaware till the last moment that their bunker had changed hands.

Outside, a trio of three-ton Bedford trucks is being laboriously unloaded by a human chain of marines and drawn-looking

Royal Army Service Corpsmen, who've had a tougher job since the landings than almost anyone. So hard do those poor bastards have to work keeping our assault troops in supplies and ammo, it's not unknown for them to drop dead with exhaustion.

No sign of any wireless operators, but that's what I need. Someone to relay the new information I have to our fighting troops.

'Ay up,' announces a sweating beefcake, as we arrive. 'The Seventh Cavalry's here!'

Immediately the prisoners are put to work unloading the trucks. Once they're occupied, I have a quiet word with the Sergeant who led us down the hill.

'Make it quick, then,' he says. 'I'll be needing you to escort this lot back to the beachhead.'

'Can't *they?*' I say, jerking my thumb at the RASC boys.

'Lieutenant Truelove's orders. Says the sooner you get out of the CO's way, the better for everyone. Now, quick, before I change my mind.'

The interior bunker is gloomy and foetid, the smell of fresh blood and raw meat cut with iodine, surgical spirit and paraffin from the lamps which are the sole source of illumination. Near the entrance, a medical orderly wearing a lance-corporal's stripe is dressing the arm of a young commando.

'Excuse me, chaps, I'm looking for a sparks.'

The commando looks up and grins. It's Mayhew.

'Jack!' I say.

'Yell –' he begins, then corrects himself to the more friendly 'Dick'.

'How are we doing?'

'Better than we could have dreamed,' he gabbles, eyes a-sparkle. 'Soon as X troop charged the weapons pit, the defence just collapsed. We passed through with B troop using the ditches either side. Spot of mortar fire on the way to town, which is where I got hit. I wanted to go on but Corporal Blackwell said I had to report back here. Jolly unfair. Expect they've taken both Features by now.'

'And the flakship?'

'Flakship?'

'Christ, we've got to find a wireless op, quickly.'

'Think I saw one round the back, trying to get a signal,' says Mayhew.

Back outside, one of the prisoners is refusing to work. 'Wo ist Hans?' he keeps asking his comrades, looking around frantically. 'Hast du Hans gesehen?'

'You speak the lingo, don't you, Coward?' says the Sergeant.

'Ah. Es tut mir leid, mein Freund,' I tell the agitated prisoner. 'Ich glaube, dass Ihr Freund Hans gestorben ist,' I say.

'Sie sprechen Deutsch?' asks the German in some surprise.

'All Englishmen do,' I say – and I know I shouldn't, but I'm afraid I wasn't a great fan of Hans and besides, there's something about the Germans that always seems to bring out the facetious in me – 'We only pretend not to for fun.'

The German isn't amused. 'You have murdered Hans!' he says.

'Not me, I promise. One of your snipers.'

'He has murdered Hans. *Der Engländer* has murdered Hans.'

From inside the trucks and along the chain of prisoners there are agitated cries.

'Was sagt er?'

'*Der Engländer* has murdered Hans!'

'Nein!'

''Ere, what's the matter with these buggers? Why've they stopped working?' asks the Sergeant.

'They think I killed one of their mates, Sarge.'

'And did you?'

'No, Sarge. It was one of their snipers.'

'Well, whether it was or it wasn't, I want this sorted out sharpish.'

I'm sure there are more tactful methods. Problem is, I just haven't the time to think what they might be. So instead, I pull my grimmest expression, cock my Schmeisser with ostentatious relish as I've seen my own Nazi guards do on rather too many occasions and shout: 'Silence! German prisoners. Your Führer has told you about the many war crimes committed by English commandos. And for once your Führer is right. I have executed one of your number already. I shall not hesitate to kill the rest of you one by one unless you go back to work, right now!'

It's a bloody good perf, though I say it myself. Based on a particularly vicious fellow I once knew called Klammer, God rest his rotten soul. After only a very brief exchange of glances, the prisoners resume their unloading.

'D'ye know, Coward,' says the Sergeant, very impressed. 'You're wasted back here.'

'Don't I know it. And, Sarge, I still need to find that sparks.'

'You'd better be off, then. And when you've found him, you mind you don't bugger off and rejoin your troop, or there'll be hell to pay,' says the Sergeant, with an audible wink in his voice.

'Yes, Sarge. Thank you, Sarge.'

On the way I pause at the bunker, where the medic has just finished bandaging Mayhew's arm. 'This man fit to show me the way to the wireless op?' I ask the medic.

'Sure. But nothing more strenuous,' says the medic Lance-Corporal, though he doesn't look as surprised as he might when, as he's leaving, Mayhew reaches with his good arm to pick up his rifle.

We find the wireless operator where Mayhew last saw him.

He's still wrestling with his set, badgered by a pair of fidgety runners clutching pencil-scrawled messages which their officers want relayed.

I nudge my way through. 'We need to get an urgent message to A and B troops.'

'Join the queue,' sighs the harassed-looking sparks. 'I've been trying for twenty minutes, but this set's knackered and I reckon both theirs must be completely u/s.'

'Could you have another go?'

'Oi, hang about. I was first,' says one of the runners.

'This is from the CO. This has priority,' says the other.

The sparks rises to his feet and takes off his headphones.

'Look, lads,' he says, 'if any of you thinks he can do a better job, be my fucking guest. But if you want my advice, I'd say you're better off on Shanks's pony.'

At this Mayhew gives me an eager look. 'I'm game,' he declares.

The first part of our journey, conducted at a steady jog, passes without incident. The sniper action at Fosse Soucy has been more or less suppressed by Y troop and, with the weapons pits in the possession of X troop, the main obstacle to the town's southern approach has now been removed. Once we get near the church, though, at the bottom part of the town's outer edge, things start to become much more volatile. From every direction there are shots, and shouts and the rapid tramp of scurrying boots, though whose you're rarely altogether sure. As I try, with some difficulty, to convey to Mayhew – his instinct is simply to trot down the centre of the street blasting away at all comers – in the chaos of urban warfare, discretion is very much the better part of valour.

'Down, you clot!' I have to hiss at one point, yanking him down by the scruff of his trouser leg. The fool was trying to take a pot shot at a German patrol we only narrowly avoided being spotted by, when at the last moment I managed to get us both behind the cover of a low garden wall.

You can understand his cockiness though. There are moments, as we make our stealthy advance, when you can look down a street and see nothing but green berets zigzagging from doorway to doorway.

But look down just the same street not thirty seconds later and all you'll see is field grey. And give it thirty seconds more and it will be empty once more. Empty that is, save for the recumbent old woman with a dark, sticky pool stretching out from her grizzled pate; and the body just beyond of a teenage boy whom you hope you don't recognise but you rather suspect you do by the fact that the ends of his outstretched, lifeless arms have no hands attached, just stumps.

The church looks a likely meeting place. I noticed some commandos go in a while ago, without apparent trouble, and they've yet to re-emerge. Saint-André de Port-en-Bessin its name is and, rather like that battleship of a cathedral they put up to frighten the Cathars at Albi, it's far bigger than you'd expect for such a one-horse town. When you're a fishing community, more vulnerable than most to the vagaries of weather and tide and natural disaster, I suppose you have to work extra hard to keep God onside.

There's only one way in. A heavy wooden door at the west end. It's shut, of course. 'Forty-seven Commando, coming through,' I bellow at the thick oak.

A scraping of bars from within, then the door swings open and a marine, B troop I'd guess, beckons me and Mayhew swiftly inside.

Like many soldiers, I often find myself drawn to a church during a battle. There's the obvious tactical point, of course, that it's invariably solid, in a prominent position, with crypts to shelter in and tall towers invaluable for observation and sniping. But then there's the numinous side of things. This belief it gives you – wholly misplaced, of course, because church spires are a priority target for artillery – that, being in God's house, you must somehow be that little bit more protected.

As we pass into the nave, the two marines guarding the entrance lower their Sten guns. Either side of the transept, beneath a dangling model of a sailing ship, wounded marines are slumped against the chapel walls, being tended by orderlies. The commander of B troop – bookish fellow, schoolmaster in civilian life, named Capt. Hobbes – emerges from the vestry.

'Coward? Aren't you supposed to be back at HQ?'

'Change of plan, sir. New intelligence about the harbour defences, which needs relaying to the forward troops.'

'What kind of intelligence?'

'We think there's a flakship moored in the harbour.'

'Hell's bells, you might be too late. Last I saw of A troop, they were readying a Bangalore to blow the wire blocking the road to the Western Feature.'

'Can you remember where, sir?'

'Rue du Phare. Steep road on the corner, about a hundred yards back from the western seafront. You'll have a job reaching it. We've had some luck on this side of the basin, but the far side's still in their hands. They've got mortars and MGs covering all the main approaches and their patrols are everywhere.'

'I'm not sure we have much choice, sir.'

'Well, good luck. And Coward, you're a cultured fellow I should imagine?'

'I hope so, sir.'

'Then just before you leave, do stop to look at the statues on the right. Medieval, I should say. Not the best of their kind, but there's a rough-hewn naïvety about them you might find affords the cheer a chap needs at times like this.'

On the way out, I do as Capt. Hobbes suggests. There's a carving of a Virgin with sculpted crescent eyebrows and a broad, benign peasant's face, carrying a pudgy little Jesus with curly, close-fitting hair, like a Roman emperor's. The one that tickles me, though, and I'm sure is what Capt. Hobbes meant, is the one of an archbishop with his crook and a comically lost expression, as if he's looked at the state of man's affairs and found them a total mystery. 'Oh, dear me! We're buggered, the whole ruddy lot of us,' he seems to be saying to the onlooker. Amen to that, I think. And after a quick final prayer for God's protection in this hour of dire need, I pass through the door that leads from ecclesiastical calm to the stench, heat and noise of bloody battle.

Rather than take the most direct route to the port, which would leave us too exposed to fire from the far side of the basin, we skirt further west, taking advantage as before of the rear gardens belonging to the houses lining the road. It's relatively safe, but our progress is slow. Too slow.

In my more melancholy moments since, I've often looked back on that day in Port-en-Bessin and berated myself for not having moved more swiftly. If only I'd been quicker to twig what Herr Flakship was on about. If only we'd ushered those prisoners faster down the hillside. If only we'd sprinted instead of jogged from Rear HQ. If only I'd lingered less in the church. If only . . . But whenever I've done so, I've always reached the same conclusion: however many minutes I might have shaved off with more impatience here and by running faster there, they would never have been quite enough to avert the disaster that befell A troop. It was one of those terrible things that happen in war, that's all.

The first I hear of it is the rapid firing of heavy-calibre guns, coming from the direction of the port. It could be ours but I very much doubt it, because our troops are only carrying small arms, and they're unlikely to have called in artillery support when their comrades are so widely dispersed. Which more likely makes it the thing I've been most dreading. A flakship carries guns designed for shooting down aircraft. You can imagine the damage they can inflict on infantry, at a range of barely 1,000 yards.

I certainly can, which is why I've abandoned the cover of those back gardens now and, with Mayhew hot on my heels, I'm running hell for leather down one side of the road leading to the Rue du Phare and the base of the Western Feature. The way may be crawling with Germans or there may be none. We'll just have to take our chances.

It plays strange tricks on the brain, the battlefield. The times when you ought most to be afraid are often those when you feel most fearless. If you've ever been out fox-hunting you'll know exactly the sensation I mean: the way everything seems to come at you in an impressionistic rush which so over-whelms the brain that it becomes detached from reality; almost as if you're no longer participating, merely a dispassionate observer.

I remember the explosion of a mortar bomb in front of me and another one behind, thinking: 'Closer than I'd prefer'; the sparks from Spandau ricochets zinging off the cobbled road; Mayhew saying: 'I'm sorry. So sorry'; seeing a patrol of maybe six Germans emerging from a hedgerow a split second before they see me, firing at them from the hip, and so taking them by surprise that instead of stopping to fight they turn and disappear whence they came; a seagull pecking something long and stringy from the hole in a dead soldier's back; a Bren gunner giving me a wave from a first-floor window; a sign reading Rue du Phare; a scattered mess of coiled wire and the tubular remnants of the Bangalore torpedo used to blow it; more bullets and ricochets from behind me; commandos, some bloodstained, some staggering, all pale, picking their way towards me through the gap; one of them saying: 'No point, mate. They've had it!'; pushing forward through the gap, none the less, surprised by how steep the hill is, so very very steep and how very slow my progress, as if in slow motion.

When all of a sudden the volume is turned right up and we're back to normal speed and it's hell. There are bullets flying everywhere, the air so thick with lead it seems scarcely imaginable that anything could pass through unscathed. Stick grenades landing, here, there and everywhere; then exploding, moments later. Flying earth and screaming shrapnel. Screaming wounded. Screaming Capt. Dangerfield coming towards me, staggering under the weight of a semi-conscious Oily Wragg. 'Back!' he shouts. 'Back! The rest are all dead.'

A glance in the direction from which he has come. Five, six, seven bodies lying on the exposed hillside where they were mown down by the flakship still pumping rounds at us, the furthest body Sgt. Price's.

16

A la Cave

You'd be amazed, the miracles you can work when you're young and fit and being hotly pursued by half a dozen stick grenades.

But once Capt. Dangerfield and I had lugged Oily Wragg's eighteen-stone dead weight off that hill, our difficulties were far from over, let me tell you. First we had to negotiate the gap through the wire, which wasn't nearly broad enough to pass through three-abreast so we had to do it sideways and gingerly, with Capt. Dangerfield at the downhill end almost collapsing under Wragg's weight, and our trousers getting continually snagged and our lower legs slashed to ribbons. You tend not to notice these things at the time because adrenalin acts like an anaesthetic. But the next day, my God, did it hit me: my trousers looked like Robinson Crusoe's after a year on the island; my calves and my shins were crisscrossed with so many welts it was as if I'd been gone over, hard, with a cat-o'-nine-tails; and the stinging was like I'd been attacked by a swarm of bees. Well, almost – out in the East once I was attacked by a swarm of bees, and I'll be honest: that hurt more.

Anyway, those cuts and slashes were the least of our worries, because glancing desperately around for what was left of our troop, we realised the whole lot had vanished. The Germans, on the other hand, appeared to be absolutely bloody everywhere.

They were firing down on us from one of the machine-gun nests on the Eastern Feature, and no sooner had we side-stepped hastily out of its sight lines behind one of the buildings just to the rear of the seafront than we spotted coming straight down the street towards us a squad of nine Germans and no way were we going to be able to take them on with just Capt. Dangerfield's Colt .45 and my Schmeisser. Especially not while burdened with that monstrous Yorkshireman.

Now, the only thing that saved us, I'm sorry to say, was poor Jack Mayhew. In the letter I wrote to his mother, afterwards, I gave him the send-off he thoroughly deserved, going out in a blaze of glory as he gallantly charged a German machine-gun post. What really happened, though, was that the last time we saw him alive he was crawling, evidently quite badly wounded, down the street towards us, about fifty yards ahead of the squad of Germans. I don't remember seeing him go down, but I think it must have been about five minutes before on the dash to Rue du Phare when I heard him call out 'I'm sorry'. You see that quite a bit with noble, idealistic, public-school types like Mayhew: they actually think that to be put out of action is a dereliction of duty.

So there he was, dear chap, crawling along, in vain search of shelter, with these Germans coming up fast behind him, which of course he didn't know.

'Jack!' I shout, though of course it's not going to do any good.

He looks up, recognises the three of us, and flashes us this huge schoolboy grin, like he's just hit the winning six from the final ball of the last over.

And, of course, it is his final ball. He's far too young and handsome to die. But, then, so was Rupert Brooke.

The Germans are almost on him now and we have a choice: do we take advantage of the temporary distraction and leg it back whence we came or try to shoot it out and give Jack a fighting chance?

Well, I'm pleased to say, a bit of both. Capt. Dangerfield looses off a couple of shots with his Colt, one of which catches the lead German dead in the centre of his chest, which is bloody good going considering he's firing left-handed. I fire a burst from my Schmeisser which wings another and sends the rest scurrying for cover, but they're made of much sterner stuff than that last patrol, and though the survivors disperse into doorways, they show no sign of beating a retreat.

'I'll cover,' I tell Capt. Dangerfield, as I duck behind the corner wall, and you can see the thought furrowing his brow – 'Shouldn't I be giving the orders round here?' – but then I have the firepower and he doesn't and anyway there isn't time. So off he staggers with his massy burden while I hold the fort.

Next time I poke my head round the corner, Jack Mayhew is still gamely pulling himself forward and up until this point the Germans have been too busy trying to kill us to pay much attention to him. But now I spot one of the Germans with his rifle aimed at Jack's head and I fell him, just in time; then three more come out into the middle of the street, cool as you like, stand there, and riddle him simultaneously and at such length you can tell they're rather enjoying it. And as I watch poor Jack's lifeless body shuddering and jerking and spurting mini fountains of blood, I take careful aim at those sadistic bastards and squeeze the trigger.

There's a click. Then nothing. My magazine's empty. I don't have any spares. And when I look behind me, Capt. Dangerfield and Oily Wragg have disappeared.

Well, I'll tell you, at this point I'm getting worried. Half my troop's been massacred. There are Germans in every alley. There's a flakship covering the seafront. There are machine guns on the Eastern and Western Features covering my every escape route. Our battle plan is in ruins. I'm all alone. My gun's out of ammo. And just round the corner, about to come after me, is a squad of Germans whose idea of fun is to pump a wounded man full of bullets.

For a hunting man you might call it poetic justice: right now I know just what goes through Charlie's mind when he's gone to ground and the hounds are casting about just above his head.

Still, you do what you can.

I try the first door I come to. It's locked.

So is the next one.

The third one is, too, and I doubt there's time to try any more, I can hear the boots approaching just round the corner. I'll just have to run and hope for the best.

'Coward!' hisses Capt. Dangerfield from the fourth doorway, and with a sigh beyond bliss I hurl myself towards it. Down a flight of steps. Darkness as the door closes behind me. Running feet and shouts in German.

'Here,' says Capt. Dangerfield, taking my hand. I follow him unsteadily forward. There is a smell of must and lees. Wine.

The darkness isn't complete. There's a hatchway at the far end through whose cracks chinks of light are streaming in. As my eyes become accustomed to the gloom, I see ranks of barrels, raised above the ground on a wooden frame.

'Quick,' says Capt. Dangerfield, quite needlessly. From next door, we can hear guttural shouts and the thump and crack of boot against splintering wood.

We have reached the far end of the cellar now. In the narrow gap between the last barrel and the wall, Wragg is propped, limp and barely conscious.

'Wragg, wake up! We need you awake!' hisses Capt. Dangerfield, slapping his face and pulling him up under his arm.

'Who the fook!' mutters Wragg, stiffening upright but still delirious.

'Damn. I should have thought,' says Capt. Dangerfield. 'We need one of us either side of him. Can you squeeze past his legs?'

'I think maybe . . . why?'

'Just do it.'

I crouch down and with some difficulty I manoeuvre myself past Wragg's boots and into the claustrophobic pocket between Oily, the barrel and the corner of the cellar wall.

'Now for the hard part,' says Capt. Dangerfield. 'We're going to lift this fellow up and keep him up so that he's wedged between the barrel and floor. Whatever happens, none of our feet must touch the floor. Got that?'

Not really, but there isn't time to argue. Now it's our door the Germans are bashing with their boots and the butts of their rifles, and they'll be breaking through any moment.

'Got him? Now lift!'

With one hand under Wragg's buttocks and another under his knee – Capt. Dangerfield is doing the same on the other side – I hoick him upwards and wedge him in more or less the right position. And if it isn't right we're stuffed because, with a final crack, the cellar door has burst open, the light is pouring in. Our scufflings covered by the noise of jackboots clattering down the steps, we just have time to pull ourselves into the requisite wedge position. Simultaneously, and this isn't easy, we have to keep Wragg held up, too.

Footsteps, cautious footsteps, coming steadily closer.

The strain of trying to hold up that bloody Yorkshireman, you would not believe. But when the choice is between a hernia or being shot, you don't spend too long agonising.

A torch beam (only a German infantryman would think to have a torch on him) searching the room, nervously, haphazardly at first, then with slow thoroughness. Our friend is searching the gaps between each cask. If he carries on like this, there is no question we're going to be discovered – and wedged in as we are, we won't have a chance to defend ourselves.

Idiot Capt. Dangerfield. Why the hell did I listen to him? He doesn't have the experience I have. He's made the wrong decision. The way I would have hidden myself, I would have made sure I had my arms free so that I could have gone down fighting.

About a third of the way across the room now. Taking his time. As, of course, your infuriatingly efficient Teuton would.

More footsteps, as one of the German's comrades comes to join him.

'Anything?' asks the newcomer.

'Nothing so far,' says our friend, continuing his slow, steady search with the torch. He's now about half-way down the room. One German, we might somehow have handled. Two, we're stuffed completely.

'Here. If they're there, you'll see their boots,' says the newcomer. He must have grabbed the torch from his comrade, and then crouched down for the beam jerks suddenly, then moves down till it's parallel with and almost touching the floor. Directly below me, the beam searches the spot where we would all have been standing if it hadn't been for Capt. Dangerfield's quite brilliant idea.

'See? Nothing,' declares the newcomer. 'Come on. What are you waiting for?'

'It's best to be sure,' says our friend, stolidly.

'You want to be sure? Here's how to be sure.'

There's a soft thud on the floor.

'What's that?'

'Come on. Hurry. It's on a ten-second fuse.'

'What?!'

The sound of German curses and rapidly retreating boots. I brace myself for the explosion. Five seconds. Four. Three. Two. One. Nothing. Maybe it's a dud.

A flash of white light. An ear-shattering noise. Singing shrapnel. The choking rasp of cordite in the throat. The smell of wine.

A voice saying something.

'What?' My ears are ringing.

'I said, are you hit?'

'Don't think so. You?'

'No.'

'I need to let go.'

'Me too. Ready?'

We ease ourselves into a standing position. Then we unjam Wragg by lifting him slightly, and prop him against the wall.

'We safe to leave, do you reckon?' I ask.

'Give 'em a bit more time to go, shall we?' says Capt. Dangerfield.

'I'm glad you said that.'

'What do you think I am? Some kind of fool?'

'No, sir.'

'Over-eager? Gung-ho?'

'Well . . .'

A long sigh from the darkness.

'Coward,' says Capt. Dangerfield. 'Do you think it would be fair to say relations between us haven't got off to the best of starts?'

We both laugh companionably.

Capt. Dangerfield goes on: 'I was wrong about you. I admit that now and I'm sorry. If I'd taken your intelligence more seriously, those chaps might never have died.'

'Do we know who they were?'

'One of them, I'm sorry to say, was Sarnt Price.'

'I saw.'

'You'd been through quite a bit together.'

'From the beginning, more or less.'

'I'm sorry,' says Capt. Dangerfield.

'It's war. You get used to it.'

'Do you? I'm not sure I'll ever forget seeing them go down like that. Hawkins. Arkwright. Calladine –'

'If you're trying to blame yourself, don't. We've all got a job to do, sometimes it gets messy and sometimes we make mistakes. But for the record, Captain, I think you're doing a pretty fine job.'

'Very decent of you to say so, Coward, but –'

'Sir, I didn't say it to be decent.'

'You can call me Guy if you like.'

'Thanks.'

'Dick, I never did get to the bottom of how it was you came to join our unit.'

'If I told you the real reason, you'd never believe me.'

'Try.'

'To look after you.'

Capt. Dangerfield laughs. 'Come now. Before Southampton, you didn't know me from Adam.'

'I didn't, no. But someone else did and that someone asked me if I'd care to watch over you. Keep you from harm.'

'And how were you supposed to do that exactly? Hold my hand? Throw yourself on top of me, every time you heard a shell? Come on, the idea's ludicrous.'

'Yes, well, I'm not sure I was altogether in my right mind when I made the arrangement.'

'I'll say, what were you: drunk?'

'I was in hospital at the time. Still quite delirious from some sort of brain fever; and she was my nurse.'

'I'm partial to nurses myself.'

'Yes, well, when I tell you who she was, you'll understand even better. She's quite a looker, ain't she, your cousin?'

'My cousin? Which one?'

'Gina. Gina Herbert.'

'Gina told you she was my cousin, did she?'

'Isn't she?'

'Well, yes, but she is the most dreadful tease. When was it you met her?'

'Oh, I've known her for years. We used to play together as children.'

'Damn it, you *are* one of the Coward boys, aren't you? The General's sons.'

'I might as well come clean.'

'But if you'd told me that right at the beginning, I might have —'

'Detested me even more, I should have thought. We weren't particularly nice to you, were we?'

'Your brother wasn't, no. But as I mentioned during bridge — Lord, was it really only the night before last that we were playing bridge? — I don't begrudge it. If it hadn't been for you Cowards, I might never have become who I am. More's the point, nor would I have married the girl I married. A girl you know rather well in fact, because —'

More footsteps.

The back of my neck prickling, heart racing.

The Germans are back. Maybe they heard us talking. Maybe they've been tipped off. This time they're not going to stop till they've got us.

Here they come. Just one by the sounds of it. Crunching through the half-broken door, down the cellar steps. Slowly, slowly.

My Schmeisser being out of ammo, I reach for my knife. Capt. Dangerfield eases his Colt .45 off its safety.

'Messieurs? Messieurs?' calls the interloper. 'Je viens vous aider.'

Bound to be a trap.

'Messieurs, the Germans have gone. You are safe now. Vite, Messieurs, Messieurs.'

'Haut les mains en l'air, Monsieur,' orders Capt. Dangerfield, before half-emerging from his hiding place. His eyes are sufficiently accustomed to the gloom to see whether his order has been obeyed. 'It's OK,' he says to me. 'He's genuine.'

The man introduces himself as Pascal Jean, a fisherman. He was watching the battle from his window and saw us go into the cellar and not come out. The battle, he says, is far from over but the side of town we're in now appears to be more or less clear of Boche. If we like, he can lead us to the house not far away where several of our comrades are holed up.

We enter through a hole that has been knocked in its rear wall. Much safer than trying to go in through the front, which looks out over the inner basin, giving it a clear field of fire against those Germans still occupying the opposite bank, but also leaving it highly vulnerable to fire from the Eastern Feature.

As we heave Wragg through the hole, the marine guarding it calls up the stairwell: 'Captain Dangerfield's here!'

From upstairs, a cheer goes up. We leave Wragg on the ground floor, where a pair of medics are already in attendance on some of the other wounded from the botched assault, and clamber carefully up the partially collapsed staircase. In an attic room at the top, their bodies so thickly sprinkled with plaster dust they might almost be ghosts, the remnants of our section are peering through loopholes they have made in the roof.

'Welcome back, sir. We was worried you wouldn't make it,' says Cpl. Blackwell, eyes still fixed firmly on the view outside. His next remark is addressed to the pint-sized Bren gunner lying prone next to him. I recognise him as the Geordie, Dinning, who made the joke on the crossing about the *Flying Scotsman*. 'See her? She's up to no good again.'

'What's the trouble, Corporal?' asks Capt. Dangerfield, pushing aside a slate so as to enlarge his viewing hole.

'See up there, sir. Girl in the red dress. Reckon she must be sweet on one of them Germans. She's been standing there, pointing out our positions.'

I can see her, too, now. Pretty thing. Damned shame.

'You know what to do, Corporal.'

'Sir. McMahon, drop 'er!'

A crack of a sniper rifle. The girl crumples.

Almost immediately the room is alive with ricochets and splinters, flying chips of tile and brickwork and sparks, as the positions on the hill return fire.

'Eleven o'clock, Dinning,' says Cpl. Blackwell, calmly noting one of the positions, oblivious to the bits of masonry tumbling near his head.

'Got it.'

A burst of Dinning's Bren.

The German fire temporarily ceases. Only to open up again from a different angle.

'We're not going anywhere till we've taken that Feature. Acting-Lieutenant Coward, your informant was right about the flakship. Do you think he was right about the pathway too?'

'Acting-Lieutenant Coward?'

'I doubt the Colonel will ratify it but yes, as long as this action lasts. Now, this zigzag pathway?'

'There's only one way to be certain. If you'll allow me four men —'

'Four men, you'll have. Corporal Blackwell, I need you here covering.'

'Sir.'

'You too, Dinning. And Simpson, I need you sniping. Anyone else who cares to volunteer to go with Lieutenant Coward, please do so now.'

There's an awkward pause. Then, to my eternal gratitude, one by one, the hands of the remaining five marines are raised.

'There's your command, then, Lieutenant Coward. Off you go. Nothing too ambitious, mind you. This is just a recce. When we make the final assault, I intend to lead it myself.'

Before we set off, the marines who are to remain in the house pool what ammo they can spare. The one guarding the ground floor furnishes me with more captured 9-mm. for my Schmeisser and a pocketful of grenades. 'Don't use 'em all at once, mind,' he chides.

''Ere, Yeller,' calls a Northern voice from a dingy corner.

'That'll be Lieutenant Coward to you, Wragg,' I reply.

'What do you do to deserve that, then, you daft booger? Nothing too dangerous, I hope.'

'This is very unlike you, Oily. Why the concern?'

'Oh, it's not you I mind about, it's just I never got to hear how the story ends.'

'Which story?'

'This girl the Captain marries. We never did hear her name, did we?'

'Good God, man, were you listening all that time?'

'There were fook-all else to do, were there, with the two of you blethering away in my lughole. You're never serious though, are you. You never really coom all this way joost because of some bint you met in 'ospital?'

'Age of chivalry bypass Yorkshire, did it?'

'Us Yorkshiremen have got more sense than to mek tits of ourselves, just on the off chance of getting our ends away. Specially when the bint's already spoken for.'

'And what exactly is that supposed to mean?'

'Well, that's why I'm so keen too find out, Yeller. Is she or isn't she the same one?'

'Who?'

'This girl you're sweet on. The one who made you come all this way. I'm laying money on her being Captain Dangerfield's new missus.'

17

The Assault

'Dick, if anything should happen to me, I should like you to give her this,' says Capt. Dangerfield, *sotto voce*, as he hands me an envelope. I don't want to look at the name on it, I really don't. Problem is, if I don't look, I'll never know, will I? So, heart clenched, I lower my eyes inch by surreptitious inch.

Gina Dangerfield.

Around me, the surface of the world begins to craze like a dried-out lake, then crack like the shell of an enormous egg, then shatter into a million pieces which tumble into the void, leaving me stranded in the vastness of a black, pitiless universe, alone on my tiny island of misery.

I want to die.

'Not wishing to tempt fate,' says Capt. Dangerfield, with a nervous laugh, 'but did you have any personal letters you'd like me to take care of?'

'Thanks,' I say, quite taken aback by the calm, icy resignation in my voice. 'But there's no one.'

He looks at me curiously for a moment, passing a tongue over his dry lips. 'Well, good luck,' he says, at last, turning away to join Q troop's commander, Capt. Gough, against the far wall of the shattered Café Terminus, where we've gathered for our final briefing.

Together with the remnants of Q troop (which bore the

brunt of the casualties during the landings), our troop has been granted the honour of taking the Eastern Feature. I use the term honour in its original Wellingtonian sense of 'total bloody suicide mission'.

Not only are the enemy deeply emplaced and more heavily armed but, so far as we can gather, they outnumber us by roughly three to one. About the only thing we have going in our favour is that they won't be expecting us to do something quite so stupid. Under cover of smoke, we plan to take a detachment of thirty men up the zigzag path to the Eastern Feature. Near the top we'll split into two groups, we'll charge, and that's as far as the plan goes, I'm afraid. The rest is in the hands of God.

Mind you, I've only myself to blame, as Capt. Dangerfield is now explaining to the roomful of filthy, jittery, weary, excited commandos.

'Thanks to Lieutenant Coward's recce mission of earlier this afternoon . . .'

A whispering across the room. Not everyone has yet heard mention of my unorthodox battlefield commission.

'. . . we now know that the path is clear of mines and relatively ill-defended. Lieutenant Coward, would you care to tell us a little more about what you found?'

'Orchids,' I hear myself, say, light-headedly, to much general amusement. God, it's good to be an officer again. And if this really is the day I am to die, I'll at least do so in the company of men who have finally chosen to like and respect me; well, laugh politely at my jokes at least.

'Lots of orchids,' I continue, milking the laughter. 'At least five varieties including a very lovely bee, so if there's enough light and the smoke barrage permits, do keep an eye open. You should have plenty of opportunities as the first 200 yards or so are clear of defences. It's only round the third bend that the trouble starts. There's a pillbox immediately on the right and, behind it, a network of trenches and further pillboxes, which unfortunately we were unable to investigate owing to an inclement shower of stick grenades.'

'Thank you, Lieutenant Coward, for that expert botanical assessment. Now, once we're past those obstacles we should by my reckoning be within ten yards of the crest, at which point I shall fire the signal for A troop to deploy left while Captain Gough leads Q troop right. After that, it's up to you. These are good soldiers we're facing but they're by no means the best. They've taken a hell of a pasting from our artillery and it's my firm belief that the moment we push hard enough, they'll fold like deckchairs. I need scarcely remind you how important this mission is. Any questions before I hand over to Captain Gough? Yes, Dinning?'

'It's them bees Lieutenant Coward mentioned,' says Dinning, to laughter and applause. 'Do they sting real bad, like? Only, the bullets I can handle, but if it's bees, if it's all the same, sir, I'll sit this one out. I'm allergic, see. Brings me out in the most terrible lumps.'

Capt. Dangerfield has scheduled the assault to begin at dusk, 2200 hours. Very sensible, I'm thinking. With luck there'll be just enough light for us to see where we're going, while not quite enough for defenders to pick us off. But it turns out there's another, more pressing reason why we need to get in there soon. Our position, it would seem, has grown more precarious than at any time since the landing.

We discover the latest bad news on the march to our start line, when Hordern spots a runner from HQ troop panting back down our line, having just delivered a message to the troop commanders.

''Ang on, mate. What's the 'urry?' says Hordern, holding him fast by his elbow.

'The hurry, mate, is that 'less you lot get a move on, we've all had it,' says the runner, trying to wrest himself from Hordern's grasp.

Coffin, McMahon and I gather round to block his exit. We've formed quite a tight little unit since our successful recce mission.

'Meaning what, exactly?' says Hordern, steering the runner round so that he's moving in the same direction we are.

'We think Point 72's been overrun. Last we heard from Rear HQ, they were under attack by at least sixty Germans. That was half an hour ago. We've heard nothing since.'

'There's our main supply line fucked, then,' says Coffin.

'There's always Uncle Sam next door,' says Hordern.

'No, mate. He's fucked, too,' says the runner.

'What?'

'Yeah, Jerry's been giving him such a hammering on the beach, he was lucky to get off at all.'

'And the good news?' says Coffin.

'Good news is that, soon as you let go of me, I'm fucking off back to Forward HQ,' says the runner. He eyes me up and down. 'You're Coward, ain't you?'

'Lieutenant Coward to you,' says Hordern.

'Field promotion? The CO's going to love that. He's been talking about having you court-martialled for going AWOL – um, sir.'

But I can't say I'm much bothered by this. Nor by the fact that our commando is now completely cut off from the rest of the Allied invasion force. All I can think about is that the beautiful, adorable girl with whom I was half certain I'd be spending the rest of my life has given herself to another.

Looking back, the wise old boy I am now would very much like to give the callow imbecile I was then a good slap. Then a vigorous shake. And perhaps after that, a few more slaps, just for the pure hell of it. I mean, really.

But which of our youthful antics does stand up to the

scrutiny of sixty years' hindsight? You may say – I would – that I was a damned fool ever to have set so much store by Gina's affections on so little evidence. And an even more damnable fool to have got so carried away as to take seriously the lunatic task she set me on what I now realise was just another of her idle, spoilt-girl's whims. And an outright, cream-faced loon for not having twigged earlier that the object of my affections and Capt. Dangerfield's new wife were one and the same.

To which I can only reply: 'I was young!' You're young your-self. You know what it's like. If you want to believe some-thing, you're not about to let a bit of inconvenient reality get in the way of your desires. You go on wishing. Anything seems possible. And if you go on wishing hard enough, you fervently tell yourself, then one day your dreams will come true.

And there's another thing you need to remember about my generation. Though in many ways war had made us older than our years – you'd see 24-year-olds commanding companies; and 30-year-olds in charge of divisions, which would never happen now – there were others in which we remained rather naïve. We could read terrain, strip a rifle, devise a battle plan, shackle a prisoner, kill our enemy silently with a knife and a thousand and one more ways besides. But show us a woman who wasn't a sister, mother or aunt, and we scarcely know where to begin.

Either she was a slut who, if you played your cards right, might vouchsafe you a quick knee-trembler in a back alley.

Or she was one of those remote visions of perfection whom you hoped one day you might be lucky enough to marry.

Gina I put very much in the latter category. If you'd told me she shat I'd never have believed you. In fact, I'm not sure I would have believed you if you'd told me she wasn't a virgin, despite all that she had told me on our walks to the cave. That was the root of my problem with Gina. It was never the person she was. It was the angel I had invented in my adolescent imagination.

But just you try telling all this to the pallid 26-year-old Dick Coward as, jaw set, eyes ablaze with thwarted passion, bitterness, self-hatred and despair, he sets off to battle for what he petulantly hopes will be his last time. Not a prayer. His mind is made up. He is resolved to die.

Not pointlessly, though, I reassure myself as we advance towards the start line. When I go, I will go heroically at the head of my troop, preferably in a way which changes the course of the battle – which, as I'm sure you know, is one of the technical prerequisites for gaining a VC.

A posthumous VC. Won't that just show 'em? My ingrate father. My poltroon of a brother! Gina! The CO. The whole bloody world!

Up until the third bend on the zigzag path, our advance on the Eastern Feature goes well. Our three Bren Carriers, which have somehow managed to escape the débâcle at Point 72, are keeping the opposition's heads down with suppressing MG fire. And our progress up the hill is being masked by clouds of smoke, laid down by our one remaining two-inch mortar.

But then, just when we need it most, the ruddy mortar decides to run out of smoke bombs. One minute we're tripping up that hill, as safe as Sunday ramblers, secure in the comfort of our puffy white blanket. The next we're thinking, 'Aye aye. This can't be right. How come I can now make out the fellow in front? And the one in front of him . . .' And suddenly, there we are, all thirty of us, as pitifully exposed as sleepwalkers who've just awoken to find themselves stark bollock-naked in the middle of the wicket in the First Test at Lord's.

From a bunker ahead a machine gun stutters, the lead man drops and so, in an instant, do the rest of us.

'Seventy-seven grenades!' a voice bellows. Lt. Truelove's. And almost simultaneously, five men rise up just long enough to free their grenades from their webbing and hurl them ahead of us. Four of them succeed. One doesn't, reminding all of us why it is you want to rid yourself of your 77 just as soon as you can.

Hideously effective, of course, your 77 grenades. I dare say you'd know them as White Phosphorus grenades – Willy Peter, as the Americans call them – and they're used for two main purposes. The first is the fairly innocuous one of laying down cover: when the phosphorus is exposed to air it burns to produce thick white smoke, such as the stuff now smothering our advance. The second – and this is why you hear the bleeding hearts get so uppity when it's used in places like Iraq – is for transforming your enemy into marshmallow toast. Soon as it sticks to your skin, white phosphorus, you've more or less had it. Impossible to extinguish it, you see. It just goes on burning: through leather, through cloth, through skin, flesh and bone, and short of cutting it out with your bayonet there's really nothing you can do.

This, I'm afraid, is what is now happening to the poor fellow who tried and failed to throw his grenade. Somehow – a bullet possibly – it has been detonated while still attached to his belt, and where this chap's stomach used to be is now an unattractive mess of charring, smoking intestines, cauterised flesh, and white-hot burning metal. He half-turns towards me, looking down, aghast, as if scarcely able to conceive that something so dreadful could possibly be happening to him and it's at this moment that I recognise him as Dent.

His screams of agony. Such screams.

He comes staggering down the hill towards me, his gaping midriff smoking like a bonfire.

'Shoot me,' he begs. 'Shoot me.'

I would, I want to, I'm trying but my trigger finger just won't respond. I'm thinking 'Dear God, this is awful. Somebody do something!' and I know it should be me, but I've become so involved with the ugliness of that wound, I can't seem to think straight.

Then Lt. Truelove is on him with his Colt .45 pressed against Dent's temple.

'Good lad!' he says with the warmest smile, and in his very last split second alive, Dent manages to return his saviour a semblance of a grin. Then his head evaporates in a mist of grey and red and white. And we're moving on, all of us, into the smoke, as if Dent had never been.

It must be around 2220 hours now. Darkness has descended on the hillside and we have reached the top of the zigzag path, the point at which Q and A troops are to split. Up until this stage, enemy resistance has proved surprisingly light. Indeed, apart from poor Dent, we've yet to lose a man. But from here on in, we can expect the going to get stickier. There are blockhouses and machine-gun nests at every turn, surrounded by minefields and coils of wire designed to funnel anyone trying to approach them straight into prepared fields of fire. It's too late to call in artillery or rocket support; we've no mortars; and we simply haven't the latitude to arrange for enfilading fire from our Brens. This is going to be a frontal assault in its purest and most brutal form: we shall split into groups and charge each individual position, guns blazing; and either the enemy will wipe us off the hill, or we shall prevail.

Everyone knows how fragile our position is, as we hit the ground and, crawling, deploy left or right in readiness for Capt. Dangerfield's signal. I don't recall being scared. More exhilarated than anything, and I'm sure it's the same for the others. Exhilaration, plus a hint of frustration. You're keyed up; you're in position; you know that the next minute is going to decide whether you live, die or, worse, get hit in some unmentionable part of your body, and you just want to get the damned business over with.

And there it is. A red flare in the sky, now parachuting downwards. You're cheering, bellowing your lungs out. The men either side of you are raising their battle-cry too, as their forebears would have done at Maldon and Hastings and Agincourt and Waterloo.

Up. Not as fast as you'd like. Nothing is. It's all in slow motion now. Unreal almost, pumped up as you are with anaesthetising adrenalin. Your senses are alive. You smell cordite and burnt grass; you smell sea tang and sweat. The noise is unimaginable. Red tracer cutting through the night. Into the inferno you advance, yelling, screaming; surrounded by your comrades yet eerily alone.

Occasionally, you'll see a khaki form in front of you, sometimes even a face you recognise, or a coil of wire to be cut or circumnavigated, or a machine-gun slit into which you can pop a grenade. From inside the bunker, a shout, then screams. Field-grey forms running; falling.

Thickening fire. All but impenetrable now. A huge blockhouse straight ahead and there's no way around it. We've got to take cover, got to, or we'll be wiped out in moments.

A trench. Swarming with commandos. Drop down to join them. Something soft underfoot. A dead German. Several dead Germans.

Still alive. However did I come through that? How did any of us?

Next to me, Dinning catches my eye. 'I knew your bees would be a problem,' he yells, as a stream of well-aimed Spandau bullets clips the lip of the trench parapet, then buzzes over our heads. He perches nonchalantly on a fire step just beneath and begins changing the steaming barrel on his Bren.

'Have you ever seen one?' I yell back.

And I uncurl my right palm and show him. I don't remember having picked it. Or rather I do, but only as if it were in a distant dream. It was when we had to hit the ground after the smoke barrage dissipated. I looked up, and there it was just a couple of inches from my nose – the most magnificent, plump bee orchid in shades of ginger and glowing viridian. Normally, I would never have thought to pluck it. But as I stared at it, I found myself filling with resentment that such a thing could blossom so cheerfully when, just a few yards ahead, a sweet boy was having his intestines incinerated; that this thing would be alive tomorrow, when most of us would surely be dead.

So I plucked it, to teach it a lesson.

'I'm afraid I need your botany student, Lieutenant,' shouts a voice behind me.

I look round. It's Capt. Dangerfield, a Colt .45 in his right hand, a Very pistol in his left. His face is flushed, his expression anxious.

'Dinning, old chap,' he says. 'On my signal, we're going to have a bash at that blockhouse. Straight in. Firing from the hip. You, me, Haines, Martley and Tomkins. Coward, I want the rest of the troop giving covering fire.'

'Sorry, I'm coming with you.'

'Lieutenant Coward, that was an order.'

'You'll remember that I have a promise to keep.'

'Then, damn it, come if you must. But, after this, consider yourself absolved. I'm quite big enough to take care of myself.'

He extends a hand. I clasp it tight.

'Well, good luck,' he says. 'And if it helps, I'm sorry.'

'What on earth for?'

'You know,' he says and before I can say more he's signalling to the four other commandos due to assault the pillbox. They reply with OK signs. Then he signals to Lt. Truelove on the left and Cpl. Blackwell on the right to begin rapid fire on the target. And no sooner has their first burst begun than he's up, with all five of us following, through a gap in the wire and towards that obstacle – a pillbox which can't be more than twenty yards away yet for the next few seconds will seem the most distant place on earth.

If there's noise, and I'm sure there is, I don't hear it. If there are bullets that come close to hitting me – and I know there are, for I'll later find the graze marks, one on my epaulette, the other on the top of my boot – I don't feel them. My gaze, my concentration, my every ounce of being are all fixed on a single purpose: I must reach that looming concrete bulk and kill its occupants before they kill me.

So far, it occurs to me with that cold, clear-headed detachment which often seems to descend on these occasions, they've been making a pretty poor hash of it. From within the slit, there are plenty of orange muzzle flashes but none of their bullets has yet found its mark, and time is running out for them, for quite shortly now we shall be on them, tossing in our grenades through the embrasure, smoking them out, and showing no mercy as they emerge, spluttering from the rear.

Capt. Dangerfield was ahead of me, but in the last moment I've edged ahead of him. He's much the faster sprinter, but he slowed his pace, just slightly, to beckon us forward and that was when I pressed home the advantage and now I'm in the lead. Quite what I'm racing for I'm not altogether sure. To reach the blockhouse first? To draw the enemy's fire and die the hero's death that covers my name in glory and – much more important – makes my father and Gina feel utterly dreadful? Buggered if I know. When you're charging an enemy position like this, believe me, you're beyond rational analysis. Either you do or you don't do. There's no time for logic, or consideration or doubt or fear. You're outside reason, outside time, existing purely in the moment. It's an extraordinary feeling. Some soldiers never stop chasing it.

Then something hard thumps into my right arm and, as I tumble leftwards, I glance round to see what it was – a bullet? A grenade? But it's not, it's Capt. Dangerfield, his left palm outstretched towards me as if he's just given me a hefty shove, perhaps, oh God, the silly brave fool, perhaps because of the dark cylinder of wood and metal which was destined to hit me, but which has now struck him, instead, in his face –

This is as much as I'm able to see before the momentum of his shove hurls me to the ground and, as I have done so often in training that it has become completely instinctive, I find myself somersaulting over my right shoulder to break my fall, aware that behind me, there has been a flash and a deafening bang.

For a while, I lie there, winded. Stunned by the blast.

When I pick myself up and look back I see Dinning on one knee, firing his Bren at the slit in the bunker. And lying next to him, two men, one wounded, one dead.

From the mouth of the bunker a white flag emerges.

Dinning stops firing.

The silence is so sudden and shocking it makes the ears ring.

The dead man is Capt. Dangerfield.

I crawl to his body just to be sure. But there's no doubt about it – he took that blast full in the face. Those handsome features are a shredded mess and his head is dripping gore. I lean close to his unhearing ear and whisper: 'My turn to apologise, old man. Sorry. Sorry for everything.'

I take his bloodied hand in mine, give it a squeeze, and remember with a lurch how warm and vital it felt when in my clasp not two minutes ago. When I let go and look up, I see commandos everywhere. The Germans from the bunker are filing out with their hands on their head; the wounded Martley is being tended by an orderly; from the darkness, from various corners of the enemy bunker system, there are cries of 'Kamerad'. Now an *Oberleutnant* with a white goatee beard has appeared. I hear him assure Lt. Truelove, in good English, that he will persuade the rest of his men to surrender.

The Eastern Feature is ours. But I take no satisfaction from this. Dazed and despondent, I stumble back towards the zigzag path, quite oblivious to the 'You all right, mate?'s and the pats on the back offered by the commandos coming in the opposite direction.

It isn't long before I have the path to myself. At first I don't know what I'm doing or where I'm going. But little by little – and the rational part of me doesn't seem to have been given much say in the matter – a plan is starting to form in my head. Something to do with Price, getting to his body at all costs. Only that way, a little voice is telling me, can I redeem myself.

Why does redemption lie that way? God knows. I think my brains have taken a knock from the grenade blast that finished off Capt. Dangerfield.

But it might also have something to do with my instinct for self-preservation telling me I have to retrieve the long letter I've been writing to Gina, so as to stop it falling into the wrong hands. Gina's hands, I mean.

Heavens, can't you just imagine it? She's just heard of the tragic selfless death of her hero husband, when along through the post comes this letter from the man who she'd sent to save him. And what does this letter say? Why only – after a series of protestations of undying love that may well make her want to bring up her breakfast – that her beloved husband is a prig, a fool and a cad of the first order.

You'll say that the chances of her ever getting this letter are slim. To which I'll say, even if they're virtually none, that's still not a risk I'm prepared to take.

The town is empty, save for the dead sprawled in the streets, and the occasional commando patrol. A marine from X troop sneaking a cigarette in a doorway confirms that our rear HQ has been overrun, but that the town is now pretty much secure. A sudden salvo which sends both of us diving for cover gives the lie to that. It seems to be directed towards the outer harbour, though, not us. We hurry to an upstairs room for a better view.

There, illuminated by tracer bullets and burning fuel, is the salvo's target. Moored against the harbour's eastern breakwater sit not one but two of those blasted German flakships, both taking hits from a warship – HMS *Ursa*, I later learn – not far offshore. We're just in time to catch two motor boats bursting into the harbour mouth, Lewis guns blazing. But it looks as if the shells from HMS *Ursa* have done their job for I don't see any fire being returned. One flakship collapses in the middle, its spine broken. The other slips slowly beneath the surface, till all that can be seen is its bridge.

'You heard what those bastards did to our lads up on that hill?' says the marine from X troop.

'My troop copped the worst of it,' I say. Then a thought suddenly occurs. I pull Capt. Dangerfield's letter from my breast pocket and say: 'I wonder whether you might do me a favour. Could you see that this makes it back safely to England?'

'Mate, if you can survive a frontal assault on that hill there, you can survive fucking anything. Give it to her yourself. I'm sure this girl – Gina Dangerfield, would that be the Captain's sister, poor girl? – will appreciate it a lot more coming from you.'

I give it to him anyway and make my way across the foot-bridge at the mouth of the inner harbour, past a group of matelots who have disembarked from the two motor boats, and up to the barbed wire at the base of the Rue du Phare. The houses around it are shuttered and dark; the road is silent.

I pick my way carefully through the wire and begin moving cautiously up the hill, keeping low so as to avoid being skylined, hugging the seaward side of the slope and making for the place where I last saw the bodies of my seven comrades.

They're still there, of course – it having been far too dangerous in daylight for our medics to try retrieving them (you'd try it for wounded soldiers of course but not dead ones) – all stiff and contorted where they fell.

The first I can't even recognise. His body is virtually unscathed but when he fell his face must have landed right in front of the nozzle of one of those concealed flame-throwers for his features have been charred beyond recognition.

A few yards further on I find Calladine, still wearing that awful doomed expression he had on as he filed down from Point 72 towards the start line. He was right, then.

I'm crawling now. The German positions are so near, you have to. God, we came so close. If it hadn't been for those flakships, we would have taken them easily. And Price and the rest might still be alive. And we might never have needed to storm the Eastern Feature. And instead of all this pain and misery, we'd all be in the port now, together, celebrating. If. If. If.

In my head, I have a clear snapshot of that vision of hell on the hill the instant before Capt. Dangerfield, Oily Wragg and I turned tail and fled for our lives. The six bodies I have crawled past so far are exactly where I remember them being. But not the seventh.

Price's is missing.

Why would the Germans do that, though? If they were going to retrieve one dead body, why not all of them? It doesn't make sense. I must be mistaken. Price must have fallen further round the hill than I remember. Or maybe lower. Or –

'Hände hoch!'

Spread-eagled, exposed, utterly undone, I know there's nothing I can do to save myself. The muzzle of my captor's rifle is barely an inch from my face.

Hands raised I pick myself, slowly, off the ground and turn to look down at my captor. His foxhole – some kind of forward observation position – has been camouflaged so perfectly you'd need almost to fall in before you'd know it was there.

With a jerk of his rifle, the German indicates that I should climb down to join him. They say the best time to escape is within the first ten minutes of being captured. But I don't even think about resisting as, my captor's muzzle pressed into the small of my back, I'm funnelled through the narrow earthen cleft which connects the OP with the main trench system.

As we emerge, another German joins us.

Together, the two men lead me further into the labyrinth of trenches. Fantastically well constructed, I can't help noticing, with sturdy concrete walls and protective overhangs, and neat little dug-outs with beds, chairs, tables and electric lights.

Finally, we reach a heavy metal door. The lead German rests his rifle against the wall so that he can wrest it open with both hands. An *Oberleutnant* is just emerging. He looks me up and down. Then observes to my captors: 'Ein anderer!'

They smile and nod.

In front of me is another flight of steps. Perhaps for the officer's benefit, I'm pushed down a bit too roughly.

At the bottom, there's another heavy steel door. My captors indicate that I should open it.

Inside, an adjutant with wire spectacles is at a desk, method-ically tearing documents into tiny strips. Scarcely looking up, he indicates that I should take a seat on the empty chair in the corner. My captor passes through a heavy curtain into a room next door. I hear him reporting my capture to someone he addresses as Herr Major.

I try to listen in, but now the adjutant says to the other German, who's standing with his rifle pointing at me: 'Put it away and make him some coffee. It'll be better for you in the end.'

The guard pulls a sour face but starts to do as he's told.

Next door, my captor is getting a rocket for leaving his post. And what if there were more commandos where I came from, the Major wants to know. On the Eastern Front, such negligence would be considered a capital offence.

And why not in France, too, asks another voice – high-pitched, nasty. Perhaps, the voice goes on, so salutary an example would serve to stiffen his comrades' resolve in the final defence.

'The final defence?' I hear the Major echo, mockingly. I'd like to listen more but perhaps I'm craning my ear too obviously or perhaps the adjutant is more observant than he looks, for he suddenly says: 'Ach, du sprichst also Deutsch?'

'I beg your pardon?'

'You were listening to the conversation,' he says in perfect English.

'Wishing I could understand it, yes. I get the impression that the poor chap who captured me is getting what we call a right-royal bollocking.'

'A right-royal bollocking. Such a rich and expressive language you have.'

'You speak it very well.'

'I try. But my colloquial English is, I fear, somewhat wanting.'

My captor, very red-faced, now emerges from behind the curtain, frantically adjusting his helmet and bustling towards the exit as if his life depended on it.

The other German, meanwhile, has made my coffee, which he serves me in a rather disgusting-looking enamel mug.

'I'm sorry that we cannot offer you tea but our empire has never extended as far as India. And the way things are now progressing, I doubt it ever will.'

He's an engaging fellow and I'd dearly love to give his conversation more attention. Problem is, the one next door is rather more pertinent to my future.

'. . . of course they must be killed,' the high-pitched nasty voice is saying. 'Those are the Führer's orders.'

'And how will their comrades treat our prisoners, do you think, Herr Hauptmann, when they discover what we have done to theirs?'

'They are not going to take any prisoners,' replies the high-pitched voice. 'Because we are not going to surrender.'

'I see,' says the Major.

'Would you rather that I just remained silent?' the adjutant asks me.

'I'm sorry,' I said. 'I was just dreaming of empire and fine India tea.'

'No, you weren't, you were listening to the Major and the *Hauptmann*. Your German is excellent, my friend. But your acting, quite atrocious.'

I sip my coffee. Revolting. But at least it's hot and warm.

'It is a pity,' says the German. 'In another world I could have asked you where you learned it and complimented you as you have complimented me. We would have got on rather well, I think.'

'We *are* getting on rather well, aren't we?'

The adjutant laughs. Then his smile fades.

'I am sorry,' he says.

'What on earth for?'

'If the *Hauptmann* should prevail. You may have gathered,

he is a committed party member. And as with so many, his heart has been hardened by the Eastern Front.'

'I'm not sure I understand your meaning.'

'If you don't know, then perhaps it is better you remain in ignorance.'

The curtain is ripped open. A man in a *Hauptmann*'s uniform appears and studies me with ostentatious contempt. His face, heavily scarred down one side with only a hole where his ear should be, is young but his eyes have the rheumy distance of an old man's and his short hair is grey. I have an awful feeling we've met before.

With a crook of his index finger, he beckons me in.

The Major is behind a desk, in front of a brimming ashtray. He lights a cigarette from the stub of its predecessor and eyes me up and down. Friendly enough face, but it's not the Major I'm worried about. The *Hauptmann* is continuing to stare at me hard. God, I really do know him, I think. When his hair was dark and he still had an ear.

'Cigarette?' says the Major.

'Thanks, but I don't,' I lie, which hurts because if there's one thing I do very much need right now it's a restorative puff. Thing is, though, I don't want to do anything that might make Kimmelman recognise me. That's his name. Franz Kimmelman. We served together on the *Ostfront* and it's a long story which I shall have to tell you another time. Suffice to say that when I left him for dead we weren't the best of friends.

'Your name?'

'Coward. Acting-Lieutenant Dick Coward,' I say, extending a hand. 'And you must be . . . ?'

'Major Thomas Wiesenbach,' he says, not shaking my hand – which doesn't altogether surprise me, but which is a pity none the less. If I'm going to persuade him not to shoot me it would help if we could establish some sort of bond.

'Herr Major, I know this man and he is a traitor,' says Kimmelman.

'Thank you, Captain, you may question him in a moment. Lieutenant Coward, you must tell me —'

'Herr Major, his name is Dieter Maier, he is a deserter from the *Wehrmacht*.'

'Is this true, Lieutenant Coward?'

'I'm frightfully sorry, Major, but I'm afraid I didn't understand hide nor hair of what your man was saying.'

'He's lying. He's lying,' shrieks Hauptmann Kimmelman. 'I can prove it.'

And, as I rather feared he might, he makes a sudden dive for my trousers. I side-step in the nick of time. But Kimmelman, now on his knees, is grabbing at my belt and shouting 'Guards! Guards!' while I try to fend him off. If he succeeds in getting my trousers off, I'm a goner.

Suddenly there's a sharp and terrible pain behind one of my knees, and I buckle on to the floor. Having hobbled me with the butt of his rifle, the guard has now seized both of my arms, giving Kimmelman free rein to go to work on my belt.

'Major,' I cry, wriggling desperately. 'By the Geneva Convention I ask you to stop this man!'

'The only convention for traitors is death,' snarls Kimmelman, as he undoes my belt. Now he's yanking at my trouser tops, as I swerve and writhe and lash out with my head, my teeth, anything I can to stop this man exposing the tattoo which will surely give me away.

'Kimmelman, stop!' says the Major.

Kimmelman does not stop.

'Kimmelman,' repeats the Major, but more in a tone of resignation than decisive command. And I know at this point that I'm lost. The Major has relinquished control. It is Kimmelman who will decide my fate.

My trousers are being pulled down. The tattoo is on the verge of being revealed. But suddenly, here's the adjutant, with a Luger pointed at the *Hauptmann*'s head.

'What the hell do you think you're doing?' asks Kimmelman.

'I believe the Major gave you an order,' says the adjutant calmly.

'I was merely trying to demonstrate –' begins Kimmelman.

'The rape of prisoners is never acceptable,' says the adjutant.

'Rape?' shrieks Kimmelman. 'How dare you, you homosexual pig? You might be interested in this man's arse but I, I was –'

'Herr Major,' says the adjutant, 'shall I have the prisoner removed until you are in a better position to continue your interrogation?'

'Thank you, Tretter,' says the Major.

The adjutant, his Luger still pointed at the *Hauptmann*, nods to the guard. I'm pulled upwards and, trousers still half-way down my legs, I'm manhandled out of the Major's office and down another passageway which leads off from the adjutant's ante-room. At the end is another steel door, with a grille on it. I have to wait on my knees, hands behind my head, while the guard unlocks it.

He pulls it open. Inside, an electric light flickers feebly. On the wall opposite is a poster declaiming Hitler's order regarding the treatment of captured commandos. Beneath it is a narrow camp-bed. Sitting on the bed, his back propped against the wall, his face bruised and speckled with congealed blood, is a man in khaki uniform. He looks at me, deeply unimpressed by what he sees.

'What did you go and get yourself captured for?' he says. 'You stupid, stupid sod.'

18

Adieu or Au Revoir?

The beach we landed on just over a fortnight ago is barely recognisable. No bodies; no wire; no mines (one hopes), no obstacles save the odd defiant Czech hedgehog and stubbornly embedded girder. The burnt-out tanks have been towed clear; the smaller of the wrecked landing craft – though not the big LCT painted 'LOOTERS WILL BE SHOT' – have been variously salvaged or cut up for scrap. The bunkers have been transformed into ops rooms, dressing stations, command posts, bomb shelters. The craters have been filled with fascines, there are corrugated metal strips to ensure that no one gets stuck, and signs so that no one gets lost. Where once was chaos, destruction and terror there now, on pain of arrest by the Military Police, reigns order and efficiency and relative calm.

Sgt. Price and I are sitting atop a sea wall, not far from where we first came ashore, watching the big ships weave in and out of the Mulberry harbour with a dexterity almost miraculous when you consider that, till war broke out, half their commanders had probably never even sailed a dinghy. We watch some of the millions of tons of supplies being hoisted and ferried and driven ashore with a swiftness that would give the work-to-rule dockers back home a coronary, and the landing craft bringing fresh waves of armour, troops and ammunition in readiness for the assault on Caen, and the Normandy breakout.

A keen young platoon of Cheshires marches briskly by. A baby-faced private is trying unsuccessfully to hide his awe at our green berets, our commando flashes and our stagnant, battle-worn air.

'Eyes front, you tosspots!' bellows his sergeant, exchanging a scowl with Price.

'I give 'em a week, tops,' mutters Price. His mood has not been improved by the week we've just spent being eaten alive by mosquitoes, cowering in trenches and shelled to buggery by 88s and Nebelwerfers and God knows what else. For all of which, I need hardly add, he blames me.

'Excuse me, Sarge,' says a timid little voice. 'Are you by any chance from 47 (RM) Commando?'

'Now, what's this? A matelot who can read and count?' says Price.

The boy who has asked the question – and he really can't be more than sixteen, but then they do recruit them young in the Navy – shrinks beneath his navy-issue hard hat.

'Only my big brother's with 47 and I was wondering whether you knew him.'

'Does he have a name?' asks Price, gruffly. He's a hard old bastard, as you know, but I'll bet like me his heart's in his mouth as he asks it. Please, we're both thinking, please let it not be one of the boys we've just buried.

'Neillands,' says the boy. 'Arthur Neillands.'

'Never heard of him. What troop?'

'Y, I think.'

'That'll be why, then,' says Price. 'We're A.'

'But you'll have a better idea what he's up to. Last Mum or I heard of him, he was training in St Ives.'

'Ah well, he's moved on since then. He took Port-en-Bessin, you heard about that?'

'No.'

'Nice to know our efforts have been so widely appreciated, eh, Price?'

'Sorry. We don't get to hear many of the names at sea. Just grid references. This port anywhere near here?'

'Not far, but your brother will have moved on by now. To somewhere else you won't have heard of called Sallenelles.'

'All right, is it?'

'Lovely. Hot showers every day. Clean sheets. Lashings of delicious grub. Not a mosquito or Nebelwerfer for miles around,' says Price.

Young Neillands looks askance at me: 'He's joking, isn't he?'

'Conceivably,' I say.

'Well, at least I know. At least I've got something to tell Mum.'

'Tell her your brother's doing all right,' says Price.

'I thought you didn't know him.'

'Yeah, but your mum's not going to know that, is she?'

Neillands smiles shyly. 'I suppose,' he says. 'Nice talking to you. Thanks.'

He begins walking away and hasn't gone far, no more than twenty yards, when the scream of a shell sends both Price and me diving sideways for cover. It's close, very close. This is what I meant earlier when I talked about the calm being 'relative'.

At the bottom of the crater all that's left of Neillands is his hard hat. I pick it up and stare at the name stencilled on to it. HMS EMERALD. It's familiar for some reason. Then I remember someone telling me that this was one of the ships that provided our support bombardment prior to the assault on Port-en-Bessin.

Damn! If only I'd remembered this a minute earlier. He would have been so proud, that lad, to know of the vital part he'd played in his big brother's finest hour. And maybe, I think to myself as the words HMS EMERALD start to blur and swim, maybe if I had remembered that detail the conversation would have gone on longer and he'd still be talking to us now, instead of . . .

I wipe my eyes with the back of my hand. There are pale streaks in the dirt and I wonder to myself: why now? I didn't when Dent and Mayhew copped one. And I didn't when I buried Calladine, and Coffin and all the other boys. I didn't because, after a time, you become inured to death as a soldier, you have to or you're in trouble. But you can't keep it up all the time. Every now and then, the surface cracks and it all comes rushing out, with the hurt, the fear, the pity, the regret. They were living, breathing human beings, all those dead boys. They wanted to go on living every bit as much as you and I do. They too wanted children, grandchildren, the love of a good woman, a ripe old age.

Price has got an arm round my shoulder and he's saying to me, in just the soft tone he did when I took a fall that snowy day on Hay Bluff with the Radnor and West Hereford and the ground was too hard and I broke my collar bone: 'It's all right, Mr Richard. Let's just get you to a medic.'

'I don't need a medic. I'll be all right. Just give me a moment.'

'Let's just let them have a look at you, all the same,' he says, steering me towards a tent with a red cross on it. 'You might need a few stitches in that arm.'

My arm?

It's only then that I become aware of the dull ache in my left bicep; and the blood dripping from the end of my fingers; and the tear and dark, sticky stain in the sleeve of my battle-dress; and the shard of twisted metal protruding from my exposed white flesh.

*   *   *

What you will, of course, be wondering is just how Price and I got out of that mess we were in two weeks ago, imprisoned on the Western Feature with my old friend Franz Kimmelman itching to fulfil his Führer's Commando Order.

Well, I'd love to be able to spin you a yarn about how we overcame our guards, seized their weapons and blasted our way to freedom. But I'm afraid the reality was a lot more prosaic: the garrison decided to surrender.

I remember we were having a blazing row at the time, Price and me. For most of the night we had been getting on as well as it's possible to do when you're lying, sardine fashion, on a single, narrow, lice-ridden bed in a cold, damp cell in the pitch blackness under threat of imminent death.

First thing we did, obviously, was run through the escape options. I had in my boots, as did Price, a length of thin serrated wire known as a Gigli, which looks like a shoelace but doubles as a very handy saw. Unfortunately, our cell being underground, there were no window bars to cut through. Nor did our usual Plan B turn out to be of much use. I pretended to writhe about on the floor with stomach pains while Price banged on the cell door and shouted for assistance, but either our captors couldn't hear or they had better things to do.

After ten minutes bellowing ourselves hoarse, we gave up. Price wanted to know how the assault had gone; I pretended to be interested in his account of his capture after being concussed by an enemy grenade, when of course all I really wanted to know was what the hell he'd done with my letter to Gina.

''Aven't got it,' says Price.

'What do you mean? I gave it to you to keep safe.'

'You wanted it posted on to Lady Gina, didn't you?'

'I *did*.'

'Well, that's just what I did. Bumped into some boys from

the RASC as we were heading to the start line. Passed it to their sergeant. Job done.'

'But, Price, I never wanted it sent.'

'You said a moment ago you did.'

'Yes, I *did*. But not any more.'

'Hardly my fault if you keep changing your mind.'

'I trusted you, Price, to look after my best interests. The fact is you have betrayed that trust.'

'Oh, I have, have I? Sooner she reads that letter, I reckon, the better for us all.'

'And what do you mean by that?'

'Nothing.'

'Have you been reading my private correspondence?'

Price doesn't answer.

'My God, that's why you sent it, isn't it? You want to make me look a fool.'

'You don't exactly make it hard.'

'Price, you are despicable!'

'She's wrong for you, that girl. Always said so.'

'Damn it, I'm quite old enough to make my own decisions. You have behaved —'

'Shh!' says Price suddenly, springing from the bed and starting to pad towards the cell door. I, meanwhile, resume my groaning noises. Well, it's worth a try.

The cell door swings open. A bright light is shone in my face.

'Please, please. I need a doctor,' I groan.

'Gentlemen,' comes the reply, 'there is really no need for this play-acting. We have come to offer you our surrender.'

And so it is that Price and I make our triumphal return into Port-en-Bessin at the head of a column of twenty-six prisoners. (There ought, incidentally, to have been more, but under the terms we agreed, those Germans who wished to run away rather than surrender were to be indulged. Among them was dear old Kimmelman.)

Now, you might think that this would be enough to put our CO in the best of moods. But not a bit of it. Having remembered – only just – to congratulate Price for having taken the surrender, the CO moves on to the business he most cares about. Which is to say he calls for my troop sergeant-major – a belligerent Scotsman by the name of Gove – and says I'm to be put on fatigues until further notice, while he decides how best to punish me for a string of alleged offences including insubordination, desertion of post, dereliction of duty and conduct prejudicial to the good order of the Commando. As for my brief promotion-in-the-field to the rank of lieutenant – I need hardly tell you that the CO refuses to ratify it. Indeed, he refuses even to acknowledge that I had anything to do with the attacks on the Eastern Feature – neither the first probing mission, nor Capt. Dangerfield's assault.

First job I'm given is to help retrieve our boys' bodies and see that they're properly buried. This I don't mind too much, as it happens. For one thing, the corpses are still fresh and more or less intact, and it's only really when they're rotten and in bits – or worse: if you've ever tried scraping a crew from the insides of a brewed-up tank, you'll know what I mean – that it becomes seriously unpleasant. For another, it gives me the chance to say my farewells.

We find a lovely spot for them, just above the Rue du Phare, where they can rest with a fine view of the sea. Obviously, the graves are only temporary. Eventually, they'll find their way to the British cemetery in Bayeux, where you can see them today. But even when you're burying your comrades as a stopgap measure, you want to do things properly: treat them with the same respect you like to think they would have afforded you if the positions had been reversed. That's what we decide, anyway – me and the three other marines on burial duty, Lee, Donald and Hogg. The ground would have been much more friable and easier to dig further down the hill. But the spot wouldn't have been nearly so fitting for a fallen warrior.

Where we can, we try to ensure that the boys we knew, we bury personally.

'Here's a handsome lad,' says Lee, peering under a canvas sheet. 'Anyone recognise him?'

'One of mine, I think,' I say, going over to inspect. 'Yes. That's Mayhew. Jack Mayhew.'

'Blimey, some blokes have all the luck. You'd never have trouble pulling with a face like that, would you?' says Lee with feeling. Understandably, for he has a face like a bucket.

'I'm not sure that he ever managed, though,' I say.

'Wot. Never got his end away? Not even once? Wot a waste. Wot a fucking, tragic waste.'

'Carpe diem,' I murmur.

'Eh?'

'Latin for: grab it while you still can.'

'A-fucking-men to that. That's going to be my motto from now on. Carp and Demon. Them Romans knew what they were talking about.'

Capt. Dangerfield is the last to be interred. I would have liked to have spent some time alone with him to tell him how sorry I am and how grateful – for at the back of my mind there will always be the lingering suspicion that he died taking the blast of the grenade that was really intended for me. But by the time I have begun digging his grave, I've been joined by half his troop, all eager to pay their last respects to the officer they so admired. The other half arrives just in time to see Lt. Truelove and me lowering him into the ground.

'You made it up, I gather,' murmurs Lt. Truelove.

'He told you that?'

'He did and I'm glad.'

The next day, more fatigues – this time at the foot of Point 72, where with two stretcher bearers named Barnard and Roberts I've been charged with cleaning up after the Germans who overran our rear HQ on the night of the seventh.

We pause for a cigarette and a brew to survey our handiwork. The dug-out still looks mildly disgusting, but you should have seen it when we arrived – soiled bandages, turds, pools of vomit, almost as if the Germans knew they weren't going to be there for long and just wanted to make things as uncomfortable as possible for our return.

'Your turn, mate,' says Barnard, indicating the two buckets of sloppy excreta awaiting incineration.

'Oh Lord. Is it really?'

With a sigh, I take a bucket in each hand, heading for the foul-smelling diesel-fuelled pyre on the far side of the road. I'm half-way across, lost in thought, wishing myself anywhere but here I dare say, when I'm suddenly aware of something rocketing round the bend towards me. There's a screech of rubber, and I'm damned near knocked over by some idiot going much too fast on a motor cycle. Fortunately it's the bucket he catches with his tyre, not me, but the result as the bucket flies upwards and dumps its contents on top of us in a shower of brown rain isn't pretty.

'What the hell do you think you're doing?' says the rider, picking himself off the ground.

'I might ask the same of you,' I say. But then I notice the other motor-cycle outrider smirking at us both a few yards ahead and the convoy which has ground to a halt in front of the fallen motor cycle and all becomes clear. Second from the front of the convoy is a staff car with pennants fluttering and two top brass in the back. One is dressed conventionally with a general's peaked cap; the other has a distinctive woollen sweater tight on his slight wiry frame and a black tank-brigade beret with two badges on it. I muster a hasty salute.

'Who is that man?' asks a reedy voice I know quite well. We have met on more than one occasion, General Bernard Montgomery and I.

'Sir, he's from 47 (RM) Commando,' calls back Monty's ADC, who has hopped from the staff car's passenger seat to investigate the hold-up.

'Forty-seven? Why, splendid,' announces Monty. 'The very unit I am here to congwatulate. Are the photogwaphers weady? Will you call them over? It looks so much better, I find, when these impwomptu meetings aren't staged.'

'Sir, I'm not sure that's wise,' says the ADC. 'He's a little, um, dirty.'

'Dirty. Well, of course he is. He's just secured the Bwitish army's wight flank. Send him over. I wish to shake his hand. And those photogwaphers. Call them up, at once.'

The ADC beckons me towards him. I come to a halt and salute. Having surveyed me for a moment with a pained expression, he reaches into a pocket, pulls out a handkerchief and begins dabbing at my uniform – as an anxious mother might do to her son on a school prize day.

'That'll have to do. Off you go.'

The three army photographers have appeared now, one American, one British, one Canadian, flashbulbs at the ready. I come to attention next to the staff car's running board and give the General my smartest salute. The flashbulbs pop.

'At ease, mawine. And tell me your name,' he says, wrinkling his nose.

'Marine Coward, sir.'

A journalist in uniform steps forward, notepad at the ready.

'Coward?' says the General, furrowing his brow and studying

me more closely. 'Why Coward, so it is you, what an extwaor-dinawy coincidence. I have with me a dispatch from the War Office, which your father asked me to pass on, recalling you for special duties.'

'Really, sir?'

'But, as a courtesy, I would pwefer to do so when your CO is pwesent. Can you spare a moment fwom your duties?' He turns to his bony-faced neighbour, who, like Monty himself, is wearing a trim moustache. For my father's generation of officers they were almost *de rigueur*: designed to stop your men noticing that your upper lip's quivering, or so one story has it. I recognise this fellow as General Miles Dempsey, commander of the British Second Army. 'Miles, do you mind if Mawine Coward sits with us? You'll wemember his father, Ajax.'

'Ajax Coward's boy, are you? I served with your papa in Flanders. It's him I have to thank for this,' he says, stroking the white and purple ribbon of his MC. With a skeletal hand General Dempsey taps the seat next to him.

I squeeze between the Generals, cringing at the thought of all that Hunnish excrement being transferred from my battledress to their freshly pressed uniforms. The Generals politely affect not to notice the wafts of shite drifting upwards to their nostrils – having both served in the trenches, they're made of sterner stuff – but even so, I feel it's only decent at least to apologise for this ruddy great elephant in the drawing-room.

'I'm very sorry about the smell.'

'Always been your style, though, hasn't it, hmm, Coward?' says Monty. 'Never happier than when you're up to your neck in it.'

'Damn it, now I remember – your brigade commander was talking about you at dinner only the other night,' says General

Dempsey. 'Can he really have got it right, though? That your papa has decided to pass on Great Meresby to whichever one of you boys has the best war?'

'I'm afraid it is, sir.'

'Wank, that's what you need,' says General Montgomery.

'Sir?'

'Wank and gongs. That's what your father's looking for. And I can pwomise plenty of opportunities for both where you're going next. Planned the opewation myself, so I should know.'

'I look forward to it very much, sir.'

We pass through a succession of checkpoints and into the ruined port, the smell of my uniform now happily smothered by the reek of spilt fuel. The once-empty streets are abustle as the rubble is cleared, the town made habitable and control assumed by the Army Port Authority. The Pipe-Line Under The Ocean (PLUTO) has already arrived and now there are fat petrol pipes snaking down every street, pumping fuel into ranks of hungry tankers. We're forced to park by the church and make the last part of the journey to the CO's waterfront HQ on foot.

'Quite extraordinary,' murmurs General Dempsey, looking up towards the defences on the Eastern Feature. 'And you took it with how many men, you say?'

'About thirty, sir.'

'Thirty, by God. I should have thought 300 too few.'

'Captain Dangerfield did a fine job.'

'Dangerfield. That's the chap who was . . .'

'Killed storming the last blockhouse. Yes, sir. He showed courage of the highest order and the course of the battle might have been very different had it not been for his sterling example.'

'Heavy hint being dropped there, eh, Miles?' says General Montgomery.

'Hint duly noted,' says General Dempsey. 'But let's leave it to your CO, shall we, to tell us which of your chaps deserves a posthumous VC. Ah. Now, is that him I see over there? Wearing a face like thunder.'

It is indeed the CO that General Dempsey has spotted and the reason for his rage is not hard to fathom. He didn't send me to shovel shit on Point 72 in order for me to return three hours later with a general on either arm, hogging the limelight that should by rights be his.

Once salutes have been exchanged and introductions effected, Monty says: 'Colonel Partwidge, your achievement here has been wemarkable and I salute you. Mawine Coward has been telling us of the bwavewy shown by Captain Dangerfield.'

'Indeed, sir,' says the CO. 'I shall be recommending him for the highest honour.'

'As has Marine Coward,' says General Dempsey, with a faint smirk.

'Marine Coward is being a little presumptuous, I would suggest, sir, being as he was nowhere near the Eastern Feature at the time.'

I shouldn't of course. It's quite the wrong thing to do. But in the awkward pause that follows, I just can't help myself.

'With respect, sir,' I say. 'I was next to Captain Dangerfield when he died.'

'Contwadicting a senior officer. Doesn't sound vewy wespectful to me,' says Monty.

'No disrespect intended, sir,' I say. 'I was merely hoping to apprise my commander fully of the disposition of his troops at the time of the incident.'

The CO has turned very pale. And it's true, I really have pushed things far further than I ought. So it's perhaps just as well that at this point General Dempsey steps in to defuse the tension.

'Very commendable, I'm sure,' he says. 'Now, perhaps, Colonel, if you'd care to lead our tour, we can allow Marine Coward to return to his duties.'

'Or wather,' says Monty, 'to pwepare for his departure. Colonel, I'm sorry I have to welieve you of two of your best men, but I bwing instructions fwom the War Office calling Mawine Coward and Sarnt Price for special duties with First Airborne Division.'

'Would that be with immediate effect, sir?' asks the CO.

'Why, yes. I believe it is. They are to be given a fortnight's shore leave, first.'

I don't know whether anyone else notices, but I certainly do: the faintest flicker of a smile twitching the CO's prim little mouth, before he says: 'Sir, I feel I must protest in the strongest terms. We're badly understrength as it is. Could their departure not be delayed until reinforcements arrive. For a fortnight at least?'

'Seems a reasonable enough request, wouldn't you say, Mawine Coward? Another fortnight in the line is much more your style, I would have thought, than two weeks' sybawitic excess in some Bayeux grand hotel.'

'Quite so,' agrees General Dempsey. 'And your dear papa, I'm sure, would wish it no other way.'

How Price got to hear of that exchange I'll never know. (From one of the marines scrounging for the fags Monty kept tossing to all and sundry, I would guess.) But hear of it he must have done because every time he volunteered me for a standing patrol in Sallenelles, he'd always say the same thing: 'Coming for some sybawitic excess at the Grand Hotel?'

There's a book to be written about that fortnight of hell. Living in trenches, plagued by rats, lice, mosquitoes, mortar stonks and 88 airbursts, I got an inkling of how it might have been that my father ended up so bonkers. Price too, come to think of it.

But we'll talk about Sallenelles some other time, for I want to tell you of an extraordinary sequence of events on the beach after I'd got that chunk of shrapnel lodged in my arm. Everything happens for a reason, I always say. And while I'm not sure that young Neillands would necessarily concur, I shall be for ever slyly grateful to whichever *Schweinehund* it was that sent the shell on to that particular section of beach at that particular moment. It meant that instead of hanging around, kicking my heels, I ended up being steered by Price to the nearest medical tent.

And you'll never guess who brushes past us in the entrance, as he hauls out a vile-smelling bucket filled to the brim with blackened old dressings. He doesn't say anything. In fact I might not even have noticed − just another German pris-oner in field grey, pressed into service as a low-grade orderly − if it hadn't been the quick, shifty look he gave Price and me.

'Good Lord, was that who I think it was?' I say to Price.

'Yes. Stupid bastard,' says Price.

'Lucky bastard, surely? You realise he was that sniper − the one Bridgeman was going to −'

'It was Bridgeman I was talking about.'

'Stupid bastard, you say? I'd say it was rather decent of him. The quality of mercy, and all that.'

'And when that evil bugger gets away, as a pound to a penny he will, and has another of our lads in his sights, what then? Will the quality of *his* mercy be strange, do you reckon?'

'I think you mean "strained".'

'Never mind that, you know what I'm getting at.'

Fortunately, I'm spared having to concede Price's point

because I've just spotted the next big coincidence. There among the crowd of wounded, nursing a very black and swollen-looking ankle, is an old and most unexpected friend.

'Fruity!'

You haven't met 'Fruity' Massingberd, yet, so you won't be as excited as I was. Went through quite a bit together in the Western Desert, Fruity and me, not to mention Crete, and I'd honestly never expected to see him alive again.

'Dick Coward, as I live and breathe.'

Once I've registered with the Medical Officer in charge of casualty clearance – I might be in for a long wait, he warns – I budge into a space next to Fruity on one of the wooden packing crates that are serving as chairs. We exchange notes, most of it bad news about the mutual friends who've been killed in the interim.

'You'll have heard about Flash, of course?' he says.

'I did, I did, poor bugger.'

'And you know Keith bought it last week?'

'How could I have done?'

'Figure of speech, dear boy. Terrible business.'

'I hope you don't mean Keith Douglas.'

'I'm sorry. Were you close?'

'Was he ever that close to anyone? Terrific poet though. Do you remember that wonderful line "It is not gunfire I hear, but a hunting horn"?'

'I've had precious little of that, the last five seasons, let me tell you. If this show goes on much longer I think I'll have forgotten what a fox looks like.'

'All the more reason for defeating that bugger Hitler quickly, then. You realise, if we let him win, hunting will be one of the first things he bans?'

Quite possibly we've been baying rather loudly. For the para-trooper perched next to me on the corner of the crate – runty fellow with a touch of the Bolsheviks about him; acted a touch peeved when I squeezed between him and Fruity – this last remark is the final straw.

'You may be fighting this war so's you can carry on hunting, mate. But the rest of us are fighting it so's we no longer have to live in a country run by the likes of you,' he says, not catching our eyes, obviously. Just announcing it, like you might from the platform at a trade-union meeting. There are one or two grunts of assent, too, which is a bit worrying. Mind you, when you've been waiting for hours and you're stuck with bits of shrapnel and such like, I don't suppose you're ever likely to be in the best of moods.

Well, you know me. Ever one to pour oil on troubled waters. Problem is, a pretty young nurse chooses just this moment to come bustling past, and puts a naughty idea in my head.

'Nurse, excuse me,' I say.

'Yes?'

'I think my friend here needs urgent treatment.'

'He's been assessed as non-urgent. He'll just have to wait his turn.'

'But, nurse, you don't understand. It's his shoulder. He's got a chip of wood lodged into it, a really big one, and I think it might be life-threatening.'

'I'll give you life-threatening, Royal!' says the para, getting off his chair and raising his fists.

'Sir!' calls the nurse to the Medical Officer.

'You, Private – what the devil do you think you're playing at?' calls the MO from behind his desk.

'He was asking for it, sir he –'

'Private, sit down now!'

The para sits down.

'Gentlemen,' continues the MO, 'this is a casualty clearing station, not the storming of the Winter Palace' (a significant

307

glance here at the private) '. . . nor the Normandy branch of White's' (a reproachful look at me). 'If you're not prepared to treat it as such, I shall have to ask you to leave. Understood?'

Before I can say anything more, Fruity has popped a lighted cigarette in my mouth and it's probably just as well, for there are few things that get my goat quite like inverted snobbery. I've seen where it leads — show trials and bullets in the back of the skull — and I'm firmly of the view that it should be sat on and squashed at every opportunity.

A few drags on that cigarette, though, and I'm feeling altogether more beneficent towards our Bolshie chum. He warms up a bit too after we've exchanged a few anecdotes about Sallenelles, which we both know very well because it was our unit that relieved his — and bloody grateful to us he ought to be, I tell him, and he almost cracks a smile. Then it's Fruity's turn to ruin things by bellowing into our conversation with what he mistakenly imagines is a whisper: 'I say, isn't that Lord Brecon's girl?'

I'm so busy wincing at the damage this remark is going to cause to my hard-won Man of the People credentials that for a brief moment the girl's identity doesn't register.

When it does, the bottom drops out of the stomach and my cheeks turn cold. I look up to check. God, it is. It really is her. And I can't immediately make up my mind whether I'm thrilled or ashamed or piqued.

She has her back turned to us because she's talking to the MO, who she has been told might have some mail for her.

'You're in luck,' says the MO, beaming up at her with the shit-eating grin of the hopelessly smitten. ('Join the queue, old boy,' I'm thinking. 'Join the queue.') He passes her a sheaf of letters, the topmost of which I recognise instantly, because damn it, it's in my handwriting.

'Gina?'

She's dressed not as a nurse, but in a uniform I can't immediately place. American? No, Free French.

'Dick!'

Her enthusiasm is gratifying, but I'm blushing madly —
like when you're at school and you've been allowed into town
with your chums and you bump into a pretty girl you know
from home and your chums regard you with a mix of envy
and disgust. He knows her? Why does he know her, lucky
beggar? What on earth does she see in a hideous poltroon like
him . . .

'Darling, what have you done to your poor arm?' she says.
Oh, God, worse and worse. It's like being mollycoddled by
your big sister on sports day.

'Just a scratch,' I say. 'Gina, do you remember Fruity? Fruity
Massingberd?'

'Yes, of course I do. How are you?'

'Oh, you know. Can't complain.'

'Dick, we've so much to catch up on, do you think the MO
would mind awfully if I treated you myself? Shall I ask?'

I feel a bit of a heel, abandoning Fruity like that, but needs
must and of course he'd have done exactly the same in my
shoes, the randy bugger. So we leave the medical tent, Gina
and I, followed by a certain amount of jealous chuntering and
the odd wolf whistle, and weave our way through crates of
supplies, jerry cans of fuel, cases of ammo, past jeeps and lorries
and Bren Carriers, into the relatively quiet corner where she
has left her vehicle, under guard.

'Thank you SO much,' she says to the young private who
has been looking after it.

'Pleasure, ma'am,' he says and clearly means it. 'Gave it a
polish for you, ma'am,' he adds, lingering.

'So I see, thank you. You're an angel. Now, if you wouldn't
mind leaving us.'

'Yes, ma'am.'

'Well?' says Gina.

'I'm impressed,' I say, inspecting the open-topped Mercedes which until recently must surely have belonged to a high-ranking German. 'Yours?'

'Colonel de Villefort's, really. He's the Free French liaison officer. I'm his driver.'

'I didn't know you spoke French.'

'I'm learning.'

'I'll bet,' I'm tempted to say, but I bite my tongue. I'm quite sure it's all perfectly innocent. She's in mourning, after all. At least, I assume she is. My God. What if the news has failed to reach her?

From inside the car she retrieves a box of sterile dressings, medical instruments, sulpha powder and iodine. She fills a billycan of water and sets it to boil.

When finally she looks up at me, I know at once that she knows. Now that we're alone, her composure has begun to collapse.

I take her hands and squeeze them gently.

'I'm so sorry,' I say. 'I let you down.'

'You did your best, I'm sure you did. Was it quick?'

'He felt nothing.'

Her blue, tear-swollen eyes search mine, wanting to believe what I'm saying is true. 'Before it happened, did he – did he say anything – about me?'

'He gave me this.' I hand her the letter. She clutches it, hands trembling, just staring at the writing on the front. The last words her husband ever wrote.

'If you'd like to read it now, in privacy, I can –'

'No, please, there's time enough for that,' she says, trying to sound brisk. 'Your arm. We don't want you losing it to gangrene.'

Having boiled her instruments, she arranges them on a strip of clean cloth on the car's bonnet. Gently, she undoes my dressing.

'Who put this on?'

'Price.'

'He did a good job.'

'Doesn't he always?'

'Where is he now?' she says, probing the wound.

'Just gone to sort out our embarkation. I didn't say – we've been called back to England. I'd been planning to drop in on you.'

'I would have liked that,' she says, her voice beginning to crack. 'If I'd known you were coming, I might not . . . gosh, it's all so confusing, I don't know, I might –'

'Ow!'

'God, Dick, I'm so, so sorry,' she says, pulling away from my arm.

'No, it's OK. Just stung a bit, that's all.'

'No, not just for that. For everything. It's all my fault. You must hate me!'

'Gina –'

'And you'd be right to hate me, too. I'm a stupid, stupid girl and I know it and I'm trying to change, I promise. It's why I came here, to be in the thick of it, because I knew I'd either grow up or end up dead, and I don't mind which, just so long as I stop being the hateful, hateful person I was.'

'Gina, stop it. You're loved. You're very loved. I love you.'

'That's sweet of you to say so but I don't deserve it. I could have got you killed. Price too. And all because of some idiot schoolgirl whim.'

'I chose to come, Gina. I didn't have to. Perhaps, hateful as you are, I'd made up my mind that you were worth it.'

She snorts. 'Then you're as big a fool as I am.'

'Maybe I am,' I say. 'Maybe we deserve each other.'

She replies with a quick, nervous smile. Then she looks away, lost in thought.

After a time, she says: 'Come on. Let's have another go at that shrapnel.'

I try hard not to jump about too much as she prods and probes, but by the time she's done there are beads of cold sweat on my forehead and I'm feeling so weak I'm ready to collapse. Gina seats me in the back of the car, under a blanket, and the next thing I know there's a mug of tea steaming under my nose and Gina's pressed up on the seat next to me, calling in my ear, 'Dick? Dick?'

I've been asleep for nearly half an hour, she tells me gently. She would have left it longer but Price is here saying if we don't leave soon we're going to miss our boat.

'He said some wonderful things about you,' she whispers.

'What, Price? Never!' I say.

'No, Guy. In his letter,' she says. 'He told you, then. About us?'

'He did.'

'And still you don't hate me, for fibbing to you like that?'

'You had your reasons, I'm sure.'

'I did. I DID. I felt so dreadful not telling you but I couldn't tell anyone. If ever my father had found out — which of course he has now.'

'Oh dear, was it bloody?'

'Frightful. A telegram arrived addressed to Mrs Guy Dangerfield and he wanted to know what it was all about. Then I read it and broke down in tears and Daddy was hovering uselessly, quite undecided whether to comfort me or throttle me. And I said: "Some father you are, I've just lost a husband." And he said: "Some daughter you are, marrying behind my back." Well, as far as I was concerned, that was it.'

'What do you mean, "it"?' I say, a bit nervous.

'I told him I wanted nothing more to do with him. I said from now on I'd make my own way in the world. And I've stuck with it, too. This job — I landed it without any help from Daddy at all. It was all down to me. With only the tiniest bit of help from one of Mummy's friends in the FO,' she says. 'What? Did I say something funny?'

I stop smiling because no, now I think about it, it isn't at all bloody funny. 'Are you going to make it up with your father?' I ask.

'Not a chance. I can't tell you how liberating it has been saying goodbye to all that silly inheritance. You don't quite realise till you've lost it what a burden it is. I want people to appreciate me for who I am, not who my father is or how much money I'm worth. That's one of the reasons I so loved Guy. He simply didn't give a damn. He would have loved me just the same if all I'd had to my name was a rusty tiara and a cast-off ballgown.'

'And I'm —' Just the same, I'm about to say, when Price leans into the car.

'Pardon me for interrupting, Lady Gina, but Mr Richard has a boat to catch,' he says.

'Yes, yes, you can have him in just one second. And Price, please, the Lady is unnecessary. Miss Gina will be quite sufficient from now on,' says Gina.

'As you wish, Miss Gina,' says Price, not unamused.

'So you see,' beams Gina, 'I'm free.'

'In a manner of speaking.'

'What do you mean?'

'Well, I'm not saying you should make your peace with your father —'

'Nor will I!'

'— but I do think that before you commit yourself irrevocably to a life without money, you ought maybe, I don't know, to suck-it-and-see first. I mean, it can come in quite useful sometimes, the odd bit of cash.'

Gina looks at me very seriously for a moment. Then breaks into a smile.

'Oh, you tease, I know you don't mean that really. You're not at all like that grisly brother of yours. You're more like Guy.'

'Do you think?'

'I've always looked up to you, Dick. You're brave, you're honest, you're steadfast, you're safe.'

'Safe?'

'Remember those walks we had down to our cave? So many other men would have tried to take advantage of me. And, do you know, I'm such a terrible, terrible girl – well, I was then – that I might not have resisted. But you, you didn't do that and I respect you all the more for it. One day, you're going to make some lucky girl the most perfect husband. In fact, if I weren't such a wretch, I'd almost think . . .'

Maddeningly, she leaves her sentence hanging.

'What, Gina? What?'

'Guy, bless him, thought the same. Here, let me read you what he says,' says Gina, opening her late husband's letter. She reads haltingly. 'I want you to get on with your life. Think of me, sometimes. But don't waste your precious youth mourning what is lost. Look to the future. Find someone who cares for you. And if it so happens to be the bearer of this letter, you have my fullest approbation.'

I wince – not least because of all the disparaging things I've written about Capt. Dangerfield in the letter she has yet to read.

'Jolly decent of him,' I say.

'He was right about so many things,' she says, with a sigh. 'Maybe he's right about this one, but it's far too soon to think about it, wouldn't you say, Dick?'

'Well, there's a lot of sense in that line about not wasting your precious youth . . .'

'Do you know, Dick, the thing I want most is for you to get the girl you deserve. I am not sure I am that girl. At least not yet.'

'Even so, it's a risk I'd be prepared to take.'

'Dick, you'd better go, Price is signalling.'

'Gina –'

'Goodbye, darling. Hope your arm gets better soon. And do write to me, if you feel like it. Here . . .' She writes down her contact address.

Then we kiss, on the lips. More briefly than I would like; but still, perhaps, more tenderly than you might expect of a couple doomed for ever to remain just good friends. She stands, waving at me, as I leave and I keep looking over my shoulder to give her yet more little waves goodbye. God knows when I'm ever going to see her again. Perhaps never if my next assignment proves as thrilling as Monty is predicting; or if that splendid Merc of hers runs over a mine or gets strafed by one of our ground-attack aircraft; or if, heaven forfend, she ends up falling for her boss.

Handsome fellow he is too, unfortunately, in his greasy, olive-skinned way. He arrives, just after Price and I have left. I'm looking back for the very last time before we disappear from view and I see she's not looking at me any more, she has been distracted by someone else – this French colonel – and what's worse, she's giving him exactly the same 'I have eyes for you only' look that not thirty seconds ago she was using on me.

'If we miss this boat because of her –' says Price, crossly, picking up the pace as we thread and barge and jostle our way towards the embarkation zone.

'Yes, yes, point taken,' I say.

'Just hope it was bleeding worth it, that's all.'

'Course it wasn't, Price. You're perfectly right, the girl's completely wrong for me. They're bonkers that family, the lot of them. It's no wonder the father's so sensitive about inbreeding.'

'Still, you've got to hand it to her, she's got spirit.'

'You've changed your tune.'

'Seen her in a new light, haven't I, now she's decided to throw in her lot with the workers.'

'Really, Price, I'd hardly call it that. Even if her father does cut her off, she'll still be getting millions from her mother.'

'Been doing your sums, have you?'

'It's not going to make the blindest difference to me. Especially not after she's opened my letter.'

'Come now. One letter's not going to change her mind either way.'

'If you're trying to ease your conscience, Price, it won't wash. You read the letter yourself. You know what a damn fool it makes me look.'

'Oh, so you're blaming me now, are you?'

'Well, you sent the bloody thing.'

'Suppose your only hope now, then, is that she never gets to read it.'

'Price, it arrived today. I saw her pick it up.'

'Ah but suppose some light-fingered person had noticed the letter in her possession and, aware of your predicament, decided out of the extreme goodness of his heart to spirit the incriminating item away. What then?' says Price.

And with a flourish, he withdraws the letter from a pocket and presses it into my hand.

'Price,' I say. 'Where would I be without you?'

Editor's Notes

'But how much of it is actually true?' This was invariably the first question publishers asked when I showed them the transcriptions of my grandfather's taped war memoirs and I can hardly blame them. The number of actions in which Dick Coward claims to have participated does indeed almost beggar belief; the fact that he lived through them to tell the tale is, as he was so fond of saying, a minor miracle.

While I have absolutely no doubt in my own mind as to the veracity of my grandfather's recollections, there are moments where his version of events diverges slightly from the recorded facts. Perhaps the most obvious of these is his use of pseudonyms. Though 47 (RM) Commando did indeed capture Port-en-Bessin on the night of 7 June 1944 in an action very much as my grandfather describes, none of his given names (save those of staff officers) tally with those of the men known to have taken part. As my grandfather once said to me: 'Don't mind having my own good name dragged through the mud, that's an autobiographer's prerogative. But I shan't be taking any risks with anyone else's. After all, some of these buggers are still alive and most of them have extensive training in the use of firearms.'

Many of my grandfather's obfuscations, deviations and pseudonyms were, I'm sure, intended to protect the innocent. Where I think it's a case of his memory playing tricks, though, or where I think his account needs further elaboration, I have provided some notes below. Any readers wishing to suggest corrections of their own are welcome to contact me care of my publisher. With luck I shall be able to include the most pertinent ones in future editions.

Jack Devereux, Great Meresby, 6 August 2025

2 Going In

p. 8. Lt. Col. (later Major-General) C.F. Phillips, about whom the men of 47 appear to have had mixed feelings, is presumably the model for Lt. Col. Partridge. Tall, decisive and a strict disciplinarian, Phillips was a CO with a reputation for getting things done. His decision to take Port-en-Bessin from the rear rather than from the seaward side undoubtedly saved many of his commandos' lives. But loved by his men he most certainly wasn't. His insistence on avoiding any form of unnecessary personal risk in battle won him few friends, especially when he himself was so ready to accuse his men of cowardice whenever they showed the slightest reluctance to press home an advantage. Afterwards, in Sallenelles, there were those who never forgave him for sending out a patrol into an area known to be mined – with quite disastrous consequences.

p. 14. 'green beret on head': Clearly, a cloth beret offered less protection from flying debris than the standard tin hat worn by line infantry, but commandos preferred it because it was lighter, more comfortable, ensured better visibility, promoted *esprit de corps* and put the fear of God into the enemy. During the landings the wearing of berets was at the discretion of the commanding officers – only 45 Commando are known to have handed in their helmets before embarkation to France – and there is photographic evidence in the Imperial War Museum's collection (B5246) showing men of 47 (RM) Commando disembarking from their LCA on D-Day wearing Mk. II steel helmets (with netting, scrim and shell dressings beneath the nets), so it's possible that Coward's memory is playing tricks. However, tin hats had definitely been exchanged for green berets by the time of the assault on Port-en-Bessin.

4 Band of Brothers

pp. 46–8. It is uncertain to which specific incident this refers, but Coward is right: more Allied troops were indeed killed training for D-Day than died during the actual landings. The worst recorded disaster was the one just off Slapton Sands, near Stokenham, south Devon on 28 April 1944 during a large-scale rehearsal (involving all 23,000 US soldiers due to land on Utah Beach) codenamed Exercise Tiger. The convoy of landing ships was ambushed in the night by nine German E-boats and 749 US servicemen were killed.

However, there have long been rumours – always denied by the US military authorities – of a 'friendly fire' incident in the same area, when owing to some sort of confusion over the use of live ammo GIs were mown down by comrades playing the role of German defenders. Among the witnesses – according to an *Observer* newspaper report in May 2004 – was Lt. Col. Edwin Wolf from Baltimore who heard several shots 'zinging' past his ear as he observed the exercise from a nearby vantage point and saw 'infantrymen on the beach fall down and remain motionless'. A Royal Engineer, Jim Cory, is reported to have seen soldiers 'mown down like ninepins' and to have counted 150 bodies. Local witnesses have claimed that the bodies were interred temporarily in a huge pit, up to two acres in size, near the village of Blackawton, then secretly exhumed and loaded on to three trains under military guard between July and August 1944.

7 Back to Basics

p. 96. Standards of fitness expected of commandos – wearing full battle order – were as follows:

Endurance:

March 25 miles;

2 miles cross-country in 15 minutes: meet the shooting
standard at the end of this;

In a forced march cover 10 miles in 100 minutes;

Crawl 100 yds. in $3\frac{1}{2}$ minutes.

Strength:

Carry a man of equal weight 200 yds. in 75 seconds;

Scale a 6 ft. wall;

Climb a rope: 18 ft. vertically, 30 ft. horizontally, 18 ft. in
descent.

Agility:

Sprint 75 yds. with loaded rifle and then meet shooting
standard;

Vault a $4\frac{1}{2}$-ft. beam;

Jump a ditch $8\frac{1}{2}$ ft. wide, landing on both feet.

Swimming:

Swim 30 yds. with rifle and boots;

Swim 100 yds. (fresh water), 200 yds. (salt water) in
clothing; remain afloat out of depth for 5 mins.

Recruits were expected to be greater than 65 inches in height, heavier than 120 lb., to have a chest girth fully expanded of at least 34 inches with a 2-inch range of movement, normal vision without glasses, normal hearing. In practice, however, all these could be overridden by a sympathetic medical officer with the wonderful get-out clause 'a deficiency in physique can be compensated for by an overabundance of spirit'. I.e. if the troop officer said, 'You can't fail Marine X, he's one of the best in my troop', the MO would take advice and pass him. Many commandos – see Arthur Delap (p. 325) – were below the minimum height and weight but performed none the worse for it.

(For further details see the excellent *From Omaha to the Scheldt – The Story of 47 Royal Marine Commando.* (Tuckwell Press) by 47 (RM) Commando's medical officer John Forfar MC.)

9 On the Beach

p. 133. Of the fourteen LCAs that carried 47 (RM) Commando ashore, five were sunk and seven others damaged while only two were fit to return to their parent ships.

10 The *Hauptmann*'s Britches

p. 149. As my grandfather aptly put it, the landings on Gold Beach were indeed a 'dog's breakfast', confirming von Moltke's dictum that 'No battle plan ever survives contact with the enemy'.

47 (RM) Commando were supposed to land on a 900-yard stretch of beach east of Le Hamel designated Jig Green. In theory this should have been already cleared by 231 Brigade's initial assault waves – first the 1st Hampshires and the 1st Dorsets, then the follow-up battalion the 2nd Devons. Unfortunately, through no fault of their own, the spearhead units became heavily bogged down.

To complicate matters further, a strong easterly current meant that each of the assault waves was pushed well to the left of its intended landing position. The luckless Hampshires found themselves where the Dorsets should have been, and ended up trapped between pillboxes, a minefield and the sweeping fire of a 75-mm. gun concealed in a heavily fortified sanatorium building in the middle of Le Hamel. Their CO was hit twice and had to be evacuated. Also out of action were their forward observation officers from the Navy and the field artillery, which meant they couldn't call on any artillery support.

The Dorsets, too, were raked with murderous fire from the sanatorium stronghold, but because they had no strongpoint immediately in the way, just some marshland, they were able to escape the beach in reasonable order and start clearing the enemy positions beyond Le Hamel at Buhot and Puits d'Herode. Behind them came the Devons, a company of which joined the Hampshires in their assault on the sanatorium, the rest advancing inland to the village of Ryes.

p. 153. The earlier air bombardment had completely failed to neutralise the enemy's heavy-gun positions, which meant that most of the mine-clearing flail tanks and bunker-busting AVRE (Armoured Vehicle Royal Engineers) specials were knocked out within minutes of landing, quickly blocking the exit routes for the vehicles trying to follow. Few even got that far. The weather was so rough that of sixteen Royal Marine Centaurs, only two actually reached the shore.

Without the Centaurs' 95-mm. howitzers or the AVREs' Petards (a mortar firing a massive 26-lb. charge of high explosive, known as a Flying Dustbin) what chance did lightly armed infantrymen have of penetrating the foot or more of reinforced concrete protecting the defending artillery and machine-gun nests? This is why those strongpoints that had been scheduled to fall like ninepins in the first few hours in fact ended up holding out – and causing mayhem – well into the afternoon.

p. 154. Brigadier Sir Alexander Stanier, Bt. – commander on D-Day of 231 Brigade, of which 47 (RM) Commando formed part – won an MC in the First World War and a DSO and bar in the Second. After the war he paid a nostalgic visit to a château he had occupied during the war. The maid who answered the door reported to her mistress, a French countess, that a brigadier had come to visit. 'Then tell him to use the servants' entrance,' replied the countess, mistakenly assuming that 'brigadier' – as it does in French – referred to the lowly rank of corporal.

Further reading:
  D-Day 1944: Gold and Juno Beaches – Ken Ford (Osprey)
  Gold Beach (Battle Zone Normandy) – Simon Trew (Sutton)

p. 168. Snipers were almost universally loathed by soldiers of both sides and when captured were often shot out of hand. They could easily be identified by the tell-tale bruises, and sometimes cuts, caused by the recoil of a telescopic sight pressed tight to a man's right eye. In his superb account of the battle for Germany *Armageddon* (Macmillan) Max Hastings records that US soldiers took a similar view of sniper rifles to Coward's commandos. 'The CO of the US 143rd Infantry reported that his men were most reluctant to use sniper rifles themselves, "because they think they will be shot if captured". This was not a delusion.'

A prisoner's survival chances depended greatly on the circumstances of his capture and the nature of the men capturing him. Often, combat troops felt considerable empathy towards the opposition and were therefore inclined to show mercy. It was those in the rear who tended to be more fickle and prone to war crimes. However, some front-line units – such as Kurt Meyer's SS Panzer-Division *Hitlerjugend*, who massacred twenty-seven Canadian prisoners just a few miles from where Coward landed – took pride in their efficient brutality. And on the Eastern Front, prisoners on both sides were invariably killed as a matter of course. But war crimes were not a purely German, Soviet or Japanese phenomenon. There are several recorded occasions (and many more anecdotal ones) in which British and American troops are known to have shot surrendering men or even killed their prisoners in cold blood. However, among troops as disciplined and well trained as 47 (RM) Commando, it is highly unlikely that such behaviour would have been tolerated, let alone condoned, by an officer.

14 Mont Cavalier

p. 234. Gendarme Dupont may partly be based on Henri Gouget, a man of considerable courage. He showed A troop the way through the town and was wounded in the face during the assault on the Western Feature. He was awarded the Croix de Guerre avec Palme.

15 Taking Flak

p. 239. Aerial photographs taken a few days before D-Day showed Port-en-Bessin's harbour to be empty, though the flakships are clearly visible in photographs taken on 6 June. Unfortunately, the news never reached the Commando, who remained in complete ignorance until they were ambushed by them as they advanced up the Western Feature. Coward's encounter with the armless boy and his attempts to persuade Lt. Col. Phillips ('Partridge') of the flakships' existence is not corroborated by any other accounts.

16 A la Cave

p. 267. Other eyewitness accounts confirm that a Frenchwoman, presumably the girlfriend of one of the German garrison, did indeed have to be taken out after being caught signalling the Commando's positions to the enemy.

17 The Assault

p. 270. Of the 420 commandos who left *Princess Josephine Charlotte* and SS *Victoria* on 6 June 1944, just 275 could be mustered three days later. Of the 145 casualties, 46 had been killed or drowned, 65 wounded, 6 captured and 28 were missing. Most of the missing were men whose LCAs had been sunk during the landings, who were picked up by returning craft and, as orders demanded, taken back to England.

p. 276–7. Dent's horrible death is not mentioned in any other accounts of the assault on the Eastern Feature but is perfectly plausible. A similar incident is recalled by Somerset Light Infantry platoon commander Sydney Jary in his wonderful memoir *18 Platoon*.

p. 281. Capt. Dangerfield's heroic, fatal charge against the concrete blockhouse appears to have been based on that of A troop's commander, Capt. Cousins. A hugely well-liked, charismatic, athletic figure, Capt. Cousins was also a strict disciplinarian. During the landing he gave the order that any man refusing to leave the LCAs should be shot. As to his background and private life, we only have Coward's account to go on. Though Cousins is known to have married shortly before D-Day, 'Doc' Forfar was unable to trace any of his relatives while researching *From Omaha to the Scheldt*. Subsequently Capt. Cousins was put forward by Lt. Col. Phillips for a posthumous VC – something many in the Commando felt he amply deserved for his initiative, leadership and act of outstanding courage. All he in the end received was a posthumous mention in dispatches.

Pint-sized Geordie Dinning may have been based on Arthur Delap, a talented cartoonist and deadly accurate Bren gunner who took part in the charge, firing from the hip. Also involved were Marines Howe, Madden and Tomlinson.

18 Adieu or Au Revoir?

p. 291. In official reports, the only member of 47 (RM) Commando recorded as having been captured on the Western Feature was Cpl. George Amos. Stunned by a stick grenade, Cpl. Amos was taken prisoner and interrogated beneath a notice detailing Hitler's notorious 1942 order that all captured commandos were to be 'slaughtered to the last man'. Amos later claimed that he believed his life had been spared because the Germans mistook him for a medical orderly. Asked to treat a soldier with a serious chest wound and another with a compound fracture of his forearm, Cpl. Amos resourcefully tried to look as if he knew what he was doing.

p. 297. According to other accounts, the dead commandos were temporarily buried by sympathetic Frenchmen in the churchyard at

Port-en-Bessin. They were later moved to the British cemetery in Bayeux.

p. 301. Coward's account tallies with a visit made to the Commando by General – soon to be promoted Field Marshal – Montgomery on 9 June. But Army Commander General Dempsey did not actually pay Port-en-Bessin a visit until the day after.

Of the Port-en-Bessin operation, General Dempsey later said: 'When all did so well it is rather invidious to pick out anyone for special mention, but the two outstanding examples of initiative and the value of tough, individual training were on my right and left flanks carried out by 47th Royal Marine Commando and the 6th Airborne Division respectively.'

General Sir Brian Horrocks, commander of the British Army's XXX Corps, meanwhile, was moved to say: 'It is doubtful whether, in their long, distinguished history, the marines have ever achieved anything finer.'

p. 302. Monty's apparent reference to Operation Market Garden looks very much like a case of Coward being wise after the event. In mid June 1944, the operation would not even have been a twinkle in the General's eye. Indeed, it was not even agreed on by Eisenhower until as late as 10 September.

After Port-en-Bessin, 47 (RM) Commando went on to distinguish itself in several actions across Northern Europe. The most deadly of these – held by many who experienced both to have been far worse than D-Day – was its part in the seaborne assault on Walcheren. This island, guarding the mouth of the Scheldt estuary – and therefore the strategically vital deep-water port of Antwerp – was far better defended than the Normandy beaches, and captured only at considerable cost.

Glossary

AVRE – Assault Vehicle, Royal Engineers

CO – Commanding Officer (ie the Lieutenant-Colonel)

Crab - tank with flails attached to a revolving drum on the front, designed to blow up mines.

DD tank – (Duplex Drive) amphibious, swimming armoured vehicle.

DSO – Distinguished Service Order. (Two narrow blue bands with broad red band in the middle) Gallantry medal, second to the Victoria Cross (VC), usually awarded only to officers of Captain or above for exceptional services under fire. Sometimes awarded to junior officers to indicate they had only narrowly missed out on a VC.

FOO – Forward Observation Officer. An observer, usually attached to frontline infantry, who serves as the eyes of an artillery battery, by radioing back with target locations.

HE – high explosive

HMG – Heavy Machine Gun

HO – Hostilities Only. Royal Navy and Royal Marines designation referring to civilians called up to serve only for the duration of the War – as opposed to career regulars.

HQ - Headquarters

LCA – Landing Craft (Assault) – Wooden landing craft carrying approx 36 troops

LCG – Landing Craft (Gun) – Support craft armed with two 4.7 in destroyer guns

LCM – Landing Craft (Mechanised) – Larger craft capable of carrying one small tank or 100 troops

LCT – Landing Craft (Tank) – Amphibious assault ship for landing tanks on beachheads.

LMG – Light Machine Gun (eg British Bren gun; German Spandau)

MC – Military Cross (white, purple and white ribbon) Third highest gallantry award (after VC and DSO), awarded to officers for 'gallantry during active operations against the enemy'.

MM – Military Medal (dark blue with three white and two red stripes in the middle) Equivalent of Military Cross awarded to Other Ranks. Discontinued since 1993 on egalitarian grounds. Now all ranks are entitled to the MC.

MMG – Medium Machine Gun (eg Vickers)

MNBDO – Mobile Naval Base Defence Organisation. Royal Marine unit which guarded naval bases.

MG – Machine Gun

MG34; MG42 – German Light Machine Guns much feared by Allied troops. Their exceptionally rapid rate of fire enabled small German infantry units to punch far above their weight. Nicknamed the Spandau by British troops.

MO – Medical Officer

MTB – Motor Torpedo Boat

NCO – Non-Commissioned Officer (eg Warrant Officer, Sergeant Major, Sergeant, Corporal, Lance-Corporal)

'O' Group – Orders Group. The briefing meeting at which officers and NCOs are given their tasks for the next engagement.

OP – Observation Post

OR – Other Ranks. All soldiers/marines who are not officers.

POW – Prisoner Of War

PW – Prisoner of War

RAF – Royal Air Force

RAMC – Royal Army Medical Corps

RAP – Regimental Aid Post. Front line treatment centre for wounded personnel.

RASC – Royal Army Service Corps. The Army's logistical wing, responsible for keeping troops in supplies.

RE – Royal Engineers

Recce – Reconnaissance.

RM – Royal Marines

RN – Royal Navy

RNVR – Royal Naval Volunteer Reserve

RSM – Regimental Sergeant Major

VC – Victoria Cross. (Crimson ribbon). The highest award for valour in the face of the enemy. Only 182 were awarded during the whole of World War II (compared to 626 in the First World War), only one of which was won by a Royal Marine.

Acknowledgements

Thanks go especially to Peter Winter (a sorely missed friend who set the ball rolling); Mickie O'Brien MC ('It's easy to be fearless when you've no imagination'); George Amos (Mr Memory); 'Chuck' Harris (never call him Cecil); Patrick Hagen (Gigli maestro); Betty Field (super secretary); Gordon 'Tim' Tye (you'd want him on your side); Ted Hartwell (for the CO's notes, the route map, the memoir).

Thanks to Professor John 'Doc' Forfar MC, author of the definitive account of the Port-en-Bessin operation, *From Omaha to the Scheldt – The Story of 47 Royal Marine Commando*.

Thanks for the inspiration, camaraderie, drinks, jokes and recorded reminiscences of Arthur Delap; Ted Battley; Arthur Thompson; John Baker; Peter Ford; Frank 'Storm Trooper 1st Class' Makings; Aubrey James; Gurnos Jones; Pat Plumb; Michael Peretz; Ken Parker; Albert Rutherford; Tom Payne; Fred Wildman; Ernie Staphnill; Tom MacAndrew.

Thanks to the 47 (RM) Commando 'family', especially Eileen Amos; Mike and Sue Parroy; Peter 'Ruddy Yorkshireman' Spears; Christine Hagen; Lannah Battley; Malcolm Ross; Sandra Tebbutt; Sammy and Kevin O'Brien; Kath Hartwell; the all-singing, all-dancing Burkinshaws; Shirley Price.

Thanks to my technical, literary, linguistic and military advisors Martin Windrow (do read his book about Dien Bien Phu, *The Last Valley*, it's a masterpiece); Major General Ken Perkins DFC; David Hearsey DFC (aka COB); Lt. Col. Ian Bennett; Hugh 'Fruity' Massingberd; Robin and Judy Neillands; Britta Bielenberg; Eric Coleman; Ian Agg; Lt. Col. Robin Matthews; Richard Delingpole; Malcolm Delingpole; Tiffany Delingpole; James Heneage; James Dow; Stephen Daneff; and to my little IWM-visiting companions Boy; War Girl.

Thanks to the Imperial War Museum, especially Grant Rogers and Martin Boswell; to Mike Jones and Colin Midson, who held their nerve when for a nasty moment it seemed as though our position would be overwhelmed. And also to Louise Miller. Thanks to Hugo de Klee, Katharina Bielenberg and Mary Tomlinson for copy-editing it, to Mark Thomas for the brilliant cover art; and everyone else at Bloomsbury, for finally getting it. Thanks to my Agent Von Straus (Iron Cross, First Class, with Oak Leaves); and to the Fawn for living with it and enduring it. (Only nine more books to go, now, deer. And think of the lovely research trips to Arnhem, Kohima and the Libyan desert . . .)